BOOK THREE OF THE TROJAN HORSE
IN THE BELLY OF THE BEAST TRILOGY

THE TROJAN HORSE
IN THE
BELLY *of the* BEAST

A Novel of the Iran Nuclear Weapons Interdiction Project

I0526410

A Novel by
CARL DOUGLASS

Former Neurosurgeon Turned Author
Who Writes with Gripping Realism

PO Box 221974 Anchorage, Alaska 99522-1974
books@publicationconsultants.com—www.publicationconsultants.com

ISBN 978-1-59433-462-7
eISBN 978-1-59433-463-4
Library of Congress Catalog Card Number: 2014936070

Manufactured in the United States of America.

The Greeks left a great hollow wooden horse filled with warriors in front of the gates of Troy. A Trojan priest suspected the plot and urgently warned the unsuspecting Trojans, *"Timeo Danaos et dona ferentes."* ["I fear Greeks, even those bearing gifts."] The line became fixed in the minds of countless generations thereafter as "BewareBeware of Greeks bearing gifts."

Virgil, *The Aeneid, Book II*

BOOK THREE

The Trojan Horse in the Belly of the Beast

The things you trust are not the same
Trust in death, trust in grief
Trust in hope is trust in pain
Who is evil, who is blind?
In the name of who you'll find
A city of souls dying for peace
Welcome to the belly of the beast

-Songwriters
Joseph A. Bellardini,
Frank Joseph Bello,
Charlie L. Benante,
Scott Ian Rosenfeld,
Daniel Alan Spitz,
-Antrax,
Lyrics of *Belly of the Beast*

CHAPTER ONE

Grande Synagtogue de Paris, (La Victoire Synagogue) [Great Synagogue of Paris (Synagogue of Victory)], June 14, 2007

Neither set of parents ever admitted to Gideon or Miriam that their marriage had been arranged. Both of the young people suspected that the long traditions of their Orthodox religion had been in play, but each preferred the fiction that they had simply fallen hopelessly in love the first night they met. Even if they were to possess full knowledge of the plotting and planning of their parents, Gideon and Miriam would only have smiled and quietly applauded the success of the intrigue.

Miriam and her parents had a strong desire for her to be married in the Grande Synagogue de Paris, but France does not recognize the marriage of foreigners as being legal. So, like many people—including many American Francophile celebrities—the Rothsbergers and the Shahnamehs entered into a minor collusion and deception. Gideon and Miriam were legally married by a county clerk in the San Francisco County courthouse with only Chava Rothsberger as their witness.

The prosaic legal courthouse marriage was ignored by the newlyweds and their families, and the complexities of the real marriage—the one sanctioned by Jewish law—absorbed most of the attention of them all for three months. That there were to be two marriages was not spoken of outside the families— no one else needed to be the wiser. Miriam flew home, and Gideon remained in San Francisco, both celibates. By mutual agreement between the parents, a standard Jewish prenuptial agreement was signed. It was simple because both families were rich beyond any need to take money from the other side in case of a divorce. There were only two other clauses in the agreement. The first was an assurance that Gideon was prevented from withholding a *get* [Jewish bill of divorce] from Miriam in case she should ever want one. The second was that Gideon would give Miriam a prenuptial gift of great value.

For that purpose, G.R. IV went to the Diamond District of midtown Manhattan on West 47th Street between Fifth and Sixth Avenues. The store was nondescript and unimposing, identified only by a small brass sign on the door, ABRAHAM GOTTESMAN AND SONS, DIAMONDS. There—by prearrangement—he met an old friend and business associate of G.R. II, the now elderly son of a friend of G.R. I named Malachi Gottesman.

"Come in, my boy. It is a pleasure to have you in our humble establishment," the old Orthodox patriarch said.

"Thank you for assisting me," Gideon said respectfully.

"You are about to be married to a woman of surpassing beauty and talent, if your grandfather and your mother and father can be believed."

"She is all of that, Mr. Gottesman."

"Please, let us be Malachi and Gideon."

Gideon nodded.

In half an hour, Malachi had given the young man a detailed description of how to buy a diamond and showed him gems of each different kind that he described. He explained the standard four Cs—cut, clarity, color, and carat—and added a fifth, cost. Malachi already knew that the Rothsberger family was fabulously wealthy, and that young Gideon would settle for nothing less than a perfect ring—stone and setting. His real concern was not to appear to have taken advantage of Gideon, which would be a violation of a deep trust that existed between the families.

Gideon patiently looked at a dozen stones—all of which had a flaw or a grading just short of perfect—and rejected them all. The last stone was truly perfect: round, brilliant, ideal cut, and internally flawless—IF grade—a stone without any internal imperfections. It was the best of the best blue white D grade stone. Malachi was frank; such magnificent stones are very rare and very expensive. The luminescent diamond sitting on a black velvet cloth was colorless, since colorless stones are rare and reflect light better than tinted diamonds. The old diamond merchant placed the stone under a fluorescent light and demonstrated that the beautiful sparkling stone had no fluorescence, a quality usually not detectable by the unaided eye. Under fluorescence, a stone may manifest a degree of milkiness. This one maintained the purity of its brilliance.

The stone was 6.19 carats. Malachi asked Gideon to describe his betrothed's fingers.

"Long and slender—a pianist's hands. They are beautiful," the ardent young man replied with an enthusiasm that brought back fond memories to the old man.

"So, she can wear a ring of such size," Malachi told him.

The negotiation began at $1.75 million.

Gideon said, "I have studied the retail prices of such stones. Tiffany's price would be closer to $1.6 million."

"True, and I must—in all candor—admit that this one was offered on the Amsterdam diamond exchange at just that price. Perhaps we could agree on that figure."

They shared a cup of tea and a period of quiet reflection.

"I would be more comfortable with a figure of … perhaps $1.2 million," said Gideon after the pause.

He knew it was pro forma haggling and expected. He also knew that his grandfather's connections with the Gottesmans were close enough that the price would be fair. He had no intention of coming across as demanding a hard and unfair bargain.

Two more figures—one descending and one ascending—were proffered before the two men agreed on the $1.6 million—the real value of the diamond. No money changed hands that day. The deal was finalized by a simple *mazel und brucha* [traditional blessing and a handshake]. Gideon left New York with a diamond in a velvet-lined jewel case and a Gemological Institute of America's [GIA's] diamond grading report. He flew from New York International to Charles de Gaulle Airport in Paris that afternoon and—on bended knee—placed it on his trembling bride-to-be's long left fourth finger the next morning.

The wedding in the Great Synagogue of Paris (Synagogue of Victory) was one of the grandest ever in the history of a city that reveled in excess and a Jewish edifice that had hosted the greatest among French and foreign Jewry since 1874. Glitterati, scholars, financiers, Orthodox rabbis, Hasidic rebbes, and government dignitaries from around the world were in attendance. By special invitation, the following people came: Hormoz Mohammad-Bagher, president of Bank Sepah, Tehran—representing the financial connections with the otherwise hostile Shi'ite world; Esfandiari Razizadeh and Razmara Tassoudji, deputies of Moqtada al-Benizir, head of the Atomic Energy Organization Iran (AEOI), and Amir Vehrahrami, chief engineer for research and development at the Bushehr nuclear plant—representing the Iranian secular world; and three people from Iran whom Gideon actually wanted to attend. They were Elizabeth Dayan and her son Elias Nichols-Dayan—expatriate American Jewish horse breeders living in the hostile Muslim country, and Rabbi Ya'akov ben Avraham, ha-Rav, the Persian Jewish rabbi who walked a social tightrope in Tehran and who had to obtain a presidential exception to be able to travel to Europe.

The synagogue is the largest in France and was built in 1874 with the financial support of the Rothschild family. It seats over 1,800 people, and every seat was taken. It serves as a setting for all official ceremonies with members of the government and is also the official seat of the Chief Rabbi of France, who—in 2007—was Pierre Diamond. The ceremony itself was conducted according to the Ashkenazi-Alsatian tradition in conformance with Jewish law and tradition. There was a *ketubah* [marriage contract] signed by two witnesses, a *chuppah* [wedding canopy], a simple gold ring owned by Gideon and given to Miriam outside the canopy to avoid breaking Jewish law, and the breaking of a glass.

He said, "Behold, you are consecrated to me with this ring according to the Law of Moses and Israel."

Miriam surprised the strict Orthodox in attendance by also presenting a ring to Gideon and quoting from the *Song of Songs*: *"Ani l'dodi, ve dodi li."* [I am my beloved's, and my beloved is mine]. The statement was inscribed on the ring itself.

All aspects of the Jewish wedding processes were adhered to—the stages of the *kiddushin* [sanctification] and the *nissuin* [the marriage itself]. Gideon was led under the *chuppah* by the two fathers and his bride by the two mothers—the *unterfirers* [lit. in Yiddish—the ones who lead under]. Under the *chuppa*, the signed *ketubah* was read aloud in the original Aramaic. The *ketubah* detailed Gideon's obligations to his wife, including provision of food, clothing, and, not the least, marital relations. This document had the standing of a legally binding agreement in the Jewish community even if it was not recognized by the government of France.

Miriam was veiled—reminding the Jewish people of how Jacob was tricked by Laban into marrying Leah before Rachel, because her face was covered by a veil. Miriam's veil was made of tulle fastened to a liny pearl coronet, and she carried a bouquet of lily of the valley and white orchids. Her nubile figure was covered by a simple silk lace gown, which had been made for her in Paris. In keeping with tradition, she walked around her groom seven times to honor the biblical command that "a woman shall surround a man."

The seven blessings were recited by the rabbi; the special wine was held to Gideon's lips by Elijah Shahnameh and to Miriam's lips by Chava Rothsberger. The glass was crushed by Gideon's right foot, and everyone in the building—except the Muslim Iranians—shouted, *"Mazel tov!"* [Congratulations!] with genuine feeling. The folding chairs were cleared away and spontaneous dancing began—the Krenzl, the Mizinke, the Horah, and the Mitzvah tantz. When the guests were finished, they formed a large circle, and the bride and groom danced by themselves, oblivious of the crowd.

A sumptuous dinner was served by liveried waiters—all in yarmulkes. The marriage wine was blessed by the rabbi, then two glasses of the wine were poured together into a third, symbolizing the creation of a new life for Gideon and Miriam Shahnameh-Rothsberger together.

Miriam walked through the crowd thanking everyone for attending and for their gifts—some extremely generous—and paid special attention to the dignitaries from Iran. Despite their resolve to preserve their national hatred for Jews, all of them were charmed out of their negativity for that one evening. Hormoz Mohammad-Bagher, president of Bank Sepah, invited her to give a solo concert in Tehran that his bank would sponsor. Miriam told him she would be thrilled to come to the land of her ancestors and to sing for them. Elizabeth Dayan and her son Elias Nichols-Dayan embraced her as family then left her; so, she could greet the rest of the guests. They walked nonchalantly away and met Gideon after he finished thanking the Iranian officials for having come such a long way to attend his wedding.

Elizabeth spoke softly, "Gideon, my boy, congratulations and all happiness. I have talked to your father and … the others. It would be a good thing for you to return to Iran as soon as possible and for your beautiful Miriam to give a concert—two, in fact. The first would be at the opera house in Tehran, and the second at our home outside the city. We have much to discuss in private there."

Her face conferred more than her utterance. Her son—the powerfully built Elias—nodded to Gideon and shook his hand firmly. They melted away into the crowd.

Finally, after the guests began to disperse, Miriam whispered to her blushing groom that she could not wait any longer, and they slipped away secretly—much to the amusement of the knowing guests. The virginal Miriam was spontaneous, giving of her entire self, and athletic. Gideon cried surrender before the first night was over. He had never even dreamt of a happier day.

§§§§§

Talar-e Vahdat Opera House, Abdolmaleki Street, Tehran, Iran, July 23, 2007

Miriam Shahnameh-Rothsberger once thought she was busy and involved during her life as an adolescent music sensation in France. She had experienced an exponential increase in her schedule when she became a professional singer. The pace of life after she married Gideon Rothsberger had been like nothing else before. She and Gideon honeymooned, traveled, gave interviews, attended business conferences, met bankers and financiers, and she performed more than ever to the delight of her husband, his business acquaintances, and paying audiences throughout Europe and the United States. She was exhausted and had to take to her bed for two days before she and Gideon flew to Tehran. Not all of the time in bed was entirely relaxing, but it was altogether restorative. She was young and healthy, and her recuperative powers were at their zenith.

The government of Iran—including its president—and Simin Aghili, the Iranian Philharmonic Concert maestro, made a place on the yearly "Triumph of the Arts in Iran Program" in Tehran. She was one of two featured soloists on a lengthy list of performers for the star-studded evening. Darya Dadvar sang *Ave Maria* and received a standing ovation. Gorgin Mousissian's Choir performed two contemporary Iranian compositions and an operatic chorus by Verdi. The orchestra accompanied all of the performers and then presented Verdi's *Requiem Giulio Cesare* [Julius Caesar] by George Frideric Handel, and Beethoven's *Symphony No. 9 in D minor.*

That brought the program to intermission. Gideon mingled with the crowd of dignitaries and rich Persians, including even a brief greeting with Supreme Leader, Grand Ayatollah Ali ibn Abi Rahimi. Elizabeth Dayan and her son Elias Nichols-Dayan—joined by Rabbi Ya'akov ben Avraham ha-Rav—passed a few pleasantries with Gideon and asked where he was hiding his lovely wife.

"She never shows herself before her appearance on stage. She is perfecting her numbers in her dressing room until they announce her."

"A perfectionist or a prima donna?" Elizabeth asked.

"Only the former," Gideon assured her.

"We will see you at the ranch next week, then, my boy. We are greatly enjoying the music. I can hardly wait to see and hear Miriam."

They turned down the hallway to their entrance portal and disappeared into the large tiered hall modeled after the Vienna State Opera. The lights dimmed once, and the audience began to return to their seats. The lights dimmed again, and the stragglers hurried. The lights dimmed for a moment while the tardy few scrambled to avoid having to clamber around in the dark to find their reserved seats. The room was dark; not even the small string of lights illuminating the front of the stage was lit. The inky darkness remained for a full minute.

Suddenly, the stage was illuminated in a dazzling array of klieg lights centered on a six-foot circle that seemed as if it were the only place the sun could reach. Out of the mine-shaft blackness, Miriam stepped into the center of the circle of light. She gave a small bow and a friendly wave to the audience, then she began to sing. With scarcely a pause between numbers, she sang two operatic arias—*Celeste Aida* from Verdi's *Aida* and *Cielo e Mar* from Ponchielli's *La Gioconda*—then quietly introduced her next number.

"Ladies and gentlemen, there is an old Iranian saying that even among the very poor, there are two books, the *Qur'an* and the poetry of Hafez and his fellow poets of Shiraz. Many of them have been performed as lead-up readings before the beginning of *ta'ziyeh* passion plays, which center around the martyrdom of the imams. Some have been set to music. I would like to sing one of the most popular for you. The great fourteenth century poet poured out his soul about being a poor boy working in a bakery. He delivered bread to the wealthy who lived in their own exclusive quarter of the city. There he gazed on a rich young woman of great beauty, but who was unattainable to the inexperienced and unknown fledgling poet."

She sang the lyrics in Persian, which were familiar to almost everyone in the audience. She was accompanied by an *alvah*—a set percussion instrument made of wooden plates played by being struck with sticks and an Azerbaijani eleven-string *tar* [lute]. The choir provided lilting contrapuntal background music. The evocative number, the popularity of the great Iranian choir, and the high clear soprano of Miriam's voice brought the audience to its feet in deafening applause.

As soon as the applause died down—for the sophisticates in the audience—she shifted into her own arrangement of Gabriel Faure's *Notre Amour*.

"Our love is something light
like the perfume that the wind
takes from the tips of the fern

so that one breathes them while dreaming
Our love is a light thing!..."

This was so reminiscent of the beauty of Persian poetry that there was no standing ovation—not even a sound came from the audience. It was as if they were collectively holding their breaths. Then the hall erupted. The sound of clapping and even the Western decadence of whooping and whistling filled the air with a sound loud enough to make the overhead chandeliers tinkle.

Miriam raised her right hand for quiet. She smiled and looked out at the audience, searching for someone.

"Ah, there they are!" she said and gestured to a pair of children sitting on the front row—a little boy and girl. "Join me *s'il vous plait* [if you please]."

The children called out from their seats, *"Avec plaisir, Madam* [with pleasure]. "

The audience began to clap as the two five-year-olds were led to the stage to share the spotlight with Miriam.

Miriam told the audience, "These are my new friends, Javaneh and Mojtaba. They are the delightful children of Ali Muhummad Sharifi and his lovely wife, Mahdis. They will sing an old favorite of children in France called *"Sur le Pont d' Avignon.*

The full orchestra began to play the accompaniment.

> *"Sur le pont d'Avignon*
> *On y danse, on y danse, Sur le pont d'Avignon*
> *On y danse tout en rond, Les beaux messieurs font comme ça*
> *Et puis encore comme ça.*
> *Les belles dames font comme ça, Et puis encore comme ça. "*

The children then sang in English:
"On the bridge of Avignon, they are dancing, they are dancing,
On the bridge of Avignon, they are dancing all around.
The handsome gentlemen go like this. And then go like that.
The pretty ladies go like this. And then go like that."

And back to French:
"Frère Jacques, Frère Jacques, Dormez vous? Dormez vous?
Sonnez les matines, Sonnez les matines, Din, din, don! Din, din, don!

And again to English:
"Are you sleeping? Are you sleeping?
Brother John? Brother John?
Morning bells are ringing, Morning bells are ringing,
Ding ding dong, Ding ding dong."

As the proud parents and everyone in the crowd who knew them or knew of them—the father was the sitting foreign minister of Iran—clapped enthusiastically. Miriam had found the way to the hearts of her audience. Everyone, everywhere, loves their children and those who show the children love. From the darkness, an old man in an old-fashioned tuxedo stepped into the light. His face was familiar to the older people in the audience. Marius Duvalier had been a favorite of two generations before when the shah still ruled Persia. Without introduction, his husky voice—accompanied by the orchestra—began an entirely familiar song made famous by the Frenchman Maurice Chevalier. His now somewhat raspy voice was not what it had been; and he halted on a word or two; but the effect of the old man's baritone voice and his obviously heartfelt affection for his song was spellbinding.

*"Chaque fois que je vois une petite fille de cinq, six ou sept
Je ne peux pas résister à l'envie joyeuse de sourire et de dire
Dieu merci pour les petites filles
pour les petites filles deviennent de plus chaque jour!*

*Dieu merci pour les petites filles
ils grandissent dans la manière la plus délicieuse!*

*Ces petits yeux tellement impuissant et attrayant
un jour clignote et vous envoyer crashin 'à travers le ceilin'*

*Dieu merci pour les petites filles
Dieu merci pour eux tous,
peu importe où, peu importe qui
sans eux, ce seraient les petits garçons faire?*

*Grâce au ciel…Dieu merci…
Dieu merci pour les petites filles!"*

He deftly switched to English.

"Each time I see a little girl of five or six or seven
I can't resist the joyous urge to smile and say
Thank heaven for little girls
for little girls get bigger every day!

Thank heaven for little girls
they grow up in the most delightful way!

Those little eyes so helpless and appealing
one day will flash and send you crashin' thru the ceilin'

Thank heaven for little girls
thank heaven for them all,
no matter where no matter who
without them, what would little boys do?

Thank heaven ... thank heaven ...
Thank heaven for little girls!"

He hugged the little boy and girl. The three faded out of the spotlight, and the applause was tumultuous. Everyone in the great opera hall was transported to a softer time—Iranians are nothing if not nostalgic. As the applause began to wane, a strikingly beautiful teenage girl—obviously Iranian, and equally obviously a special child—stepped unobtrusively into the spotlight beside Miriam. A violinist, a cellist, and a flautist appeared out of the darkness behind her.

Miriam Shahnameh, the gracious soloist—well aware of the effect that her performance was having on all the doting parents within the sound of her voice—introduced the girl.

"May I present to you the winner of the youth music competition for all of Iran in 2007, Miss Khadija Moqtada al-Benizir, daughter of the eminent scientist, Moqtada al-Benizir, and Mrs. Aisha al-Benizir."

The girl was something of a celebrity in Iran in her own right, and the mention of her father—the head of the AEOI—brought the audience to their feet. The applause drowned out Miriam's introduction.

She waited for quiet then announced Khadija's name again.

"Khadija will announce her favorite French song."

Khadija bowed and said, "I will sing ' *Clair de La Lune* first in the original French and then in English. *A Clair de La Lune* means 'in the moonlight' in French, and is a simple folk song from the eighteenth century. It is sung by adults and children alike in France and now all over the world, including here in our beloved Iran. It is best known as a children's song. The first couplet of the lyrics was sung on a recording in 1860, making it the first ever recording of a human voice."

The crowd hushed.

> *"Au clair de la lune*
> *Mon ami Pierrot*
> *Prête-moi ta plume*
> *Pour écrire un mot*
> *Ma chandelle est morte*
> *Je n'ai plus de feu*
> *Ouvre-moi ta porte*
> *Pour l'amour de Dieu"*

> "In the moonlight
> My friend Pierrot
> Lend me your pen
> So I may write a word
> My candle is out
> I've no more light
> Open your door for me
> For the love of God"

Miriam put her arm around the beautiful teenager. The orchestra began to play the most familiar piece of music in Iran. Khadija sang and, beside her, Miriam hummed in her high soprano voice.

> *"Sar zad az ofoq mehre xåvarån*
> *Foruqe dideye haqbåvarån*
> *Bahman, farre imâne mâst*
> *Payåmat ey Emåm, esteqlâl, âzâdi, naqše jâne mâst*
> *Šahidån, pičide dar guše zamân faryådetân*
> *Påyande mâni o jåvedân*
> *Jomhuriye Eslâmiye Irân"*

Then, Miriam gave her version of the "Anthem of the Islamic Republic of Iran"—this time in English.

> "Upwards on the horizon rises the Eastern Sun
> The light in the eyes of the believers in justice
> The Month of Bahman is the brilliance of our faith.
> Your message, O Imam, of independence, and freedom, is imprinted on our souls
> O Martyrs! Your clamours echo in the ears of time:
> Enduring, continuing, and eternal,
> The Islamic Republic of Iran"

When Miriam and Khadija finished the anthem, every person in the great hall was standing, even the orchestra. All civilians had their right hands over their hearts, and the men in uniform—including the ushers—stood at attention in a stiff salute. Miriam and Khadija were joined by the two Sharifi children and Marius Duvalier. They all took three well-choreographed bows and swept off the stage.

Afterwards, Miriam—with Gideon standing protectively behind her chair in the beautiful Café Opera in the corner of the great hall—greeted the adoring fans. None of them seemed to realize that she was Jewish and forgot for a joyous ecumenical evening of music that they were supposed to hate their Semitic cousins. Even the government officials and the rich business people bumped shoulders to get to shake her hand and to have her autograph their programs. The evening at the Tehran opera was an unparalleled success. Gideon was bursting with pride and was overjoyed at the opportunities his lovely young wife was going to afford him and the Iran Nuclear Interdiction Project.

CHAPTER TWO

Offices of the Supreme Leader of the Islamic Republic of Iran, Islamic Republic Street—End of Shahid Keshvar Doust Street, Tehran, Iran, July 28, 2007

"The Supreme Leader is in the north—in Kurdestan. Some kind of uprising among the peasants. He has ordered me to tell you to proceed with your meeting and to e-mail a memo on your decisions," said Hamid Hejazi, the senior guard in residence. "I will take you to an appropriate office. Follow me, please."

President Shahamatdoost and Esfandiari Razizadeh, Razmara Tassoudji, and Amir Vehrahrami—the two deputies of the AEOI and the engineer in charge of the Bushehr nuclear plant, in effect the executive officers of the Project *Jahannam Adur* [Hell's Fire]—followed the guard to a small but well-appointed working office. None of them was particularly put out that the SL was not going to be there. At least they would get some work done without the politics and personal whims of the grand ayatollah causing delays. President Shahamatdoost was pressed for time; so, he dispensed with the usual time-wasting pleasantries.

"We have all interviewed the Mouradipour girl. Much as I dislike having to consider the idea of a mere woman becoming a valuable part of our nuclear program, I was impressed with her and her credentials. She is qualified, do you agree?"

The three subordinates nodded their heads in the affirmative.

"Let me hear from each of you. When we are finished here, we will make a firm decision and either forget about her or offer her the position of director of the program."

As one of two deputies of Moqtada al-Benizir, head of the AEOI, Razizadeh was next in seniority; so, he spoke next, "President, I agree that she is qualified in almost all matters pertaining to computer and nuclear science and nuclear engineering. However, she is young and inexperienced with administrative responsibility. I recommend that my staff give her a probationary instruction period and see if she is able to handle such serious decisions. I also recommend that she be shadowed by security for her first year."

Tassouodji, the second deputy added, "She is very intelligent—quite remarkable, in fact. She can learn; she has proven that. I predict she will be invaluable in two years. She is pleasant and cooperative, modest as a good Muslim girl should be. However, in my brief discussion with her, I found her to be strong and decisive; she has definite requirements that will have to be met before she could accept a position with us."

"I presume that means a fortune in gold and the sun, the moon, and the stars," the president said acerbically.

"Not at all," said Amir Vehrahram, the engineer in charge of the Bushehr nuclear plant. "In fact, it is quite the contrary. She did not even mention money. She is a woman of simple habits, and not—as the Westerners would say—a high-maintenance woman. What she wants is trust, security, and a reasonable amount of freedom. It is more freedom than our lower-class women are granted under the law, but her requests are reasonable."

"How so?" asked the president, becoming concerned about the potential of having a strong-willed woman working around ranking men.

"She needs to be able to communicate with scientists all around Iran and the world. She needs to have telephonic and electronic access and the opportunity to use that freedom to advance our work. She needs to be able to travel widely and frequently on the project's business. She needs to be able to travel in the West in clothing that will not immediately identify her as a Muslim."

"That will require top secret clearance and credentials identifying her as a high-ranking official with privileges comparable to any that we have," said Deputy Tassouodji.

"I have put some thought into those ideas as you have been presenting them, gentlemen," said President Shahamatdoost. "You have suggested a probationary period of two years so that she can learn how things function in the country and in the nuclear energy industry. As you are well aware, we need her to bring the Project *Jahannam Adur* [Hell's Fire] to completion. I am certain that VEVAK and our computer security agents can monitor her quietly to see if she is being scrupulously honest. That is more than any of us has had to put up with, I might add."

"We can do it. Mr. President, may I supervise her work and the entire issue of security for the young woman?"

"You will work with the officers from the departments of Mullah Ali Salar Omidyar, director of the Ministry of Intelligence and Security (MOIS) and Behrouz Omidi, director of the Ministry of Intelligence and National Security of the Islamic Republic of Iran (MISIRI)—VEVAK. They will report directly to me and to the Agha. They will have veto power, but you will have day-to-day control. Understood?"

"Certainly. Your plan is exactly what I was suggesting. Have I your permission to begin the hiring process? It will require a written order from you to ensure full cooperation between the three departments involved."

"I so order you. Will an e-mail order suffice for the written document?"

"Yes, Sir. Please use the interagency encryption. I have a feeling that this young woman should work behind the scenes as much as possible and in as much secrecy as we can have and still get the work done. She seems to be one who would prefer to stay out of the limelight. I will arrange for VEVAK to dispatch an agent who is aware of the need to treat her carefully and to get her back to Tehran for the final vetting and instructions."

"Good. Anything else?"

"Just a comment, Mr. President," said Deputy Razizadeh. "You are no doubt aware of the charges being put forth by one of the members of the Majilis. He insists that he has evidence that the Taliban in Afghanistan and Iraq are working with bin Laden's al-Qaeda against us. He talks about them playing the role of the Greek Trojan horse for the Zionist regime throughout the Middle-East. I don't think he is exaggerating by much when he says that the Zionist Entity is rapidly becoming the largest training base for active terrorist operations against us. He says that this so-called 'Trojan Horse' is responsible for disruption of our oil pipelines, murders of our legislators, military commanders, intelligence agents, and our scientists. He sees the footprint of the Zionist Entity and the Great Satan everywhere and always in our spate of troubles. It is his contention that al-Qaeda is working from inside Syria with tacit government approval and protection with financing and other incentives coming from the U.S. government and the CIA as evidenced by the close relationship of Syria's top governmental officials and the Military Intelligence Directorate—the *Mukhabarat*—and the General Security Directorate—the *Idarat al-Amn al-Am*—all three divisions—and their U.S. counterparts. Finally, he tells anyone who will listen that thousands of al-Qaeda-linked terrorists from Saudi Arabia, Libya, and Jordan have entered Syria in recent months to carry on the fight against our Hezbollah and our military assets. They are provided with intelligence support by the Israeli regime—the Mossad, of course."

"Seems more than a bit far-fetched, Mr. Razizadeh," said President Shahamatdoost. "I have more faith than you in our security forces. I will have to have more substantive evidence. This Majilis functionary sounds like he is more a purveyor of hearsay and rumor than a man with genuine knowledge. Frankly, I am inclined to laugh at the very idea of a Trojan Horse from any source sitting around in our country waiting to wreak havoc. I suppose I have to ask: Does this have anything to do with our prospective nuclear engineer? And what is this legislator's name, pray tell?"

"I am only aware of rumors, not real evidence, Mr. President. And—in answer to your direct question—I don't think anybody of any importance has ever heard of Dr. Afsoon Mouradipour in our country, and only a handful of people outside her professors and fellow students in America and Sweden have any interest in her. Oh, the member of the Majilis with all of the so-called inside information is one Ali Hassan Zolein."

"Whose father was Irani Zolein, who is rumored to have had some dealings with the Shah's regime back in the day," the president stated. "I would not have expected better from his son. I will have a talk with the young man. I don't think we need to have any more talk about 'Trojan Horses' coming from Syria. Serious men in Persia will not be amused. I can think of one who will especially not be amused."

CHAPTER THREE

The Rafter D-N Horse Breeding Ranch, Shekan Kalak in Semnan Agricultural Sector, Northeast of Tehran, July 28, 2007

Elizabeth Dayan was born and reared on a ranch outside Luckenbach in the Texas hill country, thirteen miles from Fredericksburg and an hour and a half from Austin. Luckenbach was once a small but active hamlet, then pretty much a ghost town when the Wilcox family owned their ranch. It has been revived to a degree to the level of an unincorporated community in southeastern Gillespie County. The ranching business was a hard scrabble affair that amply prepared Elizabeth for her life in hostile Iran. The ranch was situated half a mile from South Grape Creek—a wispy tributary of the Pedernales River, close to what is now U.S. Highway 290. The family's access to civilization was Farm to Market Road 1376.

Elmer Wilcox—Elizabeth's widower father—raised long-horned cattle and Western Quarter horses on a ranch that could not support itself. He earned extra cash as a bartender and country music singer in Luckenbach's oldest building—a general store and saloon that is still standing. Elizabeth—who could not carry a tune in a bucket—sometimes accompanied her father. There was no movie house; and the Baptist church only had a preacher occasionally; so, despite the poor pickings, Elmer and Elizabeth Wilcox had enough of a following to keep body and soul together. The motto of the saloon had hung there since the town was founded in 1849—at least that was when the saloon was built, which inaugurated the town. It still hangs there and reads, "Everybody's Somebody in Luckenbach." That was not too hard to understand since—at times—the town's population dipped to just three citizens.

Buildings in the city consist of eight homes—two of which are abandoned—the remnants of a post office—which closed in 1971 and its zip code was discontinued—a working saloon, a general store that caters to the few tourists who happen by, a dance hall, a cotton gin, a blacksmith shop, and Lower South Grape Creek School.

Elizabeth Wilcox was an only child, and she had to be the chief cook and bottle washer, cleaning lady, ranch hand, horse breeder, farrier, and ranch accountant. There was precious little time for learning from books, and Elizabeth was largely self-taught. There was no time for religion; so, she grew up indifferent. She was intelligent enough to realize that Luckenbach did not hold a future for her. The hill country is beautiful; highways and farm roads meander with no obvious destination or particular purpose like the area's rivers. The landscape of the place where Elizabeth spent her childhood was lush and covered in trees, heavy grass, and large shrubs. It was full of natural springs and lakes, which were then and are now captivatingly beautiful.

None of that was enough to hold Elizabeth. In the same year—1952—Elmer Wilcox went bankrupt and lost the ranch, had a heart attack and died, and left his daughter penniless to fend for herself. She did quite well at it. The first thing she did was to change her last name to Dayan, after a famous Persian general she read about in a book. Then, she married a young army lieutenant who was assigned as a military attaché to the Tehran Embassy while Iran was still ruled by the Pahlavis. They loved the people and the land and elected to stay when his enlistment was up. The young couple established dual Iranian-American citizenship and built a very special horse ranch in Shekan Kalak in Semnan Agricultural Sector, northeast of Tehran. They established their brand, the Rafter D-N—named for their surnames—Dayan and Nichols. Elizabeth had no desire or intention to go back to the United States at the time they established themselves as expatriates. She certainly could not be dragged by a six-horse team back to Luckenbach, Texas. The nearest she came to nostalgia was a bit of whimsy; for decades, she continued to subscribe to the *Luckenbach Moon* online.

The brand was special because of the great care and science they applied to the establishment of their horse-breeding business. Early on, they bred Arabians, a few thoroughbreds, and a mixture of the two for racing. They took a serious calculated risk and began to breed an indigenous Iranian breed—the Caspian. The breed is a small—nine hands tall—tough horse native to northern Iran, which is believed to be one of the oldest horse or pony breeds in history. Although its body is slim and graceful, its legs and hooves are strong. The horse is known for its spirit, gentleness, intelligence, and great endurance, which made it a much better fit to the harsh terrain of Iran than the Western Quarter horses Elizabeth grew up with.

Ian did not care about religion, and Elizabeth never had any. Neither could accept Islam, especially because of its inherent intolerance and its systemic maltreatment of women. In their area in northern Tehran, there was a thriving community of Jewish businessmen and their families. It became a matter of practicality for them while doing business in Iran at the time to convert to Judaism. In public, they conformed to the traditions and mores of the society around them; but on the ranch, they remained Western transplants. The Nicholses allowed themselves to come under the wing of Rabbi Ya'akov ben Avraham, ha-Rav. He was a wise man and did not push the Nicholses to conform to his Orthodoxy.

After the revolution, he made a point of letting anyone who would listen to him know that he was a member of the Neturei Karta—an ultra-Orthodox Jewish sect opposed to Zionism and the nation of Israel. The new revolutionary regime left him and his sect alone; and he advised Ian and Elizabeth to let their neighbors know that they, too, were believers in the Neturei Karta. American rabbis from the sect visited Iran on several occasions, which gave the Tehrangeles media cause for strong criticism. The Jewish Defense Organization in the U.S. and Israel protested against one such visit by members of a Neturei Karta faction after they attended the International Conference to Review the Global Vision of the Holocaust in Tehran. All of that made the members of the sect seem inoffensive to the ruling regime in Iran. They were largely ignored, except for the excessive taxes they had to pay because they were not Muslims.

The Nicholses' big chance came in the early 1960s when they were able to enter their little horses at the Tehran Racetrack with the children of the shah and the Iranian aristocracy as jockeys wearing family silks. The shah of Iran, Mohammad Reza Pahlavi, attended some of the races and became a fan of the Nicholses' riding school. As an adroit token of appreciation, the Nicholses gave the shah's youngest son, Ali Reza, a particularly gentle and safe Caspian pony. In return, the shah touted their breed because of its clearly established Persian origins, and that led to a highly successful business for their breed in Europe. They were able to sell a large number of their Arabians and even a few very carefully bred and nurtured thoroughbreds. Elizabeth Dayan-Nichols and her husband Ian became rich.

Ian died of cholera during a four-month incarceration in Evin prison in Tehran in the early period of the Islamic revolution. His crime was being a Jew. He was eventually exonerated posthumously, but it was too late. The brutal mistreatment, intentional neglect, and the overcrowded and unsanitary conditions resulted in an epidemic. Ian Nichols died without treatment. Elizabeth was both stubborn and wise: she stayed on and ran the ranch despite the urging of her friends, family, neighbors, and the regime to leave. She was wise because she ignored the anti-American, anti-Jewish, and anti-Israel taunts and accusations she endured on a daily basis. The regime came to tolerate her and enjoyed her money. When the regime impoverished most of the remaining Jews and drove them out, she kept silent. When the anti-Israel rhetoric heated up, she held her peace. When the maltreatment of women escalated to an intolerable level, she wisely refused to protest. However, the combination of all of those discriminations became a driving force for Elizabeth. When President Shahamatdoost began to hint at a national effort to build nuclear weapons, she became determined to act.

Gideon and Miriam Rothsberger arrived at the ranch midafternoon in a rented Iran Khodro Samand LX. Elizabeth and Elias met them in the driveway and helped them carry in their few pieces of luggage.

"How wonderful it is to see both of you. We hope the trip from the airport was not too difficult or confusing," Elizabeth said.

"Not at all," Miriam said. "We only got lost twice, but Gideon did not have to ask directions either time. We had the opportunity to take the scenic route both times."

She said it with a perfectly straight face, and Elizabeth and Elias laughed heartily.

The four of them had a light lunch; then Miriam headed to a quiet back room to practice. In an hour, a small troupe of unknowns arrived in a van driven by Rabbi ben Avraham. As soon as the pleasantries were over, all of the newcomers were helped to rooms where they also could practice.

At dusk, 102 guests arrived. The guests included staid Orthodox neighbors, minor government officials, an army general and an air force colonel, an imam, and twenty-five or so children and their parents who looked as if they felt out of place in the sumptuous surroundings. In fact, the ranch house—while large—was quite simply decorated—Persian carpets on hardwood floors, comfortable dated furniture, and photographs and paintings of horses on the walls. A pretty eleven-year-old girl was introduced by her parents, then one of the younger Nichols girls took her to a room; so, she could practice.

It was an unseasonably pleasant day, perfect for an outdoor performance. The guests and performers sat together family-style and enjoyed a supper of *mirza ghasemi, borani, bademjan,* and *dokhtar-e luce* as starters. The main course was a combination plate of fish and veal dishes and fresh vegetables from the ranch. Desserts were *sholeh zard* [Persian Rice Pudding], with honey-glazed rhubarb and strawberries, and *baagh lava*. Elias and his two brothers, Zacharia and Elijah, cleared the tables and chairs and made four hemi circles facing an impromptu stage with a raised center.

Miriam occupied that center with an improvised spotlight directed at her. She created a stir, laughter, and a vigorous applause just for her costume for the operatic program. She was wearing denim bib overalls, a silk plaid shirt, cowboy boots, and a Stetson. When the audience settled down, she started her first number, *"Donna non vidi mai"* [I have never seen a woman] *by Puccini,* followed by *"Un bel di"* [One Fine Day] from Puccini's *Madama Butterfly.*

After the applause, she beckoned to an eleven-year-old girl who was dressed in a beautiful blue silk chador to join her.

"Ladies and gentlemen, this is my new friend, Eva Mariella Siavashi, the daughter of General Hossein and Mrs. Maymuna Siavashi. She and I will sing several numbers. We hope you like them."

They sang *To Believe* and *A Time for Us* in French then switched to Farsi, which Miriam had practiced endlessly at home in San Francisco before she and Gideon flew to Tehran. The sophisticated members of the audience were aware of the rather frowned upon Western favorites—*Time to Say Good-bye* and—*Who Wants to Live Forever,* and they were delighted. Gen. and Mrs. Siavashi were thrilled. They were converts to Miriam that night.

The next surprise of the evening came when Jewish cantor, Avril Azaria, was introduced by Rabbi ben Avraham. It was a total surprise to the audience and especially to Elizabeth Dayan when her daughter Kelsey sat at the piano and her youngest son Leopold began strumming a guitar. The melody was familiar to all of the Westerners in the audience but entirely new to the Iranians. Cantor Azaria began to sing *Old Man River* with his deep mellifluous bass voice.

> "Ol' man river,
> Dat ol' man river
> He mus' know sumpin'
> But don't say nuthin',

He jes' keeps rollin'
He keeps on rollin' along.

He don' plant taters
He don't plant cotton,
An' dem dat plants 'em
is soon forgotten,
But ol' man river,
He jes keeps rollin' along.

You an' me, we sweat an' strain,
Body all achin' an' racket wid pain,
Tote dat barge!
Lif' dat bale!
Git a little drunk
An' you land in jail.

Ah gits weary
An' sick of tryin'
Ah'm tired of livin'
An' skeered of dyin',
But ol' man river,
He jes' keeps rolling' along…

Don't look up
An' don't look down,
You don' dast make
De white boss frown.
Bend your knees
An' bow your head,
An' pull dat rope
Until you' dead."

Miriam returned in her cowboy garb and sang a second incongruous song as a duet with the cantor—*Back in the Saddle Again*. Elizabeth and her children laughed until they had tears in their eyes. For the final two numbers, Miriam called Eva back to center stage to join Cantor Azaria and her in a trio. Kelsey on the piano and Leopold with his guitar accompanied the trio in a heartfelt rendition of popular Iranian singer Goolgoosh's *Ahooye eshgh* [Deer of Love], first in Persian, then in English.

> *"dar peye ahooye eshgh*
> *dar peye ahooye eshgh*
> *sayad! avare shodam*
> *ta koja bayad david?*
> *yarab! bichare shodam*
> *man oghabam shah pare*
> *ghulle neshine bi shekast*
> *rishkhande bache ahooee be yek bare shodam*
> *ta koja bayad david?*
> *yarab! bichare shodam*
> *bale man bi saye shod*
> *az bas ke oftadam be khak*
> *konje khane morde*
> *bi parvaz o bikare shudam*
> *ta koja bayad david?*
> *yarab! bichare shodam."*

> "after the deer of love
> after the deer of love
> o hunter! I roved
> whither should I run?
> o God! I languished
> my eagle is the best
> he always roosts on pike, he is unbeatable
> but suddenly I was scoffed by a little deer
> whither should I run?
> o God! I languished
> my feathers got shadeless
> cause I fell on earth so much.
> I died in a corner of home
> I got featherless and workless
> whither should I run?
> o God! I languished."

Elizabeth Dayan's guests were charmed and ecstatic by the willingness of the world-renowned opera diva to sing one of Iran's most popular songs. Mrs. Dayan's party was guaranteed to be a lasting memory. Then, the trio finished the evening with Rufus Wainwright's *Hallelujah*.

> "I've heard there was a secret chord
> That David played and it pleased the Lord.
> But you don't really care for music, do you?
> And it goes like this.
> The fourth, the fifth, the minor fall, the major lift.
> The baffled king composing Hallelujah.
> Hallelujah! Hallelujah! Hallelujah! Hallelujah!
>
> "Your faith was strong but you needed proof.
> You saw her bathing on the roof.
> Her beauty and the moonlight overthrew you.
> She tied you to a kitchen chair.
> She broke your throne, she cut your hair.
> And from your lips she drew the Hallelujah.
> Hallelujah! Hallelujah! Hallelujah! Hallelujah!"

CHAPTER FOUR

The guests thanked Elizabeth and congratulated and praised Miriam and her small ensemble of singers until it began to be tedious. Elizabeth quietly made her exit, using the excuse of having to go to the ladies' room. The ever affable and courteous Miriam chatted with everyone until nearly ten o'clock, when the children's parents had to get them home to bed. The house finally became quiet. Finding herself alone and exhausted, Miriam made her way to the bedroom provided for her and Gideon by the Nichols-Dayan family. She was surprised not to find Gideon waiting for her, but she was too tired to worry. She slipped out of her clothes and into a nightgown and was asleep almost as soon as her head touched the pillow.

As soon as Elizabeth escaped from the crowd of guests, she walked out the back door and across a horse paddock to the ranch hands' quarters. They had been given the night off; so, the quarters were empty of people; and the building was dark. She flashed a small pocket Mag-Lite and made her way to a barracks room in the back. She entered and felt her way to a familiar round table in the center of the room. She pulled back the carpet the table was standing on, and found a latch for a cellar room and pulled it open. Now, she could see the light of several dim floor lamps that illuminated a set of pull-down stairs. She climbed down and walked to an adjoining room. There, seated in soft comfortable old armchairs, were her two sons, Elias and Zachariah, Gideon Rothsberger (G.R. IV), Aaron Schmuel, the Swede Ali Nylander, Rabbi Ya'akov ben Avraham, and two men and a young woman she had never seen before.

"Mother, permit me to introduce everyone. I think you know Gideon, Aaron, and Ali. This gentleman is a fellow Swede who works with Ali. His name is Johannes Hjerdstadt from Swedish army intelligence."

Johannes gave a small salute.

Elias continued and pointed at a powerful-looking Semitic man. "This is Moise Levinsky, one of our friends from Tel Aviv. Besides his business interests, he is a friend and relative of Zwi Rosenstein. I think you know him."

The Kosher Nostra gangster nodded his greeting.

"And this is Abram Cohen. He works with the Mossad as a specialist in relations with the worldwide network of the *Sayanim*," Elias continued.

"Hello, Mrs. Nichols-Dayan."

"Hello, Abram. I hope we are all going to be on a first-name basis."

Everyone nodded their agreement.

"This gentleman is David ben Yisroel—better known among his military coworkers as David Israel. He is an intelligence officer with the SAS."

"Ma'am," he said, and mimed tipping his hat to her.

"Finally, this is Elsie. She is an analyst with the Mossad with considerable field experience. She will explain the cyber actions we are going to introduce into the Iran regime's system. Aaron will give you the rundown on where you and your family fit into all of this."

"Elias and I will soon be missed; so, we need to be efficient in our communications," Elizabeth said. "Who's first?"

Elias cocked his head at Elsie.

Elsie said, "My specialty is spreading confusion in our enemy's camp. Gideon and I and a few others are tasked to learn everything we can about the computer system of the state and its nuclear program. We will be inserting viruses and worms into programs we hack into, which will let us know what is going on, and—more to the point—where we can interfere. That is where you come in and that is what poses the greatest risk for you. We have brought along a very special computer for you—one that will need a room of its very own. I have given Elias the specifications for the room, mostly about security. You must guard it and the information in it with your life. No one outside the analysts in the U.S. and Israel needs to know what the information means—it is encrypted, of course. Your house is perfectly located and can receive and send a clear signal. It is of paramount importance that we trust you. We will do all we can to earn your trust and to protect you, but there will always be an element of risk. From time to time, we will ask you to perform certain tasks on the computer. To be sure that no one has information that could be used against any of us, we ask that only you operate the computer. The other risky request we have is that you provide a safe house. We have some good people in that department. Don't be too surprised if they come knocking at your door one day soon. The password will be the name of our project."

Elizabeth said, "Good ideas."

"You and I will get together tomorrow and learn how the machine operates and how to encode messages. Also, we are grateful for the help Rabbi ben Avraham has offered. He can organize and maintain a sort of underground railroad for our people. He and his sect members have gained the grudging trust of the regime—including VEVAK—and, furthermore, they do a lot of traveling around the country for business. It just so happens that they use vans for their work."

By prearrangement, Aaron spoke next, "Moise, David, one of Johannes's men, Elias, Zachariah, and I have been an action team. Elias and Zacharia will see more action as we begin to do more work in Iran itself. Adm. Daastrup has ordered caution for now, but he predicts that Iran will become more aggressive as their progress continues to be thwarted. Incidentally, he is very much averse to the overt involvement of American military personnel in the Iran Nuclear Interdiction Project."

"Any plans I get to know about?" asked Elizabeth.

"In general, and obviously, it is best to compartmentalize knowledge," Aaron said, "but we do plan to take out two fairly important sources of income for the nuclear project and to see to the disappearance of three key players at the plants in Bushehr and ZPP."

"What is ZPP?" asked Elizabeth.

Aaron told her, "Zirconium Production Plant—which produces the necessary ingredients and alloys for nuclear reactors. Interfering in any way with production at ZPP would be a major setback for their program. To date, we have not had a way to sabotage that entity; but we have a combined strike in the works."

When Gideon got into bed, Miriam stirred enough to ask, "Where have you been?"

"Talking with Elizabeth and the family. They were thrilled with your performance. Bringing in the cantor and the children was genius. You are a genius, my love."

Miriam smiled and went back to sleep.

CHAPTER FIVE

"Basement mosque"—Jennifer Gustafsson's home, 6066 Arne Beurlings Torg, number 78, Stockholm, Sweden, September 4, 2007

This was Afsoon's third Friday meeting in the past four with VEVAK agents at the radical Shi'ite gathering place. She had discussed the idea of being employed by the government of Iran in its nuclear program in very general terms over the past year and more pointedly and in detail in the past two weeks. This meeting after prayers was obviously more serious.

The same VEVAK agents—Hassan Tajbakhsh, Mohammad Ali Nikookar, and Salar Sabeti—and the older man whom she met previously—Ayatollah Mammad Qazwini, who had informed her rather pompously that he "lived to serve his holiness, the Supreme Leader"—were there, as well as three well-dressed and distinguished-looking men she had not seen before. This was going to be an important meeting, probably the most important one since she had made her way to the "basement mosque."

She tensed.

"Hello," said the oldest of the three new men, "I am Amir Vehrahrami, chief engineer for research and development at the Bushehr nuclear plant. On my right is Esfandiari Razizadeh, and on my right is Razmara Tassoudji—deputies of Moqtada al-Benizir, head of AEOI."

The three men had been reading copies of the Iranian hard-line *Kayhan* newspaper, which they set down on the small kitchen table to acknowledge Afsoon's presence.

Afsoon declined her head slightly in a small gesture of subservience.

"I am honored to meet you, gentlemen. Please allow me to test my memory: starting from left to right, you are Hassan Tajbakhsh, Mohammad Ali Nikookar, Salar Sabeti, Ayatollah Mammad Qazwini, Amir Vehrahrami, Esfandiari Razizadeh, and, on the right, Razmara Tassoudji."

She checked each man's eyes for an indication that she was correct. It was obvious that they were pleased. There is no sound sweeter in any language or country than that of one's own name.

"I have been appointed to conduct formal contract negotiations with you, Dr. Mouradipour," said Mr. Vehrahrami. "However, first, we must come to an understanding on the most important issue in the kind of employment we will be offering you."

Afsoon watched the man's earnest face calmly.

He cleared his throat.

"Dr. Afsoon, what I am about to say to you is such a national secret of the Islamic Republic of Iran that we must have an iron-clad guarantee that you will never divulge that secret to anyone. I do not care to be threatening about that, but all of us here are under the same threat. You may leave here now, tonight, and never return if you refuse to hear my message or go forward with us. You, of course, must not reveal even the fact of this meeting. However—if you agree to hear me out—and especially if you elect to occupy a post of significance in our nuclear program—you will be bound by most serious obligations. In short, you will be executed if you divulge the secrets of our program. Am I being understood?"

Vehrahrami's face was grim but not actually threatening.

"I understand."

"What is your decision?"

Afsoon kept a calm and unrevealing facial expression but said to herself, *This is the moment of truth. Am I brave? Am I capable? Am I a spy?*

Without more than a moment's hesitation, she answered, "I agree to proceed."

There was a small sigh of relief from each of the men. They all smiled.

"Good. This is what we do and what we expect of you: we are engaged in a worldwide dedicated effort to introduce nuclear energy plants in Iran. We are fairly open about that, and you will be expected to make a contribution. However, our most secret national goal is to make nuclear weapons of mass destruction and a delivery system that we can place our bombs in the hearts of the Zionist Entity and the Great Satan."

He paused for effect and to study Afsoon's reaction.

Given the stunning quality of the revelation, she was still able to manage a well-controlled response; she raised her eyebrows and furrowed her brow slightly then said, "That certainly differs from the public announcements being made for the past several years. May I ask a question?"

"Of course."

"How far along are you?"

"Not far enough," Mr. Vehrahrami answered obliquely.

"What then do you expect of me?"

"We are short of superior nuclear scientists and computer scientists who can organize the work and get it fully on track. Be honest with me, Dr. Mouradipour, are you that capable? To put it even more bluntly, are you more capable than me? Your credentials say you are."

"It would be immodest of me to answer your last question, Mr. Vehrahrami. But the answer to your first question is yes. I believe I can make all of you believe that during a probationary year."

"For our part, and on behalf of President Mohsen Shahamatdoost and the Supreme Leader, we offer you the job of deputy engineer at the Bushehr nuclear plant, and the overall coordinator of our Project *Jahannam Adur* [Hell's Fire]—which is the code name for our nuclear weapons program. Your level and power and pay scale will be commensurate with the position. We have given this a great deal of thought. You are young and inexperienced for all of your remarkable degrees. You will serve a year of probation in your position; and—during that time—you will be under very heavy security scrutiny. It is nothing personal, but it is absolutely necessary. If you do not work out, you will be terminated at the end of twelve months."

"Terminated" did not sound like being let go with a grudging recommendation and was not very inviting to Afsoon.

"Do you agree to those terms in addition to the requirements for secrecy?"

Mr. Vehrahrami started to hand a folder with a contract in it for Afsoon to sign.

"I do. However, I have a few requirements of my own before I sign any contract. These requirements are not negotiable. I will want them as a written part of the contract. My requirements are:

1. All of you, and the Supreme Leader, and President Shahamatdoost must sign the documents alongside my signature.

2. I will wait to sign until all other signatures are on the contract.

3. The moment I sign the contract, you must provide me with full physical security protection. Frankly, I am fully aware that women occupy a secondary position in Iran, and some men—even men in high position—are known to feel free to assault a woman. I know that firsthand. You must guarantee me that anyone who attempts to force sexual actions against me will be removed and dealt with under the full measure of Islamic law. On my part, I want nothing to do with love, romance, or sex. If any man tells you otherwise as an excuse for threatening me or putting his hands on me, it will be a lie. That man must be similarly and harshly dealt with.

4. Along that same line, I am not just a good modest Shi'i woman. I am absolute about my modesty and privacy. No one for any reason is to be allowed to see me without clothing—ever. Anyone who insists that I become nude in front of another person is to be dealt with as if he or she had committed sexual assault on me. I have my reasons, and they are important to me.

5. When I am outside the nuclear energy work area, I will wear a chador, even on hot days. Inside the work area, I require that I be permitted to wear a full body pant suit—such as hazmat or air force officers wear—and sensible shoes. I wish to wear a hijab, but only a scarf—nothing that will interfere with my movements.

6. Once the probation period is over, I must have free access to the internet, to computer programs dealing with my work throughout the nation, and throughout the world. I must be able to telephone, e-mail, text, and in all other ways be allowed to communicate about matters involving my work. I understand and will honor the requirements to be appropriate.

7. I guarantee that I will keep secrets. I require that no one keep secrets from me that pertain to my work.

8. From time to time, I will need to have meetings with scientists, engineers, and perhaps others, in the course of my work. I may well have to travel within Iran to any and all of the nuclear facilities. I will likely have to travel outside the country upon occasion for such meetings--including scientific gatherings. I will be happy to have bodyguards and project security personnel with me at all times when I am outside the perimeters of my work area.

9. I wish to be able to visit my family in the United States for one week twice each year. Guards may accompany me at all times."

The men looked at each other in bemusement and back again at the placid determined face of Dr. Afsoon Mouradipour. Vehrahrami was actually pleased. Afsoon's demands had been made efficiently and forthrightly. He could see her inner steel and liked what he saw.

"Your demands are unusual and very precise. I have no problem with them and will work to see that you can be accommodated. You understand that it will take some time."

"Of course. Not too much time, I hope. My time at Stockholm University ends in a week, and I will have to be out of my campus apartment. Perhaps, I can visit my family in the United States for a while, if that is too short a time for all of the particulars to be worked out."

A trip to the Great Satan was not at all what the seven men had in mind at this juncture. Afsoon's demands were so girlish that none of them saw them as a serious stumbling block. When they called back to their superiors and explained how the meeting went, they were mildly surprised and pleased that the most important men in Iran considered it a definite plus that Dr. Mouradipour had not demanded triple the offered salary and lavish living accommodations. None of them balked. However—as expected—none of them wanted her to have an opportunity to go back to the United States until she had had a period of probation and indoctrination.

Mohammad Ali Nikookar was dispatched back to Tehran where he would pick up the top secret document signed by President Shahamatdoost and Agha Rahimi. The top two officials of the Islamic Republic of Iran added an interesting twist to the signature page. They each affixed their right thumb print and insisted that Afsoon do the same. Nikookar returned to Stockholm on the early flight the next day.

§§§§§

Stockholms Universitet [Stockholm University], Campus Roslagen Student Housing, Room 302, September 4, 2007

Afsoon walked across campus to her apartment building well aware that one of the VEVAK agents had been on the bus with her and two more were tailing her at a barely discreet distance. As soon as she entered room 302, she put her finger to her mouth to shush her two *Säkerhetspolisen* roommates, Ingrid Hakkensdatter and Marta Olson. She waggled her finger to have them follow her out into the hallway and into the stairway and down one floor.

She whispered, "I presume that our apartment has had listening devices installed. I will be followed and monitored constantly by VEVAK from now on. Have either of you ever mentioned my mission or my connection with Iran or with Swedish, American, or Israeli intelligence services?"

Both young Swedish agents answered quickly, "Never."

"Sure?"

"Never," they said again.

"It is now more important than ever. I am sure that I will be leaving Sweden for Iran in a matter of days. Even after I leave, consider the apartment to be bugged and that you are being shadowed by VEVAK."

"We are well aware, Afsoon. We catch agents watching us every now and again. We have been on full alert since you arrived in Sweden. We are as sure as agents can be that they are not aware we are anything but fellow students— a pair of empty-headed blonds who scarcely know that Iran exists, let alone are smart enough to be spies," Ingrid told her.

"I certainly hope you are right," Afsoon said. "My life depends on it."

The blonds nodded soberly.

"Here is what I need to have you do. First, tell Ali, Gideon, and 3D that the Iran nuclear higher-ups are coming to me with a signed contract from the president, the SL, and the director of AEOI. Second, tell them that the agents and an AEOI official swore me to secrecy then told me about their intentions and their progress towards producing WMDs and the missile systems to send them to Israel and the United States. They call their program Project *Jahannam Adur* [Hell's Fire]. Third, tell them they are going to put me on a year's probation and then put me in overall control and supervision of the HE uranium production, nuclear engineering, and that I am to coordinate all aspects of weapons production. To do that, I will have full control of the interdepartmental computer systems. I intend to do a major overhaul of their systems and add a few little special programs that will be—as near as it is possible—undetectable. Got all that?"

The girls nodded. They looked at each other, realizing for the first time just how important this young Iranian woman was in the overall scheme of things. From that point forward, all conversations were held in secure locations with nothing but mundane daily busy work and chitchat being communicated in the apartment. They made no effort to find the Iranian listening devices; rather, they depended on girlish drivel to bore their listeners to distraction.

"There is one more thing," Afsoon said, now showing her fatigue from the constant strain. "I need a totally secure laptop that has never been used before and will never be used again. I need to have a top secret encrypted chat with Adm. Daastrup, and I have to do it tonight around midnight."

"Easy," said Marta.

The Swedish agents—her minders—were thoroughgoing professionals, and everything Afsoon requested was done away from the apartment and before midnight. Afsoon sent a brief personal series of encrypted ultrasecret/code word instant electronic messages and received replies from Adm. Neal Daastrup, deputy director of the United States Defense Intelligence Agency. The messages were all secured by Afsoon entering her login code of the day and encrypted in the form of an XML encryption syntax using encrypted object cipher data as a base64 encoding. She included in cleartext her electronic secret decryption key signature—a series of numbers from a popular *New York Times* numerology study done for Mensa. To confuse any would-be eavesdropper, she varied each transmission with a Diffie-Hellman code—an old and difficult code to decipher, and not one that a modern counterencryption expert would be familiar with.

Afsoon: Hello, Uncle.

3D: Nice to hear from you, my bright niece.

Afsoon: I presume that you got my messages from the blonds.

3D: I did.

Afsoon: I expect the target people to contact me in no more than four or five days on the outside.

3D: And then what?

Afsoon: I will disappear from sight and communication for a while.

3D: I will let the group from 'The Farm' know. Once we have an e-mail address for you, we can get safe communications going. It will take us a while. Find a way to send a message to Elsie. Remember her?

Afsoon: I have her address.

3D: Anything else?

Afsoon: Yes. Let all of my persons in locum parentis know I am fine.

3D: Consider it done. They won't know where you are, and they can't correspond.

Afsoon: I know. One more thing.

3D: How can I help?

Afsoon: I want you to have your sister-in-law find someone for me. I will want to communicate with him eventually.

3D: He'll have to be vetted.

Afsoon: Of course. His name is Nassir Jamshidi. He is an Iranian Kurd probably now living in Iraq near Al Basrah. He is not an agent, a spy, or even a political figure. He is kind of a brother. I trust him completely. He will do anything to help me, and I am going to need him as a backup.

3D: I'll work on it.

Afsoon: Thanks. *Alea iacta est.*

3D: Indeed, my dear, the die is cast. It appears that your expensive Latin education was not entirely wasted.

Transmission ends.

Two days later, Afsoon met Mohammad Ali Nikookar in the garden of the university commons. He showed her the contract from the most powerful men in Iran. She signed her name on the signature page alongside the Iranian signatures and included her thumb print as they had done. Nikookar gave her a copy and put the other copy in his valise. Then they parted. Three days later, Afsoon Daastrup Mouradipour was back in Iran.

She was met at the airport by VEVAK agents who gave her identification papers listing her address as being on Ali Shariat Avenue near Hoseiniyeh-ye Ershad Islamic Center to establish her Iranian Islamic *asliat* [Persian authenticity], lest anyone question her post revolution *farhang-e bumi* [authentic culture]. This became her mailing address—a convenience for VEVAK to be able to monitor her mail without her knowing it, then forwarding it to her real residence in Bushehr. It was apparently important to the ruling class—who were now Afsoon's employers—that no one be able to question her bona fides as an Aryan with no taint of Jewish, Arab, Turkish, black, or even provincial Iranian: Isfahanis, Rashtis, Azaris, Kurds, Azerbaijanis, Bakhtiaris, Lors, Baluchis—the *dehatis* [peasants]. She was to be one of *them*—the new aristocracy of the Islamic state. She was aware that she would have to be very careful not to give any hint of the dialectical accents she had developed as a girl living among the *dehatis*.

CHAPTER SIX

Office of the Chief Coordinator, Bushehr I Nuclear Facility, Iran, October 12, 2011.

Afsoon purposely scheduled meetings with executives of Russia's main contractor for the Bushehr I nuclear power plant project [NPP]—Atomstroyexport—and with diplomats and nuclear engineers from the six gulf states near the nuclear power plant—Kuwait, Saudi Arabia, Oman, Bahrain, Qatar, and United Arab Emirates—at the three-star Bushehr Delvar Hotel. She could have met them in her office, now that she was the chief coordinator of nuclear engineering in Iran; but she needed access to the hotel's computers for the real purpose of her agreement to meet the foreign officials. It was worth enduring the congestion of the business section of the city to achieve that end. Her driver wove his way through automobiles, buses, motorcycles, droshkies—a type of low, four-wheeled open Russian carriage consisting of a long bench on which the passengers perched—bicycles, but also horses, donkey carts, and the occasional camel. The mixture of antiquarian and modern had existed in Iran since well before the time of the Pahlavis.

The ostensible—and in itself important—reason for the emergency meetings was the recent spate of earthquakes in and around Bushehr. The diplomats and engineers were justifiably worried about the Bushehr nuclear power plant's security. Afsoon and her staff had inspected the entire facility and found a few cracks in the concrete of several outlier buildings but none in the silo housing the now fully functioning radioactive core.

The morning session started with the obligatory tea and biscuits, fruit compotes, and juice. After almost an hour of talk about anything and everything except the earthquakes, Bushehr, or nuclear weapons, Afsoon finally brought the meeting to order. She spoke in Arabic.

"Gentlemen, I will get directly to the point. Three days ago, we had an earthquake in Bushehr City that affected the power plant location as well. It registered 3.7 on the Richter scale. The mayor estimates that about 10,000 USDs worth of damage was done to older buildings in the city. No one was killed or injured. My staff and I have spent seventy-two hours since the quake inspecting the facility. For that purpose, we shut it down entirely. We found very minor cracks in the concrete foundations of three auxiliary buildings but nothing in the main complex. The silo housing the radioactive materials is perfectly intact; and—by our measurements—no radioactivity escaped into the air or ground. We thoroughly examined the pathways of possible human exposure to effluent releases.

"Although we are probably too far from the ocean to have contaminated it, we took samples of the water a dozen times a day. We measured gamma-emitting fission products in the air using pressurized ion chambers and thermoluminescent dosimeters and by high-volume particulate samplers. Because of the remote possibility that airborne fission products could have accumulated on the ground, we are monitoring samples of garden vegetables, fruits, milk and milk products, and grasses. We are monitoring the daily catches of fish in the fishing villages of Halileh and Bandargeh along the Persian Gulf coast. The results have been consistently negative. We presume the tremor was very superficial in the ground. Any questions?"

The chairman of the Bahrain Atomic Energy Commission raised his hand, "Dr. Mouradipour, the Bushehr plant is the first civilian power plant built in the Middle-East, and its construction began decades ago. The construction cycle was unfortunately marred by long delays due to financial, political, and military issues. The Bonn firm Kraftwerk-Union A.G.—a unit of Siemens AG—started construction then backed out, leaving hundreds of thousands of parts, some of which rusted in the heat and salt air. The reactors were seriously damaged by Iraqi missile attacks. Mismatched used and damaged items were included in the reconstruction undertaken by the Russians. Iran is now the only country operating a nuclear power plant that does not belong to the nuclear safety convention designed to boost safety through peer review and mutual oversight. All of us are concerned about the age and potential deterioration of the facility. Can you reassure us? We are your neighbors—the plant is closer to five Arab Gulf capitals than it is to Tehran. We will be in the direct path of nuclear fallout in the event of a Chernobyl-level disaster. That Russian event polluted the Soviet Union and Europe and wreaked havoc. Are we safe from your facility that is built on an earthquake-prone coastal area? All of Iran sits on seismic faults and experiences an earthquake almost every day. There have been dozens of major quakes over the past several decades."

Afsoon listened thoughtfully, although none of the Bahraini's information was new to her.

"The short answer is that the facility is safe—earthquake safe. I would like to have Dr. Avraam Ivanevich Yaroslavsky, deputy director of Russia's Ministry for Atomic Energy [Minatom], answer your questions, since Atomstroyexport is now in charge of construction, reconstruction, and maintenance. Dr. Yaroslavsky."

Dr. Yaroslavsky did not speak Arabic; so, he answered in the second best foreign language for the attendees—English.

"I echo what Dr. Mouradipour has concluded. The facility is safe. Period. We have had decades to make it so. Our Russian specialists have toured the site many times to assess the damage done to the partially complete plant by the passage of time and by air raids during the Iran-Iraq War. We have brought in new equipment when it was required and spared no expense in doing so. We installed a V-320 915 MWe VVER-1000 pressurized water reactor into the existing Bushehr I building and have plans to upgrade it by the end of 2016. We have installed a light water reactor for the plant under our strict engineering regulations and have monitored all construction regularly. Incidentally, the agreement between Iran and the Russian Federation requires that all spent fuel rods be sent back to Russia for reprocessing. I say that to satisfy Iran's enemies that even if they were of a mind to do so, building a nuclear weapon would be all but impossible. The government of Russia and Minatom stands behind its work and the completed project 100 percent."

"That is fine, Dr. Yaroslavsky," interjected the chief engineer of the sultanate of Oman's Muscat nuclear energy facility, Sayyid bin Muhammad al Uthman. "What about funding? We are all aware of cost overruns, which have rendered Bushehr over budget, over time, and understaffed."

Afsoon fielded the question. Serious queries continued until lunch break from well-educated, well-informed, and serious-minded Sunnis and Shi'ites from all over the region. She was glad to get a break—which, as it often does—stretched out into an afternoon siesta. She took advantage of the lull to visit a computer in the hotel's office.

Using her computer science wizardry, Afsoon sent an encrypted e-mail. The magic of the security she had built into the secure e-mail program was due—in large part—to the ability of the program to make it appear that she was sending a message to Moscow. She was confident that it would take the best team of experts months to decrypt the message, if someone was ever to find it, examine it, suspect it, and be willing to expend such resources on it. If they did, they would discover a completely innocuous personal message from a lonely man to his lonely wife waiting back home in Moscow. When the Mossad and the DIA received the message, it was doubly decrypted to read:

ULTRA SECRET/CODE WORD, EYES ONLY
To: Deputy Director Mossad, Deputy Director Defense Intelligence Agency
From: ADM Trojan Horse
Reliability: Fully confirmed
Message: Beasts will have three packages ready in three or at the most four months. Delivery system remains in question.
Recommendation: Response necessary as soon as means are available.
OUT

Afsoon was at the computer for less than two minutes.

She spent the afternoon detailing the economic, military, equipment, and security issues that Bushehr was encountering and giving the audience the Iranian governmental party line, which she knew to be a pack of lies. She was certain that she had not been detected as she sent her message and equally certain that she had just caused herself and the project she worked on a great deal of headache. It made her smile.

Afsoon had had four years to establish herself and be able to rework the computer system linking all of the Iranian nuclear sources, resources, and facilities. At this point, she was also able to receive and to send short-burst compacted messages with confidence even though she was surveilled almost constantly. Her year of probation had been annoying and frustrating, and she had had to be out of contact with the members of the Iran Nuclear Interdiction Project for the first thirteen months. She was extraordinarily careful, made no friends or enemies, and generally kept to herself. It was a lonely life, except for one positive note: Adm. Daastrup had been able to locate Nassir Jamshidi in Iraq and to determine that he was still apolitical and not a threat to Israel or the United States. She had been able to meet him twice a year when she went out of Bushehr for meetings in Tehran. The first time they met, she brought along her rag doll *Fereshte*, the first birthday present she ever received. She and Nassir wept for joy when they were reunited even though it was only for an hour each time. He promised Afsoon that he was always her brother and would leave everything and come to her aid if ever she required it.

§§§§§

Two days after the meeting at the Bushehr Delvar Hotel, she ran into her first real test of spy craft. She was concentrating on the intricacies of loading a virus into the mainframe that would allow her access to the entire network and to bypass security. It was designed to become active only after AEOI sent an encrypted message to everyone who needed to know that the nuclear weapons and delivery system were ready to be united. Then, she would be able to cripple the missile in flight and to cause fatal errors in the bomb activation sequence.

She had learned about her virus from Gideon and Elsie and during her computer mathematics classes at Georgetown. The virus was much like a biological virus—a slow virus similar to HIV. She took advantage of the latent characteristic property of certain mathematically created viruses to hide themselves then to become active after a certain period of time inside the host software and with an appropriate initiating stimulus. In this case, it was the signal from an AEOI official sending a known encrypted message. To protect her vicious little infective agent, Afsoon programmed it to interfere with the recovery mechanisms of the host computer and of nurse recovery computers available to disinfect the system from its virus. Lacking the antivirus capacity, the computer will become fully susceptible with a very short time delay after the AEOI message was sent. The type of virus she programmed was a highly sophisticated delayed susceptible-infected-recovered-susceptible [SIRS] computer virus propagation model. She had seen it work in the George Washington computer lab and had full confidence in its effectiveness.

She was not aware of a man standing behind her, until she heard him give a little audible exhalation as she bypassed the security system she had devised for the computer network of the nuclear industry of Iran. She startled slightly and turned around.

Her worst fears were realized. The man was a recent University of Tehran nuclear physics graduate who had been hired to monitor the computers of half a dozen of the most senior computer specialists. He was a brilliant young man who was very perceptive and observant. His other quality was that he doggedly pursued the young women in the deep sub-subbasement bunker, hoping to seduce one or more of them in order to get away from the boredom of peering endlessly at a computer screen full of numbers 1-0 and 0-1. Afsoon was by far the most attractive of the women, and the young man had become somewhat fixated on her. His fascination was noted by a senior security guard—a woman—who reported him up the line. He received a reprimand and a warning. Women were a distraction, and none of them—especially the woman coordinator of the network—were to be objects of his personal or sexual interest. After that, he became cautious in the extreme.

He knew he had her dead to rights. It would be impossible for her to deny anything, because he knew where she had hidden her traitorous little virus. And … she would be ripe for the picking. He planned to blackmail her into offering him her favors in return for his silence. He planned to pluck the fruit then to report her traitorous violation to his supervisors and to earn himself a place a rung or two higher up on the ladder.

She was looking directly and unemotionally into his eyes. He leered.

"Well, Afsoon. I think I can call you that now. Correct?"

She nodded. He expected her to be sheepish, to look away; but she did neither.

"We need to talk," he said. "Do you want to have that talk here and now, or would you like to go someplace more private?"

"Private. I know just the place."

He smiled—leered, more accurately. He actually licked his lips.

Afsoon walked ahead of him and led her would-be rapist to the women's bathroom.

"Here?" he asked incredulously.

"Absolutely. It's perfectly private; it's clean; and no one is allowed to come in here for another hour when the women get their break."

He nodded his understanding. They stepped into the quiet tiled room.

"Give me a little show," he demanded.

His face became contorted with lust. He was Hassanzadeh Shakibaie from January 22, 1993, a day forever burned into her memory.

"Never again," she said to the deepest recesses of her brain. *"Never again."*

She stepped back; he stepped forward even faster. He reached out and grabbed both sides of her buttoned blouse. She stepped back further, and he ripped her blouse open. He was so rough about it that her brassiere tore apart at the same time. She was fully exposed to his leering lust-consumed eyes. He stared at her breasts, fixated on them. Afsoon was a beautiful girl, and he had never seen such beauty. He did not pay attention to her hands. He should have.

As he reached forward to touch her, she whipped her razor across his throat. Twin geysers of blood erupted from his transected carotid arteries and internal jugular veins. He could not cry out because his trachea was cut in half and blood was pouring into it, cutting off all sound and air passage. And he was dead. Afsoon quickly removed his Tehran University class ring and put it on her middle finger. She punched her face several times, leaving perfectly tell-tale indentations. She replaced the ring, then bent over and knocked her chin and forehead against the porcelain of the sink. She checked herself in the mirror. She had raised convincing bruises. She ran out of the bathroom clutching her torn blouse across her chest.

All activity ceased as she raced across the large room to the security guards' enclosure.

Her chest heaved as she tried to catch her breath. She was disheveled; her breasts mostly exposed; and she was covered with blood. She looked terrified.

The first guard to overcome shock was a woman.

"What happened?" she demanded.

"…tried to rape me." Afsoon was breathless. "Hurt me. I … I cut him."

"Who? Where?" snapped the guard supervisor.

He was now in charge. He knew all about the special protections this woman doctor was to have. It never occurred to him not to believe her. She was trembling, and fearful, but led a coterie of six guards back to the door of the women's bathroom. She could not bear to go inside. The female guard wrapped her arms around Afsoon and protected her from the eyes of men and the horrors of that room.

They took a full report; and the report was in the hands of Amir Vehrahrami—chief engineer for research and development at the Bushehr nuclear plant—in less than half an hour from the time the incident occurred. He gave a silent scream. He had sworn to protect her, and now this! Barring a miracle, his head would roll. He frantically began to determine whose heads would roll first. He checked the day's guard roster and selected the name of the supervising guard. Then he marched double time to the elevator and descended twenty-seven floors to the bunker basement computer center.

He found Afsoon sitting calmly in the guards' enclosure, a makeshift chador covering her nakedness. The rest of the workers had returned to their computers.

"Tell me what happened, Dr. Mouradipour," he asked Afsoon gently.

She did. It was not quite what happened, but with forty-five minutes to collect herself and to compose a plausible story, it was convincing—especially because everyone within the sound of her voice wanted to be convinced, and for the problem to go away.

"The rapist is dead?" Dr. Vehrahrami asked.

"Attempted rapist," Afsoon corrected. "And yes."

"Any witnesses?"

"No. I think he knew about the women's bathroom—when it was empty, and when the girls are forbidden to take breaks."

He looked at her for any indication that she was accusing him or anyone else. He saw only a tired and frightened girl.

"I want to see every security guard in that bathroom right now. Someone will pay for this. You can count on that, Dr. Mouradipour."

"Please, Dr. Vehrahrami, they are not at fault. They could not possibly have known what the man had in mind. They could not have seen him follow me out of the room from their work area. I was totally unaware of him until he surprised me in the bathroom. It would be terrible for morale, terrible for everyone in the computer bunker, and terrible for me. Please let us forget this awful thing. I cannot talk about it. I know I can get my mind back onto work if I don't have to talk about it anymore to anyone else. The rapist is dead, and no one else should be punished."

Vehrahrami thought over what Dr. Mouradipour had said. It was generous of her, the act of a true and pure Muslim girl. He nodded his head in agreement.

"You should go to your quarters to have a nap for the rest of the day. We will take care of everything here. I believe you are right about what to do. It is a good thing. Allah is pleased with you."

Afsoon did not care a fig for what Allah thought. She was pleased with herself for having gotten rid of two problems at once. She was mildly surprised that she felt no remorse. She had acted at the most primeval gut level—the *never again* level. She was safe, and that was all that mattered. She returned to her computer, explaining that she had to make sure that it was secure before she went back up to the outside world. She quickly moved all evidence of her virus to a file about birds of Iran, and left it there out of sight until it let her know that doomsday was getting near.

CHAPTER SEVEN

The White House, Oval Office, 1600 Pennsylvania Ave. NW, Washington, DC, October 12, 2011.

The White House chief of staff had made it possible for the president to hold an extraordinary meeting with the members and supporters of the Iran Nuclear Interdiction Project. The subject matter was considered to be at an ultrasecret level and too complicated for a series of electronic messages to be transmitted, discussed, and retransmitted. The president had insisted on being able to look eye to eye with the principals of the project before he would sign off on the recommendations. It sounded to him as if this was going to be the precursor to a war, and he was going to be as cautious as possible on the way in to avoid the Bush Iraq and Obama Benghazi debacles.

The Oval Office was filled to capacity. Most of the men and women who had been invited or ordered to attend knew one another or recognized the office he or she held; so, introductions were dispensed with until there was a need to know the speaker. In attendance were the DFBI, DCIA, DNIS—representing sixteen members of the intelligence community—DNSA, DDIA, DFBI, DHS, the chairperson of the Senate Intelligence Committee, CJCS, and their deputies with clearance to know about the project. G.R. IV was there to convey information on financial and computer issues. Several of them were tired and looked travel-worn, having had to leave everything and come long distances to attend.

"Who is going to give us the synopsis?" asked President Gabler.

Everyone turned to recently promoted Vice Adm. Neal Daastrup, the DDDIA.

"Mr. President, we have two assets of unimpeachable quality who have informed us that Iran will have a nuclear bomb—more than one, actually—in three months or four at the most, unless we act more aggressively than we have in the past."

"Who are these assets, Adm. Daastrup?" the DCIA asked. "It seems we are about to commit to serious actions based on two people none of us know about."

"Please let me answer that question, Director," interjected Annette Redstone, the CIA agent directly involved in the interdiction project. "Those of us who have been working on this issue directly for years do know who they are, and it is imperative that no one else knows."

"Do I get to know?" the president asked, partly tongue in cheek.

"With all due respect, Sir, you do not need to know, nor does anyone on your staff, except Lincoln Magalini."

"I don't want to waste any time on that issue. Let's hear Adm. Daastrup out."

"Thank you, Mr. President. To cut to the chase without belaboring details, let me tell you that we have first-strike capability in cyber warfare, economic warfare, sabotage, and other dirty secret warfare programs, psyops, and wet work."

"Wet work?" the chairperson of the Senate Intelligence Oversight Committee asked, hoping it did not mean what she thought it meant.

"Murder," said 3D.

"Oh," the chairperson said.

"Are all the players represented in this room, Admiral?" the president asked.

"No, Sir. We have a squad from more than one crime syndicate, the SAS, and the Mossad."

It was the president's turn to say, "Oh."

"What do you need from me, from all of us here?"

"A blank check and a carte blanche."

"Now, that is certainly short and to the point—a real world Occam's Razor," the president said with a thoughtful look on his face. "I suppose there is not enough time to debate all of this, and no need to involve the Congress," he said and nodded knowingly to the chairperson.

"That's about it, Sir. Everyone involved is going to hang their necks out on this. We will have to have this in writing. We must be able to get through to you on a moment's notice and get a Presidential Order every time we make a move. I don't need to stress that the greatest care will be taken to keep all of this secret. I think we should treat it like the Manhattan Project."

"Can we afford to do this?" the Homeland secretary asked.

"We cannot afford not to do it," 3D said.

"Tell us what we need to do," President Gabler said.

"We have prepared memos for each of you. I suggest that no one other than the president and the members of the long-standing Iran Nuclear Interdiction Project should know the components of the big picture. You all need a measure of plausible deniability; so, let me give you the high points:

"NSA, Homeland Security, the FBI, and every other intelligence organization charged with surveillance and investigation or arrest of domestic terrorists need to identify every Iranian person and asset in the country. You will have to get on the horn with the FISA court and get bales of subpoenas going today. We all know that the NSA has been surveilling American citizens for years. It is time to get into those files and find our domestic enemies.

"The president and his staff will have to order a freeze on Iranian assets like nothing we have ever seen before. There will have to be a real crackdown on cheaters who are finding quasi-legal loopholes. It is way past time for being dainty. The White House will have to begin a serious discussion with the business community to get them to cease and desist from working around the imposed sanctions. Iran does not get oil or other raw materials, machine parts, food, or anything else that sustains its government or its unfortunate innocent citizens. They must be forced to take care of the pressing problems of their populace which is growing more restless by the day as the sanctions tighten down. That is the only way the nutcases in Tehran will back off from their nuclear adventurism. We have the applicable law coverage. It is old but still in force: the 1988 amendment to the Trading with the Enemy Act.

"Law enforcement of all stripes need to back off from the Kosher Nostra and a couple of the crime families from New York and Chicago as they go about their nefarious activities on our behalf. I will keep the FBI informed about who is involved and when and what activities should be exempt from investigation and prosecution.

"Gideon Rothsberger can tell you what is needed from the economic end of things."

Gideon stood and nodded to the president.

"Mr. President, ladies and gentlemen, in addition to the freeze, we need to have U.S. banks and other lending institutions institute a full lending embargo as of today. Our overseas consortium has already done so, because the government of Iran has not made its payments—payments that we contracted to be paid in pure gold. This is a tiresome and recurrent theme, I'm afraid, but now it can be used to our advantage. We will foreclose this afternoon. I wear two hats here today. I have just told you about my economic hat. Now, I change over to my computer science hat. One of the two assets Adm. Daastrup mentioned earlier is an out-and-out computer scientist—a genius. We also have a tight-knit group of computer geeks who—when they get together in a room—have more brains than when Thomas Jefferson used to dine alone when he occupied the White House, as President Kennedy said at a dinner honoring Nobel Prize Laureates. Our geeks will launch a cyber war, the likes of which has never been seen before."

"Aren't there some laws about this sort of thing?" the chairperson of the Senate Intelligence Committee asked with a worried look on her face.

"Yes. We will apply the NSA basis of analysis and attack. We will assess our opponents as to their capacities and intentions as terrorists. It won't be on a probable cause standard, but rather a 'reasonableness' standard."

"That gives you considerable latitude," she said.

"Yes," 3D said laconically.

"And what happens when they retaliate? I, for one, don't think the Iranians are all that backward and dumb," asked the secretary of Homeland Defense.

"That is an extremely good question, Mr. Secretary. We are going to have to absorb some incoming, and it will be painful. We think we can impair their computers in all aspects, including counterattack capability. However, as you intimated, Sir, they are resourceful. Our business leaders and the people they fund are in for a bumpy ride, I am afraid. The Iranians will surely disrupt business and all computer functions in the country and probably around the Western world, I might add. However, our universities are full of geniuses and experts, and they are already seeking solutions to problems that have not even happened yet.

"Our industries and businesses, our lending institutions, our medical assets, and our military are all preparing for attack—a sort of quiet war footing. I am afraid that the result will be a limited recession all around the civilized world. For that matter, I assume that the Iranian intelligence services and the government will begin a campaign of suicide bombings and assassinations. All U.S. and Western police forces and military establishments will have to go on high alert to protect our assets—everyone in this room, important business, legal, medical, and educational leaders, and our water supplies, power grids, and even our forests. Make no mistake, this is not going to be a one-way street, and it won't be easy. One of the hardest things will be the work to maintain plausible deniability. We have put in a great deal of effort to shift the evidence of culpability to any and everyone else besides the United States—so much so that it will be chaos for the Iranians to find any evidence that will stand up. We will be in constant touch with our allies to be sure that they understand we are spreading information and misinformation on a level that will paralyze the Iranian resources."

"It would appear that we all have our work cut out for us. I suggest that we close the meeting and that we keep talk to a minimum. We need to unite as a people and fight a terrible threat, and we need to do it without having to put boots on the ground in an open war. Let's get to work."

With that, the room cleared in five minutes, and a governmental response to an imminent threat began to take shape comparable to that which preceded any of the United States' wars.

§§§§§

Office of the DDDIA, main DIA Headquarters, joint Base Anacostia-Bolling, Washington, DC, October 14, 2011

Caroline Dempsey-Conyers, Vice Admiral Daastrup's secretary of twenty-five years, answered the secret encrypted telephone in Adm. Daastrup's private office because her boss had not yet arrived in the office; in fact, he was over an hour late.

"This is a secure line, and its use is limited to a list of people with approved access," Ms. Dempsey-Conyers said brusquely.

"This is Ruth Daastrup, Adm. Daastrup's wife. My approval code is 2011-703-421-1965-RD. I have a very important message for you. You have been given instructions about passing this information on."

"Go ahead, Mrs. Daastrup. Your call is being recorded. Please speak slowly and clearly. The encryption machinery has a small lag time."

"I am calling from Bethesda National Naval Medical Center cardiac intensive care unit. My husband was admitted here at two this morning in a coma. He had a massive heart attack and will be out of commission for six to twelve months. He has had an emergency bypass operation—a CABG in medicalese—and is now fairly alert. His doctor has told him that he must not have stress anytime in the foreseeable future. He told me to call you and for you to begin processing his retirement effective today. Adm. Daastrup wants the matter to be kept as quiet as possible. Please get hold of the JCS, the DDIA, and the leaders of the Iran Nuclear Interdiction Project; so, they can replace him as soon and as smoothly as possible."

"That is the most terrible news, Mrs. Daastrup. I am so sorry. Please have his doctor call in a report to the special JCS line; so, we can officially process the changeover. Here is the number."

There was a pause on the line while Mrs. Daastrup wrote down the information.

"His doctor is Navy Captain Reginald Davies."

"I will get the ball rolling, Mrs. Daastrup. I will pray for your husband and you."

"Thank you, Caroline."

At each call, the insider members of the Iran Nuclear Interdiction Project were dismayed since they all considered 3D to be indispensable. Each of them shook his or her head and commented that the man had been working beyond any normal person's capacity for months—even years—and the recent efforts to set in motion the urgent measures to prevent the rapid progress of the Iranian nuclear energy program had stressed Adm. Daastrup beyond his poor heart's capacity.

CHAPTER EIGHT

Hencklemann's Meat Packing Plant, East Saint Louis, Missouri, October 14, 2011

Levi Schmuel and Leo "Meat Hook" Donatelli drove through the wasteland of East Saint Louis along the Mississippi River waterfront past a dozen hulks that were once major warehouses in the late 1800s and early 1900s. Two old meat packing buildings had survived and had been converted into modern businesses but still fit into the postwar apocalyptic look of the abandoned areas. One of those buildings was Hencklemann's meat packing plant, now under the titular ownership of the Drager Transport Corporation. A team of FBI forensic real estate and corporation investigators might be capable of peeling away the layers of ownership of the old building if there was any interest in doing so, but there was no such interest. At the bottom of the search, the investigators would have found that the building was owned by the Scarlotti crime syndicate—the Chicago mob.

For the better part of a century, the Chicago mob's criminal enterprises included such diverse activities as manufacture and shipping of synthetic gin during prohibition, racketeering, gun smuggling, bribery, contract killing, arson for insurance fraud, organized suburban burglary rings, coercion, larceny, skimming, hijacking, loan-sharking, drug trafficking, fencing stolen merchandise, auto accident fraud, money laundering, bank robbery, murder, illegal gambling, assault, knee-capping, extortion, running chop shops, and prostitution. The syndicate fell on hard times during the early years of the twenty-first century and lost its dominance in its former spheres of interest.

Beginning in 2009, the major interest of the Chicago mob became trafficking in illegal cigarettes. The concept was simple. The state of New York has the highest cigarette tax in the country—$4.35 per pack and rising. The national average is only $1.46. Missouri is fifty-first with a paltry 17 cents per pack. New York has instituted serious legal restrictions on the importation of cigarettes across its borders and has made it a felony to transport cigarettes that do not have the New York Cigarette Tax stamp affixed to every box. The mob bought cigarettes in the South where they were made, trucked them to the Hencklemann meat packing plant, repackaged them in innocuous boxes labeled as baby food or recycled paper hand towels, and shipped them to the overburdened New York State smokers via the black market.

That would not have attracted concentrated attention from federal law enforcement authorities had it not been for the decision of the mob in 2010 to do business with Arab terrorists. In 2011, Iran entered the business at the level of more than a billion dollars a year—a cooperative venture with the Chicago mob that returned the American criminals to somewhere near their lifestyles of fifty years ago and funded the research and development of nuclear weaponry for the Persians at an accelerated rate.

Levi and Leo drove their Cadillac up to the heavy gates of the fence behind the building. A heavy-set Sicilian brandishing an AR-15 stepped out of the enclosure's guardhouse and approached the vehicle.

"What's your business here," he demanded gruffly.

"We got an appointment with Mr. Scarlotti," Levi said.

"Who are youse?" the guard asked.

"Friends from LA," Levi replied.

The guard was dubious. It was his job to be dubious. He punched an app on his i-Phone and had a short whispered conversation.

"Okay, c'mon through. His office is on the second floor. Don't go pokin' around no place else."

Levi and Leo nodded, drove into the prison-like enclosure, and parked the caddy by the rear entrance away from the loading docks. This was their third visit, and the guards were familiar enough with them to greet them with nods as they ascended to the second floor administration office.

"Hey, Victor, good to see ya," Levi said as he and Leo swept into the boss's inner office.

"You're late," said Victor grumpily.

"Traffic," said Leo.

The three men laughed at the old joke. Fewer than ten vehicles other than Drager Transport trucks traveled the streets of the old neighborhood a week.

They shared coffee laced with Scotch and got down to business.

"Trucks all ready?" asked Levi.

"Yeah, headin' out today."

"No hitches with the union or the ragheads?"

"Everything is copacetic for today and tomorrow. These cigs are headed for the promised land."

"Awright, let's getter done," said Leo.

They shook on it. Four semitrucks a day for two days were scheduled to leave the Drager Transport warehouse for Albany, New York. The truckloads of cigarettes were valued at nearly $1.5 million each. The trucks were driven by members of the Teamsters Union and were slated to arrive three days later at a warehouse rented by VEVAK agents whose business was incorporated in the state of New York as "Persian Enterprises, LLC." Seventeen other truckloads of contraband cigarettes were already ensconced in warehouses throughout the state—warehouses owned by the Providencia crime family of New York. In all, the anticipated profit by the Iranian entrepreneurs was more than $2 billion once they were distributed to New York's black market for needy smokers. The investment by the Islamic Republic of Iran was on the order of $500 million, paid in advance to the Scarlottis who graciously handled all the details.

Each truck had a driver and a VEVAK agent as a passenger. The system was smooth and worry-free. The caravan of trucks made good time traveling through the night. They ran into a hitch just outside Springville, New York, on old highway 219. It was ten after two in the morning. The night was drizzly and foggy. The caravan was stopped by a roadblock of the New York State Highway Patrol and ATF agents.

A trooper walked up to the first truck.

"Please step out of the cab, Sir," he requested politely.

"What's the problem, Officer?" the driver asked.

"Just routine. Please step out of the vehicle."

Other troopers stepped up to the remaining three trucks and issued the same orders.

The drivers and the Iranians were escorted to a small roadside inspection tent to get out of the rain.

"Please show us your shipment invoices. Are you transporting cigarettes? If so, you will need to show us the tax payment forms and official New York stamps."

Each of the drivers hurried back to his truck and returned with the manifests.

"No cigarettes?"

"No, Sir," each of the drivers lied.

The Iranians stood in stony silence.

"We have had some instances of cigarette smuggling up this route in the past several weeks. We are going to have to inspect your cargo," said the troopers' sergeant.

One of the VEVAK agents blurted, "You have to have a warrant. We know our rights!"

"We find your trucks to be suspicious. No warrant is necessary. New York is serious about the collection of cigarette taxes, and we are acting under a mandate from the governor. You aren't thinking of impeding our investigation, are you, Sir?"

One of the teamsters elbowed the Iranian.

"No, Sir, we ain't," the teamster said.

The trailer doors were unsealed and swung open. Troopers jumped into the back of each truck and selected four boxes at random. Instead of baby food and paper products, they discovered illegal cigarettes.

"Impound the trucks and their cargoes," the sergeant ordered.

"You men are under arrest," he said to the teamsters and the VEVAK agents.

The trooper explained New York's unlawful shipment or transport of cigarettes act 1399-11, which specifies that it is unlawful to ship cigarettes to any person who is not a tax agent or wholesale dealer duly certified under article 20 of the tax law, a registered retail dealer under section 480a of the tax law, an export warehouse proprietor acting in accordance with chapter 52 of the internal revenue code, an operator of a customs bonded warehouse under section 1311 or 1555 of the United States Code, or an officer of the United States government.

"The law further states," he went on, "'Whenever a police officer designated in section 1.20 of the criminal procedure law or a peace officer designated in subdivision four of section 2.10 of such law, acting pursuant to his or her special duties, shall discover any cigarettes which have been or which are being shipped or transported in violation of this section, such person is hereby empowered and authorized to seize and take possession of such cigarettes. The penalty for each offense—that is for each *pack* of cigarettes—is a $100 fine.'"

The teamsters were placed in plastic wrist restraints. As the troopers approached the four VEVAK agents, Levi Schmuel stepped out of the shadows and nodded to the sergeant.

"Gun!" shouted the sergeant.

Troopers opened fire and killed three of the VEVAK agents before they could fire a single round from their concealed weapons. The fourth agent raced off into the night. Levi and Leo checked the bodies.

"We'll get rid of them," Levi said to the sergeant.

"Okay. We'll get the goods back to St. Louis. Pretty good night's work, all you buttleggers."

The Teamsters Union drivers were paid double overtime to transport the cargoes back to East St. Louis. They had to drive all night and the entire next day.

The remaining VEVAK agent reported by cell phone to his handler what had happened. The handler was already aware that there had been trouble because simultaneous raids had taken place at every warehouse where the Iranian supplies of illegal cigarettes were being stored. The Iranian government was out nearly $2 billion after the events of that night. The Iranians were unaware that the state of New York had no knowledge of the events. The cigarettes were resold by the Chicago mob without any interference from phony New York State troopers. For everyone but the government of Iran, it was a win-win situation. For them, a multimillion dollar per year flow of funds from New York City was halted for two years.

§§§§§

Private Office of the French Minister of Foreign Affairs, 37, Quai d'Orsay, Paris, France, October 14, 2011

U.S. Secretary of State Dalton Richards Jr. was received cordially by Francois Beauchamps, the French minister of Foreign Affairs in his private office.

"Thank you for seeing me on such short notice, Francois," Sec. Richards said as soon as the minister's door closed.

"I received your e-mail and have met with the president and the cabinet. We are in full agreement with our American allies. We share all of your concerns over the prospect of an atomic weapon in the hands of the Iranians. We are ready to give all the cooperation you need to stop those maniacs."

"I can't tell you how grateful we are, Francois. We would not ask if it were not both important and urgent. You know that, my friend."

"I do. Now let's get down to the details."

In an hour, the two top foreign officers hammered out a plan for France to cancel construction and maintenance of the Darkhovin Nuclear Power Plant—also known as Estehlal Nuclear Power Plant—located 70 kilometers south of Ahvaz, Iran, on the Karun River. The French already felt burned financially by the Iranians and were once again finding the Iranian government behind in payments. Before the 1979 Iranian Revolution, Iran had signed a multibillion-dollar contract with French company Framatome to build two 910 MW pressurized water reactors at Darkhovin. The new government never paid a single rial on the debt, and after the Revolution, France held its participation in abeyance until financial issues could be resolved.

President Mohsen Shahamatdoost's government commenced the project based on promises from the Rothsberger consortium for an infusion of a billion dollars. However, on October 12, 2011, G.R. IV held up the funding when the Shahamatdoost government failed to make two payments in gold in a row. Following that lead, Sec. Richards and Foreign Minister Beauchamps agreed that France would withdraw from the Darkhovin project, and the engineering components of the plant would be placed in storage in France. The plant would have been Iran's first indigenously designed-and-built nuclear power plant; but the American and French decision would exact a delay until at least 2016, and then only if the financial issues could be resolved to the satisfaction of the French government.

The following day, Sec. Richards persuaded Kiev to order Ukraine's Turboatom company to cancel a deal to supply a turbine for the plant in Bushehr, further impeding the progress of development in that plant. Sec. Richards and Ukranian Foreign Minister Borislav Dymtrovych Voitenko tacitly agreed that it might be better if the Russians did not learn of the decision.

Although the Bushehr Nuclear Power Plant was formally inaugurated in September 2011 and had begun making real progress in all of its nuclear power ambitions, a further result of these two financial decisions was that the main plant's operations had to revert to a "maintenance only" status for an indefinite period.

§§§§§

Mile 229, Secondary Coastal Highway between Bandar-e Abbas and Bushehr, Iran, October 14, 2011

Moqtada al-Benizir, head of the Atomic Energy Organization of Iran, his wife, Aisha, and their beautiful and talented daughter—the singer Aisha—two of al-Benizir's top aides, Amir Vehrahrami, chief engineer for research and development at the Bushehr nuclear plant, and al-Benizir's government driver were speeding up the secondary coastal road that links Bushehr to Bandar-e Abbas 311 miles to the southwest. They had combined a productive conference on the progress of peaceful nuclear energy in Iran with a delightful seaside outing.

At distance marker 229, a massive BABR 400 heavy military truck—modified from the Ukrainian MAZ-537—hurtled out of a side road and directly into the path of the speeding official government black Mercedes limousine. Witnesses testified that it was a hit-and-run. The driver of the military truck—described by bystanders as wearing a combat camouflage uniform with three chevrons—was unhurt and raced away on foot towards the shoreline and was lost to sight in the growing darkness.

No one saw Jacob "The Greaser" Cohen—a ranking Kosher Nostra officer—at the helm of the inflatable commando pickup boat that extracted the man in the uniform of an Iranian first sergeant from the sea. Nor did they see the man and the pickup crew go aboard the sleek Israeli submarine—the INS *Tannin*, called "The Crocodile" by the small Israeli navy. All occupants of al-Benizir's vehicle were pronounced dead at the scene.

President Shahamatdoost announced the deaths and declared a national day of mourning. His official statement laid the blame squarely at the feet of the Zionist Entity but did not present any evidence. Aaron Schmuel, four Mossad agents, and SAS agent Carter Miller-Partridge stayed for two days after the accident in the barn bunker at the D-K Ranch outside Tehran. They left the country by crossing the border with Iraq during the night of that second day.

§§§§§

White House, West Wing James S. Brady Press Briefing Room, 1600 Pennsylvania Ave. NW, Washington, DC, October 14, 2011

Press Secretary Jason McCarthy called for order in the press room. "Ladies and gentlemen of the press, the president has asked me to announce that because of growing concerns over the unwillingness of the government of Iran to allow IAEA inspectors into their country, the United States will add additional sanctions to the already stringent restrictions placed on Iran by the outraged civilized nations of the world. By presidential order, all Iranian assets in the United States—private, business, and governmental,—are frozen indefinitely.

"Iran has to this date been able to circumvent the United Nations' sanctions by a subterfuge. Stringent measures will now be put into place to halt any further progress of that subterfuge. There are thirty-seven companies listed under the Iranian Execution of Imam Khomeini's Order [EIKO], which bring in money from state business for the corrupt leaders and work to circumvent international sanctions on the regime. EIKO has numerous subsidiaries—one that manages and controls EIKO's international front companies, and another that manages billions of dollars in investments—which work on behalf of the Iranian government and operate in various sectors of the Iranian economy and around the world, generating billions of dollars in profits for the Iranian regime each year, according to the U.S. Treasury.

"Because of this unique private/government arrangement, EIKO has received all of the funding it needs to facilitate transactions through its access to the Iranian leadership. The Treasury identified the network for sanctions under an executive order that permits the freezing of any assets held by the Iranian leadership in the United States.

"President Gabler has also placed sanctions on Iran's currency. The rial is essentially worthless in the international marketplace. Because of the importance of the Iranian billion-dollar auto export and petroleum industries, the U.S. and its allies will henceforth ban all exchange of the rial and all sale and transport of Iranian-made vehicles.

"Further, it will now be a felony for any American individual or company to transact business with that rogue country under the provisions of the 1988 amendment to the Trading with the Enemy Act. The Department of Justice has identified and blacklisted a major network of American and European front companies serving Iran's leadership. They are now targets of prosecution. Our allies in the U.K., Canada, France, Spain, and Germany have agreed to honor these new sanction measures. Are there any questions?"

CHAPTER NINE

The Iran Centrifuge Technology Company (TESA) Assembly Complex, Natanz AEOI Enrichment Plant, Isfahan Province, Iran, October 14, 2011

Twelve Mossad commandos led by Capt. Houshang Milani and under operational control of Gen. Zwi Rosenstein did a HALO [High Altitude Low Opening] parachute drop from a Russian Mil Mi 26 helicopter at an altitude of 30,000 feet and at an airspeed of 183 miles per hour onto a sparsely forested meadow seven miles from the Natanz nuclear facility. The Russian cargo helicopter was chosen, because it was untraceable to the Mossad or the U.S. It was a sturdy reliable helicopter capable of the clandestine nighttime mission and high-altitude flight, and the U.S. had stolen one from a Russian training base in Novosibirsk the previous year. Milani's men all landed safely in a mile square area and quickly found the predetermined GPS coordinates [33°43′24.43″ N 51°43′37.55″E] southeast of the Natanz hardened Fuel Enrichment Plant [FEP] agreed upon for the LZ [landing zone]. Considerable research effort had been expended by both the Israelis and the Americans to find the ideal touchdown site near the sprawling plant.

Oxygen masks, frigid weather gear, and parachutes were quickly discarded and buried. The seven men and four women commandos formed up in an hour and synchronized their chronometers—0130. Body armor was not used on the mission because it hampered the key aspects of the practical needs of the mission—speed and mobility. They traveled light—knives, Ukrainian surplus night-vision goggles, old used Soviet Union Makarov PMM semi-automatic 9 mm pistols, water, and Russian MREs for food to last three days. They all wore Czech-issue black soft nylon clothing covering them from head to toe, including ski masks and gloves. Each had had dental implants of potassium cyanide salts in case of capture. None of them had any identification documents or telltale tattoos or scars.

The Natanz plant covers 100,000 square meters and is built 24 feet underground. The perimeter is protected by a double reinforced concrete wall 7.5 feet thick covered with 66 feet of compacted earth and rocks. The complex has two large halls and several administrative buildings. At the time of the Mossad mission, it had over 20,000 nuclear centrifuges producing 20 percent highly enriched uranium [HEU] capable of producing weapons-grade plutonium and uranium hexafluoride [UF6], or "hex," as it is commonly known among nuclear engineers. All enrichment technologies—peaceful or weapons—used on an industrial scale require a gaseous process medium. UF6 is the only suitable chemical compound of uranium, because it already has sufficiently high vapor pressure at room temperature, and Iran was desperate to produce as much of the deadly gas as possible and as secretly as possible.

The Natanz plant has finely machined high-strength alloy steel P-2 super ultracentrifuges were instruments capable of spinning a gas of uranium hexafluoride to 100,000 revolutions per minute and 5,000 supermagnets for uranium enrichment. Those centrifuges separated U-238 into 93 percent pure U-235. The nearly pure U-235 was then bombarded to make plutonium. The enrichment plant contained reprocessing cells to contain and shield the very hot plutonium.

It takes about 26 pounds of HEU to make an atomic bomb. The overall purpose of the Mossad commando raid was to impede the progress of Iranian research and development bent on producing enough HEU to make even one bomb. The important buildings of the complex were the Pilot Fuel Enrichment Plant [PFEP], the Fuel Enrichment Plant [FEP], and a large IR-1 centrifuge assembly area, which was the most vulnerable of the three. The TESA plant also manufactured uranium enrichment centrifuge parts. That assembly plant was the limited Mossad target.

Each agent was a specialist. There were two bomb experts, two Krav Maga experts for silent removal of guards—one of whom was Lt. Col. Shai Avitan—two large men to carry heavy equipment, two scouts, two snipers with their two spotters, and two officers—intentional redundancy in case of the death or incapacitation of one key member of the squad in any category. They fanned out in small groups and found the assembly plant. The close-quarter combat veterans dispatched four sentries and hid their corpses, and the squad scaled the walls using graphite grappling hooks for sound suppression and stout soft nylon climbing rope. Inside the compound, they set about executing the complex maneuvers they had practiced for months.

High explosive plastique bombs—military grade Semtex A, 94.3 percent PETN, 5.7 percent RDX mixed with the antioxidant, n-octylpthalate, in a rubber binder, similar to C4—were placed in locations provided by the Mossad operative spy on the inside. Time-delay cellphone activated fuses were attached to each of the explosives to allow a coordinated explosion that would cause the ceiling of the centrifuge assembly rooms to implode and crush the underlying sophisticated machinery and all technicians in the rooms.

The Mossad commandos retraced their steps and melted back into the night. The large helicopter touched down on the LZ at 0320 for five minutes. The commandos boarded the helicopter with highly practiced alacrity, and the stealth-protected aircraft lifted off vertically. At 20,000 feet, fourteen cellphone calls were made activating time-delay mechanisms designed to detonate five minutes after the start of the morning shift. They were flying at 30,000 feet and were 250 miles away when the synchronized blasts occurred. The explosions worked perfectly according to the bombing engineers' plans developed at the Mossad research division in Tel Aviv. The in-place spy later reported that 12,500 centrifuges were completely destroyed and 2,550 were rendered inoperative for months to come; 2,014 technicians, engineers, and scientists were killed, and another 4,887 were wounded to one degree of severity or another.

§§§§§

Camp Peary, York County, Virginia, Armed Forces Experimental Training Activity (AFETA)—Department of Defense, October 15, 2011

The gathering of the computer warriors at "The Farm" had been a feat little short of a miracle. The members were delivered by private luxury jets from Tel Aviv, Moscow, Hong Kong, and Dubai. They reveled in the comfort and coddling afforded them and arrived refreshed and ready to do battle. Elsie Silberberg represented her analyst group at the Mossad Institute; Afanasy Fedoseev, Lyosha Demidov, and Renata Leonidovna Zaslavsky disrupted their criminal activities to come from Moscow to the United States; the Chinese—Veronica Chiu and Clement Chang—came from Hong Kong, where they had been living under strict personally imposed anonymity. They were scarcely recognizable, having had facial plastic surgery. G.R. IV and the five analysts from the Sherman Kent School for Intelligence Analysis made up the American contingent.

The Chinese led off because they had the finished product that the group had agreed upon during their work over the past eight years.

"We now have a truly unique virus or worm or whatever you want to call it. Our Trojan Horse virus is ready for installation and has four important characteristics:

"First, it is easy to install once the hacker is able to enter a system.

"Second, it is easy to remove if the operator of the recipient computer knows the login and password attached to the portion of the virus dedicated to its removal.

"Third, the computer suffers no operational harm once the knowing computer operator removes it.

"Fourth, like Stuxnet, it can be turned back on its sender or sent to an opponent. We have every expectation that the Iranians will do just that.

"Fifth, we have added a devilish little signature—sort of like an artist signing a painting. In this case—because we are wicked spies—we are hiding a small embedded marker that brings up an image of a dragon once an intrepid Iranian computer security agent decrypts it. Need I say that the particular dragon image we have chosen is the same one that the official PRC encryptionists incorporate in their top secret communications to guarantee that the message is truly official and not the result of wicked foreign hackers like us inserting misinformation."

"I am a bit slow here," Gideon said. "Why allow the virus to be sent back to us and to disrupt our computer systems? I get the reasoning behind the rest of what the virus does."

"That is the insightful question, Mr. Rothsberger. I confess that the idea came from our elite spy, Afsoon. She had some free time, I suppose. And she came up with the exact methodology. The reason for her making that apparently dangerous choice is eminently sensible. She is in a key position as the head of computer communications and operations for the nuclear energy system. It is possible that she might be suspected of divulging secrets to Iran's enemies if we hackers were able to instill another disruptive virus on her watch. So our clever girl created a program that she can control and will make her look good to her watchers while also setting them up for a colossal humpty dumpty."

Gideon looked blank.

"Oh, Mr. Rothsberger, you especially should understand, given your classical education. Remember, 'Humpty Dumpty sat on a wall. Humpty Dumpty had a great fall. And all the king's horses, and all the king's men could not put Humpty Dumpty together again.'"

Gideon nodded his appreciation of the nursery rhyme's aptness as a metaphor.

"It seems to me to be a terrible choice for us to have to make. We know the retaliatory attack will come and most of what it will entail. We can stop it. I am sure the same question is in all of our minds. Why not save ourselves?"

Veronica Chiu gave the explanation. "Winston Churchill knew in November 1940 that the Germans were going to attack the British city, Coventry. He knew that because the government had advance warning from their Ultra system, which had intercepted German military radio messages encrypted with their supersecret Enigma cypher machine. Like us, he had a terrible choice to make. If he saved Coventry—especially the beloved St. Michael's Cathedral—he risked having the Germans know that the Brits had cracked the Enigma code there in Bletchley Park. He made the heart-wrenching decision to take no defensive measures. As a result, the magnificent cathedral became a ruined hulk and still stands as a monument to the horrors of the Blitzkrieg. Thousands of people were killed … but Britain won the war. The analogy could not be more apt."

"I guess you're right, but I am still not going to sleep all that well."

Clement Chang added, "What will happen is a classical combination of the old 'good news-bad news-good news' scenario. The good news is that we will succeed in disrupting computers all over Iran. That disruption will substantially interfere with their business, infrastructure, tax system, and especially will seriously set back their timetable for building a bomb. The bad news is that they will turn right around and shoot the vicious little rascal back at us, presuming that we are the originators. Even if they believe the Turks did it, they can't afford to offend them and will let it go. It will give them an excuse to harm us if just for meanness' sake. And, my friends, it will hurt. We will probably enter a short-term recession. The final good news is that Afsoon will be able to correct their computer systems within a few weeks, frustrating efforts for the nuclear energy program and will get great kudos. And the best news is that the unsuspecting dupes from Iran will not have a clue that a modern-day Trojan horse is hiding in their most crucial and secret computer program and communication system, compliments of our very own Mata

Hari. Our micro Trojan horse will just sit there waiting for the day when we tell it to surface. Afsoon or any of us will be able to open it up and let the Greeks pour out."

"Won't the initial disruption of the country's computer system anger the powers that be against our girl?"

"Not enough for them to fire her. In fact, 3D tells me that Afsoon is in line for a major promotion. The previous officer in that position met with a tragic accident. This upcoming series of events will cement her position until the very last days."

"All right," said Gideon, "I'm convinced. Let's get to work. Maybe we can finish in time to get a great steak dinner."

Chiu and Chang gave each participant a computer program to use for installing the Trojan Horse virus. They were all already well-versed in how it worked and how to install it. The final requirement for success was the employment of their vaunted hacking skills. Everyone was given a system or industry or sector to hack into, and they set to work. They were all done before the eight o'clock dinner hour.

CHAPTER TEN

Benjamin Franklin died in 1785. Thomas Jefferson succeeded him as ambassador to the Court of Saint James.
Jefferson told of being questioned about his new appointment. "I was often asked, *'C'est vous, monsieur, qui rem-
place le Docteur Franklin?'* [It is you, Sir, who replace
Dr. Franklin?] I generally answered, 'No one can replace
him, Sir. I am only his successor.'"

- TJ Autobiography, Letter to Rev. William Smith, iii, 213

Office of the Chief Coordinator, Bushehr I Nuclear Facility, Iran, 0530, October 16, 2011

Afsoon was the first to see the incoming Trojan Horse virus because—
having foreknowledge—she had been expecting it all night. It was
0530 when the telltale signs of the worm surfaced on her computer's security file. Afsoon was privy to a considerable amount of information about
the revamped virus—more accurately, a worm. It was based on the original
Stuxnet virus that someone or some country—probably the United States—
had used to attack Iran's nuclear plant computers in 2008, 2009, and 2010.
The attack was adjudged by NATO's Cooperative Cyber Defense Center of
Excellence in Estonia to be illegal. She knew that Stuxnet was the largest and
most costly development effort in the history of malware. She and G.R. IV
were part of the team that used its in-depth knowledge of computer processes
for industrial application and had an enthusiastic interest in attacking the

infrastructure of Iran, which—they were convinced—was in the process of building its own nuclear bomb. The virus attack destroyed more than 2,500 high-value ultracentrifuges and crippled another 4,000 temporarily. The computers used as vehicles of the attack were out of commission for four months. In all, the Iranian nuclear development program was set back four years and billions of dollars by the Stuxnet cybertage operation.

Afsoon had been a highly useful source of expertise on the Iranian end to help in the production of the sophisticated virus; and, as remarkable as it could be, she was also elevated in rank and responsibility and by the AEOI to help in the eradication of the vicious little virus. In fact—ironically—she was given credit as the mastermind behind the successful return of the Iranian nuclear computer system to its original virus-free function.

What was more ironic was the fact that Afsoon—working under the very noses of the Iranian security system and a score of Iranian computer scientists—was able to insert the entry wiring, that allowed the Trojan Horse virus to penetrate the system with ease.

There was more bad news for Iran's computers streaming in over her computer. The state news station reported that two of the most prominent Iranian nuclear scientists had been killed in nearly simultaneous car bomb attacks outside Shahid Beheshti University in Tehran as they left a meeting with the national computer security agency. Little Satan—the Zionist Entity—was given full blame for the incidents, although concrete evidence was lacking. The official news agency included in full the bellicose announcement by the Supreme Leader himself that the Zionist Entity and all Jews everywhere were under a fatwa, which ordered the killing on sight of any Jew encountered by any Muslim anywhere.

Everyone who came to work on time—0800—was dismayed to find that their computers crashed immediately after being booted up. Uniformed security officers and the entire plant computer security staff rushed to Afsoon's small office. It was known that she had insisted that she have an entirely separate computer system, which could only be put into contact with the standard system by entering an encrypted code only Afsoon knew. They found her hurriedly investigating the problem.

"What is this, Dr. Mouradipour?" demanded the head of computer security. "Is it the Stuxnet again?"

"No, but it is similar. I am not finding signs of permanent damage to our computers, but I am sure it will be a lengthy process requiring thousands of priceless man-hours of work to untangle our system to permit resumption of work."

Esfandiari Razizadeh and Razmara Tassoudji, deputies of Moqtada al-Benizir, head of the Atomic Energy Organization Iran (AEOI), rushed into Afsoon's already overcrowded office. The two officials were so overheated by their own piece of bad news that they were as yet unaware of the terrible computer crisis.

"Dr. Mouradipour, have you heard the news!?" they fairly shouted as they shouldered their way up to her computer chair.

"Gentlemen, there has been a great deal of bad news today. Do you refer to the killings of our two nuclear scientists in Tehran last evening or to the fact that the entire nuclear R&D computer system has crashed, apparently a victim of cybertage?"

That stopped them for a moment.

"No, but we have just learned of another catastrophe. Our beloved leader, Moqtada al-Benizir and his wife and daughter—who were named for two of the Holy Prophet's wives, may his name be blessed forever—two subdeputies of ours, and Amir Vehrahrami, our chief engineer at the plant, were killed in a hit-and-run accident. We have been dealt a terrible blow; and, of course, we presume that the Zionist Entity was behind the so-called accident."

"Then we have had nine terrible blows—eight almost irreplaceable people killed, and our computer system is not presently able to function."

"What shall we do, Dr. Mouradipour? We have to rely on you for solutions."

There was an unspoken but clear change in the hierarchy of responsibility in Bushehr. Everyone stopped talking and looked to Afsoon. She was aware of the change but was careful to avoid appearing the least bit pleased or smug. What she did in the next minutes, hours, days, and weeks would determine her success as an agent—spy—for the Iran Nuclear Interdiction Project or her mighty fall from power, and perhaps even finding herself accused of being a traitor. She looked thoughtfully at the men surrounding her and then at her computer while she composed herself and thought through the combinations and permutations of her situation before she spoke.

"Gentlemen, this is what I suggest: First, and before the end of this terrible day, the leaders in charge of our project must have a new chief engineer in place and one who has a great deal of power to make decisions and to see to it that orders are carried out effectively and efficiently. Second, we must assemble the nation's foremost experts in computer function—especially those who worked on salvaging us from the Stuxnet attack—and get them here to begin the long and tedious work of getting the computer system up and running and clean. As you know, I am thoroughly familiar with what happened with the Stuxnet attack and am ready to do my part. Third—and I hardly even need to say it—we must have absolute security and secrecy about what has happened to us. I suggest that the leaders of AEOI and of the nation keep silent or else we will scare away investors, suppliers, and helpful friends all around the world. Fourth—and beginning today—we must prepare to launch a counterattack. We have most of the counter system in place. It will only take a little more work to get it launched. Once again, I know that system—I wrote it. I volunteer to be part of that effort. Fifth, we must not make wild and unprovable accusations against Israel or the United States. However, we must have an independent organization of experts do a thorough investigation and find us evidence we can use on the world platform. The United Nations is the place to start. Russia, China, and Turkey will all be more than happy to be involved."

The rank and file of the Bushehr Nuclear Power Facility looked at Afsoon with unfeigned and largely increased admiration, and, more importantly, trust. An unspoken transfer of power and responsibility had taken place in Bushehr. The men left to get at the business of restoration infused with a newfound sense of purpose that they did not have when they first walked into Afsoon's office. By five o'clock in the afternoon, Tehran had appointed a new head of AEOI, two subdeputies, and a new chief engineer of the Bushehr facility.

The new head of AEOI, Ayatollah Ali Hossein Golzar, was a military general and an archconservative confidant of the Supreme Leader. Mullah Ali Salar Omidyar, director of the Ministry of Intelligence and Security (MOIS) arrived at quitting time to take personal control of all security matters, although he deferred to Dr. Afsoon Mouradipour when it came to technical computer concerns. The new head of engineering for the Bushehr plant, for the nuclear weapon industry of Iran, and for Project *Jahannam Adur* [Hell's Fire] was Dr. Afsoon Mouradipour. She had become the de facto leader of the system when it was verified that Dr. al-Benizir and senior engineer Amir Vehrahrami were dead. In the days to come, Afsoon was applauded not only for her brilliance but for her modesty. She humbly told anyone who approached the subject of her being Vehrahrami's successor that she felt unworthy to be in such a lofty position.

Photographers were brought to the plant to take pictures of the new head of the Bushehr facility meeting with the new chief of the AEOI and President

Shahamatdoost in front of the Building I. The pictures were prominently placed under the headline in the next day's *Islamic Republic News Agency* newspaper and forwarded to newspapers across the country. The main headline read only, "Last Official Act by Outgoing President Shahamatdoost." He had served two terms and was not allowed to serve another. Another hardliner, Hormoz Okhavat, won the presidential election over 951 political opponents. It did not hurt that Okhavat was the personal choice of Supreme Leader Grand Ayatollah Ali ibn Abi Rahimi.

Because the stress of the day and the calamities it contained, the staff stayed on to hold a minor celebration in honor of Afsoon, a singular honor given that she was only a female. Even Ayatollah Ali Hossein Golzar attended and made a point of sitting next to Afsoon. It was a stretch for him, but he complimented the woman on the success of her first day as the chief engineer. The chefs prepared a fine Persian spread: ample servings of *sabzi polow*, a dill rice dish. It was followed by a delicious dried fruit soup made from soaked red beans browned in olive oil and lamb stock, mixed with cubed boneless lamb, lentils, julienne beets, and minced onion. The dish was spiced with turmeric, cardamom, cumin, black pepper, and salt. The mixture was boiled, and then a mixture of chopped dried fruit, including apricots, prunes, pears, and peaches in light lemon juice were added. The dish was served garnished with parsley and lemon wedges. The next course was *kabab-e ozungorun*— sturgeon kebab—and *dolme-ye barg-e mo*—stuffed vine leaves. Dessert was *sholleh zard*—saffron rice pudding. Afsoon thanked them profusely for the meal and for all of their hard work to get the plant into some semblance of working order.

Every hour brought in more bad news for the Iranians. Unknown to them, Dr. Afsoon Mouradipour was both the ultimate source of the cyber attack and, ironically, the principal defender of the Iranian cyber system. Reports flowed in, telling the suffering of people and systems from a variety of forms of computer malware, especially against Iran's oil industry and Science Ministry. The *Iranian Students' News Agency* reported that Iran's Passive Defense Organization—the military unit responsible for guarding against cyber attacks—was locked in battle with a computer virus infection of an electric utility and several manufacturing industries in the southern provinces, again, focused on large oil refineries and a container port in Bandar Abbas. The *Fars News Agency* sent an air force jet to report to Afsoon that a cyber attack had also been made against the information center of the headquarters for Supporting and Protecting Works of Art and Culture, a part of the Culture Ministry.

Systems and networks rather than individual computers were targeted, with disruption rather than theft as the motive. That pointed to the Great Satan and his minions in the minds of every frustrated cybersecurity officer and technologist. It seemed that the Western hackers—although that was not yet proven—were hell-bent on the destruction of anything electronic in all of Iran. Distributed denial of service was the method—the act of terrorists, not thieves.—i.e., a torrent of conflicting traffic was being directed to a site until it collapsed. Despair was rife among the reporters.

The attackers simply took advantage of the large-scale internet transmissions used by companies and consumers in conducting their business. Large-scale "clouds" of hundreds—even thousands—of networked computer servers were being brought to a grinding and escalating halt. Gideon had found banking sites that the cyber attack identified then assaulted them with encryption requests, with the result that the networks were slowed or outright crippled. Antivirus programs in Iran were not equipped to identify—let alone defend—against the onslaught of the sophisticated new malware.

The malware had been sitting inside the prey species computer networks for years. Once initiated, the hackers from "The Farm" used and reused the infected servers to fire traffic simultaneously at each banking site until it slowed or collapsed—a sustained flood of traffic that peaked then was sustained at greater than 70 gigabits. The result was that the cybertagers cut off energy supplies and shut down power grids, gas lines, waterworks, and fracking technologies. Petroleum flow stopped in local and international markets.

Afsoon dispatched the cybersecurity officers and technologists first to limit the damage and then to prove the source. Both missions proved to be impossible to accomplish in any short-time period. The security officials learned what Afsoon already knew. The cybertagers were using botnets—networks of individual infected slave computers—which, usually, could be traced back to a single command and control center. But the security experts learned that this new infectious agent was engineered to make it all but impossible to tie it to one source, and no evidence could be elicited for Afsoon and her people to be able to point a finger at the United States and to prove it with evidence.

What they did find was distressing. Instead of locating an encrypted hint of the involvement of the Great Satan or even China, they identified bothersome hints of Russian involvement. Her researchers discovered several unmistakable Russian words embedded in the malware's code. *"Zakladka"* [Russian and Polish for "bookmark"] appeared in the malware. In the world of hackers, it was also Russian slang for "undeclared functionality" in computer software or hardware. In practical terms, the word was well-known to refer to a microphone embedded in a brick of the embassy building. The Iranian officials did not quite know what to do with that information; and when it was passed up the chain of command by top secret couriers, they were told to do nothing.

The hectic and stressful day had taken a considerable toll on Afsoon. She had come in early, and she stayed late to finish her work. To do that, she finally ordered that she be left alone to think and to do her work without being interrupted. As soon as she was alone, she sent off an encrypted e-mail.

> ULTRA TOP SECRET/CODE WORD, EYES ONLY,
> Rear Admiral Martin Torgelson, Gideon Rothsberger IV,
> Annette Redstone, CIA, and Major General Zwi Rosenstein,
> deputy director Mossad:
> Important day. Computer chaos, new directors of AEOI
> and Bushehr plant (A.M.), new and greater responsibili-
> ties for adm, including being the new director of Project
> *Jahannam Adur* [Hell's Fire].
> Retaliatory measures to be sent out tomorrow. The impact
> will be severe but temporary. Begin restoration protocols
> immediately after the attack is recognized. Sorry about the
> damage, but it cannot be helped.
> Signed: ADM Trojan Horse.

It saddened her not to have her uncle and foremost protector still on board. She had learned about Neal's heart attack almost immediately after his wife, Ruth, called his office in Anacostia. She had been assured that nothing material had changed; but it was deeply disconcerting, nonetheless. She did not know the new DDDIA Torgelson, and that made her uneasy.

CHAPTER ELEVEN

Offices of the Supreme Leader of the Islamic Republic of Iran, Islamic Republic Street—End of Shahid Keshvar Doust Street, Tehran, Iran, October 16, 2011

Agha Rahimi was attending to the inaugural ceremonies for the new president, Hormoz Okhavat, at the *Majles* [The Islamic Consultative Assembly of Iran—*Majles-e Shorâ-ye Eslami*] and could not attend the meeting. However, he did send a terse note of instruction: "If they want war, give them one."

The chief of staff of Supreme Leader Grand Ayatollah Ali ibn Abi Rahimi, Ali Hosseini Mejazi, Vice President Tajbakhsh Mavasseghi, deputy leader of the *Majles*, deputy directors of the MOIS and AEOI, and Yazid ibn Sarrafzaadeh, chief of staff of the Armed Forces of the Republic of Iran, met around the conference table. Security was intense; these were intense times. Hamid Hejazi, newly promoted chief of Rahimi's security detail at the offices, was busy minding every detail of security both in and outside the building. He insisted on being on the watch for the important men in the conference meeting at all times.

The vice president assumed the chairmanship of the meeting.

"Gentlemen, we are at war. While we do not yet have the proof to present to the United Nations Security Council, we have been attacked by the Great Satan and its monkey offspring, the Little Satan. This is a new escalation in an ongoing war with them. We have been attacked by cyber criminals before—presumably from those same corrupt hegemonous nations. This time it is more overt and coordinated. A new cyber attack has been launched at us.

The attack has done more harm than those in the past. Our new expert—the woman at Bushehr—has informed Ayatollah Golzar that the virus or worm that has infected our computers is different, more sophisticated, and more capable of spreading to any computer in contact with the computers of the nuclear industrial system.

"I ask you: are we ready to retaliate?"

"We are. The woman at Bushehr has a method of turning the attacking virus back on the perpetrators, and they will know the wrath of God."

"What is the woman's name?" asked Gen. ibn Sarrafzaadeh.

There was a moment of pause.

The deputy director of the MOIS thumbed through a notebook then answered, "Mouradipour, Dr. Mouradipour. I don't have a first name. She is very well thought of and seems to be extraordinarily intelligent and a world-class expert on computers and nuclear engineering. She has told us that she is ready to start the attack on our command. She has never been known to make statements she cannot back up."

"Fine, have her launch. We need a smile. Oh, Deputy Director, has VEVAK found any evidence of subversion, of an internal mole?"

"None yet, but the investigation is in its early stages. My personal opinion is that there is not one and that all members of our nuclear working group are honest and loyal to the Islamic Republic."

"Let us hope and enlist the aid of Allah, the all powerful."

The deputy director of the AEOI picked up his smart phone, clicked on a "favorites" link, and was instantly in contact with Dr. Afsoon Mouradipour on her private cell phone.

"Operation God's Vengeance is a go. Repeat, the retaliation plan is hereby ordered to be set into motion."

Afsoon opened her password-protected and encrypted program for the operation, clicked on "send," closed out the program, and, separately, sent an e-mail.

> ULTRA TOP SECRET/CODE WORD, EYES ONLY,
> Rear Admiral Martin Torgelson, Gideon Rothsberger IV,
> Annette Redstone, CIA, and Major General Zwi Rosenstein,
> deputy director Mossad:
> Operation God's Vengeance has been set in motion.
> Signed: ADM Trojan Horse.

Almost simultaneously, Hamid Hejazi, chief of Rahimi's security detail at the offices at the Supreme Leader and the ever watchful guard, sent his own e-mail.

> ULTRA TOP SECRET/CODE WORD, EYES ONLY, "Swede":
> Expect imminent cyber attack. Also, watch for suspicion of other assets. Top-level discussion of possible mole. No consensus and no strong incentive for investigation yet.
> Signed: Agent Ex.

§§§§§

Office of the Senior Vice President, Rothsberger Family Bankers, 423 Montgomery Street, the Financial District, San Francisco, California, October 16, 2011

Gideon had been receiving secret intel about the cyber attack in Iran; but—as yet—there had been no reporting of the event in U.S. and European news media. In preparation for the attack, he had established an entirely separate computer system for his private and personal use with a new computer, new fiber-optic wiring, new satellite company as server, and new software. Such a complete change was impossible for the bank and for other industries. The Western world would just have to trust Afsoon Daastrup Mouradipour that the coming attack could be weathered, and their computer systems could be returned to normal function.

Miriam was aware that her husband was distracted by a problem larger than the usual banking issues. She was more perceptive and intuitive than her youthful age, sheltered childhood and adolescence, her absorption in the performing arts, and her submissiveness to her Orthodox husband would lead one to conclude. Gideon was nervous and forgetful, which was so unlike him. Miriam insisted that she go to the bank with him this day and would not consider "No" as an answer.

Finally, Gideon said, "Miriam, you are smart, maybe too smart. I am involved in very delicate matters that I cannot talk to you about. You will just have to accept that and not probe."

"And be a good Orthodox or maybe even a good mafia wife?" she asked sweetly.

"Good Orthodox wife will do. Please, Miriam."

"I will keep your secrets, Gideon, but know this: I am your wife in all respects, your partner, and your confidant. Tell me what is going on. Let me work with you. I know you used me in Iran, and you were up to something there. I don't feel safe not knowing. I don't feel safe being treated like a child. I am not a child, and I am not a potted begonia. I am a grown and educated woman and more of a cactus than a begonia. I am coming to your office with you today. Consider this a major crossroads in our marriage, but I will not be shut out."

"It is for your own good, for your own safety, Miriam," Gideon said, knowing that he was fighting a losing battle with his beautiful and determined young wife.

"I have had a lifetime of hearing that very phrase, Gideon. Treat me like a woman and not a high-maintenance airhead. Let me in. Please."

"I can't deny you anything, Miriam, but my fears are valid. Let's compromise. There are things I can never tell anyone else. There are people whose lives depend on absolute secrecy. If you were to know about those people and if you were captured and forced to talk, it would be disastrous for them, for us, and for our country."

"I agree to the compromise. Thanks for calling it our country. My application for dual citizenship is almost done. I should be a French-American in less than a month."

"Great news."

As they sat in his office at Rothsberger Family Bankers in the district, Gideon filled Miriam in on the basics of the Iran Nuclear Interdiction Project, stressing the value of the effort for preserving the existence of Israel. He left out the names and positions of other participants, except for Elizabeth Nichols-Dayan and her two sons. He could not deny their involvement, because Miriam told him of her strong suspicions that came from the night she performed at the D-R Ranch.

He warned her about the computer nightmare that was to come, probably that very day.

"Miriam, we have been hard at work to prepare for this eventuality. There is a highly sophisticated U.S. pre-attack preparatory response, which was put into place when we attacked Iran's computer system controlling their nuclear ultracentrifuges. Homeland Security now has a National Cyber Security Division [NCSD], which operates what is called the Control System Security Program [CSSP]. The government has established a program run by Homeland Security, which has a computer emergency response team—

Industrial Control Systems Cyber Emergency Response Team [ICS-CERT]. I have been going to meetings twice a year for training—helping to define recommended practices—and to put out a self-assessment tool and an early-warning system. We have averted several major attacks; so, we know the system works. Even if damage does take place, the system protects servers and computers from serious or permanent damage. Thousands of technicians are now available to bring computers and computer systems back online. In a major attack, that will take time, but will eventually be successful."

A skull-and-crossbones icon flashed on the desktop monitor of the bank's system computer, heralding the arrival of the precursor and diluted virus to the eventual Trojan Horse worm that would one day strike Iran like an atomic bomb for computers. Gideon prayed that the Western world was not about to be hoist by its own petard. He booted up the bank system computers and got only as far as the screens showing an image of a mushroom-shaped cloud before they turned to crosshatching haze. No amount of manipulation could get a scintilla of work to happen on the computer.

"This is Iran's doing, then. Right, Gideon?" Miriam said.

"Like I told you. And this is just the beginning. The phones should start ringing off their hooks in about a minute."

It was half a minute. Gideon had three phones—all with agitated and furious bank executives, large account holders, and frightened investors on the other end. Gideon could not keep up; so, Miriam began fielding many of the calls. She was a quick study and easily got into the rhythm of Gideon's explanations to the callers. Gideon pressed the "call" button on his desktop; and a few seconds later, his secretary entered the room. She was about to ask her boss what was going on; but she, too, was a quick learner. She listened to Gideon and Miriam—picked up the patter—commandeered one of the phones, and began to answer the distraught callers.

Gideon let his line ring several times as he gave instructions to his secretary.

"We are not enough. Go around and get the other secretaries going on a phone bank. Teach them what to say, especially the part about the caller having to be patient. This attack will pass. I am going down to IT and see if they are able to start working on damage control like we planned. After that, I am going to sit at your desk and make a bunch of international calls. There is probably mass hysteria all over the civilized world right now. Miriam, that leaves you as the head man in here. Thanks for being here."

Miriam coquettishly looked down at her remarkable buxom figure and gave her husband a wry smile. They enjoyed a small husband-wife intimate laugh.

Similar scenarios of financial downfall were being played out all around Europe, North and South America, and the Middle-East. Iran was the clear winner in this battle, but was not likely to win friends or influence investors any time soon once the source of the computer attack became common knowledge. Al Jazeera Media Network—headquartered in Doha, Qatar—televised massive rallies by ecstatic cheering Iranians. Using previously issued, specially protected satellite phones, Gideon, representing the financial world; Levi Schmuel, representing the business world; Martin Torgelson, representing the American military; Ali Nylander, Swedish diplomat, representing European interests; Randall Caruthers from the State Department; André Lansky and Elsie Silberberg from the Mossad; and their associates and employees began a telephonic conference to explain how to deal with the destruction to business, government, military, and personal activities that was now in progress.

Sunnis in the Middle-East were hit particularly hard because of the lack of sophistication of their computer security systems, and they vowed never to forgive or to forget that it was the Shi'i that did this terrible thing. Instead of disheartening the movers and shakers and the rank and file of the West, Iran had only awakened the sleeping tiger. In four days, no one who had a television, radio, citizens' band radio, or access to a newspaper had any doubt who had launched this unprovoked attack. Iran could not speak up about the attack it was enduring without revealing state secrets; so, they had to watch in the gall of bitterness as they were vilified all over the planet.

The direct consequences of the computer virus infection lasted six months, and the worldwide recession lasted two years. The effect on electronic communications devices was mind-numbing: there was an effective shut down of 98.8 percent of telecommunications delivered via the Internet, which negatively impacted 25 percent of the citizens of the earth who were connected—well over a billion people. Equally severely affected were the landline telephone systems throughout the civilized world. There were 1.2 billion landline connections for seven billion people, 116 billion in the U.S. alone. Iran had 28 million, which were hit by their own weapon. Mobile phone capability was devastated. At the time of the cyber attack, there were 7.2 billion cell phones—more than one for every person on the planet. There were more cell phones than toilets. The United States had 328 million cell phones for its population of 312 million people, and all but a small fraction ceased to be usable within five minutes after Iran's attack. Sixty percent of Americans had smartphones and less than 0.5 percent of them remained functional.

The average U.S. home of 2.6 people had an average of 28 electronic gadgets, which might as well have been plastic knockoff dummies for all the good they could do. The annual U.S. wireless data traffic of 1.6 trillion megabytes and nearly $190 billion in total annual revenue was reduced during the first year to a paltry 9 billion MB and $8 billion in revenue. International telephone traffic dropped from 125 billion minutes to 1.1 billion during the same twelve months.

The telecommunications giants—with their massive investments in underground and undersea cable systems—were leveraged to the hilt and operated on a very thin profit margin in the best of times. Undersea networks laced the ocean floors like a giant spider web made of glass that could transmit information at the speed of light. The Iranian cybertage resulted in a reduction in messaging via TAT-14, FLAG, and Arcos-1, and many others by quantum amounts—billions of circuits and hundreds of gigabytes of data. Similar catastrophic decrements through underground fiber-optic networks heaped even greater losses on Qwest, AT&T, RCA, CenturyLink, América Móvil, Frontier Communications, Verizon, Hawaiian Telecom, Alaska Communications, and Sprint Corporation, as well as more than a thousand smaller provider companies. The catastrophic losses pushed more than one of the providers to the brink of bankruptcy.

Ironically, Iran was one of the countries worst hit by the recession caused by unleashing their weapon. Worldwide, the broad dissemination of the virus resulted in more than 500,000 industrial plants shutting down business. Every banking system in the world—other than the state bank of Iran—had to stop borrowing and lending, and every major nation declared bank holidays lasting months. The records of more than six million Facebook subscribers' contact information—including e-mail addresses and their private financial information—were hopelessly scrambled or communicated to other subscribers and to hostile creditors. LinkedIn closed down its site the first day of the cyber attack. Large health care networks, including the Mayo Clinic, Kaiser Permanente, Intermountain Health Care, and multiple Catholic insurance entities, suffered for all intents and purposes and became deaf and blind.

There was a domino effect: vendors could not produce; trucks, trains, and planes could not transport; businesses—large and small—could not stock their shelves; and consumers of all kinds had to scramble to keep ahead of the rolling disaster. Many failed. As one example, Siemens devices were especially hard hit, and the venerable company filed for Chapter 11 reorganization. Unemployment rose to 14 percent in the U.S. and even higher elsewhere.

The health of millions of Americans and Europeans was imperiled. The American FDA sent out an urgent warning to all makers and users of heart monitors, mammogram machines, x-ray machines, MRI and CT scanners, and pacemakers that their machines—and therefore the patients they served—would be jeopardized; but they were too late. The slow-moving digitization program designed to improve patient record keeping, doctor-to-doctor and doctor-to-patient communications, and to decrease medical and pharmaceutical errors throughout the Patient Protection and Affordable Care Act [PPACA] network was jammed and ground to a halt. Information technology initiatives were disrupted in 318 major hospitals. Encrypted data was beamed to outside sources—and ultimately to Iran. Only rural hospitals with antiquarian record keeping systems were spared the devastation. Much of the $30-billion funding provided by the Gabler administration was wasted.

The VA system, Intermountain Health Care, Mayo Clinic Health System, JPS Health System in Texas, and Kaiser Permanente Cardiac Catheterization labs shut down for six months. From the last quarter of 2011 to the end of 2012, the annual death rate percentage climbed four percent for each year. One notable death was that of Sheila Montrose, the vice president. Her pacemaker suddenly drove her heart rate to 300 beats per minute, and her heart could not take the stress. It was nothing short of heroic how President Gabler kept the nation's hope in the future viable. His efforts were eventually fully vindicated.

The malware virus was able to install itself on PLC devices unnoticed; so, almost no one outside the privileged few who were informed in advance by the Iran Nuclear Interdiction Project was prepared for the onslaught. The new virus teamed up with the Conficker virus to destroy many computers outright. Preparation would have required that virtually every computer outside of Iran be shut down before the virus hit and began its virulent infection. Even if they had been aware, individuals, organizations, and companies would not have been able to resist their addiction and would have booted up their computers to see if they had really been attacked. Computers with slave variable frequency converter systems were particularly vulnerable.

Almost every plant and factory that utilized computer dependent systems to start up and keep running machinery with moving parts was disrupted, and some estimates calculated that 70 percent of such machines were damaged. The cost was in the trillions of dollars. There were four different zero-day malware weapons—previously unheard of in malware attacks—and at least four different worms. As a result, no server or device escaped: Windows and Mac, Verizon and AT&T, cell phones and iPads, flash drives and laptops alike were caught up in the tsunami. The virus was promiscuous and highly infective. Early on, computer scientists and the public at large feared that the world would have to reinvent the computer to get machines that were free of the virus. While that was theoretically possible, the cost would be so astronomical that ordinary citizens would never again be able to afford a personal computer.

While the victims of the attack suffered, the computer scientists who were aware of what Dr. Afsoon Mouradipour had done celebrated. She had configured a dozen Web sites around the world outside of Iran. Those co-opted Web sites were configured as command and control servers for the malware, allowing it to be updated continuously, unknown to the information specialists in Iran. As a result, she had engineered what amounted to the perfect industrial/military espionage program. When the Western computers eventually returned to function, American, Israeli, and European intelligence services were treated to what amounted to an open door to the Iranian safe. The problem for the intelligence services was how to deal with the massive amount of data that was available. The end effect was the embedded virus had codes that updated it as needed instead of eradicating it. It now captured information and collated it as a consumer-friendly server. And Iran was totally unaware. Afsoon and her collaborators at "The Farm" learned from the Stuxnet debacle to ensure that the virus could be rerouted back to Iran in a future attack by the Trojan Virus at the will of the adept hackers working under the CIA umbrella.

During the first few days after the attack by the powerful virus, the leaders of Iran watched the beginning of the end for the West with unabashed enthusiasm. Everyone who was anyone credited Dr. Afsoon Mouradipour with the great success. She was being touted in the nuclear energy world as the next successor director of the AEOI. Her star could not have been brighter or higher in the stratosphere.

CHAPTER TWELVE

Tent Hamlet of the Shakibaie Clan, Qushchu Village, Kurdestan County, West Azerbaijan Province, Iran, October 23, 2011

Shireen, one of the four Shakibaie slave girls, brought Ahriman Shakibaie his morning coffee and the Kurdish newspaper *Rudaw*—a week old edition, which was the most recent available in the rural area of northwest Iran. His wife, Fereshten, took offense at what she considered a flirtatious look from the attractive Turcoman girl and cuffed her face as she passed by.

At first, Ahriman gave only a passing glance at the front page photograph and the headline. He focused his attention on the latest struggle of the *Hizbi Demokrati Kurdistani Iran* [Democratic Party of Iranian Kurdistan, or KDPI]—the oldest and largest Iranian-Kurd political party inside and outside of Iran—and the Islamic Republic of Iran Army [IRIA], the ground forces of the Islamic military.

Something about his glance at the photograph nettled the back of his mind. He looked at the picture again. The new head of the AEOI and the new chief engineer of the Bushehr nuclear facility were being congratulated by outgoing President Shahamatdoost. The name of the new government official meant nothing to Ahriman, but his now focused eye caught the name Afsoon for the new chief engineer. He remembered an Afsoon from the past; but then, it was a common name. He looked away, and then something drew his attention back to the photo.

He did an almost motion picture double take and let out a surprised yelp.

"She's dead!" he erupted. "That cannot be her. It cannot be!"

"Who?" asked Fereshten upon hearing the minor commotion.

Her husband looked stunned.

"What is wrong?"

"Look at this picture in the *Rudaw*."

He handed his wife the paper and stood back to avoid influencing her opinion.

"Allah help us!" she exclaimed. "It is the enticer—the girl who shamed our Hassanzadeh all those years ago. But she is dead. She was dead when they took her to Piranshahr to the county jail."

It was beyond belief. It was as if an evil spirit had come back from the dead to haunt them—a zombie.

After a moment's pause in which he calmed down, Ahriman said, "Remember, this is the miracle baby that survived freezing and the animals on the Mount of Thorns the day it was born. I guess anything is possible under Allah."

"If she did not die in jail, she should have been sent to Evin Prison to hang for her crimes against the *Qur'an*," said Fereshten.

"It is her. She is alive. She can only be where she is because she escaped from jail, probably murdered one or more guards. Now, the little trickster has worked her way into a high position in the nuclear energy program. She was always smart;, I have to give her that. It must be that she is a traitor and a spy. That's what you would expect from such a criminal."

"You have to do something, husband."

"What do you suggest? Who are such as we to be involved with criminals? If we speak up, maybe they will accuse us of being her accomplices."

"And, more likely, there will be a reward for bringing this criminal girl to the attention of the national police."

"I have a compromise. I will report her to the warden at the prison in Piranshahr. The information can go from him to the authorities, and we can appear to be only innocent people making an identification. That should still get us a reward."

Images of bales of rials shimmered across his line of vision.

§§§§§

Ahriman and Fereshten got up early and took the donkey cart into Qushchu Village the next morning. They bought two round-trip bus tickets to Piranshahr e Mokrian, the larger of the two cities in Kurdestan County. They boarded with the usual overload of peasants going to the larger city market and their menagerie of goats, piglets, chickens, geese, ducks, and children.

The rural farm couple was awed by the massive and impregnable fortress that was the Piranshahr County Jail.

"She could not have escaped from this place without wizardry. She is a witch," announced Fereshten with finality as they knocked on the side-door entrance.

"What do you people want?"

"We have come to see the warden about a matter of national security. It is very important. We swear this with our hands on the *Holy Qur'an*."

"Are you serious?"

"Absolutely. National security. Your career will be over if you fail to allow us to see the warden."

"Give me the message, and I will tell Haji Kaboudvand when he is not so busy."

Ahriman and Fereshten gave each other conspiratorial looks.

"No, Sir, we mean no disrespect; but this must be for a person of high rank."

They seemed earnest.

"It will go bad for you if you are relatives of a prisoner and are just trying to get to see him without permission from the court."

"We swear it."

With a reluctant sigh, the jailer opened the door and admitted the farm couple.

"Wait here," he said and closed and locked the door.

"Makes you shiver, and it stinks, doesn't it?" Fereshten said when the guard left them standing in the bare entry room of the jail to go and find an officer to take them to see the warden.

He was gone half an hour. He returned with another officer, this one with more gold stripes on his arm and epaulets on his shoulders. He was severe looking.

"This is your last chance to leave without punishment if you are lying," the new corrections officer said.

Ahriman and Fereshten stood their ground.

"Follow me then," the corrections officer ordered grudgingly.

They stopped at an office door. On the window to the office, in gold letters, was the name and title of its occupant, "Warden Haji Sadiq Kaboudvand".

A stern spare-framed late-middle-aged martial-appearing man beckoned them to come in. Both of the Shakibaies were nervous and trembling a little.

"Be calm, citizens. What is so important that you can only tell me?"

Ahriman told the warden about the troublesome girl whom one of the girls in their camp had brought into their tents. He left out the part about her having been left out to die on that freezing night thirty-one years ago. He told of her precociousness and her unwillingness to obey the patriarch of the clan. Fereshten had gotten tired of the tedious pace of her husband's narrative and launched into an accusatory diatribe explaining the criminal acts of the wayward girl: intentionally enticing and seducing their innocent young son, inveigling him into carnal acts, lying about it, and attempting to avoid God's punishment.

"She was convicted of enticement and lasciviousness—tazir crimes that only required judge's knowledge. She and several others were sentenced by Mullah Haji Zamaani Fard to be transferred to Evin Prison for hanging, 100 lashes, and for the guards to make sure she was not a virgin before she went to the afterlife. We know for a fact that she received the lashes. She nearly died from them. We thought she had died because we never saw her again."

"I don't understand what that has to do with me," the warden said, bemused by the rendition of such ancient history.

"Because we saw this in last week's paper," Ahriman said.

He handed the newspaper to Warden Kaboudvand. He looked carefully at the headline, the photograph—which was a very clear and professional one—and at the article.

"How can this be your daughter?" he asked.

"Not our daughter," Fereshten insisted. "Just a girl who lived in our clan tents. But we know her well and will never forget her face or her actions. She ruined our beautiful boy. He has never been the same. She must have escaped and lived a life of crime and deception to have gotten to a high position. We think she must be a criminal still and, worse, a traitor who endangers our beloved Iran."

That got the warden's attention. He was quiet for a moment then told the Shakibaies that he would investigate the situation and get back to them. The two were dismissed.

Two days later, the local constable delivered a message to the main tent in the Shakibaie clan compound. They were summoned to appear at the jail the following day and from there, they would be taken to Tehran for an interview with the chief of the Tehran Police Department. They were to speak to no one else. Only he—the warden—and the two Shakibaies were to know of the nature of their information. He had not even told the police chief the particulars, only that he was sending down two citizens of the county who had credible knowledge of traitorous activities.

That same day, a routine message about the possible criminal activities crossed the desk of Behrouz Omidi, director of the Ministry of Intelligence and National Security of the Islamic Republic of Iran [MISIRI or VEVAK]. There was a conspicuous absence of any specifics, except for the names of the individuals making a claim about a threat to national security, Ahriman and Fereshten Shakibiae. VEVAK sent the message about the upcoming meeting between the Shakibiaes and the police chief to the Supreme Leader's office without comment. Hamid Hejazi—chief of Rahimi's security detail at the offices at the Supreme Leader—handled the incoming police and intelligence services reports and filed them appropriately as to the level of their urgency. Hejazi was a very observant, well-informed, and intuitive man. He remembered the information he had read about in the Iran Nuclear Interdiction Project file about the other important agent of Adm. Daastrup's. The name "Shakibiae" jumped out. His intuition told him that this might well have something important to do with the people who had abused the agent many years ago and could not be a harbinger of good. First, he filed the report on the bottom of the stack. Then, he fired off an immediate e-mail.

> TOP SECRET/CODE WORD, EYES ONLY, REAR ADMIRAL TORGELSON:
> Swede. We may have a potential threat to your Trojan Horse agent. People named Shakibiae are coming to see the chief of police in Tehran with a message about national security. I think they may be the people who abused her years ago and nearly got her killed. They probably think she was dead. They may think she is a criminal or a traitor and probably are looking for a reward. Suggest warning Agent Trojan Horse ASAP.
> Signed: Agent Ex

Rear Adm. Martin Torgelson's alarm on his iPhone went off, signaling an emergency message. When he read it, he became instantly focused on saving his predecessor's niece and his most valuable agent. It was possible that this had nothing to do with Agent Trojan Horse, but he could not afford the risk of waiting to see. He dialed an ultrasecret number in Tehran.

"This is a secure line," was the first thing the woman's voice said.

"Elizabeth, this is the Swede. Sorry that I have no time for chitchat. Our girl, Afsoon, may be in imminent danger. Her childhood abusers seem to have recognized her somehow and are traveling to Tehran to meet with the chief of police. This may be a false alarm, but my gut tells me it is not. Please intercept the couple and take them to your bunker for questioning. Call me when you have them."

"Adm. Torgelson! How on earth are we going to be able to find them?"

"I'll have Afsoon call you. She is smart and resourceful. She will find a way if anybody can."

They hung up. Martin called the ultrasecret direct personal cellphone number for Afsoon. Elizabeth called her sons, Elias and Zachariah, to the communications room to await instructions.

"Martin?" Afsoon said, having picked up the call at the onset of vibration.

"Yes, dear girl. Listen. The Shakibiaes are going to meet with the chief of police in Tehran in the next couple of days. Anyway, they could have learned about who you are and what you are doing now."

Afsoon arrived at the obvious deduction in less than two seconds.

"My picture was taken at Bushehr when I was made chief engineer. For some unknown reason, it made the papers all over the country—probably a slow news day. The Shakibiaes must have seen it, recognized me, put two and two together, and set out to do me fatal harm."

"I agree. Any ideas how we can trace them and follow them down to Tehran? We have people who can intercept them, but we have to know where they are at a given time."

"I have one idea. You remember my sort-of brother, Nassir? He knows them perfectly well and where they live. I can reach him and get him on his way to Qushchu as fast as possible. He works in Bushehr City. I can get him a plane ride to Piranshahr quickly. He is resourceful and can finagle a quick trip to Qushchu, where he can find those monsters, hopefully."

"Take out all of the stops, but don't compromise yourself as you do it."

"Easy for you to say, Sir."

"I know. I worry about you. I feel like I know you from my meetings with 3D. Take care and watch your back."

"I always do."

§§§§§

Nassir Jamshidi was stunned to hear from Afsoon, frightened by the implicit threat to his little sister, and thrilled by the possibility that he might actually save her life. Afsoon's connections were impeccable. Nassir was on a military jet carrying papers marked urgent from the Bushehr Chief of Engineering Office. He was in Piranshahr in three hours. It was ten minutes past ten when the plane touched down. He knew he was behind the game before he had even started. He had to find rapid transportation to Qushchu quickly without drawing attention to himself. He had a moment of clairvoyance.

He found a phone in the airport and called the police station, which was located less than half a mile from the jail. He explained his urgent need to convey a message to an agent in Qushchu from a secret government institution. He had papers they could examine. A police car with lights blazing and sirens blaring pulled up to the front entrance of the airport after a few minutes, and Nassir hopped in. As they were racing back in the direction of the police station and Qushchu, one of the police officers perused Nassir's papers and was impressed.

"We need a better car," the driver said. "This wreck can only go about fifty miles an hour. We can get a better vehicle at the jail."

Nassir agreed and silently urged the officers on.

The officers parked by the side door of the jail and went in. Nassir sat in the backseat of the police car fidgeting. Every other second, he glanced over at the door to the jail, wishing it to open; so, he could get on his way. To his consternation and absolute delight, a police vehicle pulled up near the car in which he was sitting, and Ahriman and Fereshten Shakibiae—of all people—stepped out.

Nassir was not particularly religious, but he said, "*Alhamdullilah!* [Thanks be to God]."

He slid down in his seat in order not to be seen and dialed his emergency number to Afsoon. He quickly gave her a thorough description of the car, the police officers, and the car's license plate numbers.

"I will call you back when they start off," he said.

More good fortune—and another *Alhamdullilah*—for Nassir came because that car left in the direction of Tehran before his helpful officers returned to the car in which he was sitting. He called Afsoon again about the time the car with the Shakibiaes left. He resigned himself to having to maintain his cover by being taken to the miserable little village of Qushchu, where he lost another day's work before he could be returned to Bushehr.

Afsoon called Adm. Torgelson and gave him the information. Martin called Elizabeth Nichols-Dayan and conveyed the urgent message on to her. She and her sons studied a highway map and selected a perfect spot for an ambush. Everyone involved in the scenario had tachycardia and shortness of breath.

CHAPTER THIRTEEN

West Portal of the Niayesh Tunnel, Tehran, Iran, October 18, 2011

The Piranshahr police vehicle transporting Ahriman and Fereshten Shakibaie to their fateful meeting with the chief of police of Tehran—and presumably where the couple's fortunes would radically change when they received the handsome monetary reward for exposing the dreadful traitor to the Islamic revolution—entered the east portal of the Niayesh Tunnel heading into the main part of the city. The ten-kilometer-long tunnel is the longest in the capital. It connects the east to the west and has an internal route connecting the east to the south. Traffic was sparse at that time of day—midafternoon. Just outside the west portal of the tunnel, the driver encountered his first slowdown of the trip from the Piranshahr Jail to the Tehran police station. There was a police road block.

They were fifth in line to meet the Tehran metropolitan police traffic officers. When their turn came, a somewhat odd thing happened. The officers ordered the Piranshahr police to pull off into the lay-by and moved the barriers back further to the east.

"Hello. Sorry for the inconvenience, but we have had a jailbreak this morning, and we need to check your papers. We also need to inspect your vehicle. Just routine, but you understand, we have no choice in the matter. Please step out of the vehicle and take a seat in the back of our unit," the traffic patrolman said politely.

"But we're police. Why stop us?"

"Just routine, Sir. Please get into the SUV."

The men shrugged and explained to the Shakibaies what was going on. They were all a bit disgruntled but decided that it would be quicker and simpler to comply. They climbed into the SUV and waited as the patrolmen examined their police vehicle.

A patrolman stepped into the SUV and sat in the driver's seat. No one spoke.

Ahriman was getting anxious and claustrophobic. He tried to roll down the window, but it must be broken. It would not budge. He tried to open the door. It was locked from the outside. He banged on the wire separator between the driver's compartment and the passenger section. The driver did not respond. Ahriman began to shout. Fereshten joined him. The driver sat like a stone. One of the Piranshahr corrections officers banged on the separator with his night stick.

The driver did not seem to make a move, but a sudden thick cloud of gas filled the passenger compartment. All four of the northerners were taken completely by surprise and were unconscious within a minute. A second patrolman got into the passenger side.

"Let's go," he said.

The SUV started forward and was followed closely by the metro police vehicle—driven by one of the patrolmen—heading west. The small caravan exited at the next off-ramp and headed north. Since none of the passengers was conscious, the Nichols-Dayan men did not bother to secure the hands or put a black hood on the people they had just kidnapped. The anesthetized passengers were still out when the vehicles arrived at the Rafter D-N Horse Breeding Ranch. They parked at the side of the outbuilding.

Elizabeth Nichols-Dayan hurried out to the building and helped her sons drag the unconscious passengers into the barn's bunker room. They separated the two corrections officers away from the Shakibaies and secured them in wooden armchairs. The sons wrapped several windings of duct tape around the couple's wrists and ankles and the chair. They did not bother to cover their eyes or mouths.

The corrections officers were similarly secured, then the Nichols-Dayans shed their makeshift police uniforms and waited until their guests regained consciousness.

"We have no options with the couple," said Elizabeth.

"We'll take care of it, Mother," said Elias. "Just make sure no one happens to go out to the cemetery today."

The cemetery he referred to was the burial place for horses and other animals, that died on the ranch. He nodded to Zachariah, who left the room. He drove out to the cemetery and began digging a deep trench with a backhoe.

"I can't leave just yet. It's not really anything to do with being squeamish. We've got to be sure what to do with the cops."

"I can't see how we can let witnesses live, Mother. We knew we were getting into serious business when we agreed to help Adm. Daastrup and Adm. Torgelson and the rest. If you are still uncomfortable, why don't you call Afsoon?"

"I'll do just that. I know what has to be done, but maybe she'll have something else in mind. Can't hurt."

She opened the hidden door, entered the small communications room, and called Afsoon's encrypted number.

"Yes," Afsoon said.

"Can we talk?" Elizabeth asked.

"We have to be brief."

"Sure. We have no choice about what to do with the Shakibaies, but the corrections officers may be different. Don't you worry about an investigation and even a nationwide hunt for policemen?"

"I take it you have all of them?"

"Yes."

"There is no question about what has to be done."

"I understand the Shakibaies; they're monsters. But the corrections officers were only doing their job. Isn't there another way?"

"Their guilt or innocence is not the issue. They cannot live and bear witness against me. All of us would be dead within hours of their being able to contact law enforcement authorities. As for sympathy, you can forget that. These men and all of the rest of them in the Piranshahr jail raped, tormented, starved, and humiliated every woman under their authority. I saw women whom they whipped to death. No sympathy. You must swear to me that you will do what must be done. Every minute you waste makes the situation all that more dangerous. Swear that you will kill them all. I know it goes against everything you believe in, but think of all the poor girls who were their victims. You've seen my back and my privates. There's your answer."

"I know," said Elizabeth, "and I'll take care of it. Sorry to bother you."

"We are partners in an important project to save thousands, maybe millions of innocents. I'm sorry that such a good woman as you has to do such things."

When she got back to where the captives were seated before she communicated with Afsoon, they were nowhere in sight. Elias had killed them all and had loaded them in the deep bed of the old Ford and was now at the cemetery helping Zachariah prepare the trench. Glad to be prevented from having to commit murder directly, Elizabeth returned to the house and worked at appearing busy and worry free.

The trench was almost twelve feet deep carved out of extremely hard rocky desert earth. The two sons moved quickly to get the bodies ready to be dumped into the pit. They stripped them of all clothing, rings, toe rings, and anything that would aid in identifying the corpses. They rolled the bodies into the deep trench. This was a common practice to rid the ranch of corpses and to be able to use the residue as fertilizer. From what looked like an oversized pressure cooker, the men sprayed the corpses at a pressure of 60 pounds per square inch with a strong solution of sodium hydroxide—lye—in water heated to 300 degrees. The bodies immediately began to heat and to liquefy. When the men returned that night, nothing was left but a syrupy brown sludge. The hot caustic base in the hard-walled trench—which acted like a low-heat pressure cooker—had hydrolyzed the soft tissues and left some almost formless bone residue. They used the backhoe to dump rocks into the pit to crush the remaining bone fragments and to render it almost impossible for anyone to dig under the covering, because the lye, dirt, and water formed a hardened mortar locking the stones together like a flattened medieval wall. The ranch hands had learned long ago that quicklime was ineffective—even counterproductive—to the aim of getting rid of corpses, because of its desiccating effect which mummified the remains. The lye spray—on the other hand—eliminated all traces.

That did not get rid of the problem of Haji Sadiq Kaboudvand, warden of Piranshahr County jail, who was the only other person who knew about any involvement of Afsoon with the jail or that she had a criminal history. That much was learned from the Shakibaies, who became voluble when they thought that divulging their innermost secrets and life histories might save them from their murderous captors. Elizabeth called Afsoon on the secure phone and told her what she and her sons had learned.

"I'll take care of it," was all Afsoon had to say.

What she did was to convey the information to the Swede and stressed its import and the urgency of the need for a solution. Two days later, Aaron Schmuel, Mossad *katsa* [case officer] Antal Disraeli, and SAS agent Carter Miller-Partridge, crossed the border from Iraq into Piranshahr, West Azerbaijan

Province, Iran at the Piranshahr County crossing. It was easy to find Mahnaz Zarindast from the description Afsoon had given Adm. Torgelson. She was one of only four women who worked in the jail, and she was the only cook. Aaron disguised himself as a Kurdestani peddler and was able to get a quick full-face photo of the jail employee and send it to Afsoon's mobile. Afsoon confirmed that she was Mrs. Zarindast—the only person in the jail who had treated Afsoon and the other girls with any degree of kindness.

Aaron, Antal, and Carter stopped Mahnaz's dilapidated old pickup truck as she drove into town to begin her day's work. Aaron made her an offer she could not refuse. She could accept 50,000 USD and relocation under a new name in a pleasant home in a U.S. compound in al Basrah, Iraq. There she would be housed, fed, clothed—all at no cost to her—and treated well for the rest of her life. Or … they would kill her now. If she reported them, they would kill her another day. Mrs. Zarindast had no love for the Iranian system; and once she learned the specifics of what was expected of her, she became an enthusiast. She despised the autocratic, sadistic, and lecherous warden, Haji Sadiq Kaboudvand. And she loved being alive.

Aaron, Antal, and Carter believed her and made arrangements for her to carry out the project they had in mind for the warden. They gave her very careful instructions on how to do what was needed, how to get away safely, and where to meet them on the Iraq side of the border when the deed was done.

Aaron gave her a thimble-sized amber glass stoppered vial of an odorless, colorless, tasteless viscous liquid. He told her not to allow any of it to get on her skin or near her mouth or eyes. The vial contained the batrachotoxin of *Phyllobates terribilis*—the beautiful golden poison frog native to the Pacific coast of Colombia that has been used to poison arrow heads by the indigenous hunters for centuries. The toxin is a particularly poisonous steroidal alkaloid secreted from the frog's skin glands. A minute amount of less than 140 micrograms—about the size of three grains of ordinary table salt—is sufficient to kill a 70-kilogram man. Mrs. Zarindast's file contained enough poison to kill 200 men. Aaron was not about to take any risks of failure from an insufficient dose.

She told the Western agents that her best chance would be when she served the warden his noon meal. He always ate alone; so, he could cop a feel or two or more from any serving girl or woman who drew the black bean and had to serve him. Mrs. Zarindast put on a little perfume, a little lipstick, and a little rouge on her face. She smiled invitingly to the lech as she served some of his favorite foods. He had the peculiar habit for an adult man of separating each of the different foods on his plate from all the other varieties on his plate. Mrs. Zarindast took pains to place seven different foods on one large plate. His habit included eating all of his food before taking a drink, and then he quaffed his entire tumbler of juice in two or three gulps. Then, to complete the pleasure of his repast, he liked to get a little feel from a woman who could not protest.

This meal proceeded with the same routine as all of the rest. He leered at Mahnaz meaningfully and drank down the delicious sweet pomegranate juice to the last drop. Before he could raise his hand for the usual caress, he experienced almost immediate neuromuscular transmission blockade, followed by muscular and respiratory paralysis and a quiet death. He fell face forward onto the tabletop. Except in extraordinary circumstances where the batracho-toxin is suspected, and a competent toxicology laboratory is within an hour's distance—neither condition pertaining in Piranshahr, Iran, that day—the cause of death is always written off as being of natural origin, presumably a heart attack. The Haji lived a sedentary life and was—in consequence—in poor physical condition. His doctor had repeatedly warned him about the risks of his careless lifestyle, and Haji Kaboudvand ignored them all. When his body was found the following day, the cause of death was "myocardial infarction and cardiac arrest."

Mahnaz was astonished at the speed with which the deadly liquid killed the man she despised and was so abusive of the girls supposedly under his care and protection. *Inshallah* [as God wills]. It was just, and she who had seen such terrible things go on in the jail was not in the least disturbed when this waste of Allah's clean air sloughed his mortal coil. She walked briskly out of the jail and got into her truck. She drove home, picked up her identification papers—her *shenas nameh* and passport—and made her way directly to the Iraq border. Allah was with her. She was number eight in line to cross, and the border guard and customs agents from both countries were bored and waved her through perfunctorily.

Ten miles from the border, she saw a large black Suburban SUV with American flags flying from each of its antennae, just as she had been told to look for. She parked her truck. Aaron waved her to the SUV, and she got in. It did not occur to her to be afraid.

Aaron produced a thermos of ice-cold lemonade and a delicious American ready-to-eat army meal. She had hurried at everything she had done thus far that morning and was grateful for the rest in the comfortable big car's backseat and for one of the best meals she could remember. The trip to al

Basrah was exhilarating. She would not have imagined that a vehicle constrained to be earth-bound could travel at such speeds. When they drove into the American compound in al Basrah, she was greeted enthusiastically by a beautiful blond woman and an exotic Kashmiri Pandit woman from north India who introduced herself as Aisha Toskhani and filled her in on her interesting life and customs as they walked to Mrs. Zarindast's new home—a clean, bright, happy little cottage.

When she was settled in, Aaron Schmuel knocked on her door and politely handed her a thick manila envelope. She peeked inside and saw more money than she had earned her entire life—enough to keep her safe and comfortable for the rest of her days.

"Tomorrow, Mrs. Toskhani will bring you new identification papers. You are now a citizen of Iraq and are safe from the evil regime in Tehran. You will never see me again, unless you decide to speak of what you have done these past two days. You will have great cause to regret seeing me again, do you understand?"

"Perfectly. I don't know why you wanted Haji Kaboudvand dead, but I certainly had *my* reasons. The world is better off without him. I like what I have here and will do nothing to interfere with that. You have my promise, as Allah, the all powerful, is my witness."

They shook hands sealing their contract of silence.

Afsoon's secret was safe, and—for better or for worse—the family that owned the D-K Horse Breeding Ranch was now fully committed to the Iran Nuclear Interdiction Project. And the kindly jail matron was happily ensconced in the nicest place she had ever seen.

CHAPTER FOURTEEN

Office of the Senior Vice President, Rothsberger Family Bankers, 423 Montgomery Street, the Financial District, San Francisco, California, October 18, 2011

The light on his desk signaled Gideon that an important incoming call was waiting. He pushed the button to talk to his secretary first.

"Who or what is it?"

"You're not going to like it, Mr. Rothsberger, but it is a very, very angry Iranian. His name is Ali Mohamed Mustaffen, and he says that he is the director of the Central Bank of the Islamic Republic of Iran."

"Thank you, Ethel."

Gideon switched to the other line.

"Gideon Rothsberger here."

"At last. I have been kept waiting. Nobody keeps me waiting."

"What can I do for you, Mr. Director?"

"You know perfectly well what you can do for me, you cheating Jew. You can honor your commitment to release funds for our peaceful nuclear energy projects. You have been holding us up for months."

"And you have not paid the last interest installment in gold. In fact, you have not even offered to pay in rials—a currency not traded on the international money markets. We still insist on gold, and we still insist on full payment including arrears. The interest rate is now 28 percent. In one week, it will be 32 percent if we do not receive payment. And, unfortunately, all transactions will be very slow owing to the unprovoked attack on our financial and business system computer networks. I will cut to the chase: all evidence points to Iran for that attack."

"Lies! Unprovoked? That is ... how do you say ... 'the pot calling the kettle black.' We suffered severe damage to our computers, which has been most costly and time consuming for us. While we are still collecting evidence, it is obvious that the U.S. and its lackey, the Zionist Entity, were responsible!" Director Mustaffen shouted.

"I hadn't read about that. Was it in the news media?" Gideon replied with exasperating calmness.

There was a long pause while Mustaffen struggled with what he would say next.

"You will accept wire transfer payment, not gold. You will release the funds today; so, they can be in our hands by the end of the week. You will cease and desist from all of this interference. It is a Jew-American conspiracy, and we won't have it!"

"No," Gideon said with finality, further infuriating the national bank director. "We had the same discussion with your president in 2006. Because of the intercession of one of the good Jews in your country, you were able to meet your obligations. That time you were two months overdue in making your payments. Now, you are behind by four months. We will be paid in full by the end of the week or the consortium will sever all business connections with you, as provided for in our contract—our legal written contract."

There was an ominous silence on the other end of the line.

Finally, in a chillingly clear, calm voice, Mustaffen said, "You will remember and regret this conversation for the rest of your life, young man. You are warned."

"Are you threatening me?"

"I am getting your attention and demanding that you honor your commitment. I would not dream of bringing harm to you, to your lovely wife, Miriam, and your parents in San Francisco or her family in Paris. I would never threaten your father who is always in his office at the bank in the district, or your grandfather in his grand château in Paris. Give all of them my best regards."

And he hung up the phone.

§§§§§

Château Rothsberger, Village of Pauillac in the Médoc, Northwest of Bordeaux, France, October 22, 2011

Gideon had known that Ali Mohamed Mustaffen was not a man to make idle threats; so, as soon as Mustaffen hung up on him, he called his wife and ordered her to fly to New York and to stay with the family of New York Stock Exchange trader Israel Siegel, who had once been Gideon's financial mentor. He called his father G.R. III and told him of Mustaffen's threats.

"Do you think he was serious, son?" G.R. III asked.

"Absolutely. Father, none of the Iranian bankers or officials in the government could ever play poker. They do not know how to bluff. We have had all the warning we are going to get. You and Mother and the twins have to take a vacation to parts unknown to anyone else but you; and you have to do it today, please."

"I believe you, son. Thank you for the warning. I note that the cyber war is heating up in earnest—threatening murder—that is beyond the pale."

By five o'clock that afternoon, the Rothsbergers of Saint Francis Wood nabe, San Francisco, California, were on an El Al flight to Tel Aviv. They were to be the guests of the Zeev Rosenkranz family for an indefinite period. It would be hard to find a more secure place to visit than the home of the head of the Tel Aviv Kosher Nostra.

G.R. IV's grandfather took his call. He was sitting in his office working on Global Products Universal legal issues at his huge walnut desk handcrafted by Thos. Moser Company when Gideon interrupted him.

"Yes," he said.

"Grandfather, we have a problem. I have just received a serious threat from Ali Mohamed Mustaffen, director of the Central Bank of the Islamic Republic of Iran."

"What is the nature of the threat, my boy?"

"Unstated as to type, time, place, or upon whom, Grandfather. However, I do not doubt the reality of the threat even a little bit. He mentioned you personally."

"I know the director. I have been threatened by bigger men. My grandparents survived the holocaust. My parents fought with the Irgud when Israel was made a state in 1948. A punk Iranian banker hardly strikes fear into this old heart. My security force is more than adequate. Save your concerns for the rest of the family, and may Yahweh bless and protect them all."

Gideon argued with his stubborn grandfather, G.R. II, to no avail. He offered special protection from the CIA and the DIA. The old man would have none of it. Gideon gave up in frustration, fearing the worst, but hoping that G.R. II would be the least inviting target of all the G.R.s.

The most dreaded of calls came at midnight on Gideon's cell phone. He was staying in the Four Seasons Hotel in downtown Dallas—the only AAA 5 Diamond Hotel in the city—under an assumed name.

"Hello," he said tentatively.

Good news did not come at midnight in Gideon's world.

"Is this Monsieur Gideon Rothsberger IV to whom I am speaking?"

"Who is asking?"

"*Inspecteur principal* of the *Sûreté nationale*, Etienne DuGardier. Are you Mr. Rothsberger?"

"Yes, Sir."

Gideon's heart sank. This had to be more than the usual midnight bad news.

"I regret to inform you that our Bourdeaux division was called to the home of Monsieur Gideon Rothsberger II this evening. He was found to be deceased. Identification has been verified. I am sorry for your loss."

"Can you tell me, please, what happened to him, Sir?" Gideon's voice quavered, and he fought for control.

"The matter is still under investigation. Your grandfather is undergoing an autopsy as we speak. However, we have reason to suspect foul play. The first officer on the scene noted the classical facial expression, foaming at the mouth, and the odor of bitter almonds characteristic of cyanide poisoning."

"Do you have a suspect or suspects?"

"Nothing concrete yet. We will let you know when we have definite knowledge. Right now, I am authorized to tell you that one of the servants, a Moroccan man, who was a long-time employee of the Château—is unaccounted for at the present time. All other employees are presently sequestered in your grandfather's home, which is being treated as a crime scene."

"Thank heavens my grandmother did not live to see this travesty. Thank you very much for the call. I will wait anxiously for any updates you can provide."

"I assure you that the *Sûreté* will do everything in its power to bring the killer—if indeed, this was a murder—to justice."

"It is all I can ask," Gideon said; and they hung up.

Three days later, Gideon received a cellphone call forwarded from his office. It was from Ali Mohamed Mustaffen—the last person on earth Gideon expected to hear from.

"Yes, what is it?" he said brusquely.

"This is...."

"I know who it is. What do you want? You have the gall to call me after what you did?"

"I am calling only to convey my bank's condolences and those of our government for the untimely death of your respected grandfather. Nothing else."

"How thoughtful," Gideon said with undisguised sarcasm.

"Mr. Rothsberger, your grandfather probably died of natural causes—may Allah rest his soul—but even if he met with foul play, there can be no trail leading to a Persian source. If there is found to be evidence that it was murder, rest assured that we will investigate to the fullest to see if there is any Iranian complicity; and the criminal will be dealt with accordingly."

Gideon thought he was going to wretch.

"Is that all?" he asked, anxious to get off the phone, his store of courtesy strained to its limit.

"Oh, I neglected to give you a piece of what should be good news. We have found a source of temporary funding to allow us to make our payments to you. We can have a bank draft sent to you today from the Alfa-Bank in Moscow in lieu of your insistence on physical gold. That is the best we will ever be able to do, Mr. Rothsberger. Perhaps it is time for men of the world to reach a reasonable compromise. What do you think?"

"The reputation of the Alfa-Bank is good. I will tell you what I will do, Mr. Mustaffen. I will study the matter, contact the head of Alfa-Bank, and will consult with the members of our consortium. When I speak to Alfa-Bank, my first order of business will be to require them to make the payments in gold, and you will pay a premium for that. Know this, Sir. All of the efforts at intimidation are in vain, even the murder of my grandfather. We are Jews, and we have a long memory of abuse at the hands of Muslims. But we are survivors. Perhaps, we can all survive to do business, but our business will be strictly in accordance with our contract."

"That seems reasonable," said Mustaffen, certain that the computer hacking and the killing of the venerable old patriarch of the Rothsbergers had gotten young Rothsberger's attention and had resulted in his softened attitude.

The call was concluded. Gideon fought to gain personal control before calling members of the consortium—Swede, Afsoon, and the controlling members of the Iran Nuclear Interdiction Project—to be sure that it was still useful—even crucial—to keep up the façade of doing business with their enemies, the instigators of the Project *Jahannam Adur* [Hell's Fire]. As wounded as the Western world was in general and Rothsberger family especially, the crusade to stop the planned holocaust by the Shi'ite nation had to take precedence over his personal anger.

Human considerations and the Shi'ite banker's brazen bluster aside, Rothsberger & Company Bankers—under the direction of its shrewd senior vice president—had had to insist on all of its investments in the Iranian nuclear energy building program being backed by gold. This reluctance had been communicated to the government of the Islamic republic and its bankers regularly and was etched in stone—or at least an iron-clad contract with G.R. IV's banking consortium. He had a huge lever against the nuclear production program—the contract. The legal document was transparent: failure to pay the ever-mounting interest and the amortized portion of the principle that had come due—would again—in all likelihood—constitute failure of the debtor to make good on its end. That failure would kick into motion an automatic increase of the interest rate to 28 percent and then to 32 percent in a week, which would break the back of the nuclear weapons project and perhaps even that of the Islamic republic itself. Failure to make good on even this installment would trigger an automatic and final cancellation of all funding for Project *Jahannam Adur* [Hell's Fire], which would—at least—set back the completion for years, even decades.

G.R. IV's power and influence in the banking world was in the ascendancy because of the sad fact of his grandfather G.R. II's murder. Within the week, and before G.R. II's funeral, Rothsberger & Company Bankers' new president would be G.R. IV, and the new CEO of Gideon Products Universal and master of Château Rothsberger would be Gideon's father, G.R. III. Already, Gideon was beginning to feel a hint of pressure to produce a G.R. V.

CHAPTER FIFTEEN

Office of the Chief Engineer, Bushehr I Nuclear Facility, Iran, October 29, 2011

Afsoon spent her days watching the Internet news on her protected computer. Much came encrypted from the U.S. 513th Military Intelligence Brigade through the DDDIA's office. Her ostensible occupation was to marshal computer forces from all around Iran to make the necessary repairs to the computer systems attacked by the United States. The gathering of earnest young men and a smattering of women was amazed at Afsoon's brilliant management of the calamity and of her grasp of computer science and of the availability of countermeasures to deal with the virus or worm or whatever it was that had been infiltrated into the nuclear energy program's vital communication system. They—of course—were unaware that the premier engineer in the country had set the entire scenario in motion. They presumed that Afsoon was brilliant because she was leading them out of the abyss, but they would have considered her even more brilliant had they known that she already had the solution since she was the one who designed the cure along with the infection. Most of what she was doing was reality theater.

During lunch break, she sent off an encrypted e-mail to the members of the Iran Nuclear Interdiction Project:

> ULTRA TOP SECRET/CODE WORD
> All committee members:
> Results of cyber manipulation very successful. Project slowed by 6 to 12 months, at least.

Suggest no more cyber attacks until I have positive proof that there are devices ready to fire. That way, I can have time to prepare the endgame—the coup de grâce. Remember that our goal is to destroy once and for all the nuclear weapons capability and/or the will of the Iranian government to continue its project of aggression. It is not to enter into a mutually destructive cyber war. This set of mutual salvos should be enough for now. The appearance of success in getting the nuclear energy computer system back up and running will put me in an unassailable position. All of our work thus far will be greatly solidified, if I can advance in the system.

I am working on the production of a piece of software that will shift blame away from us and our countries.

Signed: AMD, The Trojan Horse

§§§§§

U.S. Energy Department Uranium Mill Tailings Remedial Action (UMTRA) Site Project Office, Moab, Utah, November 18, 2011

Western states Teamsters Union vice president Henry Gandolfo Jr. and two Italian-appearing men walked into the large temporary building that housed the office of the federal uranium waste removal project director, David Kilpatrick. They took seats on uncomfortable folding chairs and waited for Kilpatrick to get off the phone. He seemed discomfited to see them.

He looked about the cluttered work-site building anxiously.

"I thought we agreed that you wouldn't come by here. It would put the kibosh on our whole arrangement if even one whistle-blower were to see us together."

"Not to worry, my friend," said Anthony Scarlotti. "Our Chicago guys can take care of any whistle-blowers. It's possible we may have to spread around a bit more bread to keep lips zipped."

"The people in Chicago got a bit of a bone to pick with youse," said the other Italian, Dominic Tataglio.

"I know, you think everything is going too slow. But it's not like we were moving cigarettes. This stuff is monitored by federal agents from half a dozen agencies all of the time. I can hardly go to the john without some nosy cop sticking his nose into my business."

"We know all that, and we got a few of them on the take. The trucks can move this week, guaranteed."

"You know that once they do, I have to disappear out of the country and never be seen again."

"Oh, we can make sura that," Tataglio said and gave a mirthless, chilling laugh.

"And I don't mean like Jimmy Hoffa disappeared neither," said Kilpatrick emphatically.

"We don't have no intentions of doin' nothin' like that. Youse are like family. By the way, your brother-in-law and my older brother, Victor Scarlotti, is sending out a big box a frozen steaks for youse and your family. He says to say 'hi' to our little sis, Maria," said Anthony.

Kilpatrick nodded, somewhat reassured. He was already in bed with the devil, having accepted a considerable retainer from the Chicago mob. He had had the good sense to bank it offshore in the Caymans under a fake name. He could never make enough to satisfy his gorgeous young wife on his federal salary. This was his one chance to win the lottery; and Maria, her family, and Kilpatrick had planned for his and Maria's move to Sicily with new identities and a tidy fortune for almost a year. It was a perfect plan. Still, he could not shake a smoldering anxiety over the reputation for violence of the Chicago Scarlottis.

Sixteen million tons of uranium processing waste were due to be transferred from the mill tailings site on the banks of the Colorado river near Moab to a special landfill located 30 miles north in Crescent Junction, Utah. Teamsters trucks were standing by to carry the massive stock of low-value uranium ore to the Union Pacific rail yards in Moab. Three long trains waited patiently to receive the massive loads of low-value ore into their container cars.

In two days, all of the cars on all three trains—the so-called "Trains of Pain"—were filled, and they pulled out of the yards slowly and steadily at first. Each diesel 17,600 horse power UP locomotive pulled up the hill out of Moab and headed into the desert. As the careful Scarlottis predicted, the scrutiny was reduced to almost nothing for the tedious trip across the trackless desert that passed through the barren lands of Canyonlands National Park. Everything went smoothly until they came to the third junction, just off milepost 134 on Highway 191. As the trains pulled up the hill and entered an "S" curve, the entire convey of trains disappeared behind the massive red rock. At the upper curve of the "S" was a rail junction.

This was where some of the massive up-front money had been spent to have agents "on the take." The lead locomotive pulled to a stop just before the junction, because the engineer and his helper had guns pressed against the back of their heads. Being wise men and not heroes, the two leapt off the engine and ran into the desert. Their places were taken by two other engineers. The scenario was repeated on the following locomotives. It was all very smooth and free of violence. All of the trainmen had received Cayman Island transfers of hefty sums of cash months ago, and none of them made a peep of complaint that day or ever after. They all swore to having been completely astonished when their trains were co-opted.

Another trainman tripped the switch, and the trains turned northwest and away from the previous destination of Crescent Junction. More up-front money had seduced two federal agents and their secretaries to falsify the transport records. A curious inspector would learn that the three train loads of uranium ore had arrived at Crescent Junction and was now safely buried in the landfill. The standard turnaround time for the return of the trains to Moab was four days—a result of union rules enforced by the Brotherhood of Locomotive Engineers. However, records indicated that the lead train's locomotive developed a crack in the supports of its massive diesel engine, and all of the trains had to be sidetracked for inspection and repairs. Since the return trip was not at all urgent, the process took two weeks. It was only then that the computers and the officials of Union Pacific discovered that the location of the trains and their engineers and helpers was unknown.

Two changes of locomotives and some sophisticated forgeries of records along the way kept the trains moving and below the radar. Neither Union Pacific nor federal investigators could find the trains. The theft of the uranium was made a national security issue and therefore secret. The trains and their scintillating cargoes were finally off-loaded into several massive ore-hauling cargo liners whose manifests were as fictional as all of the records entered into the UP and U.S. Department of Energy computers from Moab, Utah, to Elizabeth, New Jersey. The U.S. Department of Energy was never able to obtain an exact and accurate accounting of how much uranium ore was purloined, because part of the elaborate Iran/mafia plot included burying the Moab ore in the Crescent City disposal cell and capping it with nine-foot-thick multilayered cover of concrete, soil, and rock. The records told the fiction that all of the 16 million tons was buried there, but that much no one believed.

Sea Lion shipping floated the ore on its first oceanic transit to Djibouti City on the Red Sea. There, the cargo was signed over to established Transocean cargo liners designed as dry bulk ships—which can carry cereals and commodities such as coal and iron ore. The Transocean liners carried the uranium ore cargoes to a convoluted set of destinations, finally off-loading onto trains in Pakistan, which traveled around Asia under the direction of the freight forwarder, Vernier Company, for six months. At that point in the odyssey of the ore, the cargo was transferred to Iranian-owned FreightNet freight forwarding trains in Ashgabat, Turkmenistan, and moved down to the yellow-cake processing plant in Ardekan Nuclear Fuel Unit near Yazd, Iran.

The Ardekan unit received the low-grade ore and began to turn it into yellow-cake uranium. After the ponderous amount of ore was processed down to a fraction of its original volume, it was to be sent on to the Uranium Conversion Facility [UCF] at Esfahan. At the UCF at Esfahan—using the yellow cake prepared in the Ardekan—a number of by-products—including uranium hexafluoride [UF_6], metallic uranium, and uranium oxide [UO_2]—are produced. All of these were scheduled for later use in uranium enrichment. That entire process was not completed until 2013. Chief Bushehr engineer Dr. Mouradipour was given quiet credit for administering the entire complex transaction entirely on the sly.

The coffers of the treasury of the Islamic Republic of Iran were lightened by $100 million. All along the way, money changed hands from one corrupt official to the next and for the men and women who did all of the actual physical and record-fudging work. The Scarlotti Chicago mob made $14 million for a few days' work. David Kilpatrick and his wife Maria's Cayman account swelled by $4 million. The United States government was out $42 million it had spent for the transfer and an additional $7 million spent in the fruitless investigation. The only thing they salvaged was the Union Pacific trains abandoned in the railroad yards in Elizabeth, New Jersey, and finally discovered in June 2014.

Not everything worked out well for everyone involved in the colossal theft. Maria Kilpatrick convinced David to travel to Sicily ahead of her. No one ever saw him again. Maria moved back to Chicago and lived an opulent life in the Scarlotti compound. Twenty-seven federal agents and officials lost their jobs, and eleven of them went to prison. Four of those were actually guilty. The members of the Iran Nuclear Interdiction Project and the Kosher

Nostra were unaware of the entire proceeding until the arrests of the U.S. federal officials and their heavily reported involvement in what came to be called "The Moab Uranium Train Theft" made front-page news a year after the crime took place.

CHAPTER SIXTEEN

Office of the Chief Engineer, Bushehr I Nuclear Facility, Iran, March 31, 2012

The meeting with Ayatollah Ali Hossein Golzar—who replaced the late Moqtada al-Benizir as head of AEOI—Mullah Ali Salar Omidyar, director of the Ministry of Intelligence and Security (MOIS); Behrouz Omidi, director of the Ministry of Intelligence and National Security of the Islamic Republic of Iran [MISIRI or VEVAK]; and Dr. Afsoon Mouradipour—new chief engineer of the Bushehr facility and director of the overall secret nuclear weapon engineering project—in her now central office in the Bushehr nuclear facility went better than she might ever have hoped. The occasion was a celebratory tour of the facility with its new chief engineer.

A thorough test of Afsoon's renovation and restitution measures for the computers of the nuclear engineering industry of Iran on March 7 had shown no traces of the cybertage worm. She e-mailed Golzar, Omidyar, Omidi, and her counterparts and lieutenants throughout the country with the most welcome announcement that the new cyber protection system was running successfully. Hundreds of attacks had been aborted, she told them—which was true. She did not mention that her cyber protection program in all of their computers held an undetectable Trojan Horse. The heads of AEOI, MOIS, and VEVAK were—by nature, untrusting souls—and had suggested a tour of Bushehr, the uranium mines in Saghand—125 miles from Yazd—the Natanz high security uranium enrichment facility, the Zirconium Production Plant [ZPP]—which produces the necessary ingredients and alloys for nuclear reactors—the ultrasecret Qom underground uranium enrichment facility at the

Islamic Revolutionary Guard Corps base, the Lashkar Abad plant for isotope separation and laser enrichment, the waste storage facility at Esfahan, and the Kalaye Electric Company, where nuclear centrifuge components were made and tested.

Every facility was running smoothly and efficiently, hampered only by the lack of funding. When the prestigious group finished a thorough three-day evaluation at each one of the plants, the government agency directors called the staff together and made an announcement—the same announcement at each plant.

"We owe our present highly successful function to the work all of you have done and are still doing. We are especially proud of the contributions of our new director and coordinator of the nation's nuclear system special projects division. She is—without exaggeration—a true genius and has brought our computer networks back from the dead. I can tell you now that she was the genius behind our cyber attack on the Great Satan, Little Satan, and the arrogant European countries who consider themselves to be our enemies. Because of Dr. Mouradipour, computers in the Islamic Republic of Iran are functioning at full capacity. And—because of Dr. Mouradipour—those in the countries who oppose us are not."

Every time the same speech was repeated, it was greeted with enthusiastic applause and often a standing ovation, a very unusual demonstration of approval in Iran and almost unheard of for a woman.

The government speaker—by now used to being interrupted—paused and then continued, "Dr. Mouradipour's orders are to be regarded as our orders and those of President Okhavat and our revered Supreme Leader. You are to obey them to the letter. Refer any questions on computers to her. Nothing about our special division is to be withheld from her. She will meet with you regularly; and be warned, she is a very hard-task mistress indeed. Now, let's have refreshments then get back to the work of the revolution."

After the tour of Bushehr—which included security personnel, computer safety specialists, and Afsoon's engineering staff, the government directors, and Afsoon—they enjoyed a short *halal* lunch of duck in pomegranate and walnut sauce, lamb with spinach and prunes, and rice with butter. They were served nonalcoholic Bavarian "lager" and *talebi* [cantaloupe juice] to drink. The remarkable thing about the meal was not the fine food—it was standard Persian fare—but the mixing of men and women together who were not family. Afsoon recognized that she was accepted at the level of a trusted wife in the family of the powerful men of Iran.

They sipped small cups of thick black Turkish coffee after the dishes were cleared, a signal that serious discussion was about to begin.

"Dr. Mouradipour," Ayatollah Golzar said, "we are pleased to report that our funding crisis is lessening; and, within a month, we may be able to make necessary purchases and hire sufficient workers to get the special project underway again. Our president and the Supreme Leader have been able to find ways around the accursed American sanctions that appear legal to the fools outside our inner circle. You should investigate the needs of the project and submit a list of what is required. How long will it take you to do that?"

"With respect, Sir, a printed list would not accomplish much. We must have an expert present to negotiate, to determine what products and equipment will best suit our needs, and where they can be obtained. You are well aware of the thieves and spies surrounding everything we do and of the failures of our past endeavors due to the interference by the Americans. I propose that I head up the small delegation that does the investigation and makes the decisions. If you agree, I will have to have full access to the source of funds and must be able to pay on the spot. Our much-reduced list of suppliers will not wait for the wheels of government to make slow and questioning turns."

The three directors had not expected that.

"We need to give that some thought, Dr. Mouradipour. As you know, there are rather strong restrictions on the travel of women outside the country, especially without accompanying a husband. There are some in our government who have their doubts about a woman occupying such a powerful position as yours and especially when that woman has an American background."

"How long do you think such thought would take, Ayatollah? The markets shift almost daily, and they are improving at the moment as the Western computer and economic situation is getting somewhat better. It is likely that things will get more difficult as the Westerners focus more attention on sanctions and interference with companies that would do business with us for a price."

Ali Salar Omidyar, director of MOIS, spoke next in answer to the ayatollah's concerns. "We need a decision. I propose that we call President Okhavat and get a decision right now if possible."

The ayatollah and the director of VEVAK nodded their agreement.

The call was brief and to the point. Omidyar was put through to the president immediately on the speaker phone, and he explained the issue in succinct and efficient terms. The president listened carefully, interrupting only occasionally for clarification.

"Do it," he said, and the call was concluded.

"What will you need for the trip and how long will you need to be gone, Dr. Mouradipour?"

"I will need cash—ten million American dollars or in euros. I need an immediate direct line to the Central Bank when I need to make a large payment quickly, and I must not encounter any questions or delays. The people I will talk to are skittish and will be able to sense doubt immediately. Doubt will equate with inability to pay, and that will kill the deal. We cannot afford to lose any more opportunities—past experience has brought down the number of companies willing to take the risks of being challenged by the U.S. to a precious few. I will need a set of very well-trained and skilled VEVAK security agents. They must be able to blend in to the general population at times and not look like overmuscled soldiers. I must be able to use telephone and e-mail communications with complete freedom and without delays by censorship. The security personnel may look over my shoulder at all times."

"Anything else?"

"Well … yes. Something personal. I have not seen my family for almost seven years. I would like to travel to California in America and to have a two-week visit with them. You will recall that they are Jewish. Although they know that I have converted to Islam, they do not know where I am or for whom I work. I will keep it that way. And—I'm not so sure you know—they are ultra-Orthodox Jews who are members of Neturei Karta—a Jewish sect that opposes both Zionism and Israel. Also, as a chaperone, there is a woman with whom I am sure you are familiar—Elizabeth Dayan—who runs a horse-breeding ranch in the north of Tehran. She is well-known by the past and present presidents, the Supreme Leader, many of the members of the cabinet, and other government officials, who will vouch for her. She has a wide association with both Iranian and foreign business people, and her assistance would prove to be invaluable. In addition, I have made an acquaintanceship with a young man who has come to be like a brother to me. He is an employee of the plant and has been thoroughly vetted. I am somewhat embarrassed to have to say that we have no … what you might describe as romantic involvement. He is as proper as I am."

She hesitated thoughtfully.

"And I forgot. I have almost no money. I have never even inquired as to what my compensation has been since I live and eat in the plant's facilities most of the time. I will need to get some clothes when we get to Europe; so, I can fit in successfully, and that sort of thing."

The men laughed.

"I think we can say that you have earned that much, Dr. Mouradipour. I— for one—don't see any of the requests to be unreasonable. We have come to trust you, and there is no hint of suspicions about you or your associations."

Everyone understood that a race existed between the manufacture of the bombs and financial collapse of Iran. Installing a new generation of equipment that could give the program the ability to produce nuclear fuel much faster would likely make all the difference, and time was of the essence. Because the president had approved the serious aspects of Afsoon's expedition, the personal requests where promptly approved as well.

§§§§§

Vakuum Apparat Technik (VAT), St. Gallen, Switzerland, June 24, 2012

The Vakuum Apparat Technik factory was the last stop in Afsoon's two-and-a-half month odyssey around Asia, the Middle-East, Russia, South Africa, the United States, and Europe. She and her staff and security force had met with dozens of equipment and raw materials providers in all of those places. Her success rate was 65 percent, but that yielded conspicuous results. The meeting with the men she had hired to monitor the transport of everything she had purchased for Iranian nuclear energy projects was to cap her efforts. In addition, there were a number of men and women who considered it a vested interest of their companies to see to it that there were no fatal hitches. Every meeting and every transaction had been shadowed by CIA and U.S. Department of Energy agents; and—more often than not—the legal documents Afsoon and the vendors signed were subjected to scrutiny. It was not possible for the agents to inspect every item purchased and loaded on a truck, ship, or a plane; so, they had only the invoices to rely upon. Afsoon had to learn to lie with all the confidence of a Hollywood actress or Chicago politician. The vendors already knew how.

The vendors and their intermediaries were an assortment of shady merchants, disgraced scientists, brazen thieves, smugglers, and pirates. More than one of them thought she was offering sexual favors along with payments. Nassir and her bodyguards were very convincing about the fact that she was untouchable.

Anton Grünwald, proprietor of the Vakuum Apparat Technik factory, had had a rather long and tortuous history related to providing material for Middle-Eastern nuclear enterprises and had a deservedly negative reputation with American agents and the U.S. government working to impose sanctions on Pakistan and now Iran. He worked with A.Q. Khan as the father of the Pakistan bomb wove his way through the same murky streets where no lady would go at night, and out-of-the-way manufacturers, outfitters, and back alleys from which Afsoon had just returned.

Anton was the fixer. He made high-precision equipment—it is true—fittings for IR-2 ultracentrifuges, high-tolerance aluminum and special steel pipes used in laser enrichment plants, cylindrical rotors, and replacement parts for gas centrifuge process, and was known for the quality of his plant's cylindrical rotors, which spin at high speed inside an evacuated casing to keep gaseous UF6 feeding through the system. He knew everyone who knew anything or had anything needed to make nuclear weapons, and his knowledge came at a stiff price. He was trusted by denizens of the black-market nuclear weapons world and profoundly distrusted by American, French, and German governments while he did business with many of their finest precision milling and manufacturing plants.

There were eleven principles with which Afsoon had arranged purchase and/ or transport of embargoed items: All of the equipments and raw materials she had ordered were on the no-sales-to-Iran list. Truckers, ship owners, pilots, nuclear scientists, computer wholesalers, mining engineers, and merchants served as intermediaries. They were at the meeting to be certain that they all got their fees up front. Afsoon was every bit the stickler on the business deals herself. Every box, barrel, and part—special metal and plastic sheeting, finely milled parts, fully assembled computers and centrifuges—and every barrelful of uranium ore had a shipping label attached to it. The label had a bar code that quickly identified it as belonging to the Spanish company Maquinara CME—which was as phony as the description of the box or barrel's contents.

The majority of them were being transported to the warehouses of the Iranian Ardalan company. Any inspector with a bar code reader would find that the container had benign industrial equipment or materials. Any Iranian inspector with a specially devised bar code reader—which decrypted the hidden message—knew that the real destination was Bushehr I Nuclear Energy plant with Dr. Afsoon Mouradipour as the recipient. Only a handful of very special devices were able to read the embedded GPS coding located within the heavy bond paper of the bill of lading secured to the container.

Nassir had one of them, and the two Nichols-Dayan brothers, Elias and Zachariah, had one each.

The purpose of the GPS coding was to give a continual reading to the DIA of the whereabouts of the container. The DIA—especially its deputy director—wanted to be sure that the contraband did not slip betimes away from Afsoon. Nassir was vetted by the AEOI to monitor the progress of the shipments, and the Nichols-Dayan brothers—acting as part of the private security team and as Shi'ite militiamen from Hezbollah—were careful to play their roles with finesse. They provided real-time information to the U.S. intelligence services. If the very special bar code on the bills of lading were to be discovered, it would be fatal for Afsoon, Nassir, Elias, and Zachariah, or even more suspected coconspirators.

In the meeting, Anton and Afsoon ticked off the items of the voluminous list:

-IR-2 ultracentrifuges, separate fittings, and replacement parts
-Lotng sheets of high-strength aluminum milled to the exact thickness needed for covering the bomb or for constructing the missile that would carry it
-Superplastic forming/diffusion bonding equipment used for the fabrication of sheet metal structures of advanced alloys
-Cylindrical rotors
-Fine-milled steel and aluminum replacement parts for gas ultracentrifuges
-Porous membrane of nickel or aluminum oxide
-Canisters of gaseous uranium hexafluoride (UF6)
-Computer numerical controlled (CNC) machine tools
-The newest and best 5-axis milling machines
-Alloy steel, gyroscopes, and graphite—materials to increase the range of Iranian missiles under construction
-Spin, flow, and shear-forming machines
-Filament-winding machines
-Hot isostatic presses
-High-temperature furnaces and heaters
-Vibration/shaker systems
-Flash x-ray systems
-Machine tools and precision casting used in the machining of hemishells for nuclear weapons
-And on for thirty-eight pages.

The South African mining engineer was present in the meeting to account for the collection, containerizing, and shipment of 600 tons of low-grade natural uranium ore—U-235 concentration of only 0.7 percent—and 41 tons of fuel-grade uranium worth a year's GNP of many small countries and three times that on the black market for terrorist buyers. An Iraqi arms merchant and uranium dealer who saved some product after Iraq halted its atomic bomb R&D because it was too expensive, signed on for 67 pounds of highly-enriched [H-R] uranium that he had personally packed and placed on a Transocean Company ship. A Russian Mafioso received payment for and signed off on 100 pounds of former Soviet Republic weapons-grade plutonium239 isotope.

A North Korean army colonel—with the full knowledge and complicity of his government, and despite the differences existing from a previous ill-fated business transaction between the two countries (business was business after all) delivered 400 pounds of Gelignite—an explosive material consisting of collodion cotton—a type of nitrocellulose or gun cotton, dissolved in nitroglycerine and mixed with wood pulp and potassium nitrate—and another 500 pounds of Semtex, either of which would act as the explosive to start the nuclear chain reaction. A Hell's Angel motorcycle gang captain had arranged for corrupt officials at the Marline Uranium Corporation in Virginia to siphon off 11 metric tons of uranium from its in situ leaching operation at the Swanson/Coles Hill deposit near Chatham in Pittsylvania County. It was placed on ships as iron ore bound for Japan. The Hell's Angels netted more from that one sale than their entire illicit drug sales had brought in during the first quarter of the year.

Afsoon and Nassir were exhausted after the long ordeal of procurement. Their efforts had garnered every bit of illicit nuclear arms equipment and fissionable material they could find in the black-market world. If anything were to happen to her shipments, Iran would never be able to find what it needed again even if the government could come up with enough money. Afsoon had a few ideas in mind about that which she transmitted by e-mail to the new DDDIA, cautioning him not to act in haste, but instead to take the long view. She and Nassir checked into the five-star Hotel Bayerischer Hof and slept the sleep of the dead for the next nineteen hours.

CHAPTER SEVENTEEN

White House, Oval Office, 1600 Pennsylvania Ave. NW, Washington, DC, June 24, 2012

"Thanks to all of you for making time for this meeting," President Gabler said. "Rear Adm. Torgelson from the DIA and Annette Redstone from the CIA—with the approval of their superiors—asked for this meeting. I am assured that it will be brief."

The only other people in the room were the deputy secretary of state, the president's national security advisor, the press secretary, the chief of DARPA, and the commander of the SSG-CNO.

Rear Adm. Torgelson summed up the conclusions of the intelligence community, the State Department, the JCS, and the members of the Iran Nuclear Interdiction Project. "Mr. President, we believe the cyber attacks between the West and Iran have pretty much worn themselves out, and there is nothing to be gained but a lot to lose by launching another salvo. It was extremely harmful to our country and to our allies, but we believe that the Iran bomb project has been set back for ten years. We remain vulnerable, and every cyber expert in our country, Canada, the UK, the rest of Europe, and even the Saudis are sparing no expense or time to shore up our defenses.

Our crucial agents in Iran are well on the way to effect a final closure to the threat posed by the crazy Iranians obtaining nuclear weapons and the means to deliver them. They realize that our patience—thus far—has come at a great cost, but they assure us that the all-important end to Iran's nuclear aspirations is near enough that we will not have suffered in vain. What we would like to do in the future I will leave to our two experts from DARPA and the SSG-CNO."

"I know that SSG-CNO is the acronym for the Strategic Studies Group for the Chief of Naval Operations, but you'll have to remind me what DARPA is," President Gabler said.

"Defense Advanced Research Projects Agency, Mr. President. We're the people who brought you the Internet," said Col. Avery Holmes without cracking a smile.

Everyone laughed at the standard joke perpetuated by DARPA.

"One of you give me the short version, and I suppose I'll get a detailed report and proposal a bit later," the president said.

Captain Victor Raylan answered for the two think-tank officers, "What we propose won't be very palatable, but the events of the past three-quarters of a year make our proposal necessary. As you will see from the full report, it is based on rock-solid data and has been vetted by the best minds in the country—the defense department, our top university professors, and even the Iran Nuclear Interdiction Project hackers, as well as two of their genius agents whose names even we don't know. This is what we need to have happen in our country and in the Western world, and we are going to have to be tough about it. Thus far, business and industry, the computer people, and our own military higher-ups have resisted any real control. But here goes: we are going to have to have the NSA, DARPA, the CIA, and the FBI computer and information technology people impose security measures and accountability for security on all of the manufacturers, retailers, network servers, etc., etc. It will impact PCs and every device in the civilized world. Nobody can have an old-fashioned, unprotected device anymore, because they are the most vulnerable to cybertage."

Captain Raylan took a breath, and Col. Holmes continued, "It'll sound like Big Brother, but this is definitely a period in our history where we will have to give up some freedoms in the interest of national, industrial, and personal security. Manufacturers, sellers, users, and major systems are going to have to submit their private and secret cybersecurity information to a central committee of experts. For example, the FDA will have to be tough on the vendors, hospitals, doctors, and manufacturers in their system to rid themselves of cyber vulnerabilities despite the high monetary cost. Consumers will just have to suck up the extra costs and accept that it is a new way that business must be done. Computers and devices will have to be protected by extremely effective firewalls. They are expensive and cumbersome, but now we know we can't live without them. None of these recommendations should be considered optional. The government is going to have to make laws that guarantee that everyone who tries to evade the new requirements rues the day. There will be a lot of complaining and demands for investigations and continuances and extensions to delay and procrastinate. We can't let that happen. Our enemies—especially the Iranians—are counting on just such a response from greedy capitalists."

"Let's say I agree in principle," the president said. "What will be the makeup of the central committee and who will do the enforcing?"

"We civilized people have built our lives around our wired and wireless networks controlled by computers. The question is: are we ready to work together to defend them? The Iran Nuclear Interdiction Project has been working on this for years. There are two absolute geniuses who know the issue inside and out, and they work with a set of experts who are based at Camp Peary; we call them "The Elsie Group." That entire group should be included. Homeland Security has a National Cyber Security Division [NCSD], which operates what is called the Control System Security Program [CSSP]. The government has established a program run by Homeland Security, which has a computer emergency response team—Industrial Control Systems Cyber Emergency Response Team [ICS-CERT]. They need to be on board fully.

"The FBI currently leads the national effort to investigate high-tech crimes, including cyber-based terrorism, espionage, computer intrusions, and major cyber fraud. Their assets include the National Cyber Investigative Joint Task Force, ready-to-roll Cyber Task Forces, InfraGard for protecting infrastructure, the National Cyber-Forensics and Training Alliance, the Strategic Alliance Cyber Crime Working Group, and Cyber Action Teams. Each of those FBI groups should be represented, as well as be key enforcers in the field. And there is the DOJ Computer Crime and Intellectual Property Section. The DIA works closely with them, and both should be part of the governing committee and part of the field force."

"How about outside our national boundaries?"

"We don't want to leave that out. I mentioned the "Elsie Group." Part of that group of brainiacs is a contingent from the CIA's Sherman Kent School for Intelligence Analysis, which is located in Reston, Virginia. They are great analysts and fiendish cyber fighters. The CIA's Counterterrorist Center [CTC] has a great counter-cyberterror division. The National Intelligence Service has been fighting cyberterrorism since its inception. They should not be left out of the picture."

"That would be a huge committee; and, if I know them, the project would be scuttled by interagency bickering," the president said.

"That would be where you come in, Mr. President," said Col. Holmes. "You would have to be the head of that committee. The day-to-day work would be done by someone you appoint—maybe a general or an admiral—someone with real clout. We agree that the whole effort would never get off the ground without a serious understanding that the work will get done; the initiatives will be enforced with stringent laws; and that agencies protecting their fiefdoms will see new leaders for the agencies."

"Could work. And yes, it would make me unpopular. But that's why Harry Truman put the sign on his desk, THE BUCK STOPS HERE. Let's get a committee going to set up the rules and plans of action and get the DOJ to write it up in nice legal language," the president said—then as an afterthought—he concluded, "I also agree that we should let sleeping dogs lie—no more U.S. cyber attacks until Iran starts to play nasty again. If that's what your superagents need, Adm. Torgelson, let them have it."

CHAPTER EIGHTEEN

Home of Daniel and Esther Mouradipour, 375 Trousdale Place, Beverly Hills, California, June 30, 2012

Her VEVAK minders left Afsoon off at Ali and the Twelve Imams mosque in downtown Los Angeles after picking her up at LAX when her plane arrived from Paris. Afsoon sensed no suspicion from them, and—in fact, to the contrary—they were deferential. In the limited Iranian intelligence community, Afsoon was regarded as something of a heroine. She was accompanied and chaperoned by Elizabeth Dayan all the way from Paris to Los Angeles. It was the first time Elizabeth had been back to the United States since she got married. It was an uncomfortable experience for her. Ali ibn Massoud, the original VEVAK contact agent in the Ali and the Twelve Imams mosque, and Mullah Omar were waiting on the steps of the mosque to greet them.

"Welcome back to the land of the Great Satan, dear sister," the Mullah said with a smile. "We have heard good things about you from our Twelver brethren."

"It is kind of you to say. I am very tired from my travels and a bit over-whelmed with all the American confusion. It will take me some time to adjust, I fear."

Afsoon thanked the VEVAK agents who had shadowed her since she left Bushehr in April. Ali held open the door of the mosque's minivan—carefully nondescript and free of signage—and drove her and Elizabeth to Beverly Hills.

"Would it be better for me to drop you off some distance from your parents' home, Sister?" Ali asked.

"That won't be necessary. Thank you, Brother. I make no apologies and keep no secret of my religious choice. Mrs. Dayan makes no apologies for anything."

Elizabeth gave her an affectionate smile.

Afsoon was wearing a long plain dark maroon dress that covered her from the neck to her wrists and ankles and a silk hijab scarf printed with a muted design.

"Thank you, Brother Ali. I look forward to seeing you again when I leave for Persia in two weeks."

She and Elizabeth walked up the front walk knowing that they were being watched and knowing that their watchers were very skilled, because she had not caught a glimpse of any of them. She knocked on the door and was quickly swept inside by Esther Mouradipour's fervent embrace and away from the prying eyes of her watchers from three countries. Once inside, the scene was a surprise birthday party, anniversary, welcome-home, and dream-come-true for the lonely spy. She embarrassed herself by beginning to cry. Elizabeth Dayan, Brenda Daastrup, Esther Mouradipour, and her sisters, Abigail, Mary, and Ruth, all smothered her in a rough embrace. It was not Georgetown, but it was home nonetheless.

Everyone from everywhere was there: her adopted brothers and sisters, Daniel, Michael, Evan, Abigail, Mary, and Ruth; her cover-story siblings, big brother Abraham, sister Ruth, little brother Eli—who was no longer little—sweet little sister Kelsey—still sweet but grown-up—and big sister Rivka—who was showing her middle age—her cousins Stephen and Dietrich, and the twins—Martha and Elizabeth—Neal and Ruth's children; and Gideon's sisters, Tahmineh and Leila Rothsberger.

The "older" generation waited their turn to engulf the returned family prodigal. G.R. IV and Miriam, G.R. III and Chava Rothsberger; Neal and Ruth, Daniel and Brenda Daastrup; Rebecca Hershowitz, Chava's mother and Gideon's grandmother; Marta Olson and Ingrid Hakkensdatter, agents of the Swedish *FMUndSäkC*, her roommates and protectors from Stockholm; Elsie Silberberg from the Mossad, and the usually very reserved horse rancher, Elizabeth Dayan, all got a hug from Afsoon, who entirely forgot her aversion to physical contact with other people. She impressed them by calling off each of their names accurately, some of which she had not seen for over a decade. They all cried when she did. Afsoon cried again.

The consummate spy, genius scientist, important administrator in an industry with more than 20,000 employees, the keeper of secrets that were of history-changing importance, the woman who had killed and had sent others to their deaths had been through the valley of the shadow of death twice and remained standing; and the lonely introvert whose only friend and confidant outside the people in this room was still in Iran was overwhelmed with the sheer joy of the moment. When Brenda clasped Afsoon in her loving arms, the important cog in the machine to undo all that the vicious Iranian regime intended to foist on an innocent world became the innocent two-year-old sprite in the arms of the first mother she had ever known, sweet Yasmin, her wet nurse in long-ago Qushchu village. She was clutching her beloved rag doll, *Fereshte;* and she gave in to all of the emotions that were pent up inside her tormented soul.

Once order returned to the emotional gathering, Afsoon renewed acquaintanceships and met Gideon's beautiful and talented—and now pregnant—wife. She and Miriam hit it off and became sisters in five minutes. Afsoon still loved Gideon; and he loved her; but now it was a pure and platonic thing. She played games with the children, hugged the family dog, enchanted the men with exotic Persian stories and adventures, and helped the women prepare supper as if it was just another Friday seder meal. It was not a time for serious discussions—just unleashed familial love and being at home. There would be two weeks for being serious.

§§§§§

During the night, everyone—except the Mouradipour family—exited out the back door of the house and eased through the large backyard and into the next yard east of the Mouradipour mansion. They were picked up by a city bus leased for that place and that time and delivered to the Hyatt Regency Century Plaza Hotel in Beverly Hills. The DIA had reserved a full floor for the family, friends, and officials who joined them. Everyone was registered under a fictitious name, and the hotel administration and staff were compensated for not asking questions.

The morning started with a kosher breakfast for the Mouradipour family, including Afsoon Mouradipour. Afsoon pitched in to help with all of the chores and enjoyed the tranquil domesticity and idle chatter. At ten o'clock, all of the Mouradipour women left for a Rodeo Drive shopping spree. Three State Department Diplomatic Security Service SUVs accompanied them. The DSS presence aroused no suspicions on the part of the VEVAK agents surveilling the house through telescopes from a mile away. It was no less than they expected and presumed that an Iranian official of Dr. Mouradipour's stature should be afforded. They did not detect the DIA agents who were watching the watchers. The men of the family drove in the direction of LA ostensibly on business. Since they took the direction away from Afsoon, the small VEVAK contingent decided it was not worth the manpower to follow them.

Afsoon and her female relatives were easy to follow. They made no attempt at evasion, and they did not appear to have even a hint that they were being tailed. At one o'clock, the women left off from their shopping labors and walked to 218 North Rodeo Drive to the Urasawa Restaurant, one of the trendiest and most expensive eating places in the world—$600 a person. Beyond the great food, the restaurant provided a private upstairs dining room, which they had reserved for lunch and where they could not be observed. The ladies were greeted by Hiroyuki Urasawa himself and escorted to their tables by the maître de. The head waiter—like all of the waiters—was Japanese.

He said, "Every dish is a work of Japanese art and a labor of love from our people to yours. If there is anything we can do for you, please let me know."

Restaurant security closed the area off from the public. The DSS agents took up places inside the restaurant on the first floor and outside on the streets around the building and at all entrances and exits. They were overtly conspicuous. The VEVAK agents held back, being more leery of detection and making their presence an international incident than they were worried about the safety of their target, Dr. Afsoon Mouradipour. The agents—selected by Mullah Ali Salar Omidyar, director of the Ministry of Intelligence and Security [MOIS] himself—did not worry a whit about the possibility that Dr. Mouradipour would defect or have a clandestine meeting with opponents of Iran.

It was a languid multicourse meal, strong on service, and served on 300-year-old tableware, which took two and a half hours and another half an hour for the ladies to dawdle over the excellent coffee. The courses were prepared by their own chef at a grill in the center of the collection of tables. The courses arrived one at a time: *goma dofu*—sesame-seed tofu—sashimi of toro; Spanish mackerel and wild Japanese red snapper; *junsai*—chilled then fried Kyoto eggplant—egg custard with sea urchin; Japanese chive gelée; caviar with gold flakes; sashimi of toro; *yoromushi*—red snapper, sea urchin, shiitake and shrimp with mountain potato and egg white—*ishiyaki*—toro cubes marinated in soy and sake, grilled on a hot rock with tosazu dipping sauce of soy, bonito, vinegar and sweet sake—Kobe beef grilled over wood; and on for twenty-eight courses, more than any individual or even a family could eat. The meal concluded with a regional sake—Kubota Manju from Niigata.

Somewhere between the sashimi of toro and the yoromushi, Afsoon slipped away and left the back way northeast onto Dayton Way, then changed direction to go southeast on North Beverly Drive to Wilshire Boulevard. She walked a short distance and stood in front of the Gersh Agency, where she caught a cab to the Hyatt Regency Century Plaza Hotel. She paid the driver, got out, and walked briskly—head down—to the rear entrance of the hotel where she met her case manager—the DDDIA, Adm. Torgelson—and her uncle Neal Daastrup, who was there in an unofficial capacity. There were two behemoth DIA bodyguards.

They took a back stairway up six flights to a floor entirely set aside for corporate conference rooms. Security was serious—hotel, DIA, DSS, and IDF—none of whom was in uniform.

This meeting was entirely different from the family gathering of the night before, except that there were nearly as many people there. Afsoon was impressed with what it must have taken to get all of those important people into Los Angeles and into the hotel unrecognized. 3D was still an impressive man, but he deferred to his successor, Adm. Torgelson. In addition to the two admirals—seated around the long conference table and in two rows behind those chairs—were G.R. III and IV, Daniel and Abraham Mouradipour, Levi and Aaron Schmuel, Annette Redstone, Max Rosenstein, David Henderson, Antal Disraeli, Elsie Silberberg, Lt. Col. Shai Avitan, Veronica Chiu, Clement Chang, Renata Leonidovna Zaslavsky, Elizabeth Nichols-Dayan and her two sons, Elias and Zachariah, Ali Nylander, and Carter Miller-Partridge.

It certainly was not lost on Afsoon that she was looking at a grouping that included business interests, computer hacking experts, the IDF, the SAS, the murky world of international spies—the Mossad, DIA, CIA—Iranian heroes, international criminals; and people who were risking their lives to provide a successful cover story for her. It was a United Nations of dedicated foes of Iranian nuclear adventurers and bigots—America, Israel, Sweden, China, Russia, England, and Iran were represented. To a man and a woman, they all despised and hated the ruling regime of the Islamic Republic of Iran.

Adm. Torgelson spoke first. "I am not going to have much to say until the end; and even then, I will only make a couple of brief announcements. I believe our time will be best spent by first hearing what the two gentlemen standing over there in the corner of the room have to say."

He pointed at Army Col. Avery Holmes and Navy Captain Victor Raylan—heads of DARPA and the SSG-CNO respectively.

"I won't go into the full exposition of those acronyms. Col. Holmes and Captain Raylan have prepared a White Paper that will flesh out the details for you. Understand that none of those papers will be allowed to leave this room."

Everyone nodded their understanding and assent.

"So, we'll hear from Captain Raylan."

The chief of the Strategic Studies Group for the Chief of Naval Operation prefaced his remarks with a sobering announcement. "We have studied the entire history and operation of the Iran Nuclear Interdiction Project. Success-wise, it is a mixed bag. The goal has always been to stop the madmen in Iran from lighting the nuclear spark off and blowing us all away. The success—thus far—is that we have delayed them by something like ten years. That has come at a huge financial cost and use of manpower. The failure is that we have not killed their Project *Jahannam Adur* [Hell's Fire]. It stutters and stumbles inexorably along like the villain in the old movie *The Terminator*.

"The direct financial cost to us is now somewhere over a billion dollars, and the indirect costs stemming from the Iranian cyber attack is in the trillions. It is admitted that the world's sanctions against the Iranian regime have cost their people almost everything, and they are beginning to starve and to riot in streets that are crumbling like the rest of Iran's infrastructure. That has not deterred the "axis of evil" there, as former President George W. Bush put it. They are sociopaths and are willing to sacrifice anything for their cause. Our heroic agent embedded deep in their nuclear energy for WMDs knows that only too well. This is the bottom line, ladies and gentlemen: President Gabler and his Council of Economic Advisors have come to the decision to require a different approach to a solution, one that will not bankrupt our great countries."

Afsoon looked shocked. Was all of her work and exposure to danger about to come to naught?

Col. Holmes continued where Capt. Raylan left off. "Take it easy, everyone. No one is suggesting that the project be abandoned. However, Capt. Raylan and I have come to lay out the plan that the president, the PMs of Israel and the UK, and all of the intelligence services have hashed out. First of all, Afsoon is still the lynchpin of the whole project. All aspects of what you have been doing are still to be part of the final solution, but they have to be put on hold for now. The U.S. will keep tightening the screws on the regime with its sanctions, but we are now going to go after what we started out to do in a more direct fashion. Here are the details."

Col. Holmes and Captain Raylan tag-teamed to give the outline of what they called "Plan B," admitting that the old original attack would still be in force as "Plan A" whenever it was needed. Annette Redstone from the CIA and Antal Disraeli from the Mossad presented the on-the-ground strategy and how it could be carried out. Afsoon Daastrup Mouradipour kept silent but—for the first time since she had agreed to be part of the project—she was afraid.

The American and Israeli analysts finished their outline of the new plan in an hour and a half.

The salient points in the conclusion were: [From Redstone] "Ronald Reagan recognized that the Cold War had reached a level of a hugely dangerous and expensive ever-escalating stalemate. He saw the true weak spot in the U.S.S.R., which was their vulnerability in terms of wealth. He ordered an unprecedented escalation, which—put in its simplest terms—was to enter into an escalation of costs that the Soviets could not match. In the end, we outspent them until the economy of the U.S.S.R. collapsed; and they imploded as a power. Similarly, we must make a dramatic change. The current recession—the worst in the world's history but hopefully not as long-lived as the one in the dirty thirties—has made it impractical to continue on our present course.

We are playing a game of brinksmanship with the Iran regime. We fire a secret salvo at them, and they fire back in a disturbingly similar escalating and harmful stalemate to what we have seen in the Cold War and in Vietnam. Then we were far richer than our enemies and could afford to engage in a program of outspending them. Because they do not care about their own people or anyone else, the Iranians will keep on trying to get the bomb to be able to extort us at any cost. Our capacity to spend has been severely compromised; so, we must take a fresh tack. We spent enough to keep their bomb-making capacity at bay and put it off for more than a decade with Plan A. Now, it is time to finish what we started. We won't have another decade to do so."

[From Disraeli] "We know the Iranian regime is on thin ice diplomatically and militarily—even from the religious standpoint. They are a pariah with their only two national friends—Syria and North Korea—neither of which will support them when push comes to shove. Russia gives support only to the point that they can annoy the United States, but they will not go to war with America for such a minor mission goal. The regime has pushed its efforts to the point of bankruptcy to get the bomb and will put everything it has into a final push. It is very high-stakes gamesmanship indeed. Plan B will call their bluff—it is the endgame, and Dr. Mouradipour is the main player. We will get together with you, Afsoon, and spell out your role in detail and give you all you need to know and to have to get your part accomplished."

He gave Afsoon a reassuring look and a smile.

Rear Adm. Torgelson stood up and said, "That is a lot to digest and is a new twist on this already complicated effort. We will all get our assignments in the next few weeks. However—right now—Afsoon has to get back to her lunch on Rodeo Drive to keep her cover intact. So, at the risk of being overly abrupt, I want to tell her something in front of all of you; it will come as a considerable surprise to her. Afsoon, you have been unaware of the fact that you are a ranking officer in the United States Army; and now I am announcing that you have just been promoted to the rank of full colonel." A few of the attendees began to clap, but Martin held up his hand for quietness. "You have also just been promoted to full professor at the Armed Forces University. You have been on the faculty for the past twelve years. If you don't believe that, you can look up your impressive teaching and publishing record in the DOJ files. Oh, and you have a substantial amount of back pay coming."

Afsoon gave her uncle—who had remained stoically quiet—a look of consternation.

Martin concluded, "We have not forgotten you or what you have accomplished. As much as it pains me to say, you have to go back into the belly of the beast. The world is counting on you, even if they don't know it."

He gestured to Afsoon to follow him. She paused just long enough to give G.R. III and IV, 3D, and the Schmuels a hug. Martin and his two bodyguards hurried her back down the stairs and into a van marked "Beverly Hills Linen Service" and whisked her back to the Urasawa Restaurant to be with her family as they left; so, the attentive VEVAK agents would be none the wiser or the least bit nervous.

CHAPTER NINETEEN

Office of the President, Rothsberger Family Bankers, 423 Montgomery Street, the Financial District, San Francisco, California, July 27, 2014

The Central Bank of the Russian Federation had taken over the majority of Iran's national indebtedness over the past two years. To maintain a fiction of plausible denial when the United States challenged the federation for funding the Iranian bomb production program, Russia blandly explained that the money was coming from the Sberbank. Neither Gideon nor the U.S. Treasury was new to the world of banking, and they knew that the Central Bank owned a 60-percent stake in Sberbank. The Central Bank had $561 billion in physical gold, and their stockpile was increasing every year. The mineral industry of Russia was already the world's largest and most profitable owing to their vast hard-rock gold deposits in Siberia and the Russian far east—which produced between 38 and 40 tons a year—and to the fact that gold prices were steadily climbing. By the end of the first quarter of 2015, they were expected to double their stocks of physical gold because of a dramatic new discovery in the Kupol deposit.

That presented something of a problem for the Russians—their possession of so much gold and allowing it to reach the world's gold market would almost certainly drive gold prices down, making their industrial expenses a self-defeating effort. They faced a situation similar to that which brought down the DeBeers diamond monopoly. The DeBeers cartel controlled too many diamonds, and other diamond finds—including large fields in Russia—began a ruthless competition. In order to remain financially afloat, DeBeers began selling off large quantities of good diamonds at discount prices. That changed the world diamond market status quo. Now, diamond prices were controlled by the market and not by DeBeers. Russia feared the same fate for its national treasure in gold.

The solution selected by the federation and its central bank was to supply gold to nations that were in a state of disfavor with the rest of the mercantile nations. Iran, Ecuador, Paraguay, Venezuela, Cuba, and Myanmar fit that description. They all had worthless currency, and only raw materials to offer as collateral. They were all hungry for gold to be able to pay their creditors and thereby to remain in business. It was a matter of quiet pleasure to the rulers of the former Soviet Union that they could blunt the impact of American sanctions against those rogue countries and rub the American governmental nose in the fact. It was something of a tightrope to walk because neither Russia nor any of those states wanted to have a complete diplomatic and trade break with the U.S. since they all depended on American importation for survival of their economies. Only Iran plowed ahead with its anti-American policies, not the least of which was its determination to produce nuclear WMDs.

The Russians were walking on tiptoes between Iran and the U.S. They chose a compromise: supply the gold to Iran; so, the defiant Shi'ite country could proceed with its nuclear ambitions and pay its ever more strident creditors. At the same time, they upped the ante of stress on the Iranian regime by increasing the interest payment schedule almost every year. The principal and the interest now owed to Russia was bothersome to the Russians and alarming to the Iranians, who could no longer pay their debts, maintain their infrastructure, feed and transport their people, *and* build their bomb. The Russians were no fools when it came to finances; it was evident that collecting on the ever-mounting debt being accumulated by Iran was likely to be a problem. There was collateral that could be taken, but the Russian Federation was reluctant to resort to force, not knowing how the U.S. would react.

That was what brought Vadim Bogdanyevich Onipchenko, chairman of the Central Bank of Russia, to G.R. IV's office in the district that day. The secretary of the U.S. Treasury, Thomas Wildemere, and the deputy chairman of the Board of Governors of the Federal Reserve System, Angus Thacker III, accompanied the Russian. They were all in San Francisco for the annual G-8 conference, and Gideon's office was convenient. His staff had prepared a quick and efficient lunch.

"Your communication to our office was clear and to the point, Mr. Rothsberger," Chairman Onipchenko said to open the conversation. "I agreed to come because you convinced me that you could persuade my friends, Secretary Wildemere and Deputy Chairman Thacker, to meet in a private setting; and I underline the importance of 'private.' May I presume that we are all gentlemen here and that there is no recording being made?"

"You certainly may. It would not be in any of our interests to do such a thing. We can all speak freely. You won't read about it in *Pravda* or the *New York Times*," Gideon told him.

"I will give you my opinion. Of course, I don't speak for Treasury or the Fed or any other governmental institution. Politically, the Russian Federation has its differences with the U.S., and every now and again it has to feel good to get in a dig. However, we are all pragmatists. Doing business with Iran is a difficult and often unrewarding experience, both for private companies and for governments. I will be frank; the banking consortium I head has no complaint about you funding the government of Iran. As a result of your willingness to step in and make it possible for them to meet our demands for payment in physical gold, we are up-to-date with them. We have grown weary of the difficulty of getting our interest paid, and it was only because of your generosity to the Islamic government that they finally paid the principal. Our contract with them ends in December of this year, and we are very reluctant to renew it. They are hell-bent on making a bomb—I think every schoolchild in the civilized world knows that. They are willing to let their people starve and their country to disintegrate to accomplish that. I am doubtful that you really want them to succeed any more than the U.S. does."

"Off the record, of course, we see them as a destabilizing influence in the region; and we certainly do not want a nuclear device to explode anywhere near us. To be blunt about it, we are wary that anything we might do to collect on the principal owed us might cause the U.S. to intervene. We don't want that either."

Secretary Wildemere spoke for the United States. "Chairman, short of an all-out conflict in the region, we would not stand in your way to obtain collateral for your debt. I have the full authorization of the president to guarantee you that if your government will act with its usual careful restraint."

"Thank you for that, Mr. Secretary. We are both old enough to remember the Cold War; there was complete restraint on the part of both of our nations when it came to nuclear weapon use. I will tell you what we have in mind. If it should appear in *Pravda* or the *New York Times*—as you put it—I will deny that it was ever even mentioned. In short, if we have full knowledge that the United States will keep out of it, we will move certain of our forces in and take control of three of Iran's petroleum pipelines and will transfer the product to our own use until their debt is paid. At that point, we will not grant them so much as an ounce of gold in the foreseeable future. What do you have in mind?"

"Upon formal agreement, the U.S. government will look the other way."

"And our banking consortium—the only other source of funds for Iranian projects—will cancel our contract and leave them without money," Gideon said firmly.

The secretary added, "We have decided some time ago to take a hard line, even when it comes to humanitarian considerations. The Iranian regime is incapable of reasoning or of bargaining in good faith. They regularly cite the mandate of their religion as if that were something that mattered to us. Our sanctions will intensify to the level of a naval blockade on the day that you take over their petroleum business."

Gideon said, "Like all other sensible people, we do not want the genocide-minded Iranians to have weapons of mass destruction. I am in possession of some intelligence that indicates they are not so far off from accomplishing just that. They have put almost their last ruble, dollar, and rial into their project. If it were to be destroyed—including the infrastructure to rebuild—their economy would collapse."

"War?" asked Chairman Onipchenko, Secretary Wildemere, and Deputy Chairman Thacker almost as a chorus of alarm.

"Of course not. However, if something were to happen to their manufacturing capability, how would the Russian Federation react?" Gideon asked.

"I can't speak for the government," Chairman Onipchenko said, "but in the spirit of your concession on the pipeline, I am pretty sure that the Federation would take no action—some harsh words, perhaps, but no action. I will bring it up when I get back to Moscow."

"We need full coordination. I hope you gentlemen can get President Gabler and President Golodyayev together in the reasonably near future to come up with a plan. I don't have the influence to make the political contacts—that is your purview; but I do believe I can locate people who can offer an acceptable plan, including details of time and place."

"It's time for us to get back to boring meetings, but we will get to work as soon as we get back to Washington," Chairman Thacker said.

"And Moscow," Chairman Onipchenko echoed.

CHAPTER TWENTY

Hôtel de Shahnameh, No. 2 Rue Gozlin, Faubourg Saint Germain, 7th Arrondise-ment, Paris, France, Home of Elijah and Ruth Shahnameh, December 5, 2015

Gideon Rothsberger V—the two-and-three-quarters-year-old curly-headed no-good-for-nothing rascal, as his doting father referred to him—and his petit cherubic nine-month-old little sister, whom everyone called Esther—because she was the family queen, played with wild abandon. Her real name was Ruth miriam—after her mother—and she and her brother noisily moved about the spacious kitchen floor in search of trouble. The two Rothsberger children of the latest generation were in the huge old Shahnameh residence to celebrate Hanukkah 2015 with their French family.

The famous late-nineteenth-century-to-early-twentieth-century architect Jules Aimé Lavirotte built—among other notable structures—23 avenue de Messine, 3 Square Rapp, 6 rue de Messine, the Céramic Hôtel, the Lavirotte Building, the Lycée italien Léonard-de-Vinci, and the original Hôtel Baron Rothschild at No. 2 Rue Gozlin in Faubourg Saint Germain. The latter grand home was completed in 1918. It was bought, sold, and improved three times before the founder of the Shahnameh dynasty—Elijah's father, Seth—purchased it in 1949. He and his wife modernized the beautiful classical-style home and established it as the Hôtel de Shahnameh, one of the most beautiful and most French in all of Paris. Elijah inherited the Rue Gozlin home and a country villa, as well as a fortune in land, diamonds, and successful investments when his parents died two weeks apart in 1982.

The preparations for Hanukkah had been in progress for the past two weeks, and the twenty-eight children of the Shahnameh extended family were gathered in Hôtel de Shahnameh for the week-long festivities scheduled to begin formally the next day, December 6, and to end on the evening of Monday, December 14. Gideon IV thought the house looked a lot like Christmas, except that there was no "Hanukkah Bush," as some of his reformed friends referred to their unorthodox Christmas trees.

It was a beautiful place and a beautiful time, but Gideon was anxious and distracted. At her insistence, Miriam was about to have a business meeting with several members of the Iran Nuclear Interdiction Project later that morning. Although—also at her insistence—Miriam was well aware of at least the major aspects of the program and had made some minor contributions to it, this would be her first real business meeting with the serious people of the project. It was a business meeting—a spy business meeting—and Gideon was ill-at-ease about the prospect of his lovely wife and mother of his children becoming more involved.

It was inevitable. He knew that. Miriam was too bright, too caring, and too loyal to be left out. So, he had reluctantly agreed to her meeting agents of the Iran Nuclear Interdiction Project. The least suspect place to do so was within the confines of the fortress-like Hôtel de Shahnameh, her girlhood home. Someone wiser than he made a decision and arranged for the prominent women in the project to be the ones who approached her. Unknown to Miriam, the contingent of women arrived in the middle of the night while she was asleep.

Miriam was fully aware of the presence of agents and fully aware that those agents were going to grant her access to one of the most important secrets in French and American history. She was not aware that they would all be women, and she had only a skewed and truncated understanding of what was going to transpire.

Gideon escorted her to the south tower great room and kissed her a temporary good-bye while he went back to the main central section of the mansion to entertain his rambunctious offsprings. He carried Ruth and shepherded G.R. V for a walk up and back on the very short city block between the Place du Quebec—at the rue Bonaparte—and the rue des Ciseaux.

Miriam knew some of the women and was surprised and mildly amused to see that everyone in the spacious room was female: Annette Redstone from the American CIA; Elsie Silberberg from the Mossad; Veronica Chiu and Renata Leonidovna Zaslavsky from the "Elsie" hacker group; Elizabeth

Nichols-Dayan from the D-R Horse Breeding Ranch; Chava Rothsberger, her mother-in-law; Rebecca Dayan-Hershowitz, Gideon's grandmother; and Sanna Kullberg, special advisor, Homeland Security Affairs for Sweden. Annette was the most senior officer and the best informed of the women; so, she led off.

"Miriam, thank you for allowing us to come to your beautiful home. We have talked to Gideon, and he let us know that you have been informed and have been making a contribution to our project to get rid of Iranian nuclear weapons. We need your help in a specific facet of our operation, and the senior officers of the project—which involves several different agencies from several nations—have given us their blessing. I'm afraid we have to be quite formal here, because there is so much at stake. Before we go much further, let me ask you a question: why do you want to be involved?"

By way of an answer, Miriam held up the front page of yesterday evening's *Le Monde*. The title was self-explanatory: "SCHOOL BOMBING BY HEZBOLLAH IN TEL YITZHAK, ISRAEL, 63 Children and 14 Teachers and School Staff killed, 145 Wounded."

"That is the main reason. I could go on with my list. How about FGM, or human trafficking, and sexual slavery? Or brutal and demeaning polygamy? Or forcing women into inhumane costumes and preventing them from doing normal activities, working outside their homes, or getting a decent education? And making them vassals of men ... and, oh yes, there's that little thing about them making an atomic bomb to erase poor little Israel from the earth—a twenty-first century holocaust!?"

"I couldn't have put it better if I had prepared for a week, Miriam," said Annette. "So, are you willing to learn some secrets? Once you do, you cannot breathe a word of what you have learned to anyone outside the need-to-know group that forms the leadership of the Iran Nuclear Interdiction Project. Do you understand that?"

"I do."

"Furthermore, you must understand that penalties will be most severe if you reveal such information to any unauthorized person for any reason."

"I understand."

"Sign here."

Annette handed her an official-secrets-act document from both the French and American governments.

"All right, we will tell you what you need to know, but no more. That is as much as we know and as much as we are allowed to tell you."

Annette explained the role of the American government and its intelligence agencies. Elsie told Miriam about the Mossad's part in the project and about the activities of the "Elsie" group of computer hackers. Sanna detailed the actions and plans of the Swedish intelligence services; and Miriam's family women told about the long computer and financial attack on the Iranian nuclear weapons plans, projects, and funding efforts. None of them mentioned any names of other project members or anything about specific dates. The name of Afsoon Daastrup Mouradipour was never allowed to be mentioned.

Annette and Elsie then explained the specific role planned for Miriam herself. When they did, Miriam reacted for the first time. She gave a little gasp and put her hand over her mouth and blinked hard.

"You okay?"

"Yes. That's quite a leap for me. I will have to toughen up."

"You will, but you will have help and training. Your part is crucial," said Annette, and the rest of the women added sober head nods of agreement.

CHAPTER TWENTY-ONE

"Tous les changements, même les plus souhaités ont leur mélancolie, car ce que nous quittons, c'est une partie de nous-mêmes; il faut mourir à une vie pour entrer dans une autre."
["All changes, even the most longed for, have their melancholy; for what we leave behind us is a part of ourselves; we must die to one life before we can enter another."]

Anatole France, French Novelist, and winner of the Nobel Prize for Literature in 1921
The Crime of Sylvestre Bonnard (1881), *Part II, Chapter 4*

Office of the Deputy Chief of the Atomic Energy Organization of Iran [AEOI], Bushehr I Nuclear Facility, Iran, December 29, 2015

Dr. Afsoon Mouradipour was pensive, or perhaps it was ennui. For the past several months, she had ruminated about the time she spent with the Mouradipour family and all of her closest friends and family in Beverly Hills, California, in June of 2012. Her visit with Daniel and Brenda Daastrup six years earlier—September 2006—now came to mind vividly and with an intrusive frequency as well. It seemed a lifetime ago, and she was not handling the separation from almost everyone she cared about very well. For the past several weeks, she had taken to holding her now frayed-around-the-ages little rag doll *Fereshte* on her lap when she worked—a kind of security blanket. She was anxious and depressed—both mild and not enough for her to risk visiting a doctor anywhere in Iran. She was sure she could shake off her dampened enthusiasm for life by throwing herself deeper and harder into her work.

She pushed her comfortable swivel chair back from her computer modem, stretched, and made one more inspection of the banks of computers before making her way up two floors to her apartment. She made quick spot inspections to see that all of the computers still had her software embedded into the programs she had invaded. Everything was still a go for the new plan—the intensively modified Plan B—hers, the DIA, the Mossad, the government of the United States, and particularly the new senior officers on board, Col. Holmes and Captain Raylan from DARPA and SSG-CNO, respectively. With Plan A, Afsoon had been in a comfortably hands-off position; with Plan B, she was far more committed and obliged to act more overtly. She granted herself the human frailty of being afraid, because with Plan B, she was putting herself and her one lifelong friend in increasing danger. The stakes were getting higher with each passing week. Security was being heightened; even she was being interrogated regularly. She lived with an icy grip of fear on her heart.

Afsoon kept up with her former world through highly encrypted e-mails that would seem obtuse and almost meaningless even if they were to be intercepted. Gideon and Martin Torgelson were as faithful about that aspect of communications with her as they were with keeping her abreast of developments from the military and intelligence agencies of the Western nations committed to stopping the Iranians from having an atomic bomb—ever. She was just now becoming able to accept that her uncle Neal was out of the loop. Increasingly, she now focused on the majority of that set of communications, because the pace and intensity of activity was an exposition of what she was doing.

What she was doing involved her oldest friend and mutually accepted brother, Nassir Jamshidi. He had help from Arab-Israeli agents of the Mossad and from certain Haredi sect members of the Neturei Karta in Iran, which had had a profound change of heart. Elizabeth Dayan and Rabbi Ya'akov ben Avraham, ha-Rav—a rabbi and a son of a rabbi, a Jew and an Iranian—had found and vetted willing workers from the ostensibly anti-Israel Jewish sect willing to work for the antinuclear cause despite all of the patently obvious risks and inconveniences of Plan B of the Trojan Horse operation. Nassir and all of the Jewish volunteers underwent extensive training so that they could pass for Persian Shi'ites and be able to secure employment in the Iranian atomic energy industry. Afsoon's powerful position in the AEOI greased a lot of skids. By the end of February 2015, sixteen men loyal to her and Nassir were in strategic positions throughout the Iranian nuclear weapons industry. The men were fiercely loyal to Afsoon, but were equally convinced of the intrinsically correct concept that jingoistically religious bigots should never be able to launch an obliterative attack on the tiny country of Israel or to attempt such an attack on the United States, which her devoted coconspirators regarded as the most generous and big-hearted nation on the planet.

For the Neturei Karta in Iran, the scales had dropped from their eyes. Jews were still being murdered—mostly secretly—but it did not take any kind of genius to realize that whereas there had been Jews in Iran since Biblical times—2,700 years ago—by the time of the rise of Islam, they became far fewer in number and second-class citizens. At the time of the establishment of the state of Israel in 1948, there were almost 150,000 Jews living in Iran. By 1978—the year before the Islamic revolution—there was some forced emigration, and less than 100,000 remained. Within a year of the revolution, about 30,000 Iranian Jews immigrated to Israel, and additional thousands fled the United States and Western Europe. By the mid-1990s, the population of Persian Jews had dropped to around 35,000, many of them able to stay in the country only because they swore firm allegiance to Iran and against Israel. It was to no avail. By 2011, there were less than 9,000. By the end of 2015, there were somewhere in the neighborhood of 4,500 Jews left, mostly old. And most of the attrition after 2011 was from killing.

The following night—December 30—Afsoon, Nassir, and their long-time coagents left Bushehr and traveled 45 minutes by AEOI corporate jet the roughly 300 miles to Ardekan Nuclear Fuel Unit near Yazd, Iran. Afsoon was as responsible for the Ardekan unit as she was for Bushehr. The unit received low-grade ore from South Africa and the United States, depleted uranium [DU] from Japan, Namibia's Rossing Uranium Limited—in which Iran had the ownership of 25 percent of the stock acquired over a nearly twenty-year period—the uranium mines in Saghand, Iran, Kazakhstan's Nur Afxar Gostar company, and from unscrupulous officials of the Cameco Corporation of Australia, the world's largest uranium producer. At the Yazd plant, ponderous amounts of ore were processed down to a fraction of their original volume, and then sent on to the Uranium Conversion Facility [UCF] at Esfahan.

No one met their plane. By careful prearrangement, not a soul knew that they would be arriving, especially at that time of night—0110. Two large black SUVs were parked just off the tarmac, and the eighteen pseudoaficionados of nuclear weaponry were at the main gate of the Ardekan unit. The alert guards outside the perimeter fence stepped to the driver's side of each of the vehicles and tapped insistently on the windows.

Each driver opened his window and peered into the security officer's face.

"What is your business here and at this time of night?" the officer demanded imperiously.

"Dr. Afsoon Mouradipour and the instant inspection team are here for a surprise security check."

The driver handed over an impressive set of credentials and authorizations. There was not a man or woman in the entire Iranian nuclear energy industry who did not know of Dr. Mouradipour. Her orders to carry out surprise inspections without interference were signed by the director of the AEOI himself, Ayatollah Ali Hossein Golzar. Upon seeing the papers identifying one of the occupants as the official next to god and an authorization from god himself—at least so far as any lowly worker bee in the system was concerned—the guards snapped to attention with a posture and salute as stiff as one of the Buddhas of Bamiyan from pre-Islamic Persian history and waved the two SUVs through.

As the SUVs began to roll, Afsoon leaned out of her window enough to say, "You are not to breathe a word about this inspection. Do not call into anyone in the buildings. Is that understood?"

"Yes, Deputy Director, fully understood," the trembling stone-stiff guards said as the SUVs passed out of sight.

First hurdle passed," Afsoon said to herself.

The vehicles pulled to a stop at the rear entrance of the main uranium enrichment building. Afsoon got out first and strode briskly up the stairs and knocked sharply on the door. An armed guard opened the door, his H-K machine gun pointing at Afsoon's chest. She said nothing. She handed the sleepy man the magical papers, and he flung the door wide open and ushered the eighteen surprise guests into the main processing area.

"As our orders from the ayatollah indicate, we are here to conduct the first of several unannounced inspections of the AEOI facilities. It is required that you never speak of this inspection so that the surprise at each location, and every time, will achieve the desired reaction—constant readiness, because no one can predict when a formal security evaluation will come to a given facility. You needn't be tense, Mr...?"

"Estuani, Ma'am."

"Yes, Mr. Estuani. Your security record is impeccable, and we are certain that our inspection will add to your already fine record. You and your men will accompany one of my people to your security office where you will remain until we are done. Presuming that we will find nothing seriously amiss, you will be able to return to your work before the night is over."

Elias Nichols-Dayan led the twelve security guards to their offices where they enjoyed a comfortable chat and a cup of coffee.

"Second hurdle passed," Afsoon said to herself.

Afsoon and the rest of the men set to work at a feverish pace. They unloaded supplies and found places to secrete the materiel that would be crucial on the day that Afsoon's Plan B for the Trojan Horse would commence but out of sight and mind until then.

"Third hurdle passed."

Afsoon and her men left Yazd at 0221. Their plane landed on an auxillary landing strip adjacent to the main airport tarmacs one hour and thirty-four minutes later at 0318. They were inside the main entrance of the Uranium Conversion Facility [UCF] fifteen minutes later. The vast floors of the main work areas were like the inside of a gigantic beehive. There was a buzz of ultracentrifuges doing their part to further the enormous effort of converting the yellow cake received from Yazd into a number of by-products, including uranium hexafluoride [UF_6], metallic uranium, and uranium oxide (UO_2)— well on their way toward becoming highly enriched [HE] uranium.

The team split up into two-man teams and raced into each of the six facilities of the UCF: First, the Miniature Neutron Source Reactor for the production of short-lived radioisotopes for the light water research reactor. Iran used this Chinese-made reactor for neutron activation analysis. It was fueled with about one kilogram of weapon-grade uranium; second, the light water subcritical reactor [LWSCR], another Chinese product; third, the heavy water zero-power reactor [HWZPR], yet another Chinese contribution—this one used for research; fourth, the fuel fabrication laboratory [FFL] used for small-scale fuel pellet production; fifth, the uranium chemistry laboratory [UCL], where Afsoon spent most of her time when she was in Isfahan; and sixth, the graphite subcritical reactor [GSCR], a training reactor, built as a gift of the kind citizens of the People's Republic of China.

Unlike the response Afsoon's squad received at Yazd, the senior security guard on duty in the main facility insisted on a prolonged and assiduous scrutiny of every line, paragraph, and page of the carefully forged documents submitted by the antinuclear-weapons spy unit. Finally, he reluctantly allowed them access.

However, as a parting shot, as Afsoon and her men dispersed, he said, "But I am going to call this in to the higher-ups."

Afsoon nodded to Zachariah, who dropped back when Afsoon and the others began their carefully rehearsed work in the whirring facility. It took each team between an hour and fifteen minutes and three hours to complete their work.

Zachariah was waiting for the assembled anti-Iranian weapons agents at the exit door at 0532. The first hints of dawn were beginning to be manifest, which made Afsoon anxious.

"How did it go?" Afsoon asked as soon as the two of them were able to talk.

"He is now a bona fide martyr," Zachariah said matter-of-factly.

"How do we explain his body?"

"We don't. I found the sign-in cards in the security office files. Seems he never did make it in to work. His car was found at a roadside stop between Falavarjan, where he lived, and the UCF, where he worked. Looks like a highway robbery—lots of that in these parts."

Afsoon raised an eyebrow.

"The Mossad and their *Sayanim* in Esfahan arranged it all. The poor fellow had a broken neck—actually happened as an 'industrial accident' here in the plant, but we fudged a little. I found him dialing on a security phone. His belongings were all taken, and the inside of the car was torn apart. The resident Mossad agent for Esfahan assured me that everything has been taken care of, and we are out of the picture."

During the last night of 2015, Afsoon and her team repeated their activities—this time at the Natanz nuclear plant, where hardened nuclear fuel pellets were produced—as in the FFL—but on a much larger scale. At Natanz, the pellets were subsequently formed into nuclear rods. That portion of the Natanz plant was where the team focused its efforts and was able to get in and get out in less than two hours. During the wee hours of the same night—New Year's Eve—the team used password-protected numerical codes to enter the ultrasecret facility at Qom, where the low-enriched uranium [LEU] from Natanz was enriched to a bomb's worth of HEU every six months. The good *jinnis* of Iran were with them. There were no incidents; and—as 2016 appeared on the world's calendars—the Trojan Horse project within the Islamic Republic of Iran and the antinuclear weapons team spies were on time and over budget—as usual, and—for the moment—safe.

CHAPTER TWENTY-TWO

Who is evil, who is blind?
In the name of who you'll find
You're not supposed to question faith
But how do you accept this fate?
Million, you walk this earth without a heart
Madness, tear the innocent's souls apart
Martyrs, shovel your conscience into the grave
Monsters, A city of souls dying for peace
Welcome to the belly of the beast

-Lyrics-*Belly of the Beast*, Anthrax
Songwriters: Joseph A. Bellardini,
Frank Joseph Bello, Charlie L. Benante,
Scott Ian Rosenfeld, Daniel Alan Spitz

Hotel Saraban, Natanz, Iran, January 12, 2016

Two Irish sheet aluminum tubing businessmen were checked into the dull but quasi-functional rooms on the top floor of the two-story elongated rectangular hotel Saraban hotel, with an, ornate dome set incongruously on the center of its roof. The hotel was a two-star—even as Iranian tourism rated it—but it had the advantage of being obscure; i.e., VEVAK had no interest in it. Aaron Schmuel was registered as Devlin O'Leary, and Levi Oistrakh as Liam MacGiolla. Levi's choice of MacGiolla was a source of amusement for Aaron because Levi—the Israeli Jew—was laying on the Irish authenticity more than a bit too thick—the name translates to "son of the devotee to Jesus." They had paid for a three-day stay with a phony VISA card, which at least was good for the cost if not for identification.

Aaron now worked regularly for both the DIA and for Mossad, and Levi's boss was Zeev Rosenkrantz in Tel Aviv. Both had red hair. Had the VEVAK been aware of them, they would have disregarded both as espionage suspects—they were too obviously what they said they were, a couple of down-on-their-luck, hard-drinking, carrot-top Irishmen willing to shave a corner or two to make a buck. As spies, they would stand out like barber poles.

At midnight, the two men transformed themselves. They dressed head to toe in mat black ballistic nylon ninja-type uniforms, black high-top soft-sole shoes, and Kevlar vests, and armed themselves to their figurative teeth. The most important part of their armament was a sackful of single use—therefore untraceable—cell phones. The most important advantage of the phones was that they could reach an obscure receiver from five miles away. The local Mossad agent had procured for them a dilapidated and nondescript-appearing truck with a new Ford F-350-engine and supercharger, bulletproof windows and tires, and pop-up hardened steel windshield and back window shields. They drove out to the Sheikh Abdolsamad Mosque on 17th Shahnvar Road and parked in a small copse of trees at the edge of the grounds. The mosque was the only tourist attraction in the area; and—even in the day—no one but local devotees ever entered it.

There were two reasons for their visit to the mosque. The first was to meet with several of Afsoon Mouradipour's agents, and the second—following that visit—was to secure the use of the empty garage building on the grounds. Men approached their truck, giving a set of flashlight signals—three long, two short—pause—two long then three short. Aaron returned the signal. In a few minutes, the two newcomers and Aaron and Levi coordinated plans; and the outsiders turned over four cell phones and instructions about how to call and the number for each phone to Afsoon's men. Afsoon had programmed the phones to be able to activate receiver phones inside the Natanz nuclear facility buildings with great reliability. The calls could be made from five miles away, and would start a sequence that would take an hour to complete. The GPS card had been removed from the phones to cripple attempts at locating the user of the phone. This would provide Aaron and Levi a considerable lead time on any pursuers if any should gain knowledge of their existence.

Once Afsoon's handpicked men left with their phones and their instructions, Aaron and Levi entered the outbuilding on the Natanz nuclear plant grounds. They did it the old-fashioned way: first, they deactivated the electric-wired shock fence; and then they cut through the lowest wires enough to let themselves through. They left themselves a readily accessible escape route. They walked through the pitch-blackness of the wintery night—gaining a small advantage over total blindness by using the excellent military grade Gen 3 Night Vision goggles from Night Vision Systems provided by Rear Adm. Torgelson—to the rear door of the building. The door was unlocked. Levi felt his way to the far right-hand corner and moved a large old box that appeared heavy but was actually very light. He moved it to the side, and the two of them opened a trapdoor in the floor. As instructed, the local agents had emptied the eight-foot-deep gravelike chamber completely. There were twelve 100-pound bags of quick-drying cement, a large plastic tank of water, and shovels to mix the cement and water into concrete. There was enough to fill in the coffinlike chamber four feet deep. No one would be wiser when—in several years—someone should decide to take a peek inside. They would find a concrete box exactly as the original builders had left it, except, of course, there would be a somewhat shallower box.

Three heavy large tarpaulins were folded neatly in the corner opposite the secret subfloor of the barn. There were several tools—including saws and axes—placed in the building for their future use, along with two 9mm handguns with baffle-suppressor silencers and enough ammunition for a week's standoff if it came to that.

§§§§§

Offices of the Leader of the Islamic Republic of Iran, Islamic Republic Street—End of Shahid Keshvar Doust Street, Tehran, Iran, January 13, 2016

Col. Dariush Aghdashloo, commander of the Agha's private security force, and Lt. Col. Hamid Hejazi, second in command to Col. Aghdashloo and onsite commander, ushered the president of the republic, Hormoz Okhavat, Yazid ibn Sarrafzaadeh, chief of staff of the Armed Forces of the Republic of Iran, and Ayatollah Ali Hossein Golzar, head of the Atomic Energy Organization Iran [AEOI] to the Supreme Leader's receiving room.

The SL came abruptly to the point as soon as the nation's most important leaders—other than himself—were seated.

"There will be a great celebration in Natanz for the opening of the new reactor. My plans to be in attendance must be a state secret until the very day for obvious security reasons. The other reason for secrecy is that the woman in operational charge of nuclear energy projects has assured me that we now have twelve bombs ready to strike the Little Satan as soon as the missiles are ready. That is your responsibility, General Sarrafzaadeh."

"Overall, yes. But Dr. Mouradipour is also the overall supervisor of missile construction for the weapons. The manufacture of the nuclear devices had to have top priority owing to budgetary issues, but we have the component parts all ready to be assembled at Natanz as well. That should take less than a week, transport to Bushehr another three days, then we can run an atmospheric test. Presuming that will be a success—and everything Dr. Mouradipour does is blessed with success through the mercies of Allah—we will be able to strike the Zionist entity in twelve days, fourteen at the latest."

"It is difficult to be patient, but Allah wills it. We must obey and be patient. The rewards will be beyond our greatest hopes. Think of it—no more Israel. The Jews will be dealt a crippling blow. I have it on good intelligence that the fool American president, Gabler, will make a fuss; but he won't counterattack with nuclear weapons. The Americans learned caution during their Cold War with the Russians, and they won't be able to make decisions to strike us until it is too late to do so. The cowardly Europeans will hold them back. In three words, 'It's a go,'" said the SL.

"And a cause to celebrate. The nation has had a very difficult time for the past three or four years, and a little of Allah's joy will lighten the mood in the country," the general said.

"General, President Okhavat, and Ayatollah Golzar, I commend you for your accomplishments. It is long overdue to be ready to strike a true blow—a *Jahannam Adur* [Hell's Fire]—on our infernal enemies. But…," he let it linger., "…but the internal unrest must be brought to an end. My patience is exhausted. What are your plans, General?"

"Boots on the ground and real bullets, Agha. We have not been able to get control of the mobs any other way. The president and I are in agreement. We sympathize with the citizens. Indeed, some are starving, but it is the fault of the Great Satan's sanctions. The restrictions they imposed are now enforced by their terrible political power, and by the presence of their navy. Despite knowing that, we are a society of law and order—the Sharia and the *Qur'an*—and we cannot let the forces of darkness and treason to the revolution gather strength. The time to act is now. You will be targeted in Esfahan, and that would appear to be the place to show our determination. With your approval, of course, Agha."

"You have it. The rioters are an insult to Islam. It shall come to a stop in Esfahan."

President Okhavat spoke for the first time. "I am in full agreement."

He was always in full agreement with the SL; it was how he came to be president.

"The plans for the celebration are complete and ready for your approval. Because of the woman's great knowledge of the area, the facilities, and her control of the security forces, she has been given a strong hand in the preparation of the ceremonies. Gen. Sarrafzaadeh's forces, along with my household security, are more than adequate to handle security in Esfahan itself, where the real threat lies. The people will recognize your great courage, Grand Ayatollah, for standing up to them where they will be out in force fomenting revolution. The sixteenth will be a great day; we could almost call it 'The Day,'" the president said.

Grand Ayatollah Rahimi offered only one minor correction. "No, my friends, 'The Day' will be the one when we watch the contemptible Zionist entity disappear from the earth and from history. I feel like a child waiting for Eid al-Adha. The news is so wonderful that I can hardly contain myself."

The president laughed. "I am the same way. And—in fact—I look forward to the evening's entertainment. The committee has done all it can to ensure the best the world has to offer. We have the American star of musical films, Ali Reza Sharifzadeh, who has agreed to a contract; our own opera sensation, Mamman Dehdashty, will be the headliner. The French are sending their acrobatic entertainers, the Cirque de Soliel—compliments of the Jewish opera singer, Mrs. Rothsberger, who will also sing for you. And the Chinese State Circus will be a huge attraction for our people. I spoke with Chairman Chou the other night. These people they are sending are the best of the best—trained in the Chinese tradition of *Ma Xi* [hippodrome, horse theatre]. No horses, though. I think the evening will be wonderful. We must remember to send the committee and the nuclear science woman a small thank-you message. I will handle that, Agha."

"Good. It should be an evening to remember. I can almost see the newspaper headlines now!"

Half an hour later, Rear Adm. Torgelson, the DDDIA, received the following e-mail from Hamid Hejazi:

Chapter Twenty-Two

ULTRA TOP SECRET/CODE WORD, EYES ONLY,
R-A Torgelson
AEOI ready with twelve fully active plutonium warheads.
Missiles ready by 16th, and attack on Israel expected that day."
Signed: Agent Ex

§§§§§

Off-limits Security Area, Nuclear Energy Facility, Bushehr, Iran, January 13, 2016

Dr. Afsoon Mouradipour and her trusted team of scientists, engineers, and security officers gathered in the top secret holding room in the lowest sub-basement of the Bushehr facility. This was a special unveiling for the men who had struggled with her for nearly two decades to obtain a functional thermo-nuclear weapon. Their products were pure fission weapons—the traditional first type to be built by a nation state. They were about to unveil a dozen of them. Everyone was wearing a nuclear hazmat suit just in case.

Afsoon was brief and to the point as usual. "Gentlemen, may I present...," and the velvet curtain whipped aside.

Twelve outsize gleaming bare metal, silver-colored footballs—weighing 16 kilograms/35 pounds each—sat on pedestals behind a protective clear plastic barrier. Each football was an uncompressed oblong-shaped delta-phase pluto-nium-239 core unit, which still needed to be covered with explosive material and computer-controlled wiring. The beauty of the highly—perfectly—polished metal was only seen in this form, unadulterated by anything asymmetrical. Although the men had all been involved in one stage or another of the project, it was the first time any of them—except Afsoon—had seen all twelve together at one time.

The men were silent for a time. Then they responded with broad smiles and high fives. It was how exuberance was expressed by exhausted scientists and engineers. After the others left to go back to their duties, Afsoon stayed behind to wait for the technologists who would complete the assembly. That was pro-jected to take about six hours. Before they came, however, she donned protec-tive gloves and reached through the armholes in the protective cover and made a few adjustments of her own. When the technologists arrived, she was sitting on a comfortable chair absorbing technological specifications provided her by her chief engineer. She smiled at the techs and signaled them to proceed.

CHAPTER TWENTY-THREE

'Tis no sin to cheat the devil.
-Daniel Defoe

Office of the President, Rothsberger Family Bankers, 423 Montgomery Street, the Financial District, San Francisco, California, January 15, 2016

G ideon sat back on the hind legs of his office chair, put his fingers behind his head, and interlocked his fingers. His face wore an expression of profound satisfaction. There had been a detail in Plan B of the Iran Nuclear Interdiction Project, as they now called it—that seemed unlikely and improbable—but the Iranians had given him his out. They were a week late in their payment, and Gideon had just received an e-mail from Ali Mohamed Mustaffen, director of the Central Bank of the Islamic Republic of Iran, at five o'clock in the afternoon:

> "Problems with gold shipment. Negotiations with Russian Federation underway, but they are slowing progress. We have been placed at a great inconvenience to have to make payments in gold and now demand a change. We can make our most recent payment and all future ones in Deeds of Trust from Bank Sepah in Tehran based on government property in and around Tehran as security. To arrange transfer of the funds—cash in rials—contact Hormoz Mohammad-Bagher, president of the bank."
> -Ali Mohamed Mustaffen,
> Director, Central Bank of
> The Islamic Republic of Iran

Mustaffen, the arrogant anti-Semite had given him the out—the excuse, if you will—he needed. Gideon took considerable pleasure in his reply:

"No. The Iranian rial is worthless."
-Gideon Emmanuel Rothsberger, IV,
President Iran Nuclear Project Funding
Consortium.

Gideon took even more pleasure from his next act; it was simple—he pushed a single button on his smartphone. That sent an encrypted message prepared months ago in conjunction with DDDIA Rear Adm. Torgelson. The message led to the freezing of all Iranian assets throughout the G-12 nations. All bank and other lending institutions transactions ceased less than a minute later. It was four-thirty in the morning in Tehran. The director must be working long hours, Gideon thought.

At nine the next morning, Tehran time, the Iran Stock Exchange opened for only five minutes then ceased trading, as all Iranian stock values collapsed. Gideon would have given a small fortune to see the look on the smug old bigot's face at that moment.

§§§§§

Camp Peary, York County, Virginia, Armed Forces Experimental Training Activity (AFETA)—Department of Defense, January 15, 2016

The "Elsie" group relaxed around their conference table, each fiddling with the computer in front of him or her. They were waiting for a call from Rear Adm. Torgelson. When it came, Elsie Silberberg opened her iPhone and saw a brief text. She turned to the others.

"Let's get to work," she said.

The bulk of the work was already done. With a minimum of keystrokes and clicks of a mouse, the American, Russian, Israeli, and Chinese injected poison into virtually every computer in Iran. The Trojan Horse virus had been per-fected over the past fifteen years. It was not much more than a remake of the old Stuxnet virus but with two important twists. The first was that the first keystroke on a computer in Iran sent a picture of a skull-and-cross-bones and a spherical bomb with its fuse lit; that was the contribution of the two

Russian boys. One second after the caricature appeared, the recipient computer crashed; and the crash was permanent. The second twist had been contributed by Afsoon Daastrup Mouradipour. The Trojan Horse virus had an antivirus embedded with codes, which update Stuxnet instead of eradicating it and keep it in a constant killing mode. The antivirus element prevented any computer thus infected from being used to send harmful computer software back to the system that infected it.

For the past fifteen years, beginning with the Howard Ryan presidency and continued by the Glen Gabler administration, the companies, universities, factories, service organizations, medical facilities and institutions, and all research facilities throughout the G-12 nations had been required to include specific, expensive, and very effective antivirus software. The software was kept as secret as the Manhattan project, and there had been no WikiLeaks or NSA Edward Snowden treason to endanger the protection system. Like the Star Wars concept of the Cold War era—designed to shoot down incoming enemy aircraft and missiles—the resources of the civilized world were effectively and efficiently marshaled against attacks on any and all computers in the G-12 nations.

Similar anti-infection agencies and systems throughout the civilized world targeted Iran and North Korea and even random recreational trackers. In the U.S., organizations as diverse as the FDA, the FBI, the Treasury Department, Homeland Security Department, the IRS, the NSA and CIA, Department of Justice, and the DOD joined forces with their counterparts in two dozen countries to save their economies. It was a dramatic alliance—the like of which had never been seen before, because the common interest was the same as the individual interest.

With their mouse clicks and keystrokes, the "Elsie" group triggered a worldwide response. Computers whirred; technologists returned from vacations; soldiers, police officers, and intelligence operatives joined forces in a coordinated defensive front. In the U.S., the men and women of the FDA's Task Force sent out instructions to every manufacturer, seller, vendor, and user of medical services. Homeland Security's National Cyber Security Division [NCSD] and its Control System Security Program [CSSP] went into action and invaded (in computer-speak) business, industrial, and personal computers to protect them—all of which was agreed to by the users in order to have access to the Internet. Homeland Security's computer emergency response team—Industrial Control Systems Cyber Emergency Response Team [ICS-CERT]—sent its agents and technologists into secure offices of businesses, industries, and the military and all branches of federal, state, and local government. It was so well preplanned that they blanketed the country in a matter of hours.

The FBI currently led the national effort to investigate high-tech crimes, including cyber-based terrorism, espionage, computer intrusions, and major cyber fraud and put all of its assets into play the second the "Elsie" Group sent its message. Those assets included the National Cyber Investigative Joint Task Force, ready-to-roll Cyber Task Forces, InfraGard for protecting infrastructure, the National Cyber-Forensics and Training Alliance, the Strategic Alliance Cyber Crime Working Group, and Cyber Action Teams. Analysis, investigation, and action agents went into war mode to become the key enforcers in the field.

The DOJ Computer Crime and Intellectual Property Section was ready with requests for subpoenas and no-knock warrants, and had access lines on standby with the Federal Intelligence Security Agency Court [FISA]. The DIA worked closely with all of them because they were in front of the entire situation, having been involved in the long-term, hugely expensive Iran Nuclear Interdiction Project. They joined the FBI as part of the field force. Coordinated measures went into effect throughout the systems of the G-20 nations. All of this took place without anyone who did not have the clearance to know having any idea that WW III was occurring, and scarcely a bullet was being fired.

Everyone involved in the sweeping counterattack measures initially complained that it sounded like "Big Brother from *1984*," but as they began to give up some freedoms in the interest of national, industrial, and personal security, they bought into the cooperative vision. Manufacturers, sellers, users, and major systems finally became willing to submit their private and secret cybersecurity information to a central committee of experts—a committee of officials with unassailable and impeccable credentials for efficacy and honesty. The Iranians and North Koreans who counted on the greedy capitalists and individualists of the decadent Western democratic world being unable to band together were wrong—dead wrong.

Anyone who sought to get around the countervirus protective shields rued the day. Detection, investigation, arrest, conviction, and punishment occurred in world-record time for what was usually a tedious and sluggish process. Only a handful of computers were infected, and the G-20 economies were not noticeably affected. It was the equivalent of the Homeland Security National Terrorism Advisory System threat level Red and entirely comparable to the unprecedented mobilization of the nation's armed forces that occurred during and after the thirteen-day Cuban Missile Crisis standoff in October 1962. In 2016—as in 1962—there were no notable shooting battles as a result of the Red level.

CHAPTER TWENTY-FOUR

Defense Advanced Research Projects Agency [DARPA], Security and Intelligence Directorate, 675 North Randolph Street Arlington, Virginia, January 15, 2016

One of the mottos that arose spontaneously among the agents and officers of DARPA and the SSG-CNO fifteen years previously when the Iranian computer hackers nearly wrecked the economies of the West was "Never Again." With the full cooperation of the DOD, NSA, and the DOJ, the two military agencies had collected warehouses full of easily accessed information on the Iranians and North Koreans, which made it possible to be selective and accurate whenever a known hacker—official or otherwise—from one of those two countries began to tap on his or her computer keys. Actually, DARPA and SSG-CNO were quite as well capable of monitoring and intercepting computer efforts by Middle-Eastern jihadists, Chinese and Russian hacker/attackers, freelance cybertagers, and American survivalist militia members as they were with Iran and North Korea. They just chose to focus their immediate attention on the two nations that posed the greatest threat.

In the spring of 2013, a thirty-year-old NSA contractor committed treason and leaked a significant amount of information regarding the NSA's top secret mass surveillance efforts, which brought unwanted worldwide attention to the secretive organization and the technologies at its disposal. Those technologies made it possible for the NSA and the U.S. 513th Military Intelligence Brigade to thwart Iran's efforts to commit cybertage on the civilized world's computers on numerous occasions, and helped the agency shut down the Iranian counter-cyber attack almost wholly when it was attempted on January 15 and 16, 2016. The scope of the NSA's capabilities was made apparent when the agency announced completion of a data center in the west desert of Utah, costing well over a billion dollars for the facility, its super-computers, and its security. That center was only one of many such centers working in secret around the United States. New and different technologies were required to augment and usually to replace traditional SQL computer language, which stores data in tables, columns, and rows. The new technolo-gies—MongoDB, Cassandra, and Simple DB [generally known as noSQL or "not only SQL"]—made it possible for the NSA to store strings of words such as are found in e-mails and text messages, photographs, or digital video data.

The same technology that private companies such as IBM used to iden-tify fraudulent insurance claims and identity theft required less than thirty minutes using NoSQL compared to days or weeks on SQL. This enabled the companies—and with a private-government cooperative endeavor—to gain access to Iranian cyber attackers in a matter of seconds and to shut them down. Mistakes in interpretation were reduced to a minuscule percent of the data retrieval and interpretation by the introduction of so-called "natural lan-guage" processing—i.e., the word "bomb" could be separated into its possible reference to an explosive device or a more benign term, meaning "a failure" such as a Broadway play that "bombed." In addition, the NSA was instru-mental in foiling multiple physical threats by VEVAK, including assassina-tion plots involving Israeli, American, Canadian, British, and Saudi Arabian diplomats, scientists, and engineers.

DARPA—the "no-idea-is-too-wacky" research division of the DOD—and SSG-CNO made contributions to NSA and several other counter-cybertage agencies involved in protecting the economies of the Western democra-cies. DARPA created a genius-level computer strategy called the Active Authentication cybersecurity program. The program was capable of moni-toring any individual in the world; and, concentrating on computer users in Iran and North Korea, analysts were automatically and almost instanta-neously able to identify an individual user who would be likely to pose a threat. The technology to make such identifications was complex beyond that of traditional computers and certainly of any individual or agency to accomplish acting alone. The technology was able to analyze—and therefore to identify—distinctive patterns of *how* the nation's enemies use technology: patterns of speed, hesitations in typing, keystroking, swiping a mouse, key "dwell-time" to the submillisecond differences in individuals, tapping on the punch sensors on a smartphone, and using biometrics to identify individuals based on physical and behavioral traits. The biometrics were so elaborate and precise that the cybersecurity program became able to catalogue the muscle memories of tens of thousands of Iranian and North Korean hackers and cybertagers. U.S. and other G-12 countries secretly inserted accelerometers and gyroscopes into all smartphones sold to customers in the enemy countries, which allowed DARPA, SSG-CNO, and all of their military, governmental, law enforcement, and business clients to know what, where, and when a suspected terrorist was using his/her smartphone data functions.

On the fifteenth and sixteenth of January, every agent, technologist, programmer, secretary, and administrator of DARPA worked nearly straight through that forty-eight-hour crisis period. They were the people in the shadows, the people up in the night, so that the rest of the citizens could sleep in their beds in security, and the sheepdogs that kept the wolf at bay.

As the sixteenth was almost behind them, Army Col. Avery Holmes and Navy Captain Victor Raylan touched base by secure telephone to see if each agreed that the crisis was now over, and their agencies could return to the more nearly normal routine.

"So, Victor, can we hit the head and get into our bunks, my friend?" Col. Holmes asked.

"I think so, Avery," Capt. Raylan responded. "I think we dodged this bullet."

"But there's still the bomb in the hands of maniacs."

"Yes, there's still that. Somebody else has to deal with that little issue. I can't think any more."

CHAPTER TWENTY-FIVE

The Day

Esfahan Shahid Beheshti International Airport VIP Lounge, January 16, 2016, 0810

The Supreme Leader of the Islamic Republic of Iran, Grand Ayatollah Ali ibn Abi Rahimi and his first wife, Roshanak; Ali Muhummad Sharifi, foreign minister of Iran, his second wife, Mahdis, and his two talented children, Javaneh and Mojtaba; and Miriam Rothsberger were escorted from their plane to State Limousine 1 by Hamid Hejazi, second in command of the security forces guarding the SL. Limousine 2 provided a comfortable ride from the airport to the Nuclear Power Facility at Katanz for President Okhavat, General ibn Sarrafzaadeh, Col. Dariush Aghdashloo, chief of the SL's security detail, and their wives. Limousine 3 held a contingent of Revolutionary Guards—the elite personal security division of the SL's household. Each of the limos was made by Iran Khodro [IKCO] for the exclusive use of the Supreme Leader, his household, and dignitaries honored by the SL.

The elites of the day's program were provided with a small box of sandwiches, brownies, pomegranate juice, and dolmothes. The limos were comfortable and provided a smooth ride, which belied the bulletproof tires, windows, passenger compartment, and the weight of the vehicle itself and its security material—nine tons—and its eight-inch-thick military-grade armor. VEVAK had been extraordinarily thorough in their provision of security within the airport itself; they stopped and frisked passengers, baggage handlers, and flight attendants. They went through every trash can, bathroom stall, and mailbox searching for bombs in anticipation of Rahimi's visit—no different from what the SAVAK did during the Pahlavi era.

Agha Rahimi placed a casual hand on Miriam's thigh. It was unexpected, entirely inappropriate, and very much not appreciated by the virtuous Orthodox Jewish wife and mother. Besides, she was afraid that the SL would discover her secret. Roshanak missed nothing where her husband was concerned and was no stranger to his lechery. She promptly reached across and removed his hand. Neither woman spoke a word. The Supreme Leader acted as if nothing had happened.

The limousines were preceded by three military security vehicles and followed by another three troop carriers full of Islamic Revolutionary Guard Corps [IRGC], making the caravan an impressive sight to behold and one befitting the grandeur of its occupants. Peace and quiet reigned until the caravan exited the secure military gates on the north side of the airport.

Then, all hell broke loose. A violently angry mob of rioters—easily 100,000 of them—flooded the highway and side streets. More than 10,000 frenzied thin-faced spectators wedged their way between Limo 1 and the security vehicles in front of them. In that crowd were forty Mossad, CIA, DIA, and political opposition members who whipped up the crowd of starving Iranian citizens to a vociferous frenzy. Molotov cocktails began exploding on the military vehicles, and the soldiers began to fire into the crowd with fully automatic machine guns.

The nearly 20,000 members of the Supreme Leader's household security staff were driving around the city in an assortment of vehicles on the lookout for dissenters when the riot seemed to spring from the ground in the vicinity of the international airport. They communicated with each other and coordinated a mobile attack on the outlying groups of placard carriers and screaming dissidents. The results were horrific. Thousands of men, women, and children fell victim to submachine gunfire. The initial success of the security forces gave them false confidence and led them to fail to recognize that they were driving in a compact vehicular cavalry directly into a pincer of well-armed opponents of the regime. Their vehicles died of bazooka fire and LAWS rockets. The security forces—of which 1,000 were women—began leaping from their burning vehicles and directly into the withering fire of thousands of machine guns. The losses on both sides mounted into the thousands, and the confusion became complete.

Grenades fell into the troop carriers behind the limousine carrying the SL, and in less than thirty seconds, his limo was an unprotected island in a sea of screaming citizens—each of which believed that they had no other choice left to them by the government than to fight. Hamid Hejazi ordered the chauffeur to exit the main highway and to drive over anyone who got in the way of the SL's limo.

Three minutes after turning onto the side street, the limo was away from the crowd. The white-faced occupants only then breathed a sigh of relief. Even within the sumptuous cabin, the sounds of war could be heard. The chauffeur gunned the limo's massive engine to its maximum torque, and the car barreled out of the city at breakneck speed. The chauffeur was the instructor in the elite defensive driving school for the Revolutionary Guards and had the additional distinction of having been personally selected by Hamid Hejazi, the SL's security force second in command.

"Fine man, our driver," the SL commented. "Remind me to reward him with a medal."

They were going 120 miles per hour and were halfway to the Katanz facility when the front tire exploded, and the limo driver had the fight of his life to keep control. He ploughed into a sand berm beside a large van parked there, evidently having experienced engine problems.

"Is everything all right, Sergeant?" Hejazi asked.

"Nearly perfect," the driver said.

Then he and Hejazi pulled out their machine pistols and shot every occupant of the limo's cabin dead, except Miriam and the SL. He was purple with rage.

Miriam hiked up her skirt, extracted a 9mm Glock from its holster strapped to her upper-right thigh, and put a single bullet into the head of the Supreme Leader of Iran. From the time the driver said that everything was "nearly perfect" until everyone except Miriam and the two security guards was dead, less than eight seconds had elapsed. Miriam had practiced her part in the assassination thousands of times with the help of her lady friends in the Iran Nuclear Interdiction Project.

As rehearsed, the three leaped from the limo and stripped down to their underwear—even Miriam's vaunted modesty was abandoned. Men from the "disabled" van—including Aaron Schmuel, whom Miriam recognized, and Levi Oistrakh, who was new to her—brought them clothing suitable for ordinary citizens going about their business. Miriam joined the contingent of Mossad and DIA agents in the back of the van, and Hamid Hejazi and the chauffeur, Ibrihim ibn Ali, ibn Muhammad piloted the limousine away as soon as its wheel was replaced. All telephonic and radio communication was turned off, and the two vehicles drove at breakneck speed to the Katanz

Nuclear Power Facility and parked in front of the large doors of the previously reconnoitered outbuilding.

Aaron and Levi opened the doors, and Hamid drove the limo into the interior of the building while his sergeant drove the van. Everyone helped to move the bodies out of the limo and place them along the side of the pit in the far corner of the open area. It was hard on Miriam to see the children and their mother, all of whom were presumably innocents in the lethal scenario. She had been coached and trained to expect this eventuality by her lady friends. Nevertheless, it was hard to look at them and do what was necessary to dispose of the bodies.

Aaron climbed down into the pit while Miriam, Levi, and the Supreme Leader's former security detail stripped all of the corpses. They carefully lowered the bodies—one at a time—to Aaron, who laid them out in a single serried row so as to be as shallow as possible when covered with concrete. Levi started up the cement mixer, and the other two men began adding cement and water to mix concrete. It was brutal work—choking dust, heavy cement bags, sloshing water, and hellish heat in the stifling atmosphere of the almost airless building. It took them two hours to cover the bodies. Then they lowered the pit cover and drilled screw holes in the floor to make it a permanent covering.

When that ghoulish task was completed, they filled the cabin of the limousine with cans of gasoline and set it ablaze. It had the effect of lighting a quiet bomb. The heat was almost overpowering but fairly brief. Finally, Aaron relented and allowed Hamid to open two windows of the building facing away from the main reactor building where the ceremonies were to be held. The three killers, Hamid, and the chauffeur worked feverishly to cover the charred remains of the limousine with the tarps piled across the room for just that purpose. Then, they clambered into the van to get away before Afsoon lit the fuses.

§§§§§

Katanz Nuclear Power Plant, Main Reactor Building, January 16, 2016, 0830

News of the violent riot in Esfahan and the all-out response of the Republican Guard—which had been underway for twenty minutes—had not yet gotten to the crowd of dignitaries gathered on folding chairs facing a raised stage where the most senior officials and speakers were already taking their seats. No one knew that the Supreme Leader and the president had been separated from their security detail in the mêlée and were missing. They certainly were unaware that eight people—including the Supreme Leader—were located less than a mile from where they were all sitting, and no one then living would ever see them again or that the disappearance of the limousine and its occupants would become a national historical mystery for more than a hundred years.

The dais was fully occupied. The dignitaries included Hormoz Mohammad-Bagher, president of Bank Sepah; Ayatollah Ali Hossein Golzar, head of the AEOI; Vice President Reza Mohammad Hessami; Behrouz Omidi, director of the Ministry of Intelligence and National Security [MISIRI]; Mullah Ali Salar Omidyar, director of the Ministry of Intelligence and Security [MOIS]; eight full professors of science, physics, and nuclear energy; four presidents of universities; and the ministers of Justice, Industries and Business, Industries and Mines, and Labor and Social Affairs.

The only dignitary not present was Dr. Afsoon Mouradipour. She did not give her assistant any indication about why she was late or if she was going to attend the most important gathering of her professional life. He took the initiative and welcomed the most important officials in the Islamic Republic to the formal announcement of Iran having nuclear weapons and the missiles to be detonated to the Zionist entity. It was his proudest moment, and he savored every second of it.

At 0800, Afsoon was satisfied that the architects of Project *Jahannam Adur* [Hell's Fire] were tightly gathered in one concentrated area. During the past three nights, she and her coconspirators had connected several hundred pounds of gelignite with timer fuses around the area of the reactor, including the open area where the dignitaries were seated. She switched the control switches to "on" and set the timer for 10:00. She checked to see that her handgun was loaded and a round was chambered. No matter what, she could not be stopped or arrested. She hated the thought of biting down on her false molar and releasing the cyanide, but nothing could compare to the torture to which she would be subjected if she were to be discovered.

"Dr. Mouradipour!" the urgent voice of a girl from the secretarial pool rang out immediately behind her. "They need...," and the girl's voice turned shrill and stopped mid-sentence as she took in what the famous nuclear scientist was doing.

The girl's face formed a scream that was cut off with sudden and final abruptness as Afsoon wheeled about and fired a single round into the T-zone of her face and blew the girl's brain stem to pieces. There was a brief huffing sound from the baffle-suppressed handgun muzzle and a "splat" noise as the bullet entered the top of her nose. She was dead before she could vocalize. Afsoon caught her before she could make any noise by falling against the cluttered desk. Afsoon had a very brief moment of pause, knowing that she had just killed a girl who was for all intents and purposes an innocent. She was surprised at herself for not being analytical about it or feeling the slightest remorse.

She hurriedly descended the stairs from her fourth floor office and headed towards the exit leading to the executive parking lot.

An exit guard yelled at her as she went through the door without checking out with him. She kept moving.

"Halt!" he yelled. "Stop or I'll shoot."

Afsoon made a nearly complete about-face, gun out and ready. As good as his word, the alert and well-trained guard fired off a round, which struck Afsoon in her left shoulder. It was a clean through-and-through wound and did not cause any critical damage, but it was like being run through with a dull hot poker. The pain was so surprising and intense that she thought she would faint. She was facing her opponent who was beginning to squeeze off a second shot. Her automatic brain took over, and she fired before he could. It was another accurate head shot, and he became an immediate noncombatant.

She slapped herself out of her developing stupor, reholstered her gun, and ran as fast as she could to her car. She was fighting panic, nausea, and a feeling of blackness closing in on her. Once inside her car and out of sight of any potential pursuers, she bit her tongue brutally. The acute severe pain of that bite caused an immediate surge of adrenalin, and she woke up. In fifteen seconds, she was fully alert and had her brain back. Her left deltoid was burning, aching, and now stiffening. She forced the almost crippled arm to help her back out of her parking place and to get her heading out to the highway. She approached the main gate sentry who—recognizing her and her car—waved her through. She had the presence of mind to reach across her chest and shoot the man so that he could not be a witness against her in the aftermath of the impending explosion.

She looked frequently into her rear and side-view mirrors and was relieved to see no pursuers. There were no people out and about because the security precautions had been strict—even stringent—to create a *cordon sanitaire* around the Katanz facility.

Inside the main reactor building, speeches, joyous cheering, clapping, high fives, and spontaneous interruptions, which, in one variation or another, greeted the marvelous news that "today—The Day—the evil Zionist entity and all its collection of 'the sons of Zion'—whom our Allah described as the sons of apes and pigs—will not survive."

She was nearly two hundred miles away to the north on Highway 65 and pleased to see that the bleeding had stopped coming from her shoulder when the blast went off. She took note of the time—1000, but could not hear the explosion, of course.

Aaron, Levi, and Miriam raced through the rear exit to the huge property of the Katanz facility and sped out towards the main highway towards Esfahan, churning up a trailing cloud of dust. That road intersected the Katanz main entrance just before it made a T junction with the highway. The cloud of dust gave them away. A uniformed security guard stood in the middle of the dirt road holding an AK-47 in one hand and holding up the other hand for them to stop. Aaron slowed down the van and approached submissively. The guard walked towards the front of the van, and Aaron gunned it straight at the guard—to his total consternation. He reacted by freezing in place, and Aaron ran him down. A second guard leveled his AK-47 at the car and began firing at the escapees on full auto. Miriam flung herself down between the back-seats. Aaron hunched down as low as he could get and still see out the wind-shield. Levi lowered his window and began to fire in the general direction of the guard but was totally ineffective owing to the jouncing motions of the van as it struggled to keep its purchase on the road. The guard changed the vector of his shots, elevated the muzzle, and raked six bullets into Levi's head and face. He dropped his machine pistol out the window and slumped over dead.

Escape was the obvious thing to do, but he and Miriam would join Levi among the dead if the guard was able to report the incident. Aaron knew about the cyber and telephone attack by the U.S. and Israel, but he could not be sure that it reached down to the level of this particular guard's phone. He did a bootlegger's turn and roared back in the direction of where the guard had been when he fired at them. The return of the van and the fact that it was aimed right at him so unnerved the man that he dropped his Kalasnikov, turned, and ran. It was a brief incredibly rough off-road ride after a man run-ning and zigzagging for his life. He was no match for the vehicle traveling

60 miles per hour to his 10. He stopped and turned to face the van with his hands in the air in total submission. Aaron stepped out of the van and fired a quick three-shot burst, which killed the hapless guard instantly.

Aaron and Miriam did what they could to cover the two dead guards and to get Levi's body into the back of the van and out of sight. They sped off in the same direction—north—that Afsoon had taken. Miriam was pale and shaking as her adrenalin rush tapered off, but she kept calm. Neither she nor Aaron spoke until they met Afsoon in the designated place—behind a nondescript international chain motel. It was 1010. From ten o'clock on, for several minutes, the ground shook as if a low-grade earthquake was taking place; otherwise, there was no real indication of what had transpired at Bushehr.

A ten-year-old shepherd boy moved his small herd of sheep and goats around Abraham's Hill, a low green knob with a view of the famous Bushehr plant. It was 0945, and young Mohamed had been up and busy since his family offered their first prayer of the day—the *fajr*. He was sleepy; his fine small herd of Raeini and Siahmouie goats and Asfari and Arabi sheep were beginning to lie down under the few bushes on the top of the hill to get out of the cold. The boy was an expert—even at his young age—at least at managing the physical end of the goat and sheep business. He participated in the twice-annual birthing and slaughtering. He was skillful at helping his father and older brothers produce the meat, milk, wool, goat fuzz and hair, skins, and valuable guts. For all of the changes that had taken place in Iran over the years that the elders of the family could remember, they were proudest of the fact passed down from generation to generation that this hilly region was the origin of the world's first wool sheep.

Mohamed had watched much of the building of the Bushehr Nuclear Facility, but was only a bit curious rather than really interested in it. It was not important, since it had nothing to do with sheep or goats. That morning had been one of unusual activity; big cars, soldiers, grand clerics, and men in suits poured into the doors of the main building. Since he could not read, Mohamed had no real inkling of what went on in the complex. He began to become uncomfortably cold sitting there on the hilltop watching the goings-on five miles in the distance. He presumed that his animals would be getting cold as well—maybe too cold—so the dutiful boy began stirring them into motion. He had no timepiece, but the sun was at or very near the ten o'clock hour, time to have a cup of the sweetened tea his mother had sent.

Suddenly, the ground shook violently. Mohamed might have ignored it as just another earthquake since Bushehr had an average of one a day, but this rolling of the earth was accompanied by a huge, low-pitched boom that seemed to come from the bowels of the earth. The earth lifted up nearly a hundred feet in the air then settled back down in a thick cloud of dust. A force that Mohamed could not see knocked him to the ground, as if a great wind had bowled him over. Except—prior to that moment—the wintery air had been still. Mohamed was in great pain. Something in that wind had burned him horribly; his clothes had disappeared or somehow melted away, and his flesh was scorched well down into his muscles. He screamed.

All around him, the goats and sheep died, some still standing against a rock or large bush. In the city of Bushehr, people died and turned to stone or dust where they stood like the men from Greek mythology who had had the audacity to rest their gazes on the Medusa. The fury of the earthquake or whatever it was had largely spent itself by the time it was felt in the nearby fishing villages of Halileh and Bandargeh along the Persian Gulf coast.

Because the blast occurred so deep in the earth and within a heavily reinforced bunker of concrete topped by nearly thirty feet of compacted dirt and rocks, the incredibly massive explosion had largely expended itself downward and outward in the Bushehr 1 main reactor site. Twelve plutonium239 bombs had gone off simultaneously, creating a crater nearly a mile deep. The walls of the crater were molten glass. Radiation billowed out of the seams and cracks of the crater and wafted north to Turkey on The Day.

Coincidentally, an earthquake did occur shortly before the blast at 0952. Young Mohamed did not even feel it, but it was recorded in Western monitoring stations as being 3.6 on the Richter scale. The massive focal earth movement that occurred eight minutes later was considered to be an aftershock. Such temblors were commonplace in the region.

§§§§§

Shahrak-e-Daneshgah [Tehran University Town], January 16, 2016, 1000

SAS Agent Carter Miller-Partridge watched with a proprietary smile as his chosen Indian agents mixed with the angry crowd of Tehran University students milling about the university town square. They were highly skilled—gifted and trained *agents provocateurs*—and were his men in whom he took great pride. From 0745, they had been unobtrusively herding the progressively frenzied crowd of young people in the direction of the adjacent Khodro Iran Khodro Company [IKCO] manufacturing plant. The screaming had been on a crescendo from the beginning, and now—five minutes to ten—the students, their partisan agitators, and Miller-Partridge's *agents provocateurs* were banging on the front gates of the factory. The lone remaining security guard was in sympathy with the rioters since he had not been paid his wages by the company for the past two months while President Okhavat's despised government spent all of Iran's money on the worthless atomic bomb. He opened the heavy steel padlock and stepped aside quickly to allow the burgeoning crowd to crush their way through. From somewhere in the crowd, Molotov cocktails appeared. From somewhere very near Miller-Partridge, two flamethrowers appeared and turned the entire plant into a holocaust that consumed the buildings, machinery, stockpiled vehicles, and the factory workers—most of whom became innocent victims—in the resulting inferno.

The SAS agent and his men made their way back through the crowd, found their old Ford van, and drove north towards the rendezvous point at the D-R Horse Breeding Ranch. They were on the northern outskirts of Tehran before the army arrived in the area of the automobile plant to take back control.

§§§§§

Petroleum Linkage Terminus at the Border Crossing from Iran to Doğubayazıt, Turkey, January 16, 2013, 1000

The crucial petroleum pipeline linkup point near the Iran-Turkey border—Doğubayazıt, Turkey, the nearest city—was severely undermanned, especially in the security division due to the mandatory layoffs of trained personnel. Funding shortages resulted from the deferral of funds to the nuclear project, the stinginess of the American and European lenders, and the American sanctions imposed on the nation. As a result, the Swedish commando force led by Johannes Hjerdstadt, agent of *FMUndSäkC* [Swedish Army Intelligence] had an easy time planting explosives at strategic sites where pipelines coming in from different directions linked up. His team included: Ali Nylander—a ranking member of the Iran Nuclear Interdiction Project; five experienced Swedish commandoes and sappers; and Amos Jukes, an American CIA agent who reported directly to Annette Redstone and was the only American on the sabotage team.

Two security agents—an unarmed boy of sixteen and an old man—had the misfortune to drive by the site where Hjerdstadt's men were attaching limpet mines at an X junction of the pipeline. They were killed by machine gunfire as they attempted to flee. Otherwise, the mission was a training-book success. At 1000, a two-mile segment of pipelines in four directions exploded and ripped open and destroyed the pipes, valves, and supports. The fine crude oil burst into flames, which burned for sixteen days because the petroleum system crews could not locate the site of the sabotage. The saboteurs watched from a low hilltop four miles to the south as oil transport vital to the Iranian economy ground to a halt. The pipelines crossing at that junction flowed into the Pan-European pipeline, the Bourgas, Bulgaria to Vlore, Albania and, at another connection, flowed from the Bourgas to the Alexandropolous, Greece line.

§§§§§

Evin Prison, Tehran, Iran, January 16, 2016, 0800 to 1522

The animus, hatred, and fear of the infamous main prison in Iran boiled over on the morning of January 16 with some help from a Mossad-run spy ring led by David Henderson, Mossad agent, and Krav Maga expert Sergeant Ruth McGuire, and included the sons of Moise Levinsky and Jacob "The Greaser" Cohen, ranking officers in the Kosher Nostra. More than 150,000 people with long memories gathered from all parts of Tehran on Evin Prison. Guards shot almost 100 of them before realizing that the prison and its security personnel were doomed. They followed the warden out through a secret rear exit. When all of them had evacuated the prison and were marching double-time away from it, the Mossad operatives opened fire in a pincer tactic. None of the employees survived. That signaled the start of an all-out military style attack. Fifteen of the more than a thousand political parties opposed to the regime established by the Supreme Leader, former president Ahmedinijad, and present president Okhavat united for the first time ever to join in the bombardment of the despised symbol of the tyranny of Supreme Leader Rahimi's regime. Mortars, LAWs rockets, shoulder-fired surface-to-surface missiles, flamethrowers, AK-47s, handguns, baseball bats, and rocks were hurled in fury at the walls and gates of the institution of cruelty and injustice. The crowd breached the walls and two of the gates at a little past noon, and, in an hour, rounded up and slaughtered the assistant warden and every corrections officer, janitor, and secretary remaining in the place.

The crowd parted in sober silence as the women imprisoned there and who had suffered unspeakable abuses walked out of the hellhole. Those who limped or could not walk were carried by strong men. Those who were bedridden or dying were carried on makeshift stretchers to equally makeshift ambulances—largely commandeered private vehicles—and transported to hospitals around the city. The transporters saw to it that the women received preferential treatment before the other patients in the hospitals and in the place of any person identified as a sympathizer or official of the despised regime.

The countryside was in a state of near-civil war by sunset. It was unclear as darkness fell whether the army with its superior weaponry and discipline or the dedicated insurgents would prevail. It was also unclear how many deserters would swell the ranks of the opposition.

CHAPTER TWENTY-SIX

The Day After

The Rafter D-N Horse Breeding Ranch, Shekan Kalak in Semnan Agricultural Sector, Northeast of Tehran, January 17, 2016, 1218

A fsoon struggled to remain conscious. She found her mind wandering; and, at times, she lost concentration and had to swerve to keep from running off the road. Fortunately, the highway was well-kept asphalt and four lanes wide, which gave her a margin of error. She used her encrypted mobile— a phone unaffected by the cybertage of the morning—to get in touch with Aaron and Nassir with their STUs [Secure Telephone Units]. Aaron gave a very terse description of his location but left out details of his and Miriam's escape. Nassir had been successful in setting off a chain of Semtek bombs around the secret Qom facility and was sure that it had been severely crippled. Qom is 96 miles southwest of Tehran and 246 miles from Shahrekord. He was encountering some clashes between the army and dissidents as he traveled between the two cities, but fewer as he went south. He expected to meet at the first rendezvous in about 45 minutes.

Afsoon was bone-weary and thankful to see the BP motorway service area at the Shahrekord turnoff south of Esfahan. Her hold on consciousness was fading. She pulled to a stop behind the truck parking area, put a blanket over her left shoulder and chest to cover the blood—which she noted was copious—and fell unconscious slumped onto the steering wheel.

Half an hour later—1010—Aaron and Miriam pulled into the BP service area and drove around to be sure there was no one paying attention to them and to locate Afsoon.

"There she is!" exclaimed Miriam, distraught. "I think she might be dead."

Aaron drove the van up to the driver's side of Afsoon's car, and he and Miriam quickly got out and rushed to her. Aaron looked around one last time; no one was watching. He flung open the door to Afsoon's car, and Miriam shook her gently. She gasped as she saw the blood on Afsoon's lab coat and blouse.

Afsoon roused and looked about in confusion.

"Where … where am I? Who…?"

"It's me, Miriam."

Afsoon did not seem to understand.

"Gideon's wife."

"Oh," Afsoon said and gave a wan smile. "Good."

Miriam and Aaron half helped and half carried Afsoon over to the van and put her on the floor where she could lie down. She looked somewhat better with her legs on the same level of her head. She was no longer bleeding.

"Nassir will be here in a few minutes," Afsoon managed to say.

"We'll wait," Aaron assured her.

Afsoon fidgeted about with her hands, hunting for something.

"What is it, Afsoon?" Miriam asked.

"Where is *Fereshte*? Where is she?"

Miriam gave Aaron a blank look.

Aaron said, "There's no one else here, Afsoon. Everything's all right."

"No, it's not," Afsoon said. "It never will be."

She turned her head to the side and was quiet.

Nassir and two of his men pulled up beside the van twenty minutes later. He and Afsoon had a gentle embrace; and, seeing that she was stable, he and Aaron agreed that it was time to get out of there. Everyone clambered into the van with Nassir driving, and began the last leg of the trip to Tehran and, hopefully, to escape the whirlwind of civil war threatening to engulf them. They were retracing the route down from which they had come to escape, and now they were heading back into danger, but they were determined to keep to their carefully prearranged escape plan. Aaron rode shotgun with a machine pistol and a combat shotgun on his lap, watching every person and vehicle they passed.

They slowed their pace at the Abadeh-Shiraz Saadatshahr Tunnel located between Saadatshahr and Qaderabad, which was closed down to a single lane of traffic for repairs and lighting related works. They again met construction delays on the highway between Shiraz and Firouzabad. By being aggressive and ignoring the protests of other drivers, they drove along the margin of the asphalt most of the way and made better time than they might have hoped. Aaron, Nassir, and Miriam were becoming increasingly worried and frustrated at the slowdowns that were preventing them from getting Afsoon to medical care.

The fighting between small army squads and scattered groups of dissidents became larger in scope, more frequent, and deadly as they came into the southern outskirts into Tehran. The danger to the escapees was escalating.

Nassir said to Aaron, "Turn right at the next road. We can't make it going straight through. I know some back roads to the ranch."

They were entering Kahrizak. The road to the Holy Shrine of Imam Khomenei and Bereshte-e Zahra was on the left and clogged with misguided pilgrims caught in a pincer between larger army forces and condensed huge crowds of armed rioters. Heavy gunfire was concentrated to their left; so, Nassir's suggestion to turn right was not one that could be avoided. The road was not well marked and not in good condition, but the van was up to it. Afsoon was jounced and knocked around at each rut and hole in the gravel road and moaned involuntarily. Miriam cradled her head and shoulders against her own body to lessen the trauma.

They kept to the road that followed the northeast side of the Lar River—which was tedious and slow—but the route had the advantage of putting distance between them and the concentration of fighting nearer the center of the capital city. It was shortly after noon when they arrived at the Rafter D-N Ranch.

Elizabeth, Elias, and Zacharia Nichols-Dayan rushed out of the ranch house when the dust plume from the van announced their arrival. The sons ran back to the house and brought out a stretcher for Afsoon. Elizabeth supervised Afsoon's care; Zacharia drove the van to a barn and secreted it behind a stack of hay bales.

It took Elizabeth less than five minutes to recognize that Afsoon was sicker than she knew how to manage. She called Dr. Abbas Homayoun, the elderly Nichols-Dayan family doctor for fifty years.

"Dr. Homayoun, this is Elizabeth. I need your help in an emergency."

"Horse or person?"

"Person, and it is not something you can talk about. Please drive right over."

He was there in half an hour. Not knowing quite what to expect, he brought his wife Ahuva to act as his nurse. Elias met them at the door and hurried the old couple to Afsoon's bedside. He and Ahuva cut off Afsoon's blood-soaked lab coat, blouse, and brassiere. She was conscious enough to assist. She was so covered in blood that he could not be sure of the extent of the actual wound.

"Hot water, soap, and towels," he ordered.

Zachariah brought them immediately.

Dr. Homayoun, Ahuva, Elizabeth, and Miriam proceeded to wash off the blood gently but firmly enough that Afsoon moaned but stifled a real outcry. The exit and entrance bullet holes in her shoulder were obvious. Dr. Homayoun put his nose to the entrance wound and sniffed.

"Not infected yet."

"Ahuva, some iodine please. Afsoon, my dear, I'm sorry but this will hurt."

It did—terribly. Some of the brown liquid passed all the way through the wound front to back. Afsoon cried out as the burning became too intense. She arched her back, lifting herself up from the bed. Ahuva put her hand underneath the writhing young woman, and, feeling the scars, motioned to her husband to look. She turned Afsoon to her side, and the doctor and all of the women were able to see the heavy keloids. They all turned their eyes away, having looked at an obscenity.

"Whipped with a knotted leather cat o' nine tails … probably with glass shards embedded in the knots. Poor dear girl," the doctor said, speaking for them all. "We must save her. The monsters cannot have the last say in her life."

The doctor and his nurses worked with grim determination. He started an intravenous line and ran in three bottles of dextrose in normal saline [D_5NS] over the next eight hours. When the intravenous infusion was complete, Afsoon was alert and conscious enough to talk coherently. Elizabeth fed her a thin soup of lamb's broth and boiled vegetables. The doctor gave her a small box of iron tablets and told her to take one twice a day until they were gone.

"You are anemic from blood loss, my dear. But you are young, and you will survive. You will need your strength for what is to come."

"I'm still hungry," Afsoon said and smiled at the kindly old Orthodox Jewish physician.

"Have you some calf's liver, Elizabeth?"

She nodded to Elias, and he produced a large lobe of liver from the freezer. They thawed it and sautéed it with bacon and onions. The liver provided much-needed nourishment for the entire family and the doctor and his wife.

"Eat it as often as you can get it for the next three months, Afsoon. It will do you a world of good."

She nodded and squeezed his hand in gratitude, which made him blush. Despite his medical training, he was still Orthodox enough to be embarrassed from an intentional touch by a woman not his wife.

By nine that evening, the rest of the saboteurs straggled in with their tales to tell. David Henderson and Sergeant Ruth McGuire from the Mossad; the sons of Moise Levinsky and Jacob "The Greaser" Cohen, Seth and Micah—from the Kosher Nostra; Johannes Hjerdstadt, agent of *FMUndSäkC*, Ali Nylander, and three of their five Swedish commandos and sappers; Amos Jukes, the American CIA agent; Carter Miller-Partridge and his two Indian SAS agents—Ghurkas Thapa Dhanbahadur and Ghhetri Krishnabahadur; Mossad *katsa* Antal Disraeli, and three Mossad junior agents; Hamid Hejazi and the chauffeur and Ibrihim ibn Ali, ibn Muhammad all made it to the rendezvous more or less intact. Two of the Swedish commandos had been killed in the initial moments of their escape and had to be stripped of their clothing and dumped without ceremony alongside the road. Ibrihim had sustained a creasing bullet wound across the right side of his scalp but with no skull or brain injury. Micah took a round in his right buttock and did not want to talk about it. Dr. Homayoun and his nurses were able to repair the damage in minutes.

Elizabeth, Aaron, Afsoon, Miriam, Hamid, Ruth, Amos, Seth Levinsky, Nassir, and the doctor and his wife held a quick and decisive meeting once the doctor and nursing chores were finished.

Elizabeth had a way of cutting to the chase without embroideries or euphemisms. "Our time in Iran is finished. There is utter confusion and chaos in the entire country right now; but one day soon, the powers in Tehran will figure it out and will come for us. We have to leave here tonight under the cover of darkness and hide out in the forest until we can make a run for the Iraq border. Like it or not, that will take us closer to the army and the Revolutionary Guard than any of us want; and we will probably have to fight our way out at some points. Let's hear your suggestions."

Nassir answered, "I know one thing we need to do. We need to assume new identities. Afsoon and I have had experience. I think I can get hold of our friends among the Bakhtiari nomads who have pretty much abandoned their ancestral animal drive trails in the Zagros Mountains to live near the Caspian Sea during the summer. It will be cold enough that they are probably moving the animals towards the coast even now. I have friends in Qom who can find them, and they can put us in their traditional clothes and move us with them across the border at the tripoint boundary with Turkey at Kuh e-Dalanper. They trust the two of us, and they hate the Tehran regime."

"Go to it," Aaron said, and everyone nodded their heads in agreement.

Elias said, "We have some guns, ammunition, and horses, but we'll need some extra pack horses and some stores for the trip."

"Hamid and I will take care of that tonight," said Aaron.

Ibrihim and Ali stepped alongside Aaron, indicating their willingness to help in what would undoubtedly be an illegal venture.

Dr. Homayoun quietly asserted himself. "My wife and I are dead people if we stay. Someone will have seen us and put two and two together that we aided you. It is time posthumous that we got out of Iran. We have been fooling ourselves for decades that we can live with Muslims—whether it is our home or not. Our Neturei Karta rabbinical council has issued a *posek* [*psak halakha*, ruling of law—to stop or cease], bringing the process of legal debate to finality. We will cease to criticize Israel or to deny its right to exist. All of us who can will leave this land of oppression to become Jews free to practice our religion. We have been dislocated before, mocked, discriminated against, even murdered; but Judaism has a soul, and the chosen people live on despite every pogrom and holocaust.

"Almost every city in Iran has a Jewish attraction, shrine, or historical site. We will sorely miss the Esther and Mordechai and the Habakkuk shrines of Hamedan, the tomb of Daniel in Susa, and the Peighambariyeh mausoleum in Qazvin. Over my long life here, I have loved visiting the tombs of several of our outstanding Jewish scholars in Iran, such as Harav Ohr Shraga in Yazd and Moshe-Ha-Lavi in Kashan; but we will leave; or we will die. We know we have to go. I can help. We can load a wagon with enough medical supplies to make the nomads happy for years. It will require some special help tonight—some nightshift work for the likes of you."

Everyone smiled and nodded their agreement that the old Jewish couple had earned their place.

Carter Miller-Partridge and Sergeant Ruth McGuire volunteered for what was an obvious need for a quick B&E. They were joined by Carter's Ghurka agents, Thapa Chanbahadur, Ghhetri Krishnabahadur, and Antal Disraeli.

Carter said, "And in our copious free time, we can split up and hit the armory in Tajrish neighborhood. I reconnoitered it when we drove in. The neighborhood is one of the oldest parts of Tehran and is located along the northern edge of Tehran. It is popular with the upper classes, and, for our purposes, has a favorable location along Tehran's northern hills. The rich and famous will be hunkered down in their homes, and my bet is that there will only be a skeleton security crew on watch. All the rest of the troops will be out murdering innocent civilians. It's good and dark in there by the Saadabad Palace. The Tajrish bazaar will be empty tonight, and the roofed passageway will be pitch-dark. During a normal day, thousands of people pass through on a pilgrimage to Emamzadeh Saleh or to the bazaar to buy stuff, but I bet it will be empty tonight. I don't anticipate any real trouble."

"Elizabeth, I think my men and I can serve best as scouts; and, along with Zachariah, we can find a reasonably safe campsite where we can wait for the nomad guides. By the way, I'd like you to meet Gideon Meier and Rudolf Ashensky," Antal said.

The young Mossad agents nodded and shook hands with the matriarch.

"Can you arrange a rendezvous point with the Bakhtiaris by tomorrow evening, Nassir? I'm afraid we will be out of cellphone range by the time we are at the temporary camp."

"I will try my best," Nassir said with a grim set to his jaw.

There were no Murphy's Law mishaps during the night. Before first light the next morning, an impressive pack train of horses stolen from neighboring Muslim horse breeders was ready for loading in the back pasture behind a stand of assorted indigenous trees. A large pile of food, clothing, armaments, ammunition, winter clothing, medical supplies, kitchen and camp necessities, and wagons were assembled.

Nassir's job was the hardest. He called everyone he could think of and had no success because of the shutdown of usual telephone service. He asked Afsoon for suggestions.

She thought for a few minutes then said, "Find an old-fashioned citizen-band radio. There is no reason why that system should have been affected by the cyber attack on Iran."

"Why didn't I think of that?" he said.

Elizabeth laughed, "You don't have to look far. We have a set in the attic. Haven't used it since we got the Internet. Come with me and help me get it down."

Nassir and Afsoon made it their sole purpose in life during that day to find the nomads. They bounced a smattering of C-B lingo, which was probably woefully out of date and largely taken from old American movies. They did the best they could to get some kind of message out around the globe and to sound like American truck drivers as they did. They finally landed on the call sign of an American expat aficionado living in Van, Turkey. Nassir and

Afsoon early on had to concede that they could not manage the American-tinged C-B lingo well enough to get the job done. Elizabeth had to be brought into the team.

The contact that produced results went like this—with Elias translating for the gathered listeners:

ELIZABETH	ELIAS
Elizabeth—"Driver."	"Polite for 'Don't know your name.'"
C-B Operator—"This is Wild Turk, kick it in."	"Willingness to respond."
Elizabeth—"I have a 10:33. "What's your 20?"	"I have an emergency. What's your location?"
A real emergency?"	"Channel 9 is reserved for emergencies."
Elizabeth—"No doubt."	"Yes."
C-B Operator— "What's yourhandle?"	"What is your C-B call sign?"
Elizabeth—"Horse Woman."	
C-B Operator—"Don't compute."	"I can't find your sign listed."
Elizabeth—"I been off for years."	
C-B Operator—"Sure you're not a hacker or an outbander?"	"Hacker is a person operating a radio transmission without regard for standard rules or etiquette. Outbander is a person who operates an illegally modified CB radio, usually broadcasting outside the regulated frequencies."
Elizabeth—"I'm not. I'm a sidebander. I repeat, what's your 20, Wild Turk?"	"A sidebander is a CB station using SSB modulation—and updated technology.
Pause	
C-B Operator—"I'll take a chance. Van, Turkey."	
Elizabeth—"You sound American."	"Expatriate."

C-B Operator—"Expat. How about you?"

"Expatriate, too."

Elizabeth—"Part of my 10:33, can't say now."

"Part of my emergency."

C-B Operator—"Little business with the bears?"

"Police."

Elizabeth—"Bad bears east of you."

C-B Operator—"Like Iran bad bears?"

Elizabeth—"That's affirmative. Have to change my 20."

"Yes, I have to change my current location."

C-B Operator—"That's your 10:33? Has to be PDQ?"

"That's your emergency? Has to be pretty damn quick."

Elizabeth—"You know it, Wild Turk. Can you kick it in and help?"

"That's right. Can you respond and help?"

C-B Operator—"I'm an expat because the U.S. county mounties don't like the cut a my jib. I'll help. How?"

"I have trouble with U.S. law enforcement; they don't like me."

Elizabeth—"Need to find some nomads by the Caspian. Bakhtiari."

Pause

C-B Operator—"Taking the scenic route?"

"Running and hiding in obscure places?"

Elizabeth—"Affirmative."

C-B Operator—"I got a good neighbor over in Astera. He's a chief hood lifter over there. I'll get him on the horn."

"I have a friend in Astera. He's a chief service manager in a truck repair garage there. I'll get him on my C-B."

Long Pause. Nearly an hour. Several operators began attempting to contact Wild Turk.

C-B Operator—"Breaker, breaker. Need Horse Woman back."

"He's telling other CB users that he wants to start a transmission to Horse Woman on a different channel."

Elizabeth—"Tuned in."

C-B Operator—"Need to go to 1-1, too much traffic on 9. Getting some static." "Need to change to channel 11; there are too many listeners on channel 9."

Elizabeth—"10-4." "Understood."

C-B Operator—"I'll give over to the hood lifter. I'll be 10-10 on the side." "I'll stop broadcasting, but I'll be listening in."

Astera Operator—
"You Horse Woman?"

Elizabeth—"Affirmative."

Astera Operator—"I'll help. I know the 20 of your good neighbors, the travelers. I can get one on the hook, but it'll take a couple." "I know the location of your friends, the nomads. I can get one on my broadcast band, but it will take a couple of minutes (or hours)."

Elizabeth—"Hours?"

Astera Operator—"Yeah. They're not on the big slab. Gotta motor over some dirt." "Yes. They're not on the four-lane highway. I'll have to drive on a dirt road or even cross-country."

Elizabeth—"10-4. We'll be waiting. Thanks."

Astera Operator—"No prob. Had a few run-ins with the bears. And the VEVAK for that matter. Don't like 'em. Okay, I'm gone." "He's finished transmitting for the time being."

Elizabeth and the others waited anxiously for two hours for Astera Man to return to C-B channel 11. They were all laughing at the weirdness of the conversation between what seemed ostensibly to be some sort of English, understandable only because Elias could translate.

Astera Operator—"Had a good ride."

Elizabeth—"Find the travelers?"

Astera Operator—"Affirmative."

Elizabeth—"How do we talk
to them?"

Astera Operator—"I got one at my
20 now."

Elizabeth—"Really?"

Astera Operator—"Yeah, but there's
a bit of a prob."

Elizabeth—"Give me the worst."

Astera Operator—"Can't understand "I don't speak his language. You'll
a thing this one says. You're gonna have to talk to him in his lan-
have to jibber-jabber with him." guage if you can."

Elizabeth—"Farsi?"

Astera Operator—"Negatory. Some "No, they speak some
Bakhtiari jibber-jabber." Bakhtiari language."

Elizabeth looked like she might be defeated.

"Let me try," Afsoon said. "Between Nassir and me, we should be able to
find a language that will work."

"Have at it," Elizabeth said.

Elizabeth—"I have a jibber-jabberer.
Put the traveler on."

Pause

Astera Operator—"Here's your good
neighbor, let's hope."

Afsoon—[Speaking Azerbaijani] "Do
you understand me?"

Bakhtiari—"Yes. Who are you?"

Afsoon told him, reminding him of her escape from the jail bus on the
Valfajr highway at the edge of Shinabad in Ostan-e Azerbaijan-e Gharbi in
February 1993. He remembered. He paused for a moment. She told him that
there would be many people in their party. He explained that they were poor

nomads and could not afford to give shelter, food, and transport for a large party. It would put the clan in danger. He asked if they could pay and told her it would be expensive. Nassir signaled Afsoon to let him negotiate.

Nassir—"What would be fair, Brother?"

Pause

Bakhtiari—"Horses, cattle, sheep."

Nassir—"We have horses."

Bakhtiari—"How many?"

Pause

Nassir—"Maybe ten."

Bakhtiari—"Not enough. Be realistic."

Nassir—"Maybe twenty, no more. That is all we have."

Bakhtiari—"Not enough. Any cattle, sheep?"

Nassir—"No."

Bakhtiari—"Anything else of value?"

Pause

Nassir—"Guns and ammunition."

Bakhtiari—"Enough for the clan?"

Nassir—"Plenty."

Bakhtiari—"Done."

Nassir's pauses were to look at Elizabeth and Elias for approval. Elizabeth's heart sunk when she realized she would lose all of her beautiful Caspian breeding stock, and it would be the devil's own task to start over. But it was the difference between life and death—probably a very unpleasant death.

Aaron, Antal, and Seth all interrupted to guarantee that their organizations and governments would make it good. Neither Elizabeth nor her compatriots could be certain that they could make it happen, but there was not another viable choice. Every member of the Nichols-Dayan escape party was determined to keep their end of the bargain with the Bakhtiaris—if only for the fact that they knew from past experience that the nomads were a particularly unforgiving race. But they also knew that—for the moment—they faced a very uncertain future.

CHAPTER TWENTY-SEVEN

The Scenic Route

Bakhtiari Nomad Camp, Alborz Mountain Range Bordering the Western Margin of the Caspian Sea, Northern Iran, West of Rasht, January 22, 2016

The escapees were loaded and ready to leave the Rafter D-N Ranch at 0430 on the 17th while it was still dark enough to provide cover. Elizabeth, Elias, and Zachariah gave every ranch hand a week off to express their appreciation for the years of service they had rendered the family. None of the hands had seen the influx of bedraggled guests, and they were unaware of the plans of the escape. Nonetheless—everyone knew that once they left—the ranch hands would know soon enough and shortly thereafter, so would VEVAK.

Once their horses stepped off the northeastern border of the property, there would be no turning back, and they would probably never see their homeland again. Elias and Zachariah adjusted the panniers on the pack horses one more time. Every rider wrapped a cloth around the muzzle of his horse and the pack horse for which he or she was responsible. Miriam was one of the best riders among them because of the training in dressage she had enjoyed in Les Ecrinelles riding school based at Saint Sauveur en Rue. It was part of her becoming a young lady of sophistication through her finishing school in Lyon. She was assigned to calm the panic of the hardened Mossad agents and Kosher Nostra members who had never been on a horse. Everyone laughed, but no one balked at her good-humored help. Afsoon appeared tired, presumably from lack of sleep due to the pain in her arm and blood loss.

They were approximately 45 miles from their rendezvous with the Bakhtiaris as the crow flies, but it was a difficult country and slow going. The distance they traveled was considerably farther because they had to wander about to be able to keep inside the patchy groves of trees in the lowlands. When they got to the foothills of the Alborz Mountains, the trails were steeper; and the snow became ever deeper.

The nights were cold, and Afsoon and the doctor and his wife grew weary and less able to keep up. They fell into their sleeping bags as soon as the company stopped, and would have passed on having food if Elizabeth and Miriam had not sternly insisted. Dr. Homayoun and Ahuva began to be concerned about Afsoon on the second night in camp.

"She has a fever," Ahuva said.

"I'm all right," Afsoon said. "Don't worry. I can keep up."

"Let's have a look at that wound, Afsoon. I know you are a stoic, but we have to be realistic."

Reluctantly, Afsoon allowed the doctor and his wife to open her shirt. The pain was dreadful, and the wound was bright red and swollen. Pus had leaked out from under the bandage and caused the blouse to stick to it. Removal of the bandage made her grind her teeth and grimace, but she did not make a sound.

"Afsoon, my dear, I have some antibiotics. I was afraid you would get some trouble. I have pen and strep. That has been my mainstay for thirty years. I am sure it will do the job here. But, Daughter, I am going to have to open the wound to let the pus drain. I'm sorry. It will hurt a great deal," said Dr. Homayoun.

Elizabeth brought her a thick strap to bite on. She, Miriam, and Ahuva knelt beside her to hold her down. Dr. Homayoun injected the antibiotics, then he placed a snowpack on the tender area to serve as a local anesthetic—an inadequate one, but at least it would dull some of the worst acute pain. Once the wound was icy and numb to the touch, he used a clean rough towel soaked in water made by heating snow and sprinkled with laundry detergent to scrub the wound. The infection was acute, and Afsoon's nerve endings were at their most sensitive. It was like having a severely infected ingrown toenail removed with dull pliers. She bit down violently on the leather strap in a valiant effort not to scream. Everyone in the party feared that she would make enough noise to bring an army patrol into camp.

The pain of cleaning the wound paled in comparison to what came next.

Dr. Homayoun said, "Afsoon, I beg your pardon for what I am about to do. Hold on tight. Elizabeth, hold her head; so, she won't thrash around and hurt herself. Nassir, come and help hold her legs."

Afsoon nodded, and Dr. Homayoun made a deep vertical incision with a disposable scalpel. Afsoon screamed inwardly but refused to let out even a whisper of a sound. When the doctor made a horizontal cut, Afsoon fainted. The "X" opened widely and a pocket of purulent fluid and necrotic muscle issued forth. Dr. Homayoun worked swiftly while his patient was unconscious and scrubbed the wound vigorously to leave it clean and wide open. He sprinkled sulfa powder in the wound and compressed it vigorously to staunch the bleeding that accompanied his deep debridement. Finally, it was over; and Afsoon fell into a ragged dreamless sleep.

The next morning, her color was better; but her arm was useless.

"It will be all right once the infection begins to die down, Afsoon," the doctor told her.

Afsoon was doubtful but knew that she had to soldier on. She drank half a quart of chicken broth and ate a slice of wheat toast soaked in warm milk. It was difficult to force the food down, but she felt better for having made the effort. When she tried to stand, she became light-headed; and, even with a half-hour's rest, she was unable to mount her horse.

The men fashioned a travois from pine boughs, with the soft needles providing some insulation against the snow and the battering she had to endure as the travois bounced along behind one of the pack horses. She intermittently fell asleep or unconscious; it was difficult to tell which. Nassir rode along beside her the entire way.

She was no better the next night when she camped, and the men and women who were familiar with such signs and symptoms shook their heads in doubt.

Nassir said, "You don't know her. She is the toughest human being you will ever meet. She is going to make it. Don't you dare give up on her. She was left out on a freezing mountaintop the day she was born, and she lived. She had a terrible FGM by a monster with a filthy knife and nearly bled to death. Her sister died of the same …"operation" or whatever you want to call it, but Afsoon lived. She was raped and flogged with a cat o' nine tails until you could see her ribs on her back. She was in a coma when she was taken to a prison where she was starved and mistreated every day. But … she lived. She endured almost twenty years of being the lone secret agent among people who would have tortured her to death if they knew. She knew fear like no one else has ever known. But she kept the faith, and she lived. She will live through this."

Nassir's passion transcended the objectivity of every other escapee. They began to believe.

Before dusk the next day, five riders came into camp—Zachariah, Antal Disraeli, Gideon Meier, Rudolf Ashensky, and a blue-robed nomad mounted on a small sturdy pony. His face was veiled.

"We're not too far from the Bakhtiari's main camp partway up on Mount Damavand. It's the tallest mountain in Iran, and it is covered with about ten feet of snow. We are safe there for a little while; but our friends have to leave urgently or else their animals will freeze; and the people will starve."

He looked over at the nomad who as standing patiently by his horse.

"This is Najaf Sardar Bakhtiari. His brother is the headman of the clan who has agreed to lead us to the Turkish border. It is comforting to know that they are very seasoned fighters and that they hate the Rahimi regime. The SL had their father executed then beheaded, and the Evin prison guards were filmed playing football with his head. No love lost there."

The following morning, Afsoon was better but still could not keep upright in the saddle. She endured another travois ride up horse trails that led ever upward through the deep snow. They rode into the large nomad camp at midafternoon on January 22. They were expected and something of a festive atmosphere was in the air. These were a people who seldom saw outsiders, and instinctively mistrusted them when they did. However, Zachariah, Antal, and Antal's two subordinates had won them over—they were as tough as the Bakhtiaris and were good-natured when they were battered in several of the rough masculine games the tribe enjoyed. In addition, the promise of a bounteous reward sat in the back of every man, woman, and child's mind.

Two days later, the magic of nomad decamping unfolded. It was a scene of organized confusion and efficiency born of centuries of practice. Nearly a hundred horses and donkeys balked at being loaded, but were generally patient beasts of burden treated reasonably well. Headman Saad ad-Daula Khan signaled to his followers to move out, and the long train began lethargically to move. The pace picked up shortly so that they were able to make about five miles the first day as they slogged through the snow down the eastern slope of the mountain near the southern coast of the Caspian Sea, and, after that, to go between eight and eleven miles a day. Saad led them down a ravine to an abandoned gravel road hard-packed with ice and snow.

The road was the forerunner of a future four-lane highway. The view looking back was amazingly beautiful and pristine—snowy conical peaks, most likely dormant volcanoes. The nearly 17,000-foot high peak of Damawand itself emitted irregular puffs of sulfur smoke from fumaroles near the summit crater. It is the highest volcano in Asia.

Aaron and Elizabeth questioned the headman about the choice. He admitted that they ran a greater danger of attack along the road that served as the western edge of the narrow plain that led to the Caspian coast. He was confident that the army was busy murdering innocent civilians elsewhere and had no reason to bother a migrating train of nomads passing through snow country where rich people cavorted at a number of world-class ski resorts. He pointed them out as they rode by: Dizin, Shemshak, Tochal, and Darband. The effect was tranquilizing. A fairly well-kept road, magnificent scenery, the sights and sounds of people having fun. They had not seen a police or military presence since they reached the bottom of Damawand. Afsoon's health was returning; and she could now ride, which helped the caravan to move along more rapidly.

At night, clan history teller Amirreza Moshiri sang the highlights of the memorized history of the Chahar Lang division of the Bakhtiaris—the four-legs—going back more than two thousand years. A beautiful middle-aged woman named Nadia Amirbakhtiar sang the epic Bakhtiari folk song *Shir-e-Ali Merdoon*, which complemented Amirreza's storytelling. The children were given sweets and put into their warm sleeping cocoons made of leopard and brown bear skin. The adults had a veritable feast of chukar partridge and grey-necked bunting, then retired to their black goat-hair tents. They were camped in a dense wild oak, beech, and hazel tree wood, which enclosed them and hid them from possible prying eyes of the government. The fears and trepidations of the fugitives were beginning to ease. Nonetheless, both the nomads and their guests maintained a regular armed watch.

The aura of pastoral winter tranquility was shortly to prove illusory.

CHAPTER TWENTY-EIGHT

Meeting the Beast

On the Old Road North and West of Rasht, Twenty-one Miles from the Coast of the Caspian Sea, January 27, 2016

They were fortified by a hearty breakfast of Bakhtiari yogurt enriched with green raisins, pistachios, and coarse whole grain unleavened bread smeared with fatty goat butter. They drank whole unpasteurized milk and Turkish tea, then the caravan went into its ancestral camp takedown and travel mode. In less than an hour, they were back on the road. The fugitives were tense, edgy, and felt a growing insecurity because they were getting closer to cities.

Their lack of ease was prophetic. They had traveled about five miles when a rifle shot knocked Fereydoon Alipour, the camp cook, from his horse. Headman Saad ad-Daula Khan gave only the slightest of hand signals, and the long caravan wheeled to the left and into the trees. It was tough going through the soft deep snow, and the horses and donkeys struggled. Finally, the frantic Bakhtiaris and fugitives had to dismount and pull their mounts and pack animals into the cover of trees until neither man nor animal could keep going. Mrs. Homayoun was gasping for breath. The exertion for the old woman was too much; she sat down in the snow and leaned against a bush, struggling to catch her breath. Only her husband could offer her help. Everyone else had formed a defensive perimeter and began waging a pitched battle against a company of regular Iranian army soldiers. On the defensive side of the ledger, there was a plus—they were better armed and better disciplined than the soldiers who were little more than raw recruits drafted to fight in the ongoing crisis demanding the attention of every citizen in the country at that point.

Gideon Meier and a Bakhtiari sentry named Shapour Del-anchin rose up and began firing with automatic weapons, and both of them were cut down by return machine gunfire. The disciplined Bakhtiari and fugitives instituted a steady fusillade of small arms fire and a series of well-timed and well-placed grenade return fire. Afsoon dug deep into her exhaustion and found a reservoir of strength sufficient to bring up her Kalasnikov and to put out controlled fire that began picking off Iranian soldiers below them foolish enough to raise their heads. This gave heart to the other embattled members of the caravan, and soon they saw small breaks in the ranks. A woman and her young son were the next to die. Saad waved his hand to indicate an operation to flank their attackers, and the men—and even the women—moved into position to form a pincer attack. Afsoon forced her way through the thigh-deep snow—firing as she went—although she soon became too exhausted even to walk, let alone fight. She rested to catch her breath; then, under withering fire, she slogged through the deep snow to drag the first wounded man to safety and finally two women and a child before she collapsed in the snow. An AK-47 round grazed her right thigh, but otherwise she was unhurt.

The pincer caught the army company in a deadly withering cross fire, and they began to fall like trees in a high wind. They were not battle-experienced enough to stand their ground in an organized defense—and, within minutes—they panicked and began to run away from the scene of carnage. When the Bakhtiaris began to scream their war cry, the young soldiers threw away their weapons and made a rout out of their surprise attack.

The nomad and fugitive men mounted their horses and pushed them down the hill, killing straggler soldiers as they rode down the hillside like the devil's own cavalry. They were everywhere—the four horsemen of the apocalypse rolled into one. None of the hapless and terrified soldiers survived. It was over in less than half an hour. The women gathered up the weapons, ammunition, and rations from the men and their temporary camp and stripped the soldiers of their warm clothing and boots. Gloves were a scarcity among the Bakhtiari, and they found an ample supply—some still in their packing crates and some on the men themselves.

When it was quiet again, Nassir picked Afsoon up in his arms and placed her on the still warm body of a dead horse. Miriam—having seen the elderly woman sag down off her horse into the snow at the start of the skirmish—

hurriedly looked for Dr. and Mrs. Homayoun. Ahuva was lying cradled on her elderly husband's lap. She had died of heart attack from her exertions. Dr. Homayoun rocked her back and forth, humming the strains of an old Persian Jewish funeral dirge. Nearby, the wife of Fereydoon Alipour was crying in a soft keening voice, afraid to give full vent to her overwhelming angst for fear of alerting more of the enemy. Gideon Meier and Shapour Del-anchin, the Bakhtiari sentry, were being laid out with respect by the Bakhtiari, Israeli, American, and British warriors. The ground was hard frozen and covered with nearly four feet of snow in most areas. A suitable burial was impossible for anyone. The first priority had to be hiding of the evidence of the skirmish. When the army discovered the massacre, they would come after the caravan with a vengeance. They might even suspect that there were Western military men among the Bakhtiaris, and possibly even Western agitators who could bear the blame for the deadly chaos threatening to engulf Persia.

Every able-bodied person—even children—rushed to cover the bodies with rocks and snow. The spring melt would not come for another three or four months, and they hoped to keep the evidence of the battle a secret until they were at least well away from the area. When the area looked more like a winter scene than a deadly encounter, Saad ordered the people to get ready to move out and on the double.

The people quickly gathered around the burial sites of their kindred dead. Dr. Homayoun, a devout Orthodox patriarch, intoned the Mourner's Kaddish, which spoke for everyone, even those who did not understand the words, but recognized the feelings: *"Yit'gadal v'yit'kadash sh'mei raba [Amein]. B'al'ma di v'ra khir'utei v'yam'likh mal'khutei b'chayeikhon uv'yomeikhon, uv'chayei d'khol beit yis'ra'eil, ba'agala uviz'man kariv v'im'ru: Amein."* [May His great Name grow exalted and sanctified Amen in the world that He created as He willed. May He give reign to His kingship in your lifetimes and in your days, and in the lifetimes of the entire Family of Israel, swiftly and soon. Now say:]

And Elizabeth, Elias, Zacharia, Antal, Rudolf, and Miriam—the Jews—intoned the response: *"Y'hei sh'mei raba m'varakh l'alam ul'al'mei al'maya"* [Amen. May His great Name be blessed forever and ever], and on down the ritual words to *"Oseh shalom bim'romav hu ya'aseh shalom,"* [He Who makes peace in His heights, may He make peace,] a sentiment all would be willing to echo.

The Bakhtiari were silent and respectful. When the Jews were done, they moved to where Shapour Del-anchin, Fereydoon Alipour, Amilie Bakhtiari and her son, Ali Asghar, would sleep the long sleep under the snow. They began the tribe's rendition of *Maqam-e Gahgeryu*—the time for mourning. The lyrics were particular to each tribe and subtribe and reflected more the mythology of the Bakhtiari people than the anguish of mourning. Mourning is part of the mythology and is very prevalent in Bakhtiari funeral music. "*Gahgeryu*" is one of the vehicles of this mythologic manifestation, and there was a mixture of vehemence and sorrow in Saad's people as they rendered their impassioned respects to the recent dead and their reverence for their noble people. The tune—the *maqam*—was—as it always is—an improvisation. Those still living produced stringed instruments, and the people accompanied the players in this rare moment of deep sadness.

It was time—past time—to move on. The caravan mounted as a unit and rode through the snow to the road. It was a dangerous move, but a faster route. If they were caught by the army mired in the deep snow, it would be a turkey shoot, with the Bakhtiaris and the fugitives assuming the roles of turkeys. It was imperative that they gain distance. Saad drove them mercilessly. Nassir tied Afsoon to her saddle and kept hold of her by a rope around both of their waists. They drove on hour after hour, until children fell from their horses, too near unconscious to be mindful of what they were doing. Finally, several mothers announced that they could not go on any further. Either the clan would stop here and fight to their deaths or perhaps Allah, the Merciful, would will that they should live another day. *Inshallah*. The deep Shi'ite core of the nomads was a source of strength and courage, and they moved into the forest and circled the animals and wagons around them. Sentry duty was now half the men on for four hours then the other half would replace them. They ate dry rations in silence.

Afsoon's shoulder wound began to bleed again. Her leg throbbed. Nassir and the doctor removed and replaced the shoulder bandage. The wound, though oozing some blood, looked clean and considerably improved over the time of debridement. The graze wound on her thigh would leave another scar, but it would hardly be noticed among the enduring marks that testified to her painful past.

CHAPTER TWENTY-NINE

The Defense

Fort Detrick, Fredrick, Maryland, Satellite Office of the Deputy Director of the Defense Intelligence Agency, January 27, 2016

Rear Adm. Martin Torgelson assumed the office of DDDIA in 2011 when Neal Daastrup was temporarily incapacitated by his heart attack—3D had already met the mandatory retirement age before his health issues forced him out. Out of respect, the appellation "3D" stuck with Vice Adm. Daastrup, Ret.; so, Torgelson had become known as the "Swede." He answered to the new director, the DIA, and then to President Oliver Sandstone, who had appointed him. Unlike his two predecessors, Sandstone was an overt hawk, and the attitude towards such miscreants as the North Korean, Sudanese, Egyptian, and Iranian kleptocratic tyrannies was nothing like the kid-glove approach of presidents Ryan and Gabler. He certainly was not going to win the Nobel Peace Prize like another predecessor had who bad-mouthed the United States all around the world and was nominated for the prize during the first twelve days of his first administration.

Torgelson received an alarming call on the twenty-sixth and again, today, the twenty-seventh. The woman and her team from the Iran Nuclear Interdiction Project who wreaked havoc on the Iranian plans to obliterate Israel with a nuc was in deep trouble. She had been shot during her escape from the Bushehr plant, and now was apparently infected and sick. The call today was alarming for two reasons: it did not come from the Trojan Horse herself but from one of her agents, about whom Torgelson knew nothing—a man named Nassir

Jamshidi. He hoped the call was legitimate and not someone who had gotten control of Trojan Horse's special encrypted phone. Presuming that the caller was who he said he was, the news was almost as dire. Trojan Horse and her confederates were under attack by regular army troops in some godforsaken winter wonderland way up by the Caspian Sea.

Adm. Torgelson placed a conference call to the DDIA, the DCIA, the president's national security advisor, the secretary of defense, and to the president.

"Gentlemen, Mr. President," he said, "we have a crisis happening today, and we need to correct it as soon as possible."

President Sandstone said, "The Iran situation?"

"Yes, Sir. A specific problem going on as we speak."

Adm. Torgelson explained something of what Afsoon and the others had been doing for the past fifteen years and about the culmination of all those years of effort and planning that occurred on the sixteenth without divulging Afsoon's identity.

"Our Trojan Horse has given up the best parts of her life for us, Mr. President. I think she deserves the Congressional Medal of Honor and am going to recommend that to you officially once all of this is behind us. Right now, we need to save her and the brave men and women who are in such immediate grave danger because they are helping her."

"Tell me what you have in mind, Admiral."

Torgelson gave the president the short version. The president acquiesced; and, on the other lines, he heard the rest of the government officials add their agreement.

President Sandstone then said, "Secretary Augmar, work with the NSA and Adm. Torgelson and get this done. I want those people brought in out of the cold—safe and sound, if at all possible."

CHAPTER THIRTY

In the Cold

Wild Country at the Junction of Eastern Turkey, Northern Iraq, and Northwestern Iran ["Kurdestan"], January 29, 2016, 0415

Army Ranger Col. Matthew Spikeburg, Navy Seal Captain Nick Orfanakis, and SAS Col. Sir Walter Heckfield-Brown, had been up for twenty-four hours, along with the men and women of their commands preparing for and arriving at the designated location. There were seventy-two elite soldiers and sailors—the best of the best short-notice commanders of the night, men and women with whom you would gladly hunt tigers in the dark. Along with them—and equally well armed—were three civilians: Gideon Rothsberger—whose wife was one of the heroes out there in the cold; Levi Schmuel, a businessman and probably an organized crime chieftain—whose son was there as well; and Ephriam Meyer from the Mossad. No one sitting at the ready on that bitter morning was a stranger to armed conflict. Their mission came directly from the president of the United States, but their personal passions were also a powerful driving force. The financial wherewithal for the mission came from the Rothsberger family, so that there could be plausible deniability to lessen the impact of what would likely involve a cross-border incursion into the territory of Iran.

The cold was biting, and their breaths were heavy with condensation in the air. Silence was the order of the day, and they were well camouflaged and hidden behind the low hills of the area. The miracle of C-130s had brought for them tanks, armored cars, crew-served machine guns, flamethrowers, bazookas, rocket-propelled grenade launchers, rapid mobility small troop carriers—you name it. The machines had been fitted out with special grease and oils to prevent freezing down to -45 degrees. It was -21 degrees as the men and machines huddled in the night.

They strained their eyes looking through the latest and finest night vision glasses, looking from their position on the Iraq side for any signs of movement from the Iran side, which was only 50 yards to the east. They were within shouting distance of the tripoint boundary point, Kuh e-Dalanper-e Bozorg—37° 08' 44" N and 44° 47' 05" E—where Iran, Iraq, and Turkey meet and more than four hours of land travel is needed to reach the nearest small city. The selection of their location was nearly perfect. They were hidden from view by the hillocks in front of them and had a direct, unimpeded run across the border. The countryside was semiarid, and the land area was not cultivated or fenced. The landscape was mostly covered with natural mosaic vegetation and few large boulders—in short, the small expeditionary force had a clear initial shot.

§§§§§§

Five miles to the east—on the Iran side—the harried Bakhtiari and fugitives had encountered twenty miles of sporadic attacks, which were growing more intense as they approached the border with Iraq. The semiarid area had two advantages for them. The ground was frozen solid, and the fleeing nomads and their guests did not have to contend with mud. The second advantage was that the snow was only about a foot deep, and, in many areas, less. Of course, those advantages applied to their pursuers as well. Aaron, Carter, Hamid, and Headman Saad ad-Daula Khan split up the leadership responsibilities. Aaron and Carter served as the rear guards to fend off the skirmishers from the army. The latest attackers were the most heavily armed yet. The army was now deadly serious and newly cautious. Too many young army privates had lost their lives to inspire confidence that the caravan was a soft target.

Saad, his wife, Elizabeth, and Miriam kept order and progress among the women, children, the wounded, and the animals. The oldest of the boys were armed and served as roving sentries constantly circling the contained group of vulnerable people. Afsoon was only able to stand temporarily and was relegated to the center of the protective circle with the injured.

Hamid, Elias, and Zachariah led a forward contingent of good fighters to scout the way, and, more importantly, to prevent a surprise attack coming from the front by soldiers who might have circled around in front of them.

The first predawn light began to turn the sky gray. Suddenly, the air was filled with gunfire and screams, and the sky lit up with aerial bombardment. The people fell and hugged the frozen ground as bullets whizzed, HM 12 60mm mortars whumped, 2S1 Gvozdika howitzer rounds and Fajr-5 self-propelled artillery rockets roared like freight trains, and MGA-3 heavy machine guns mounted a ceaseless staccato and ricocheted above them. The Iranian army rolled up in all its might from behind them and from both sides. Saad told his men to kill the women and children when the army broke through, and to prepare themselves to die like Bakhtiari warriors.

§§§§§

At the commencement of the cacophony, Col. Spikeburg, Captain Orfanakis, and SAS Col. Heckfield-Brown simultaneously gave the hand signal to attack. The force was small and highly mobile. The company bugler sounded the old cavalry call, signaling the order to gallop forward into harm's way with deadly intent. The mechanized force—heedless of the illusory line of the border— roared forward with all lights blazing and sirens blaring. Rocketeers fired dozens of flairs, which lit up the sky like noonday. By the time they crossed the border, the armed vehicles were going nearly 70 miles per hour. The commandos on foot sprinted in a mad murderous dash directly at the oncoming enemy. It was easy to differentiate: the Iranian soldiers were all in olive-drab and all young. The Bakhtiari men were in vivid blue desert gowns with their faces veiled, and they were waving long razor-sharp swords. The women and children in the center of it all were prostrate and below the fray.

At first, a ripple of surprise started in the closest ranks of the Iranian officers and soldiers. Then, every soldier became aware deep into his bone marrow that demon-warriors were upon them. As the accurate firepower of the allies began decimating the Iranians, their colonel, Mohammad Ali Fontana, shouted orders to retreat. The retreat became hurried, then chaotic, then pan-icky. The fire coming from the west was deadly and decisive. The Bakhtiaris and the fugitive men turned on the fleeing Iranian soldiers and picked them off like shotguns firing into a flock of pigeons.

Saad, Aaron, and all the others were as dumbfounded as the Iranians; but the killers from the other side were obviously their people, *their killers*. And a joyous shouting could be heard over and above the crackling machine gun-fire, interspersed with heavy pounding of mortars, grenades, shoulder-fired rockets, and small cannons. The Iranians ceased fire and ran pell-mell away, heedless of the orders of their colonel, the majors, the captains, and even the first sergeants. Living was all that mattered now, and the only chance to live was to be far away to the east.

Medics, doctors, and nurses rushed in behind the fighters and began an orderly triage and battlefield emergency treatment of the wounded. All of the "wounded and dead" who fit the definition that drove the rescue force were among the Bakhtiaris and the fugitives—wounded Iranians were ignored, and dead Iranians did not factor into the count. Four brave Bakhtiari warriors were dead, and two of the fugitives. None of the protected women, children, and wounded in the center of the maelstrom were hit. Afsoon was enlivened by the process and found strength to rise and to begin to help the newly wounded.

Daylight poured in, and Col. Spikeburg ordered his men to load all of the wounded onto ambulance trucks and to move back to Iraq on the double. The allied fighters ran behind them, followed by the armored vehicles. There was no resistance from the vaunted Iranian army. In great haste, the wounded were gurneyed aboard the C-130 that had landed during the attack by the allies.

The angels who carried Afsoon on a stretcher had no idea who she was. Heavily armed vehicles entered the belly of the great plane, then light vehicles, then men. The plane took off for the Forward Operating Base Warrior, and Ramadi U.S. Military Bases in Iraqi Kurdestan. A second C-130 landed, and the remaining people who wanted to do so walked aboard and took seats along the walls of the cavernous belly of the plane. Gideon and Miriam were dirty, sweaty, and bloody—other people's blood—but they paid their appearance and bodily odor no heed as they locked in what appeared likely to be a permanent conjoined twin attachment. Elizabeth and Zachariah helped bear the litter holding the body of Elias and set it gently down to rest. Elizabeth—who never cried—wept unashamedly. Zachariah slumped.

The remaining able-bodied Bakhtiaris—which fortunately was the vast majority of the clan—refused exfiltration. Instead, they gathered up the herd of fine Caspian ponies that had been so lovingly nurtured by the Nichols-Dayan ranch, formed up into their ages-old traditional rankings, and rode off to the north. Their wounded traveled with the fugitives like Afsoon and the medics. Their dead were placed on pack horses for burial services where the people could share their mourning rituals in privacy and peace.

Gideon put it succinctly to Miriam: "The Iran Nuclear Interdiction Project is over—successful and over."

She added, "And Project *Jahannam Adur* [Hell's Fire] is no more."

That was a truism that would hold forever.

CHAPTER THIRTY-ONE

Out of the Belly of the Beast
And in from the Cold

U.S. Military Headquarters Air Base Hospital, Ar Ramadi—the capital of Al Anbar Governorate—Iraq, January 29, 2016, 1852

Daniel and Brenda Daastrup arrived two hours after Afsoon was placed in a comfortable hospital bed on clean sheets—the first she had enjoyed in nearly two weeks. She was given a heavy dose of modern antibiotics, two liters of D_5NS intravenously, and a large bowl of chicken noodle soup and wheat toast. She was alert and smiling when the Daastrups entered her room. The occasion was joyous, and serious questions were reserved for later. Brenda and Afsoon held hands throughout their conversation.

"Where is Uncle Neal?" Afsoon asked once the preliminary family catch-up was complete.

"He wanted to be here more than anything, you know that. But, he is sick, Afsoon, dear."

"What's wrong?"

"You know he had a heart attack a few years back and in the past few months developed something called ITP—Idiopathic Thrombocytopenic Purpura—which destroys blood platelets; so, he can't clot his blood well. He is on steroids, which the doctors hope will bring his count back up. If that doesn't work, he'll have to have his spleen taken out. The spleen destroys old red blood cells and other cells like platelets. Maybe if it is removed, he will be able to make more than he loses. It is up in the air right now."

"What causes it?"

"No idea. The doctors don't have anything that tells them why he got this."

"Is he going to live?"

"Not sure."

Brenda was uncertain whether or not all of this unvarnished truth-telling was wise, but Afsoon seemed to be able to take it.

"Could you guys help me to have a little walk?"

"Sure, sweetie," Daniel said and stepped to her bed to get her up.

She was initially rather awkward because her left arm was fixed across her chest with a bulky bandage, and she had a minor limp from her thigh wound.

"How are Daniel, Abigail, Mary, Ruth, Evan, and Michael?" Afsoon remembered to ask.

"Doing great!" both Daniel and Brenda said at the same time.

They showed her the family album, which showed them to be all grown-up. The album included several pictures of Afsoon taken over the years that Neal should not have given them but could not resist. She was touched as she always was when she saw herself included in the nuclear family of the Daastrups.

"Do you know where my friend, my sort of Iranian brother is? I know he made it out."

"Sorry," Brenda shrugged.

"Could you do me a favor and try to find out?"

"We'll do our best," Daniel said with conviction.

§§§§§

Rear Adm. Martin Torgelson flew in to the airbase and was taken immediately to the headquarters building of Camp Blue Diamond, where he met Col. Spikeburg, Captain Orfanakis, SAS Col. Heckfield-Brown, Carter Miller-Partridge, Aaron Schmuel, Hamid, and G.R. IV in the basement morgue. Together, they paid their respects to their fallen comrades—Elias Nichols-Dayan; Ghurkas Thapa Dhanbahadur and Ghhetri Krishnabahadur; Gideon Meier; Micah Cohen; and four Bakhtiari warriors whose names were not yet known to them. Camp Blue Diamond graves registration NCOs took down the necessary information and arranged for all of the men to be sent to proper resting places, including Arlington, Luckenbach, Texas, Tel Aviv, and the Ghurka cemetery in San Tin Barracks, Hong Kong.

Adm. Torgelson requested that the commanding officer of Camp Blue Diamond arrange for transportation back to civilization of all the combatants. He gave each of them a stern warning about maintaining full secrecy about everything that had happened in Iran and to take the secrets to their graves. When those arrangements were completed, Adm. Torgelson brought up the subject of putting Afsoon up for the Medal. His casual suggestion was greeted with unreserved enthusiasm.

§§§§§

Tehran Times
Iran's Leading International Daily
January 17, 2016

ANTI-ISLAMIC RIOTERS CREATE ALARM

The Supreme Leader, President Okhavat, their wives, and several ranking officials of the government were caught in a spontaneous violent riot near Esfahan this morning. Army troops and the Supreme Leader's personal guard units responded. At the time of this exclusive report, there is no report of where Agha Rahimi and the president have been taken for their safety. The army general staff assures our reporter that the riot is limited to the Esfahan area and is rapidly coming under control. Army and security officials assure the *Times* that rubber bullets and other noninjurious measures have been used, and there have been no civilian casualties. No army or security personnel have been injured.

••••••

January 19, 2016

COMMUNIST AND GOVERNMENT OPPOSITION FORCES FOMENT NATIONWIDE UNREST

Anti-Islamic agitators, acting under the coordination of Mohammed Sarqoui, the leader of the treasonous opposition to our beloved Supreme Leader and our elected president have stirred up riots throughout the major and even many smaller cities around Iran. Fires, destruction of property, bombings, murders, rapes, and thievery were rampant until the army was forced to declare martial law and to cancel habeas corpus temporarily.

Security personnel and several army divisions have been called up to quell the unrest. Our *Times* reporters have seen considerable devastation caused by the rioters and much sadness among the citizens. The *Times* can also report with pride that innocent civilians who obey curfew laws are safe and have not been harmed in any way by security measures. There have been casualties among the heavily armed traitors to the revolution and scores have been arrested as our valiant soldiers and law enforcement officers bring the situation back to normal.

●●●●●●

January 21, 2016

EARTHQUAKES IN ESFAHAN and BUSHEHR PROVINCES. UNREST CONTINUES

Fragmentary reports have come in to the *Times,* which indicate that a series of very powerful earthquakes have occurred in Esfahan and Bushehr provinces, and there are reports of scattered areas of serious damage and loss of life. Unconfirmed reports indicate that a massive quake has severely damaged the peaceful nuclear production plant at Bushehr and that an explosion and fire at Katanz has possibly leveled the main structures. There is no report of foul play on the part of the traitorous rioters in the area.

We are not able to confirm the location of our dear leader, Agha Rahimi, or our beloved President Okhavat at this time. There have been several reports indicating that they are in protected security areas, that they may have been injured and are hospitalized, and that they may have been killed by the demons who have caused such destruction throughout the country. None of these reports has been verified.

In other news, our beloved and sacred Qom has been severely damaged by rioters. A special energy plant in the holy city has been burned to the ground. Army units continue to fight insurgents there. When asked if we were in a civil war, Acting Vice-President Tajbakhsh Mavasseghi, serving temporarily as the leader of our nation, was adamant. "No!" he said with great emphasis.

Industry, governmental, medical care, and military leaders assure us that the problem with our internet and telephone system is well on its way to being solved. Certain government officials, who communicated with the *Times* with a guarantee of anonymity, have reported that dissident groups are responsible and that they have been working with the government of the Great Satan to assist the imposition of their terrible sanctions. When asked what motive the opposition had, Vice President Mavasseghi replied, "They hope to cripple the Iranian economy so that their political agenda can go forward, and they can take power. Allah is with our Supreme Leader, and he has let us know that such a thing will never happen."

●●●●●●

January 29, 2016

DETAILS OF THE DESTRUCTIVE EARTHQUAKE IN BUSHEHR AND KATANZ
Reports of Serious Loss of Life—High Officials
and Common Citizen Workers

Final reports from the beleaguered provinces of Bushehr and Katanz indicate that earthquake damage and fires have killed almost 2,200 plant workers and another 1,200 citizens of Katanz and Bushehr cities. Fortunately, Allah, be praised, no nuclear explosion or nuclear emissions have taken place, according to AEOI officials who have done a thorough investigation of the scene. Army officials have cordoned the area off for the sake of safety and security.

Reports to the *Times* indicate that among the dead and missing are: Hormoz Mohammad-Bagher, president of Bank Sepah; Ayatollah Ali Hossein Golzar, head of the AEOI; Vice President Reza Mohammad Hessami; Behrouz Omidi, director of the Ministry of Intelligence and National Security [MISIRI]; Mullah Ali Salar Omidyar, director of the Ministry of Intelligence and Security [MOIS]; Dr. Afsoon Mouradipour, who was the director of peaceful nuclear energy production for Iran; eight full professors of science, physics, and nuclear energy; four presidents of universities; and the ministers of Justice, Industries and Business, Industries and Mines, and Labor and Social Affairs. The nation has suffered a great loss, and our flags will fly at half-staff for the rest of this week.

●●●●●●

February 12, 2016

Los Angeles Times

CIVIL WAR IN IRAN?
American-born Professor among Those Killed

In recent days, the *Times* has reported sketchy and fragmentary information about serious unrest, earthquakes, explosions, and fires in Iran. Among the facilities destroyed, it is reported that the infamous Evin Prison in Tehran was burned to the ground by angry rioters. Coincidentally, the nation's Islamic government shut down the internet, telephone system, and social media sites in an apparent crackdown on dissidents. Much of the information coming from the Islamic Republic is anecdotal and cannot be fully verified. The best the *Times* can determine is that communications resources have been severely crippled, probably intentionally; there have been serious earthquakes with massive damage in the northern and western provinces of Iran and widespread rioting throughout the country. There may be a frank civil war in progress, but it is too early to be definitive in that description. The Supreme Leader, Grand Ayatollah Rahimi, and President Okhavat have not been seen in public for over a month, and some speculate that they are in a secure location for their safety until the period of unrest can be brought under control by law enforcement and military officials.

Conservative estimates are that at least 22,000 employees of the major nuclear energy plants in Bushehr, Katanz, Zirconium Production Plant—known as ZPP—Lashkar Abad, Esfahan, Kalaye Electric Company, several laser enrichment facilities in the area, the yellow-cake processing plant in Ardekan Nuclear Fuel Unit near Yazd, Iran, and the principle uranium mines in Saghand have been killed or critically injured. The reputed secret nuclear facility in the Iranian holy city of Qom was burned to the ground by rioters—that much has been confirmed by *Times* staffers. Some reports coming from the *Associated Press* indicate that destruction has been so severe in those plants that Iran's peaceful nuclear energy program has been set back a century, if not forever.

For the past two decades, the West has accused Iran of working to produce nuclear weaponry. The acting leader of Iran, Vice President Tajbakhsh Mavasseghi, denies that claim categorically. He insists that his country has suffered an incalculable loss in its investment in peaceful nuclear energy, but will resume R&D efforts once the results of the natural disaster have been repaired. He and a number of European opponents of American efforts to impede Iran's peaceful nuclear efforts have suggested that the United States may be behind the current problems Iran is facing—including the damage to the nuclear industry. President Sandstone has issued an emphatic denial. "We have not had any part in the calamities apparently facing the nation of Iran. In fact, we have offered any assistance the Iranians may require to alleviate this huge human disaster. They have refused our offer."

Closer to home, the *Times* has received a confirmation that a prominent Beverly Hills nuclear scientist, Dr. Afsoon Mouradipour—who received her postgraduate degrees from U.C. Berkeley—was among the casualties in the Katanz fire. She was an expatriate American citizen, who left her Orthodox Jewish religion and converted to Islam prior to accepting a crucial position in the peaceful Iranian nuclear production industry. She leaves behind her parents, Dr. Daniel and Esther Mouradipour—who are prominent in the Tehrangeles Persian community—and her brothers and sisters, Abraham, Isaac, Ruth, Eli, Kelsey, Rivka, Gilda, and Aaragail. Dr. Afsoon was much admired in the Tehrangeles community and at U.C. Berkeley, where she was prominent in university activities.

CHAPTER THIRTY-TWO

The Calm after the Storm

And a youth said, speak to us of friendship. And he answered, saying: your friend is your needs answered. He is your field which you sow with love and reap with thanksgiving. And he is your board and your fireside. For you come to him with your hunger, and you seek him for peace.

-Khalil Gibran, *The Prophet*, p. 58, 1973

The White House, Oval Office, 1600 Pennsylvania Ave NW, Washington, DC, January 29, 2019, 0800

Afsoon was busy and happy with herself and her life during the three years she had been back to live in the United States in relative obscurity. She still lived something of a fiction but a comfortable one. She was Afsoon Daastrup again, active duty army colonel, holder of two masters degrees and two Ph.D.s. She taught and did research in nuclear physics, nuclear engineering, and computer science at the Armed Forces University. Her résumé included items indicating that she had held her current position for fifteen years and had advanced through the academic ranks from instructor in 2005 after obtaining her Ph.D. from U.C. Berkeley until 2018 when she became a full tenured university professor. Her résumé included some truth:

she received a BA degree in physics with a minor in nuclear physics from Georgetown University in 1999 and a master's in nuclear engineering in 2002. Her masters in computer science from U.C. Berkeley—awarded in 2004—would have appeared murky to someone who ran a forensics analysis on the strict facts. She received her Ph.D. in nuclear engineering from U.C. Berkeley as well and under similar circumstances. Everyone said she deserved the masters and the Ph.D. based on her work; but in actual fact, it was Afsoon Mouradipour's Ph.D. that Afsoon Daastrup was trading on. Once again, serious officials of the intelligence community influenced Berkeley to place the award of the Ph.D. in their records. Similarly—on paper—she received a Ph.D. in computer science from *Stockholms Universitet* the year after she started her teaching career. Once again, that was the result of the influence of intelligence officers—this time the Swedish kind.

She was given the Morris Janowitz Career Achievement Award by the Inter-University Seminar on Armed Forces and Society in 2016 for "achievement as a small number of senior scholars whose careers most demonstrate excellence in the study of armed forces and society and important service to the discipline." She received that recognition upon the recommendation of the DDDIA and the DIA, as well as from the secretary of defense. In fact, she had not been in the country during that period. The students in the Armed Forces University voted her the best science teacher in the university in 2017 and the best teacher in the university in 2018; she did not need a spy working for her in the background for that achievement.

Afsoon lived at home with Brenda and Daniel. Her adopted siblings were all off to school and work. The family's annual pictures included her among them every year from 2016 to 2019. Nassir Jamshidi was now a graduate student at Georgetown University and doing well, although he was not a genius—a fact he was quick to admit. He was living and matriculating under an assumed name, Saman—which he shortened to Sam—De Silva, and the fiction that his family had emigrated from Sri Lanka two generations ago. He was safe in his new identity because the beneficent intelligence community granted him placement in the FBI's witness protection program and gave him $200,000 to get him going in America. He and Afsoon were discreet, but they got together as often as they could. He married an American girl of Western European extraction in 2018, and they were expecting a baby.

§§§§§

Along with the peace, tranquility, familial association, and academic and military success, Afsoon had some negative times. In the spring of 2017, her uncle Neal died of his ITP. It was a painful and lingering death; and—for a time—Afsoon felt bereft, as if she had lost her father. Of all the members of the Iran Nuclear Interdiction Project, she had kept up a frequent and cordial relationship with him and his wife, Ruth, and the Rothsbergers. She and Miriam were real friends, and each of them exulted in the other's accomplishments. She and Gideon were the only ones with whom she felt at all comfortable in discussing their experiences. It seemed too dangerous to talk about it to anyone else, except her cover parents, the Mouradipours, in a watered-down version.

G.R. III died suddenly in the summer of 2018 from an apparent heart attack. As a result, Gideon and Miriam had to relocate to Paris and took the family to live in Château Rothsberger. The distance and Gideon's responsibilities—as well as Miriam's stardom in French opera—led to a lessening of contact and to the ability to have the couple as confidants.

Secrets remained firmly entrenched as an integral part of Afsoon's life. In 2019, she received a new one—the pinnacle of her life and one of her best days—dimmed only because she could not talk about it to anyone, except her very small inner circle for the next thirty years.

§§§§§

A very select group of people gathered in the Oval Office for what might have been shown on national television if circumstances were different. Every person had had to be vetted for top secret clearance, and few of them had had much experience with government. Afsoon, her parents, her cover parents, Elizabeth and Zachariah Nichols-Dayan, Gideon and Miriam Rothsberger, Nassir Jamshidi, Carter Miller-Partridge, Antal Disraeli, Elsie Silberberg, Zwi Rosenstein, Annette Redstone, Avery Holmes, Victor Raylan, Ali Nylander, Rebecca Hershowitz, Chava Dayan-Hershowitz Rothsberger, Rear Adm. Martin Torgelson, and Sec. Def. Jason Augmar stood quietly in the president's office, waiting for the president to return from his press announcement on the east lawn.

Afsoon was in full dress uniform with shoes that Nassir had polished for two days. This was the first time she had been in a dress army uniform, and, in fact, one of very few times in her twenty-plus-year career in the army— her record being as public as any other army officer, but a good deal less genuine—she had worn a uniform of the United States armed forces. The observers were quiet and perfectly respectful as President Sandstone entered the room. Having practiced for the occasion, Afsoon stood at rigid attention and saluted her commander -in -chief. He smiled at her and shook her hand.

"Everyone, please sit," he said. "Be at ease. This a great occasion."

Afsoon relaxed a fraction.

"Col. Daastrup, please stand with me."

Afsoon presented herself to the president.

"It is my privilege and honor to present you with medals you have earned; but, owing to the nature of your service, you were unable to receive. It is past time that you did."

He handed her a maroon box decorated with gold inlays that held a Purple Heart, Good Conduct Medal, National Defense Medal and ribbon, National Defense Service Medal, Global War on Terrorism Service Medal, Armed Forces Service Medal, Overseas Service Ribbon, the Special Iran Antinuclear Service Medal—awarded to only seven individuals—and, set apart, the Distinguished Service Medal.

"Thank you, Mr. President. I feel humble in accepting these important awards."

"No, Col. Daastrup, it is I—speaking for a grateful nation—who thank you. And there is more."

He gave her a broad smile. "Here is a record of your back pay including hazard additions. It was too complicated to factor in twenty years of pay grade changes; so, the Department of Defense elected to make your pay retroactive to the day you entered Iran, and reckoned your pay at your present grade throughout your career abroad. You will find on the bottom line a very substantial sum, which should help you as you approach the time of retirement from the army."

Afsoon bowed her head a little and said, "Thank you very much, Sir."

"And now, Col. Daastrup, ladies and gentlemen, fellow Americans, it is with the greatest of pleasure but with some sadness that I make the award presentation for which you have all gathered here today. As some of you may know, Col. Daastrup is only the second woman in the history of the country to receive the Medal. The other one was Dr. Mary Edwards Walker, the first woman surgeon in the union army for her long service during the Civil War. Among her acts of heroism—and it is not lost on me that there is a decided similarity to Col. Daastrup—she stayed behind after the battle of Chattanooga to tend the wounded and became a prisoner of war of the Confederacy."

He handed Afsoon a parchment. Then he read in its entirety the citation: "A. Daastrup, Colonel, United States Army, in my capacity as president of the United States and commander in chief of the Armed Forces and acting for the Congress, I award you the Congressional Medal of Honor. The Medal is the highest honor that can be bestowed on a member of the Armed Forces. For conspicuous gallantry and intrepidity at the risk of her life above and beyond the call of duty while serving...."

The parchment that Afsoon was holding and the copy from which the president was reading contained the entirety of the description of her heroism. The copy that she would be able to keep was entirely redacted after the words, "while serving."

When he finished reading the citation, the president placed the handsome medal and its blue ribbon around Afsoon's neck.

"With the appreciation of a grateful nation, Col. Daastrup."

She gave him a smart salute.

"I mentioned earlier that there is a note of sadness in presenting this award. I wish that every American could know what you did and why; but our national security requires that you wait, and that this award and medal remain a secret for thirty long years. You will take a nearly completely redacted copy of the citation if you wish; but even that cannot be made public. The original from which we read today will be kept in a Department of Defense archive until that period has elapsed. I hope that all of us can remain alive long enough to witness that great day. Now, Colonel, would you like to say a few words for posterity?"

"A few, Mr. President. Like every other Medal recipient, I feel more than humbled; I feel undeserving. I am aware of the magnificent feats of bravery and valor of my predecessors; and I cannot help but feel that we should be honoring them instead of me today. The term 'hero' is bandied about rather loosely these days. I am of the opinion that heroes are those who never came home or came back to us blind, crippled, and crazy. Comrades of mine paid the ultimate price in this silent war with Iran just as heroes of more publicized wars of the past. Perhaps it is fitting that I represent them—the ones who cannot speak for themselves and will remain lost to history. In that vein, I thank the United States for its unfailing and unflinching support of me and of my fellow fighters in the Iran Nuclear Interdiction Project."

She turned to the president and assembled well-wishers and gave them one last salute.

THE TWELVERS

You've got to be taught to hate and fear,
You've got to be taught from year to year,
It's got to be drummed in your dear little ear,
You've got to be carefully taught.

You've got to be taught to be afraid
Of people whose eyes are oddly made,
And people whose skin is a diff'rent shade,
You've got to be carefully taught.

You've got to be taught before it's too late,
Before you are six or seven or eight,
To hate all the people your relatives hate,
You've got to be carefully taught!

-*You've Got To Be Carefully Taught*,
   Lyrics from the musical *South Pacific*,
   Rodgers and Hammerstein, 1949-

I n the previous discussion about Islam—see the set-off section following the end of Book Two—the main focus was on the Sunni, which constitute the vast majority of the world's Muslim population—90 percent. The next largest group—and a distant second—is the Shi'i. Although the term "Twelvers" is often used synonymously with the term "Shi'i," that is not strictly correct. A small minority of Shi'i believers are not Twelvers—a minority so small, in fact, that this discussion will not include them. Before discussing the beliefs and consequences of those beliefs held by the Twelvers, it is necessary to know that there is a violent impasse between the Sunni and the Shi'i. It is no exaggeration to state that wherever there are Muslim populations, there is violence and strife whether it stems from age-old antagonisms between the believers in the Sunni and Shi'i traditions, a perception by Sunnis that the Iranian revolution was a threat to Sunni dominance, a reaction by one branch or the other of Islam to persecution by the opposite branch, to the so-called forces of hegemony and Zionism intent upon weakening Arabs, or to secular Muslims trying to stem the tide of virulently intolerant activists from the other persuasions or vice versa.

The reasons leading to the differences between the Twelvers and the Sunni will occupy a majority of this presentation—but for the moment—consider a very brief set of examples of the results of those reasons and differences. Wherever and whenever Sunnis and Shi'ites intersect, there is strife, often bloody, homicidal, and suicidal. Both factions consider beliefs that are not exactly the same as their own to be those of *kaffirs*, polytheists, and non-Muslims, even if they are Muslims of the same superficially general type. There is a contest to find converts or to destroy the *kaffirs* they encounter; and—as a result—there is a pattern of antipathy and violence that has only increased in recent years with the jingoistic extremes of Khomeini Twelvers versus Wahhabi Sunnis.

As far back as the tenth Abassid caliph, al-Mutawakkil [A.D. 822-861], the tomb of the Shi'ites revered saint, the third Imam, Hussein ibn Ali in Karbala, was demolished on the orders of the reigning caliph, followed by group beheadings of Shi'is, and of other Shi'is being buried alive or being confined alive within the walls of government buildings under construction.

On the obverse side of the coin, Shah Ismail Safavi—Ismail I [1487–1524]—initiated a totalitarian religious policy to recognize Shi'ism as the official religion of the Safavid Empire; and the fact that modern Iran remains an officially Shi'i—Twelver—state is a direct result of Ismail's actions. However, most of Ismail's subjects were Sunni, which led him to enforce official Shi'ism with violence, putting to death any who opposed him. Under this pressure by the minority Shi'ite ruler, Safavid subjects either converted or pretended to convert; thus, ushering in the dominance of Shi'ism in Iran that persists to this day.

Shi'i throughout South Asia suffered virulent persecution by many Sunni rulers and Mongol emperors, which resulted in the killings of Shi'i scholars and simple common Shi'is. Shi'is in Kashmir endured an atrocious period of their history. Plunder, loot, and massacres—which came to be known as *Taarajs*—largely devastated the community. There were ten such *Taarajs*—also known as *Taraj-e-Shia*—between the fourteenth to nineteenth centuries, from 1548 to 1872, during which Shi'i homes were plundered, people slaughtered, libraries burnt, and their sacred sites systematically desecrated. Sunni-Shi'i clashes also occurred sporadically during the twentieth century in South Asia, especially between 1904 and 1908 in the United Provinces (Uttar Pradesh) area of northern India. These clashes resulted from the public cursing of the first three caliphs by Shi'is and the praising of them by Sunnis. To put a stop to the violence, public demonstrations were banned in 1909 on the three most sensitive days for the Twelvers: Ashura, Chehlum, and Ali's death on 21 Ramadan. The violence resurfaced in 1935-1936 and again in 1939 when many thousands of Sunni and Shi'is defied the ban on public demonstrations and took to the streets.

The tension and violence between Twelvers and Sunni appears to be interminable and unchangeable given the implacable intolerance of both sides. Sectarian violence persists to the present day from Pakistan to Yemen, and is a major element of friction, discord, and instability throughout the Middle-East. Tensions between the two communities intensify during power struggles, such as the recent Bahraini uprising, the Iraq War, and most recently, the Syrian civil war of 2010-plus.

Following the 1979 Iranian Revolution, Shi'i in the Al-Ahsa Governorate—which makes up much of the Eastern Province of Saudi Arabia—ignored the predominately Sunni governmental ban on mourning ceremonies commemorating Yawm Al-Ashura. When police broke them up, three days of rampage ensued, with cars being burned, banks being attacked, and shops being looted. At least seventeen Shi'i were killed. In February 1980, disturbances were less "spontaneous" and even bloodier.

Following the initial turmoil emanating from the advent of the Iranian Islamic revolution, Sunni-Twelver strife increased exponentially, especially in Iraq and Pakistan. Where Iranian revolutionaries saw Islamic revolutionary stirrings, Sunnis saw mostly Shi'i rabble-rousers seeking to overturn the centuries-old order with Sunnis on top and the Shi'ites on the bottom. There is no question that there was a remarkable change in the Twelvers with the revolution and that it led to a very violent Sunni reaction—beginning in Pakistan and spreading to the rest of the Muslim world—culminating in the fratricidal Iran-Iraq War of 1980-1988, at least in the Sunni perception.

Three changes occurred to upset the balance of power: the Islamic revolution in Iran, its violent aftermath, and the American military intervention in Iraq in 2003. The impact on the Middle-East and upon Sunni-Shi'i relations was a sea change. The origins of the Iran-Iraq conflict came from the usual sources. The Shi'i suffered persecution under postcolonial Iraqi governments from 1932, finally erupting into full-scale rebellions in 1935 and 1936. Shias were severely persecuted during the Ba'ath Party rule, especially under Saddam Hussein. Under the tyrannical Saddam regime, public Shi'i festivals such as Ashura were banned outright. Every Shi'i clerical family of any consequence in Iraq suffered torture and murder. Saddam's regime executed forty-eight major Shi'i clerics, and tens of thousands of Iranians and Arabs of Iranian origin were expelled in 1979 and 1980, and a further 75,000 in 1989.

The Shi'is of Iraq openly revolted against Saddam following the Gulf War in 1991, when they were encouraged by Saddam's defeat in Kuwait and the simultaneous Kurdish uprising in the north. Saddam, however, was weakened but not beaten. Shi'i opposition to the government was brutally suppressed, resulting in an estimated 50,000 to 100,000 casualties and successive savage repressions by Saddam's armed forces. The Gulf War exacted a dreadful toll on Iraqis. Even then, deaths from American and allied military collateral damage paled in comparison to the cycle of Sunni-Shi'i revenge killing. There was an interesting difference in the methods used by the different factions: Sunni used car bombs, while the Twelvers employed death squads.

Suicide bombers have blown themselves up; Sunni suicide bombers have targeted thousands of civilians, but also Shi'i mosques, shrines, wedding and funeral processions, markets, hospitals, offices, and streets. A host of Sunni insurgent organizations sprang up. Elsewhere, from 1987–2007, almost 4,000 Muslim people were estimated to have died in sectarian fighting in Pakistan. A considerable driving force for the seemingly endless sectarian strive is Al-Qaeda, which works with local Sunni groups dedicated to killing "Shi'i apostates" and "foreign powers trying to sow discord among the peace-loving Muslims of Pakistan." Al-Qaeda and other Wahhabi groups to this day advocate persecution of the Shia as heretics. Such groups claim responsibility for violent attacks and suicide bombings at Shi'i gatherings at mosques and shrines and at Shi'i funerals.

In Afghanistan—in 1998 alone,—more than 8,000 noncombatants were killed when the Taliban attacked the cities of Mazar-i-Sharif and Bamiyan, where many Hazaras [poor Shi'ites] live. The Taliban commander and governor banned prayer at Shi'i mosques. The commander stated "The Hazaras are not Muslims, and now we have to kill Hazaras. You either accept to be Muslims or leave Afghanistan." As recently as mid-2013, the fratricidal Syrian civil war became overtly sectarian between Alawites—a mystical branch of the Twelver school of Shia Islam—and Sunnis. With the involvement of the Twelver radical group, Hezbollah, the fighting in Syria reignited tensions between Sunnis and Shi'ites, spilling over into Lebanon and Iraq.

Such wanton destructive behavior between religious factions seems inexplicable to most Westerners who subscribe to a different religious philosophy and practice. After all, both main factions of Islam are "People of the Qibla"—those who turn toward Mecca. The Twelvers, however—early on—set themselves apart from the Sunnis whom they considered to be heretics, even *kaffirs*/infidels.

Christian Memories tend to be short; how many young Western people—even educated people—can articulate the causes and consequences of the Christian crusades, the wars between Protestants and Catholics, the gross intolerance by the dominant Protestant religion in America towards Jews, Catholics, and Mormons, the Inquisition, the homicidal reign of John Calvin in Geneva, and the systematic slaughter of the indigenous Americans by the Catholic Church in South America. It is history that is well out of mind.

You would think that the antecedents of conflict among the adherents of Islam—going back 1,333 years to the Battle of Karbala and the martyrdom of Al-Hussein ibn Ali ibn Abi Talib (Ali's son) in A.D. 680 (some scholars say 661)—would have long since passed into the mists of time and memory.

Not so, the events of that era are so vivid to the Sunni and the Twelvers that they could have happened last week. Here is a brief synopsis of the history of why such hatred persists.

Al-Hussein ibn Ali ibn Abi Talib was the son of Ali ibn Abi Talib, the first Shi'i imam, and Fatimah Zahra, daughter of the Prophet Muhammad, which made him an important figure in Islam since he was a member of the *Ahl al-Bayt*—the household of Muhammad—and *Ahl al-Kisa*, as well as being the third Shi'i imam. After the death of the Prophet and the murder of the second caliph, Umar, the six remaining companions of the Prophet, including Ali, debated which of them should be the next caliph. The choice narrowed to two: Ali, a member of the Household of Muhammad, and Uthman, a man from a corrupt family. Despite those facts so obvious to Ali's followers and family, Uthman was chosen. The followers of Ali developed what would become a millennial antipathy towards the Sunni, who colluded in a conspiracy and accepted the concept of election of the caliph rather than the obvious choice of the divine right leader coming from the Prophet's direct family. When Uthman was murdered in his palace during an army rebellion in 655, Ali was persuaded by the insurgents and the remaining two companions of the Prophet to accept the caliphate, which he did. However—even by that time—the divisions were too deep, and Islam remained seriously divided thereafter.

Hussein or Ali, as preferred by different factions, is regarded highly by both the Shia and the Sunni as a martyr, because he refused to pledge allegiance to Yazid I—the Umayyad caliph. He refused to pledge allegiance to what he considered the unjust and oppressive rule of the Umayyads. As a consequence, he left Medina—his hometown—from which he travelled to Mecca; and then after the people of Kufa sent letters to him—pledging him allegiance,—he set off for Kufa. The people of Kufa then broke their pledge; and, on the way, his caravan was intercepted; he was killed and beheaded in the Battle of Karbala in 680 by Shimr Ibn Thil-Jawshan.

The seminal event in Shi'i history is the martyrdom of Hussein, who came to symbolize resistance to tyranny. The annual memorial for him, his family, his children, and his *As'haab* [companions] is called *Ashura* [the tenth day of Muharram] and is a day of mourning for Shi'i Muslims. *Ashura* is celebrated by mass marching and self-flagellation severe enough to spill considerable amounts of blood and is associated with violence almost every year and in every place the marching takes place. Anger at Hussein's death became a rallying cry during that historic era that helped undermine and ultimately to overthrow the Umayyad Caliphate.

The dominant characteristic of the followers of the Shi'i or Twelver sects—which is as true today as it was over a thousand years ago—is a total unwillingness to compromise and a total willingness to fight against overwhelming odds. It has persisted as such until the present day—a fact that Sunnis consider anchoritic and un-Islamic. Sunnis have fought against *Ashura* for over a millennium, because it suggests evildoing by their forebears, represents a rallying point for opponents of the Sunnis, and highlights the divisions in Islam.

Muawiyah I, the first Umayyad caliph, and his aides made use of every possible means to put aside past disputes and remove the household of Muhammad and the followers of Ali and his sons and thus obliterate the name of Ali and his family. Muawiyah ordered public curses of Ali and his major supporters, including Hasan and Hussein, and established a pattern of denigration of the Shi'i—the followers of Ali—that persists until now.

The people of Kufa—near Karbala, the site of the defining battle—believed that leadership of the Muslim community belonged to the descendants of Muhammad. That established a minority Islamic group that matured into the Shi'i of Iran. They still contend that the guidelines set by Ali, who had strongly upheld the sole right of the family of Muhammad—through the descendants of the Prophet Muhammad's daughter Fatima—to divinely decreed leadership of the Muslim community. Twelvers believe that the descendants of Muhammad through his daughter and his son-in-law and cousin, Ali, are the best source of knowledge about the *Qur'an* and Islam, the most trusted carriers and protectors of Muhammad's *Sunnah* (traditions), and the most worthy of emulation. The Shi'i are the Puritans of Islam. All others are heretics. Intermittently, the Shi'i have launched holy wars to defend their principle.

Twelvers recognize the succession of Ali, Muhammad's cousin, son-in-law, and the first man to accept Islam (second only to Muhammad's wife Khadijah), the male head of the people of the Prophet's household, and the father of Muhammad's only bloodline, as opposed to that of the caliphate recognized by Sunni Muslims. Twelvers also believe that Ali was appointed successor by Muhammad's direct order on many occasions, and that he was therefore the rightful leader of the Muslim faith. The bloodline of Ali—the *Alawiya*—are the rightful successors of the Prophet and of his appointed one, Ali. The Sunnis stoutly deny that right and the assertions of the Shi'i that they are the *ordained* protectors of the traditions.

The impact of the tragedy of Karbala on the religious conscience of Muslims has always been deep and goes beyond its consecration of the passion and penitence motives in Shi'ism. It caused the whippings of *Ashura* for the Shi'i Muslims who have tried to repent and to expiate the sins of their forefathers for having failed to protect and to save Hussein. It is the foremost tradition separating the Sunnis and the Shi'i. Hussein's grave became the most visited place of Ziyarat for Shias. The Imam Hussein Shrine was later built over his grave. In 850, Abbasid Caliph al-Mutawakkil destroyed his shrine in order to stop Shi'i pilgrimages, and the Shi'i have never forgiven the Sunnis for that outrage. Nonetheless, pilgrimages continued to what is now a holy site of pilgrimage for Shi'i Muslims. The commemoration of Hussein ibn Ali—accepted as the third imam of Shi'i Islam, A.D. 669–680—has become a national holiday in Iran.

The Twelver Shi'i brand of Islam became the state religion of the Safavid dynasty in Persia in the sixteenth century—1502—with the Twelvers receiving significant support, protection, and funding from the Persian state; and major theological centers were built up and preserved as holy places. Adherents of Shi'ism are commonly referred to as Twelvers, derived from their belief in twelve divinely ordained leaders, known as the Twelve Imams. They believe that the holy messianic—and all-powerful—Mahdi will be the returned Twelfth Imam who disappeared and is believed by Twelvers to be in *ghayba* [occultation]. This is an enduring belief that the messianic figure, or Mahdi—who, in Shi'i thought, is an infallible male descendant of the founder of Islam, Muhammad—was born, has never died—but disappeared—and will one day return and fill the world with justice and peace.

Hujjat ibn al-Hasan al-Mahdi is believed by Twelver Shi'i Muslims to be the Mahdi—an ultimate savior of humankind and the final imam of the historically recognized Twelve Imams. He will emerge with Isa (Jesus Christ) in the *Yaum al-Qiyamah*—literally, Day of the Resurrection or Day of the Standing—in order to fulfill their mission of bringing peace and justice to the world.

Twelver Shi'i believe that al-Mahdi—the historical person—was born in A.D. 869 and assumed the imamate at five years of age following the death of his father. After a seventy-two-year period—known as the Minor Occultation in 941—he is believed to have sent his followers a letter in which he declared the beginning of Major Occultation, during which the Mahdi—while still alive—is not in contact with his followers. That period of waiting for the Mahdi to return—after what has now been over a thousand years—still persists.

Sunnis and minority Shi'is believe that the Mahdi has not yet been born, and his exact identity is only known to Allah. Belief in the appearance of Hidden Imam or Mahdi helps Shi'is to endure under unbearable situations and to hope for a just future pending the return of Mahdi. The Hidden Imam is considered to be the Imam of the Time, to hold authority over the community and to guide and protect individuals and the Shi'i community.

Muslims in general derive their Sharia, or religious law, from the *Qur'an* and the *Sunnah*. The difference between Sunni and Shi'i Sharia stems from the belief held by the Shi'i that Muhammad assigned Ali to be the *Khalifa* [steward]. Perhaps more importantly—according to Twelvers—an imam or a caliph cannot be democratically elected and has to be nominated by Allah. Sunnis believe that their caliphs were popular and had a greater vote; so, they were made caliphs. In practice, Twelvers religiously follow hadith [sayings of the Prophet] and his descendants—the Twelve Imams—while the

Sunnis do not emphasize those sayings to the same degree in their interpretation of the law. More rankling to the Sunnis is that Shi'i belief results in them being unwilling to accept the examples, verdicts, and sayings of Abu Bakr, Umar, and Uthman ibn Affan, who are considered by Sunnis to be the first three caliphs.

Sunnis consider Shi'ites to be heretics, because they consider the Twelve Imams and Muhammad and his daughter Fatimah to be the "Fourteen Infallibles" chosen by divine decree, and because they accept the examples and verdicts of this special group. Sunnis consider only Muhammad and the *Qur'an* to hold the infallible truths of Islam and the origin of the Sharia.

Both the Sunni and the Shi'i hold that only Muhammad, the Messenger, ever received divine revelation, but the Shi'i believe that their Twelve Imams have a very close relationship with Allah, through which Allah guides them; and the imam in turn guides the people infallibly. This concept is core to Shi'i Islam and is based on the concept that God would not leave humanity without access to divine guidance. To the Sunni, this smacks of disrespect for Muhammad as the only Messenger, and constitutes heresy. There is a consensus by all four schools of Sunni Islamic jurisprudence—the Maliki, Hanbali, Hanafi, and Shafii—that Shi'ites holding such a belief are apostates from Islam and should be put to death. Where the Shi'ite imam is an infallible communicator of Allah's will, the Sunni imam is a prayer leader.

With the Iranian Revolution, the Twelver Ayatollah Khomeini and his supporters established a new theory of governance for the Islamic Republic of Iran. It was based on Khomeini's theory of guardianship of the law as the rule of the Islamic jurist, and jurists as legitimate "legatees" of Muhammad. Strictly speaking, in Islam, there is no clergy, no ordained priestly class to carry out special religious rites and functions. At least, this is certainly true for Sunni Islam.

However, in postrevolutionary Twelver Islam, there came to be a distinctive class of theologians who were charged with the interpretation of the religious law and whose decisions were binding on the Shi'i faithful as both religious and secular law. Another feature that Sunnis decry is that Shi'i Islam shares with Roman Catholicism the belief that pious, holy people after their death can intercede for the living. There developed in Iran a definite hierarchy of theologians; the lowest is the common mullah, a preacher, and the highest rank to which only the most learned theologians may aspire to is the Ayatollah, who is infallible and whose decrees are binding on earth and in heaven. The Supreme Leader—who must be an Islamic jurist—holds all power similar to the dominance of Muhammad himself. Sunni critics recoil at what they see as the transgressions of Twelver scholars who are gradually acquiring for themselves the powers and responsibilities of the Prophet and the Hidden Imam.

Sources: *Walden University Online—LookLex Encyclopedia*; *OpenCourseWare*, University of Notre Dame. *Faith, Practice, and Law in Sunni and Shi'i Islam. ugu.edu—University of Georgia online*; *Wikipedia.* Michael Axworthy, *A History of Iran: Empire of the Mind*; Ervand Abrahamian, *A History of Modern Iran*; Nikki R. Keddie, *Modern Iran: Roots and Results of Revolution*; Hamid Dabashi, *Iran: A People Interrupted*; Amnesty International, *Iran: Violation of Human Rights, 1991*; *Iran, Lonely Planet*, Andrew Burke and Mark Elliott, 2008, *Islam*, ed. John Alden Williams, 1961; *Islam*, 5th Ed, Cesar E. Farah, Ph.D.; Dore Gold, *Hatred's Kingdom: How Saudi Arabia Supports the New Global Terrorism*; Milton Viorst, *In the Shadow of the Prophet: The Struggle for the Soul of Islam*, Wilfried Buchta, *Who Rules Iran?*, 2000.

EPILOGUE

EPILOGUE

But helpless pieces in the game He plays
Upon this chequer-board of Nights and Days
He hither and thither moves, and checks
... and slays
Then one by one, back in the Closet lays.

-Rubaiyat of Omar Khayyam,
by Omar Khayyám (A.D. 1048-1131)
Persian poet, mathematician, and astronomer-
-Edward Fitzgerald *translation—first edition,* 1859

The White House, East Room, 1600 Pennsylvania Ave. NW, Washington, DC, January 31, 2050

On the third of January, President Umberto Gonzales was informed that a most remarkable photo-op was about to present itself at the end of the month. His NSA, Douglas Nissel, had discovered that the thirty-year secrecy period had expired for a number of events that occurred in the period of ten to fifteen years leading up to 2020. Historians from all over the world gathered at the National Archives every year at this time to learn the great secrets of the past. They were unanimously annoyed when they received an entire file of almost completely redacted materials relating to Iran-American relations during the period. National Archives director Peter Inouye explained that the outgoing president had requested that the information remain classified until the end of the month. President Gonzales learned why and concurred with the wishes of President Agnes Maxwell Cunningham, with whom he maintained cordial relations.

The historians were invited to a black-tie affair in the East Room for the presentation of the materials, which had rested in the special security files area of the National Archives for so many decades—some for as long as fifty years. It was an unprecedented formal occasion, and there was a tingle of anticipation regarding why the president was making such a dramatic affair out of what was usually a mundane opening of dusty files—most of which were of only arcane interest to scholars.

Besides the academics, the capacious and ornate East Room of the White House—the largest room in the president's mansion—held the entire cabinet, the Joint Chiefs of Staff, the leaders of both houses of Congress, and all nine members of the Supreme Court. The foremost members of the faculty and administration of the Armed Forces University were seated in the front-row chairs. The Lansdowne portrait of George Washington painted by Gilbert Stuart in 1797—and rescued from the enemy-set fire in 1814—and a companion portrait of Martha Washington painted by Eliphalet F. Andrews in 1878, looked benevolently down on the assembled dignitaries.

President Gonzales entered the room followed by his security team, and the marine band began to play *Hail to the Chief.* Everyone stood until the president gestured from the podium for them to get comfortable.

"My fellow Americans, friends and visitors, brothers and sisters, it gives me great pleasure to welcome you here today. This is a day of revelation that has been a long time in coming. It is a day of celebration for several reasons. First of all, we are going to celebrate the birthday of a genuine American hero. We only know that it is her birthday because her girlhood best friend and adoptive brother told us how she came to choose this as her birth month. So, my friends, this is a party. Have a good time.

"The second reason we will celebrate is that at long last, we can give our honoree the award she earned so long ago but could not be made public until today. Finally, while we will honor Maj. Gen. Afsoon Daastrup personally, she represents the great accomplishments of more than three decades ago. She was part of a secret war that prevented a war. The United States and its friends were able to bring the world back from the brink of a nuclear holocaust that Iran had so assiduously planned. The battles fought then were unheralded—even unknown—to anyone but a few intelligence officers who carried the brunt of the action. It was largely a war of brains and technology rather than of guns and bombs. The principal actor in that long-ago and almost unknown drama was Gen. Daastrup.

"General, would you kindly stand beside me at the podium?" he requested.

Gen. Daastrup was in her full dress uniform complete with medals, except for the most singular award of her life. She stepped up to the president and gave him a smart salute.

"Ladies and gentlemen, allow me to present a genuine hero. Because of the top secret nature of her involvement, you—the public—are about to learn for the first time why she is here today. She has already received her award, but has been sworn to silence for the past thirty years. A handful of other people were present in the Oval Office the morning of January 29, 2019 when she was awarded the Congressional Medal of Honor by then President Oliver Sandstone. I ask you to note her other medals, and that she received her second star two months ago. As of tomorrow morning, she will be retired officially from the military she has served for most of her life and from her university where she has received every honor that can come to an academician."

He placed the blue ribbon and the Medal around Afsoon's neck.

"I will now read her citation. Note that Gen. Daastrup is only the second woman ever to be awarded the Medal." He put on his half glasses. "Afsoon Daastrup, Major General, United States Army, is awarded the highest honor that can be bestowed on a member of the United States Armed Forces for conspicuous gallantry and intrepidity at the risk of her life above and beyond the call of duty while serving in the Iran Nuclear Interdiction Project. Gen. Daastrup—like only one other recipient of the Medal—is not being honored for a single action but rather for the patient and intrepid endurance of her lonely status as a brave intelligence officer. She was at the eye of the storm when the Iranian government set out on a great misadventure—that of preparing to mount a nuclear attack on its neighbors, which would undoubtedly have resulted in a worldwide nuclear conflagration had it not been for the brilliant subterfuge, uncommon bravery, and willingness to sacrifice herself for the greater good demonstrated by Gen. Daastrup."

The language of the award went on for two more pages to allow the audience—who, after that day, would be the world—to understand the magnitude of the accomplishments of the Iran Nuclear Interdiction Project and the magnificent men and women who literally saved the world. The august audience gave Afsoon a standing ovation that rocked the room for half an hour. Printouts of the highlights of that era were passed out to the assembled dignitaries in the East Room, with two extra pages of references to publications and electronic data sites that would give scholars many years of study and thousands of publications generated by the work of the journalists and academics in the room that day and abroad in the country and the world.

§§§§§

Afsoon retired to live in quiet obscurity with her beloved brother Nassir and his family in Georgetown after the death of her parents. She and Nassir lived next door to the Daastrup compound, which housed her adopted brothers and sisters—Daniel, Abigail, Mary, Ruth, Evan, and Michael Daastrup and her adopted cousins—Stephen, Martha, Elizabeth, and Dietrich and their large and boisterous families. She died June 2, 2083. Despite her advanced age of 103, she did not die of old age—a condition to which she would never admit—but in an automobile accident that also took the life of her devoted great-grandniece, Annika Daastrup.

Neal Daastrup had a chronic debilitating condition—idiopathic thrombocytopenic purpura—and knew that the end was near for him. He had a stroke while giving a lecture at the West Point Military Academy on the events of the "Belly of the Beast" War as he dubbed it. It was only a year after Afsoon's triumphant appearance at the White House. His wife Ruth lived another seven years and died of a vicious new strain of influenza. Daniel Daastrup died a year after his younger brother Neal of carcinoma of the lung—a particularly galling diagnosis for him because he had never been a smoker. Brenda, his wife—and Afsoon's mother—died at the age of eighty-seven, having lived her last five years in a senior care center for Alzheimer's victims.

Nassir Jamshidi, aka Saman "Sam" De Silva—Afsoon's adoptive brother and lifelong friend—became a highly successful entrepreneur and humanitarian. He died of malaria in the Congo while on a mission sponsored by the United Nations to help the Africans learn how to drill wells and how to irrigate. His particular project had been to educate the poverty-stricken people about how to produce sufficient clean culinary water to sustain their villages in perpetuity. He was eighty-two when he died. Travel conditions were so difficult that he was buried in a Methodist mission cemetery in the heart of the jungle of the Democratic Republic of the Congo.

Gideon—G.R. IV—was already one of the wealthiest men in the world when he succeeded his father, G.R. III, as chairman of the parent Rothsberger company, Gideon Products Universal. He retired at the age of fifty-five and dedicated the rest of his life to Jewish humanitarian projects and to the furtherance of the security of the state of Israel. In 2061, when he was eighty-one years old, he was honored by being given the Israel Prize for his lifetime achievement and exceptional contribution to the nation. He died of a glioblastoma multiforme brain tumor shortly before his eighty-ninth birthday. His son, G.R. V—although very young even by Rothsberger standards—was able to take over as the president and CEO and to hold the reins of power until his death at the age of ninety-two. His son and grandson ably filled his positions when his hold on power was finally relinquished.

Miriam Rothsberger received the Israel Prize in her own right in honor of her contributions to the Iran Nuclear Interdiction Project and for her lifetime contribution to the humanities, social sciences, and Jewish studies. She became a world-renowned opera diva and had an unusually long singing career spanning forty years. She taught singing to select young women from all over the world who learned from one of the greats in her small concert hall in Château Rothsberger in Paris. She died of breast cancer in 2080 at the age of ninety-one.

Rebecca Hershowitz—G.R. IV's redoubtable maternal grandmother—died in 2033 of pneumonia as a complication of diabetes. She left her entire fortune to an assortment of Jewish charities. She was awarded the Presidential Medal of Freedom for her behind-the-scenes work to prevent the Iranian-made holocaust but did not live long enough to see that award become known to the public. Chava Dayan-Hershowitz Rothsberger—mother of G.R. IV—became the matriarch of the family after the death of her husband. She was appointed to the board of directors of Rothsberger and Company Bankers, where she excelled in real estate finance and was awarded the Presidential Medal of Freedom for her courage and honesty in requiring transparency in mortgage finance while the country was descending into the abyss of the Great Recession of 2008. President Barack Obama included in his farewell speech a tribute to the grande dame of American philanthropists, the particular honor coming from her life's work to create more than a thousand successful schools for minorities throughout the country. She lived until 2062, when she died in her sleep of an apparent rupture of a cerebral aneurysm.

Lt. Col. Shai Avitan died in combat during the 2019 "Hezbollah Weeklong War." Major General Zwi Rosenstein had a heart attack while climbing the Golan Heights with a group of Mossad agents during that same war. He died two days later. Zeev Rosenkranz, Max Rosenstein, Moise Levinsky, Levi Schmuel, and Jacob "The Greaser" Cohen—the senior rulers of the Kosher Nostra—all died in Israel's toughest jail—Ayalon maximum security prison—in the late 2040s after being convicted of murder, extortion, and masterminding a professional ongoing criminal enterprise. At the last, none of their attempts at extortion, bribery, or influence peddling availed them. Their Iran Nuclear Weapons Interdiction Project exploits were never known outside their group of comrades -in -arms.

André Lansky quietly retired as head of the Mossad in 2022, with only a handful of people ever knowing of his role in preserving his country's security. He lived out his retirement in a pleasant but modest villa on the Tel Aviv coast. No one knew for certain the cause of his death in 2031.

The members of the Mossad Institute analyst group—who contributed so greatly to the success of the Iran Nuclear Interdiction Project—all retired on modest pensions. They maintained their cordial relationship with the Rothsbergers and Afsoon. The last member of the group died in 2073.

Abraham Mouradipour and his sister Ruth died in an airplane crash in Ethiopia when they were transporting a small of group of Ethiopian Jews left in the Horn of Africa to new homes in Israel during Yom Kippur in 2042. Little brother Eli died of pancreatic carcinoma when he was twenty-two. Only sisters Kelsey and Rivka outlived their parents, Daniel and Esther. The patriarch and matriarch of the Mouradipour family and their two daughters visited Afsoon frequently and attended her Medal award ceremony both times it was held at the White House. Afsoon enjoyed many vacations in Beverly Hills and in Newport Beach with her cover family. The two cover "parents" died within two years of each other—2024 and 2026—of causes incident to old age.

§§§§§

The most remarkable outcome of the entire Iran Nuclear Interdiction Project or the "Belly of the Beast or Iran Trojan Horse War," as it was variously known, was what happened in Iran itself. The government of the Islamic Republic of Iran for twenty years never publicly admitted that it had been involved in the production of nuclear weapons, that their production plants had been sabotaged and destroyed by nonIslamic outsiders, or that atomic bombs had detonated in Bushehr rather than a huge earthquake had occurred. They were too busy attempting to reconstruct their nation impoverished by the misguided massive expenditures for the nuclear weapons project and their own reputations. The economy collapsed; and the nation was bankrupt, not that the Islamists ruling the country would ever admit it. They simply—and with a variety of excuses—refused to pay their debts.

That was a stopgap for a short period of time—five years—but; in the longer term, it was disastrous for the haughty and intolerant nation. Imports and exports dried up until Iran had to accept a role of a poverty-stricken pariah country. There was an American speculative fiction television series—*Life After People* on the History Channel—during the early years of the twenty-first century, which showed a sobering vision of what the industrialized world would look like at intervals of years, decades, and centuries after the instantaneous disappearance of all human beings. Buildings were not maintained and gradually crumbled; precious documents, art objects, and documents crumbled into dust; plants fractured through sidewalks and highways, destroying the infrastructure. Cities became ghost towns. After the Trojan Horse war, Iran looked much like that.

In the real world of postapocalyptic Iran, transportation languished so that people living at any distance from supply centers found food, fuel, building supplies, and working vehicles in short supply. By 2030, the economy had reverted to that of a thousand years earlier: agrarian, small farms; political jurisdictions were reduced to small communities, even down to clan hamlets. Neighborhoods were abandoned; and, finally, whole cities that had flourished for hundreds—even thousands of years—fell into desolation as people migrated away from them and into the countryside.

Early on, strongman rule and dog-eat-dog conditions prevailed. By 2040, however, there was nothing to steal or to control worth expending effort and scarce resources for; and a sort of tired peace began to exist in the country. The Bakhtiaris and other nomads and pastoral minorities went on with their lives much as they had since people moved away from hunter-gatherer status. They had enough to eat, homespun clothing that sufficed for their needs, and had horses, donkeys, and camels for transportation and hauling. Life remained harsh; but—in comparison to the lot of city dwellers—quite acceptable.

Hezbollah and Hamas were the first casualties to governmental cutbacks. Then the vaunted defense forces gave way to warlord militias. The 120,000-

man strong Revolutionary Guard [IRGC]—created in May 1979 by Grand Ayatollah Khomeini—developed into a multibillion-dollar business empire and became the third wealthiest organization in Iran prior to the collapse of the economy after 2016. From the onset of the revolution, the IRGC was among the most autonomous power centers in Iran; and it resisted subordination to any civilian authority, from the presidential executive to the clerical control apparatus embodied in the Supreme Leader's representatives throughout its existence.

Many millionaire guardsmen abandoned the country and lived like princes in Europe while their countrymen struggled and starved. The Rashimi family similarly fared well. Their wide-reaching business connections—including interests in European manufacturers, African mobile phone companies, and international commodities markets—flourished as the nation they left behind dwindled into near oblivion. The Guard was once considered invincible; after the fall, it was scarcely a presence in Iran. The Revolutionary Guard newspaper, *Sobhe Sadeq*, published its last edition in 2022. Military materiel and equipment like airplanes, missiles, and tanks could not be maintained, and ammunition was hard to come by; so, finally, the warlike character of the Iranian elites subsided into something more like ennui than aggressiveness.

The once arrogant and pugnacious Iranian military evaporated and was reduced to a small regular military [the *artesh*] limited in lack of resources to defend Iran's borders and maintain internal order—a necessary accommodation to the Iranian constitution established by Grand Ayatollah Khomeini in 1980. No outside military defenders appeared on the scene to shore up Iran's crumbling defense forces. Syrian President Bashar al-Assad—Iran's closest Arab ally—had his own problems as he attempted to keep his power when the "Arab Spring" hit Syria with a revolution. He was out of power and an exile in Moscow under the protection of President Vladimir Putin by mid-2016. Neither Russia nor China—the only putative defenders of Iran—contributed military aid to the crumbling economy and military-industrial complex of the Shi'ite empire.

Four successive election cycles beginning in 2020 provided a platform for revenge-seeking firebrands who preached the religion of atomic weapons as the Holy Grail for Iran. Social media persisted almost unhindered with resupply coming from the outside world. The aggressive hotheads were eventually defeated by quiet whispering through Facebook, Twitter, and clandestine e-mail sites. The whispers were about peace. No more nukes, no more terrorist adventures. Even if the privileged elite did not realize what had happened, the people did. They defeated every candidate that preached nuclear WMDs. Finally, a small, stable central government emerged that eschewed anything but a limited defensive security force—rather like post WWII Japan.

There was a dramatic change in Iranian demographics over the thirty years following the catastrophic period beginning in 2016. In 2010, there were an estimated four to five million Iranians living abroad, mostly in North America, Europe, Persian Gulf states, Turkey, Australia, and the broader Middle-East. For the most part, they emigrated after the Iranian Revolution in 1979. By 2012, there were an estimated 1,340,000 Iranian-born expatriates. In 2016—after the economic collapse—that number rose to 2,112,000. By 2020, there were 2,489,000; in 2030, that number had grown to 4,899,685.

Their combined net worth in 2006 was $1.3 trillion. In 2000, the Iran Press Service reported that Iranian expatriates had invested between $200 billion and $400 billion in the United States, Europe, and China, but almost nothing in Iran. In Dubai alone, Iranian expatriates invested an estimated $200 billion in the years before the collapse. The investment numbers trebled by 2030 and quintupled by 2050. In response to altered allegiances and shame over the Islamic Republic's human rights abuses, many Iranian immigrants to the U.S., Europe, the U.K., and Australia distanced themselves from their nationality and instead came to identify themselves primarily on the basis of their ethnic or religious affiliations.

In 2011, there were eleven functioning synagogues—many of them with Hebrew schools—in Tehran. The 2030 census revealed that there were no functioning synagogues or Hebrew schools. Many—like the Yusef Abad Synagogue—were converted to mosques or Islamic centers. There were almost no Jews left in the entire country. The directors of the census found none but speculated that a few—perhaps no more than a 100—could have escaped the census takers. Although prior to 2016, Israeli officials and American Jewish communal leaders urged Iranian Jews to leave their home country, there were initially many holdouts. Wealthy expatriate Persian Jews established a fund to offer incentives to Iranian Jews to emigrate to Israel; but for five years, few took them up on the offer. The Society of Iranian Jews—a prominent Iranian Jewish business and religious organization—dismissed this as "immature political enticement" and said that their national identity was not for sale. When it became apparent that a small-scale holocaust was underway, the few remaining Jews attempted to flee with little more than the clothes on their backs. For many of them, it was too late, and they were caught up in the xenophobic dragnets that sought their lives.

Similarly, by 2030, there was a near complete absence of Indians, Pakistanis, Chinese, and Turks—whom many considered to be the backbone of Iranian business, especially foreign trade. The economic collapse attending the expulsion of foreign business people and the absolute discouragement of native Iranian bazaaris led to a decline in import/export, financial, and industrial business that left the nation a mere husk of the dynamic competitor of 2010. Double and triple digit inflation made a joke out of the rial and—as a result—of business transactions as simple as buying and selling bread.

Embargos and sanctions stopped the petroleum business of Iran and left refineries and drilling equipment to rust in the desert. The Esfahan Oil Refining Company with 176 trillion rials (about $13.8 billion) of revenues in 2012 went bankrupt in 2023, and the Bandar Abbas Oil Refining Company—the leading Iranian exporter with $2.9 billion of exports in 2012—followed suit the next year. The Iran Khodro car manufacturing group failed that same year, 2024.

Iran's mineral exports were at $2.3 billion in 2012 and less than $10 million in 2025, according to the IRNA. Iran's caviar exportation reached three tons in 2012, but by 2025, there was no fishing or shipping industry left, and no market outside the country. Iran Electronics Industries [IEI Military], which designed, developed, and produced electronics for aerospace and military applications both domestic and for export, ceased to exist by the end of the year 2029. The Tehran Stock Exchange closed its doors February 11, 2039—ironically, the national day of celebration of the 1979 revolution.

There was one conspicuous area of economic success. Iran became a global engine of economic growth in the farming and distribution of heroin, marijuana, and cocaine. The World Health Organization estimated that in 2030, 64 percent of all young adult Iranians were either users, addicts, or purveyors of drugs.

Even among the Iranian Shi'i, there was recorded a conspicuous census blank. Before the fall, Twelvers constituted the majority of the population in Iran—90 percent—and approximately 94 percent of the Shi'i. Of the remaining population, less than 3 percent were non-Twelvers and 1 to 2 percent were nonMuslims. By 2030, there were no Ismailis—The Seveners—or Zaidis—the Fivers—left in Iran.

The 2030 census and all subsequent counts revealed a net decline in population. In 2010, there were 75 million Iranians. In 2020, there were 79 million—mostly owing to a high fertility rate. In 2030, there were 69 million. The decline at that time was found to be related to emigration of many affluent families, a declining birthrate, and an increasing death rate among those who remained. In 2040, the census found 62 million, and in 2050, 58 million. By 2060, the decline hit 52 million. By then, the birthrate, death rate, and emigration rates had stabilized with yearly counts varying only by two or three hundred thousand year to year. From 2020 on, the rate of immigration into Iran was negligible.

The influence of outside opinions streaming in through the social media networks that condemned the maltreatment of women and minorities became so powerful that even the next seven Supreme Leaders became champions of the rights of all members of Iranian society, especially for women. The chador all but disappeared. Rapists were tried, convicted, and punished at a rate never before imagined. The pervasive mythology that accompanied the revolution of 1979 called "cultural revival" and "regaining the past" gradually faded in intensity. The idea that *Gharb* (the West) had to be abandoned both conceptually and as a way of life softened to a level of disinterest.

Life as enjoyed in the West became a national aspiration, at least among the young. The ailment referred to as *gharbzadegi*—or "*Weststruckness*"—which the revolutionary ayatollahs decried as a loss of cultural identity—became more or less acceptable. The will to fight everything not Twelver as defined by the radical Shi'ite regime of the past softened until it was frowned upon by the oldest generation but no longer condemned.

Only after all of these profound societal changes had taken place; and a new and less virulently intolerant regime emerged and took root, did the outside world begin to pay some heed to the overtures being made by the new and much chastened Iranian ecclesiastical hierarchy and government regime—still essentially one and the same. The grasping power of the Shi'i religion waned, and, for most of the world, became little more than a footnote of history—a condition mourned by almost no one outside the territory of Iran and southern Iraq.

DOES IRAN HAVE NUCLEAR WEAPONS?

They're rioting in Africa, they're starving in Spain.
There's hurricanes in Florida, and Texas needs rain.
The whole world is festering with unhappy souls.
The French hate the Germans, the Germans hate the Poles.
Italians hate Yugoslavs, South Africans hate the Dutch.
And I don't like anybody very much!

But we can be tranquil, and thankful, and proud,
For man's been endowed with a mushroom-shaped cloud.
And we know for certain that some lovely day
Someone will set the spark off, and we will all be blown away.

They're rioting in Africa, there's strife in Iran.
What nature doesn't do to us, will be done by our fellow man.
-*They're Rioting in Africa,* Lyrics by the Kingston Trio

To the query posed in the title, Iran says "No," and they have no intention of using nuclear energy for anything other than peaceful energy for the benefit of the Iranian people. The U.S. CIA and intelligence services of Israel say "Not yet," but Iran has every intention of having such weapons and will use them against Israel as soon as they are fully ready. No one except the highest officials of the Islamic Republic of Iran and the leaders of the Atomic Energy Organization of Iran [the AEOI] know for certain whether or not Iran is working on producing weapons of mass destruction, and, if so, how advanced is their progress. Aside from the assertions of the citizens of the world who fear a nuclear holocaust above all else and the self-serving denials of the Iranian regime, there *is* some objective information available. Even then, we are left with the pessimism expressed by Alfred North Whitehead: "There are no whole truths: all truths are half-truths. It is trying to treat them as whole truths that plays to the devil."

On July 6, 2013, former British Foreign Secretary Jack Straw rejected as baseless the allegation that there may be a military dimension to Iran's nuclear energy program by emphasizing that there is no evidence for such a claim. He said on the BBC, "There is no evidence, not from the IAEA [the International Atomic Energy Agency], not from the Americans.... There is no evidence that they (Iranians) are involved in building a bomb." He referred to the 2007 U.S. National Intelligence Estimate (NIE) that verified Iran was not after nuclear arms. The NIE report—prepared by sixteen US intelligence agencies—confirmed with "high confidence" the peaceful nature of Iran's nuclear program. A similar report was also published in 2011.

Straw welcomed the election of Hassan Rohani as Iran's next president in the June 14, 2013, vote, saying, "What I have been urging the government is that we do our best to reengage with Iranians, because there is a chance now that we can."

Rohani, who was Iran's former chief nuclear negotiator from October 2003 to August 2005, won Iran's eleventh presidential election. Straw was adamant that the U.S., Israel, and some of their allies falsely claim that Iran is pursuing non-civilian objectives in its nuclear energy program, with Washington and the European Union using the unfounded claim as a pretext to impose illegal sanctions on Iran.

In the *New York Times*, on August 1, 2013, Rick Gladstone wrote an article entitled, "Sending Message to Iran, House Approves Tougher Sanctions." He said, "The House overwhelmingly approved legislation on Wednesday that would impose the toughest sanctions yet on Iran, calling the measure a critical step to cripple the country's disputed nuclear program." On July 26, 2013, writing as an Op-Ed guest columnist, Jonathan Tepperman, for the *Times*, entitled an article, *Israel vs. Iran, Again*. He said, "Earlier this month, Prime Minister Benjamin Netanyahu of Israel went on American television to remind the world—in case anyone had forgotten—that the threat from Iran remains very much alive. Speaking on *Face the Nation*, Netanyahu warned that the Islamic Republic is once again approaching a nuclear redline, and hinted that if the United States doesn't take action soon, he will...."

Netanyahu won't—and shouldn't—get the kind of response he's hoping for. Simply put, that's because both his language and Israel's behavior make it harder and harder to take his warnings seriously.... Now, let me be clear: I'm not trying to argue that Israel doesn't have any reason to worry about Iran. Given Israel's size and location, the Obama administration's current preoccupation with Egypt and Syria, and Washington's seeming willingness to engage Iran's new president in yet another round of talks, Netanyahu's anxiety is understandable (if excessive)."

Tehran strongly rejects the allegations regarding its nuclear energy activities, maintaining that as a committed signatory to the Non-Proliferation Treaty (NPT) and a member of the IAEA, it has the right to use nuclear technology for peaceful purposes. According to *Wikipedia*, "Iran is not known to currently possess weapons of mass destruction (WMD) and has signed treaties repudiating the possession of weapons of mass destruction, including the Biological Weapons Convention, the Chemical Weapons Convention, and the Nuclear Non-Proliferation Treaty (NPT)."

Wikipedia listed a timeline of U.S. announcements and actions related to its contention that Iran was maintaining a stubborn secrecy about its nuclear program, which makes the program highly suspect:

- In 2005, the United States stated that Iran has violated both Article III and Article II of the NPT. The IAEA Board of Governors, in a rare divided vote, found Iran in noncompliance with its NPT safeguards agreement for a 1985–2003 "policy of concealment" regarding its efforts to develop enrichment and reprocessing technologies. The United States, the IAEA, and others consider these technologies to be of particular concern because they can be used to produce fissile material for use in nuclear weapons.

- The United States has argued that Iran's concealment of efforts to develop sensitive nuclear technology is *prima facie* evidence of Iran's intention to develop nuclear weapons—or at a minimum—to develop a latent nuclear weapons capability. Others have noted that while possession of the technology "contributes to the latency of nonnuclear weapon states in their potential to acquire nuclear weapons," such latency is not necessarily evidence of intent to proceed toward the acquisition of nuclear weapons, since "intent is in the eye of the beholder."

- The United States has also provided information to the IAEA on Iranian studies related to weapons design and activities, including the intention of diverting a civilian nuclear energy program to the manufacture of weapons, based on a laptop computer reportedly linked to Iranian weapons programs. The United States has pointed to other information reported by the IAEA, including the "Green Salt" project, the possession of a document on manufacturing uranium metal hemispheres, and other links between Iran's military and its nuclear program, as further indications of a military intent to Iran's nuclear program. The IAEA has said U.S. intelligence provided to it through 2007 has proven inaccurate or not led to significant discoveries inside Iran; however, the U.S. and others have recently provided more intelligence to the agency.

- The United States acknowledges Iran's right to nuclear power, and has joined with the EU-3, Russia, and China in offering nuclear and other economic and technological cooperation with Iran if it suspends uranium enrichment. This cooperation would include an assured supply of fuel for Iran's nuclear reactors.

- A potential reason behind U.S. resistance to an Iranian nuclear program lies in Middle-Eastern geopolitics. In essence, the U.S. feels that it must guard against even the possibility of Iran obtaining nuclear weapons capability. Some nuclear technology is dual use; i.e., it can be used for peaceful energy generation and to develop nuclear weapons, a situation that resulted in India's nuclear weapons program in the 1960s. A nuclear-armed Iran would dramatically change the balance of power in the Middle-East, weakening U.S. influence. It could also encourage other Middle-Eastern nations to develop nuclear weapons of their own, further reducing U.S. influence in a critical region.

- In 2003, the United States insisted that Tehran be "held accountable" for seeking to build nuclear arms in violation of its agreements. In June 2005, U.S. Secretary of State Condoleezza Rice required former IAEA head Mohamed ElBaradei to either "toughen his stance on Iran" or fail to be chosen for a third term as IAEA head. The IAEA has on some occasions criticized the stance of the U.S. on Iran's program. The United States denounced Iran's successful enrichment of uranium to fuel grade in April 2006, with spokesman Scott McClellan saying, they "continue to show that Iran is moving in the wrong direction." In November 2006, Seymour Hersh described a classified draft assessment by the Central Intelligence Agency "challenging the White House's assumptions about how close Iran might be to building a nuclear bomb. He continued, "The CIA found no conclusive evidence, as yet, of a secret Iranian nuclear-weapons program running parallel to the civilian operations that Iran has declared to the International Atomic Energy Agency," adding that a current senior intelligence official confirmed the assessment.

• In March 2006, the U.S. State Department opened an Office of Iranian Affairs (OIA) overseen by Elizabeth Cheney, the daughter of Vice President Dick Cheney. The office's mission was reportedly to promote a democratic transition in Iran and to help "defeat" the Iranian regime. Iran argued the office was tasked with drawing up plans to overthrow its government. One Iranian reformer said after the office opened that many "partners are simply too afraid to work with us anymore," and that the office had "a chilling effect." The U.S. Congress has reportedly appropriated more than $120 million to fund the project. Investigative journalist Seymour Hersh further revealed in July 2008 that Congress also agreed to a $400-million funding request for a major escalation in covert operations inside Iran.

China, Russia, and Kazakhstan have all been accused of supplying enriched uranium ore to Iran; and all of them—including Iran—deny the allegations, as well as denying any seismic evidence of nuclear testing. There is ample and undisputed evidence that Iran has sufficient delivery missiles to accommodate a nuclear arsenal. There is also well-established evidence that Iran has deep secret facilities in several areas related to nuclear energy production. It is argued that there would be no real need for such secrecy for plants intent on pursuing peaceful energy production. There have been unverified reports that Iranian scientists and military officers have served as clandestine whistle-blowers to inform the outside world that Iran, indeed, has a nuclear weapons program. The IAEA has expressed concerns that Iran has the capability to produce either peaceful uranium or weapons-grade enriched uranium and could decide to build weapons. Furthermore, it is well established that Iran worked closely with A.Q. Khan, the father of the Pakistan nuclear bomb.

The evidence for an Iranian nuclear-weapon program is not there or is, at most, subject to considerable conjecture by parties that are not disinterested. The present novel is fiction and is significantly attuned to the conjecture. The Iranians have established a closed society rife with secrets, which does not contribute to a sense of well-being in a nuclear-attack-conscious outside world. The outlandish statements by immediate past president Ahmadinejad and Supreme Leader Khamenei have certainly done nothing to instill confidence in a jittery world. The polemic rantings of hatred of Jews, of Israel, of the United States, and of the West in general, accompanied by grossly inflammatory claims that they wish to annihilate those who differ in opinion and practice from their extremely intolerant religious views—including the very concept of democracy—raise defensive hackles among most people who follow the issues.

The Iranian senior government officials sound like some combination of Maximillian Robespierre, Genghis Khan, Adolf Hitler, Mao Tse Tung, and Popes Urban II and Alexander VI with their threats of mass destruction of enemies and world dominance gained through war (or in the case of the Iranians, jihad). The Iranian tirades suggest to common people that—despite evidence to the contrary—Iran does have nuclear-weapon ambitions and an entrenched desire to destroy Israel despite the fact that they have to know that mutually assured destruction would be the result. Most people—including this author—distrust religious fanatics—particularly those who fantasize that their God wills them to wreak destruction on their opponents—which will assure their dominance in the postapocalyptic world. I am a chicken when it comes to nuclear conflict; so, this author will reserve judgment as history and the news informs him.

-THE END-

Those who play with the devil's toys will be brought by degrees to wield his sword.

-R. Buckminster Fuller

CAST OF CHARACTERS
[MOST IMPORTANT CONTINUING CHARACTERS*]

IRAN

Nawsheen Shakibaie	Afsoon's birth mother, fourth wife of Ahriman
*Ahriman Shakibaie	Afsoon's birth father, master of a tent hamlet near Qushchu, Kurdestan County, West Azerbaijan Province, Iran
*Fereshten Shakibaie	Ahriman's first wife
*Azadeh Shakibaie	Ahriman's fourth wife
*Afsoon Daastrup—Afsoon Mouradipour	Biological daughter of Nawsheen and Ahriman Shakibaie, adopted daughter of Neal and Brenda Daastrup. Mourapidour is a cover name.
*Astera Shakibaie	Ahriman's third wife
*Yasmin	Wet nurse and surrogate mother to Afsoon
Kamin Shakibaie	Ahriman and Fereshten's third son, Afsoon's half-brother
Muhammad Shakibaie	Ahriman and Fereshten's son, Afsoon's half-brother
Shokofeh	Astera's servant
Farhad Sharifi	Shepherd boy, illicit lover of Astera

*Firudin Jamshidi	Afsoon's temporary paternal guardian in rural Kurdestan County, West Azerbaijan Province, Iran
*Mariella Jamshidi	Afsoon's temporary maternal guardian in rural Kurdestan village
*Nassir Jamshidi	Loving "brother" of Afsoon in rural Kurdestan village
*Elaheh Jamshidi	Daughter of Firudin and Mariella Jamshidi
Mozaffarian and Gorgani Jamshidi	Elder sons of Firudin and Mariella Jamshidi
Dina Jamshidi	Daughter of Firudin and Mariella Jamshidi
Fatemah Shakibaie	New—fourth—wife of Ahriman after the death of Astera
The Dashnaksutyun	Armenian bandits
*Fereshte [angel].	Afsoon's beloved rag doll, made for her by Nassir
Imam Ali Abedi	Cleric who preformed FGMs
Imam Zamaani Fard	Cleric in Kandovan who conducted Dina's funeral
*Grand Ayatollah Ali ibn Abi Rahimi	Supreme Leader of Iran—the Agha, the SL
Saif-al-din and his wife, Parveen	Temporary guardians of Afsoon in Kandovan Village, Kurdestan County, West Azerbaijan Province, Iran
*Hassanzadeh Shakibaie	Eldest son of Ahriman and Fereshten Shakibaie
Shireen	Shakibaie slave girl
*The Bakhtiaris	Bedouin nomads from the Zagros Mountains
Mullah Haji Zamaani Fard	Circuit judge at Piranshahr jail
Shafiqah Kadivar	Afsoon's employer at a wool carpet factory in Amarrh, Iraq
Sergeant Naomeh Nikahd	Municipal police, Al Basrah, Iraq

Aisha Toskhani	Kashmiri pandit woman in charge of humanitarian relief center, Al Basrah, Iraq
Dr. Sylvia Asad	Physician at the humanitarian relief center, Al Basrah, Iraq
Haji Naazem Zadeh Harandi	Scholar, librarian, teacher at the humanitarian relief center, Al Basrah, Iraq
Roshanak Rahimi	Wife of Supreme Leader Grand Ayatollah Ali ibn Abi Rahimi
Ali Hosseini Mejazi	Chief of staff of Supreme Leader Grand Ayatollah Ali ibn Abi Rahimi
*Mohsen Shahamatdoost and successor Hormoz Okhavat	Presidents of the Republic of Iran
Yazid ibn Sarrafzaadeh	Chief of staff of the armed forces of the Republic of Iran
*Moqtada al-Benizir and Ayatollah Ali Hossein Golzar his successor after al-Benizir was murdered. Aisha and Khadija	Head of the Atomic Energy Organization Iran (AEOI), his wife and daughter (a singer)
*Mullah Ali Salar Omidyar	Director of the Ministry of Intelligence and Security (MOIS)
*Behrouz Omidi	Director of the Ministry of Intelligence and National Security of the Islamic Republic of Iran (MISIRI) or VEVAK.
Abdul Qadeer (AQ) Khan	Smuggler of uranium enrichment and nuclear-weapon technology to Muslim countries
*Hamid Hejazi	SL guard, Agent Ex
*Daniel and Brenda Daastrup	Georgetown, Washington, D.C. Daniel is Neal Daastrup's brother, and Brenda, his sister-in-law. They are the adoptive parents of Afsoon.
Dr. Nawal El Mubarak	Egyptian feminist physician and surgeon who repaired Afsoon's recto-vaginal fistula

*Ali Mohamed Mustaffen	Director of the Central Bank of the Islamic Republic of Iran
Ali Muhummad Sharifi, Mahdis and Javaneh, Mojtaba	Iranian foreign minister, his wife and children (singers)
Col. Dariush Aghdashloo	On-site commander of the Agha's private security force.

1. Daron Naderi
2. Ayatollah Mohammad Esmail Rahmanipour
3. Ali Hossein Rahnavardand
4. Bobak Larijani
5. Col. Darius Aghdashloo
	The management of the SL's household and directors of his personal guard [SL Agha Rahimi's oldest friends, if the Supreme Leader of Iran's Muslims could actually have friends in the usual sense]:
	  1. Head of amputee war veterans
	  2. Currently a member of parliament
	  3. Director of IRGC intelligence
	  4. Head of the guard corps and member of the Security Council
	  5. Second in command to Rahnavard.

*Project *Jahannam Adur* [Hell's Fire]	Iranian project for manufacture of nuclear weapons, placing them in missiles, and delivering the missiles on Israel and the U.S.
*Elizabeth Dayan-Nichols	American expat living in Iran, horse rancher, and spy for the Iran Nuclear Interdiction Project
*Elias, Zachariah, Elijah, Kelsey, Leopold, and Pearl Nichols-Dayan	Children of Elizabeth and coconspirators. Elias is an active agent with Aaron Schmuel in Iran.
*Rabbi Ya'akov ben Avraham	Persian Jewish rabbi who ostensibly is a loyal citizen of Iran and secretly becomes an agent for the American-run Iran Nuclear Interdiction Project. Member of Neturei Karta—ultra-Orthodox Jews, a Jewish sect that opposes both Zionism and Israel.
Esfandiari Razizadeh	Deputy of Moqtada al-Benizir, head of the Atomic Energy Organization Iran (AEOI)

Razmara Tassoudji	Deputy of Moqtada al-Benizir, head of the Atomic Energy Organization Iran (AEOI)
*Amir Vehrahrami	Chief engineer for research and development at the Bushehr nuclear plant
*Hormoz Mohammad-Bagher	President of Bank Sepah, Tehran
Cantor Avril Azaria	Jewish singer
Ali Hassan Zolein	Member of the Majilis who spoke of Israeli Trojan Horse
Ayatollah Ali Hossein Golzar	New head of AEOI after al-Benizir's murder
Arash Behdad	Finance minister of Iran
Saad ad-Daula Khan	Bakhtiari headman near the Caspian Sea
Muhammad	Bakhtiari headman who helped Afsoon escape from jail
Shapour Del-anchin, Fereydoon Alipour, Amilie Bakhtiari, and Ali Asghar	Bakhtiari tribespeople killed during Afsoon's escape
Dr. Abbas and Mrs. Ahuva Homayoun	Afsoon's doctor and nurse during the escape
Ghurkas Thapa Dhanbahadur and Ghhetri Krishnabahadur	Carter Miller-Partridge's two Indian SAS agents

ISRAEL

*Major General Zwi Rosenstein	Deputy director Mossad
Zeev Rosenkranz	Chief of Tel Aviv Israeli mafia—"Kosher Nostra"
*Max Rosenstein	Zwi's brother and second in command of Kosher Nostra
*Moise Levinsky	Ranking Kosher Nostra officer
*Jacob "The Greaser" Cohen	Ranking Kosher Nostra officer

*General André Lansky	Director of the Mossad
David Henderson	Mossad agent and Krav Maga expert
Sergeant Ruth McGuire	Mossad analyst
*Levi, Miriam, Rebecca, Alice, Abraham, Constance, Michael, Harry, Daniel, Avril, Julius, and Elsie	Mossad Institute analyst group
SLHAN1__@#%@ *trickmagicphantom.	G.R. IV's Mossad login code
Antal Disraeli	Mossad *katsa*—case officer
*Elsie Silberberg	Electronic communications analyst, friend of G.R. IV

UNITED STATES

*Gideon Emmanuel Rothsberger I, II, III, IV—[G.R. I, II, III, IV]	Line of wealthy Orthodox Jewish bankers, G.R. III and IV are members of the *Sayanim*. I is deceased, II is CEO of Gideon Products Universal, III is president of Rothsberger & Company Bankers, and IV is senior vice president of the bank. Part of the Iran Nuclear Interdiction Project.
*Chava Dayan-Hershowitz Rothsberger	Mother of G.R. IV
Tahmineh and Leila Rothsberger	Twin daughters of G.R. III and Chava, and sisters of G.R. IV
Nathan Rothsberger	Uncle of G.R. IV who opposes him for the position of senior vice president and president-elect of Rothsberger & Company Bankers
*Rebecca Hershowitz	Mother of Chava and grandmother of G.R. IV
Dr. ben Schulberg	Chava's obstetrician
Joseph ben Aaron,	Rothsberger's butler

Ruth Kline	G.R. IV's nanny Abba Cogen
Abba Cogen	G.R. IV's *mohel* [circumcisor]
Rabbi Bergen	Rothsberger's rabbi
*Aaron Schmuel	School bully, later friend of G.R. IV, action agent of the DIA in the Iran Nuclear Interdiction Project
*Levi Schmuel	Aaron's father, member of Kosher Nostra
*Lt. Col. Shai Avitan	Martial arts instructor, IDF. Krav Maga expert
Gilda Rogdonavich	Master's thesis, *Gifted Child*, about G.R. IV
President Tate-Waring	President of U.C. Berkeley
Tom Bradshaw	Senate majority leader
*Ali ibn Massoud	VEVAK contact agent in the Ali and the Twelve Imams mosque
Dr. Stephen Ammon Rhodes	U.C. Berkeley math professor for G.R. IV
Dr. Willard Lazar	Head of the department of computer science—G.R. IV's major professor at Berkeley
Dr. Stanley Protel Thatcher	Head of the MIT computer science department
Miriam bat Ezekiel	Message courier—member of the *Sayanim*
Dr. Kristina Shimazaki	G.R. IV's MIT major professor in mathematics
Drs. Leif Erik Nielson and Karl L. Nielson	MIT economics department cochairs
*Rear Adm. Martin Torgelson	Assumed the office of DDDIA in 2011 when Neal Daastrup retired. The appellation "3D" stuck with Vice Adm. Daastrup, so Torgelson became known as the "Swede."
Rabbi Pinchas ben Yisroel, ha-Rav	Headmaster, Saint Francis Woods Hebrew Academy
Leopold Antal Lavigne	Dean of students, Saint Francis Woods Hebrew Academy

Professor Samson Bernstein	UC Berkeley Professor and tutor for G.R. IV in elementary and high school
*Howard Ryan, Glen Gabler, Agnes Maxwell Cunningham, Oliver Sandstone, Umberto Gonzales	Presidents of the U.S.
*Army Col. Avery Holmes and Navy Captain Victor Raylan	Heads of DARPA and the SSG-CNO, respectively. [Defense Advanced Research Projects Agency and Strategic Studies Group for the Chief of Naval Operations]

SWEDEN

Jonas Zillacus	Ambassador to the United States
*Ali Nylander	Consular agent in charge of trade and economic affairs
Dr. Arvid Bergström	Counselor for Swedish defense
Counselor Ms. Sanna Kullberg	Special Advisor, Homeland Security Affairs
Magnus Bielvenstram	Minister-Counselor, Trade and Economic Affairs
*Johannes Hjerdstadt	Ostensibly, the undersecretary for embassy affairs. Actually, an agent of *FMUndSäkC* [Swedish Army Intelligence].
*Marta Olson	Agent of *FMUndSäkC* protecting Afsoon in Sweden
*Ingrid Hakkensdatter	Agent of *FMUndSäkC* protecting Afsoon in Sweden
Nick Staphanakis	DIA agent protecting Afsoon in Sweden
Michael Grodmore	DIA agent protecting Afsoon in Sweden
Hassan Tajbakhsh	VEVAK agent following/protecting Afsoon
Mohammad Ali Nikookar	VEVAK agent following/protecting Afsoon

Ayatollah Mammad Qazwini	Senior VEVAK agent in Sweden
Salar Sabeti	VEVAK agent in Sweden who first approached Afsoon at the Universit
Ali Hossein	VEVAK agent in Sweden

FRANCE

*Miriam Shahnameh	Maiden name of Gideon's wife—opera singer
Elijah and Ruth Shahnameh	French Orthodox Jews, parents of Miriam
Gideon Rothsberger V and Ruth	G.R IV and Miriam R's children
Marius Duvalier	Elderly French singer

NORTH KOREA

Gen. Gangjon Chung-a	North Korean general-head of the DRNK Institute of Atomic Energy
Col. Dockko Yong-Jin and Dr. Soung Hong-jik	Members of the DRNK Institute of Atomic Energy

AUTHOR CARL DOUGLASS, a former neurosurgeon turned full time author, writes with gripping realism because in all his books he has been there and done that in some measure. He grew up in a small town where fighting was the rule, not the exception. He was determined to escape the sameness of geography, intellectual outlook, and career prospects of the majority of his contemporaries. In complete naiveté, he applied to only one well-known major university for his undergraduate work, and to everyone's surprise, he was accepted. He found himself out of his league scholastically and had to work like a Hannibal to find a way or make one to succeed in that rarefied atmosphere. His goal of success was to become a neurosurgeon, and he did it. His career in academia and the military as well as his work as a medical humanitarian provided the background to produce the riveting tales that have made their way into his remarkable books.